DEAD OF EVE

BY

PAM GODWIN

Dead of Eve

by
Pam Godwin

Science may have found a cure for most evils;
but it has found no remedy for the worst of them all-
the apathy of human beings.

Helen Keller

CHAPTER ONE: HANDPRINT

"You are looking at very disturbing shots of the fighting that has erupted on the White House lawn behind me. Riots, just like this one, have ripped across every town, in every country. The situation has been compounded by the continued silence from presidential cabinet members. Their whereabouts, and their health, are still unknown. It would seem the U.S. has collapsed like all the nations before it. All we can do now is hope and pray. This is Mitch Case with MCSB World News reporting on assignment in...aaah. No. No...aaaaahh..."

The camera angle rotated, tumbled. Mitch's screams transformed to gurgles. The sideways view of trampled grass, smoke, and red and blue lights filled the TV screen.

I hit the power button on the remote and vanished the clip I'd seen numerous times. News broadcasts were on continuous replay. How long had it been since the cameras stopped rolling? Four...five weeks?

I lay in bed next to glass doors that opened to a screened sun room on the deck. The room overlooked wilting bushes, overgrown shrubs, and an algae infested in-ground pool. There was a time, not too long before then, when I loved that view from my bed.

Lightning bugs flickered through the screen. The sun bowed behind the maple trees bordering the property. Silver-green leaves waved in the residual light. The shift from spring to summer used to be my favorite time of year in Missouri. I would prop the doors open and welcome the richness of soil and clay, the sweet smell of the earth drying out after the rainy season.

But the doors remained closed and a musty staleness choked the room. I sank into the pillow. My hip bones threatened to poke through the cotton sheet. My dinner sat on the night stand untouched.

Dull strands of hair knotted around me. I plucked at the ends. Only a couple of months earlier, I took pride in my fit physique. A vegetarian. A five miles a day runner. I lifted weights with Joel every morning. But that was before. In two months, twenty pounds of muscle seemed to dissolve from my body, leaving a frail shell to hold what was left of my soul.

Hairs on my nape prickled. The shadows concealing the deck thickened and gathered. There, just beyond the sun room, a section of the darkness contracted. Was it…was someone there?

The deck was two stories up. Joel had chopped off the stairs to secure our home from looters and other threats. He said it would take a ninja or a forty-foot ladder to access the deck from the outside.

The only way in was through the barricaded front door. And I would've heard the garage doors. Certain I was alone, I hugged myself and squinted at the deck.

A small form emerged on the other side of the glass door. My shoulders bunched to my ears against a stampede of goose bumps. The uncropped outline of a child solidified. Darkness gravitated toward two cavernous holes where eyes should've been. A teddy bear dangled from one hand.

"Aaron?" I gasped and tried to sit up. My arms shook with the effort.

The shadows dispersed into nothingness. I rubbed my eyes. Another nightmare? But I was awake. My breathing quickened and I wrestled to control it. It wasn't real. It couldn't have been Aaron. I watched my boy die two months prior.

The silence broke with a giggle and the patter of feet. A fleshy palm flattened against the glass then receded into the dark. I gripped the sheets and worked my throat against a lump. An oily handprint remained.

The garage doors squeaking vaulted me back to reality. Joel must be home from wherever it was he went. If not him…ah well, maybe my wish for death would finally come.

Each lock on the interior door snicked, one by one. What incited him to leave every day? Pre-outbreak, he kept our garage stockpiled with water and non-perishables. We should've had another month of basic survival supplies. I knew a shit storm brewed outside, but didn't care. Instead, I focused on the handprint—didn't dwell on the fact it couldn't be real—and tucked back into that safe place in my mind. The place where I climbed the corporate ladder, laughed and drank with friends, and tucked children into bed at night.

His boots landed with purpose along the wood floors. Should I feign sleep? He'd just wake me to eat.

The stomping stilled. Gun oil flooded the room, overlaying his usual scent of Cavendish pipe tobacco. He leaned on the door jamb. "Did you at least try to eat?"

I bit my cheek. Maybe he'd give up and go away.

He wore his armor carrier vest rigged with bullet proof plates and a hydration system. It outfitted a tactical custom radio, a first aid pouch, and mag pouches for his M4 carbine and Glock 19 pistol. Married to a gun dealer for fifteen years, I'd learned to catalogue the details of his equipment.

"Ba-y." A firm tone. He never hesitated to battle wills with me. And he used his pet name, aware the way he called me *baby*, silencing the *b*, softened my stubbornness.

The stare down commenced. He'd win it with patience, a virtue ingrained through a lifetime passion in martial arts. I couldn't fault him for it since he treated me to several years of self-defense tutelage. Though, indulging him meant that while my girlfriends' husbands were pampering them with pedicures and dinner theater, Joel was grinding my face in sweaty wrestling mats and bruising more than my ego. Was the part of me that enjoyed those activities gone for good?

He hit the quick release on the vest and slid it off. His fatigues rasped at his thighs as he crossed the room.

Did he glance at the glass door? At our boy's handprint? Nah, I was the only head case.

The mattress dipped. He scooted next to me and scooped a spoonful of corn. "Open." The spoon floated an inch from my mouth. "We're not doing this tonight."

The heart-breaking look dampening his blue eyes made me wince. His face aged so much in two months. Wrinkles creased his forehead. Dark circles furrowed the tender skin around his lids and silver streaked the goatee under his scowl.

He was ruggedly handsome. Built like a wrestler, his strong neck and big legs intimidated lesser men. Thick brown hair curled on his shoulders, contrasting his graying facial hair. He reminded me of a mountain man. Fitting, given our living conditions.

He adopted survivalist ideals years prior. I used to tease him for his fascination with it. He consumed every book and documentary he found on the subject. A garage loaded with medical supplies, gloves and masks prepared us for the threat of bird flu. We caught rain water in barrels around the house. Supplemented electricity with solar panels on the roof. Self-sufficient and ready for world abolition. He'd claimed, "Lack of preparation can wound the strongest families." I accused him of suffering from paranoia. Two months earlier, I ate my words.

"Evie." His impatient tone snapped me back to the hovering spoon. "I'm not asking again."

That was true. In a few moments, he'd be shoving the salty corn down my throat. I opened my mouth and swallowed the cold mush.

He handed me a glass of water. "Keep it down this time." His eyes searched my face.

In the years I'd known him, I'd never seen him so sad, so detached. We met in high school. Together longer than apart, we both turned thirty-three that year. And I blamed myself for putting the pain in the stare that held me.

I surrendered and choked down the last of the corn, salad and black beans. The corner of his lips levitated as I ate. So loving, that smile. How long had it been since we kissed? Damn, I missed our passion and spontaneity.

The tiny handprint glinted on the glass behind him. Should I tell him about it? I pressed my tongue against the back of my teeth. It would confirm his suspicions about my state of mind. He'd make me talk. About the nightmares. About everything.

"Thanks." I rolled to my side and breathed through the nausea that came with eating.

"I pulled some mint from the garden this morning. You want hot tea?"

I nodded. We grew our own produce in our backyard greenhouse. Another convenience owed to his survivalist foresight.

He kissed the crown of my head and stalked to the kitchen with my dishes. I grated my teeth and squeezed my eyes shut. I didn't understand his drive. How could he keep going through the motions every day? He did everything essential to keep the two of us alive while I lay in bed and aimed for the contrary. I died the day our children died. And I committed to dying every day since.

The covers tangled around my legs as I fought sleep and the awaiting nightmare. My nightmares didn't kill me. They just reminded me why I wanted to die.

"Joel?"

His head poked in the doorway. "Going to sleep?"

"Yeah."

He put his pistol on the side table. Slid off his boots. Dropped his fatigues with riggers belt still attached. Arranged the pants over the boots to ensure quick dress, fireman style. Then he settled behind me and pulled me close. His finger traced circles on my back.

I laid my cheek on his chest and paced my breaths with his. Within minutes, sleep took me.

I perched on the floor in Annie's room and brushed her doll's hair.

She bounced in her closet, picking out a dress to wear. "Round and round the garden. Like a teddy bear." Her angelic voice pealed behind me. "One step..." Her feet rustled on the carpet. "Two steps..."

The corners of my mouth tugged up. I braced for the tickle.

"Tickle you under there." Her tiny hands squirmed along my sides.

I twisted to return the tickle.

All white eyes sunk into her skull. Spiny pincers replaced dainty hands. Pus oozed from her pores and plastered her hair and dress. Her skin glowed green, covered in tiny hairs and thin enough to reveal the fluids pumping underneath. Dusty lips cracked and fell away. A spear-shaped tube emerged from the hole that disfigured her mouth.

She held out her arms. The claws snapped open. Black blood leaked down her chin and the mouth-like thing moved. "Will you sing the Teddy Bear song with me, Mama?"

I jerked out of her reach and screamed.

As if increase of appetite had grown
By what it fed on, and yet, within a month—
Let me not think on't—Frailty, thy name is woman!—

William Shakespeare, *Hamlet Act 1, scene 2, 144—146*

CHAPTER TWO: FRAILTY, THY NAME IS WOMAN

Arms hooked under my knees and back, lifting, pulling me close. "Shh. You're okay." Joel rocked us and murmured words I didn't hear. When my shivering tapered off, he whispered, "Talk to me, Baby."

"Just another dream."

He stroked a finger down my cheek and raised my chin. "Tell me."

I shook my head and screwed my eyes shut.

"Is it the A's?"

I slid off his lap and lay on my side.

He rested a hand on my hip. "I've let you have your silence for two months. We're going to talk about Annie and Aaron very soon." I cringed when he said the A's names.

"But there's something more urgent we need to discuss." His voice was grim.

I rolled back. His fingers thrummed his knee. Shadowed eyes flicked back and forth.

"I'm listening."

He cleared his throat. "Have you turned on the CB radio? Do you know what's going on out there?"

"CB's been silent for days." Maybe weeks.

His mouth tilted down. "There's no kids, no old people...no women."

No kids. Somehow I knew. Didn't stop the burn simmering in my chest.

"Evie, they're saying women didn't survive this thing."

I shrugged and waved a hand over my body. "Obviously *they* are wrong."

"Women are gone. Dead." His eyes blazed. "And those who didn't die...their fate was worse."

"A fate worse than death." I whispered it, lived it, despised it.

He sucked in his cheeks. "Don't. Don't go there."

No, I'd plunge back into my fated solitude later. After I convinced him to leave me be. "Then get to your point."

"I've done my own investigation. In the two-hundred mile radius of this house, the rumors are true."

"You know this because you've searched through every house in the metropolitan area." Fucking melodrama.

He stood and swiped a hand over his mouth. "I knocked on doors and talked to men passing through from other cities. No one has seen another woman or child in at least four weeks."

"What about broadcasts from other parts of the country?" Surely the radio or internet would've debunked his fears.

"Same thing. The amateur radio stations claim this is a world-wide phenomenon."

A knot formed in my belly. "The ham operators are now our only source of communication?"

He rubbed his nodding head. "Attacks by the infected have grown out of control. They call them aphids and say they hunt in packs. The stories I've heard, the things I've seen..."

The things he'd seen? Unease stole through me. What risks did he take to get that information? "Aphids? Like the little green bugs in our garden?"

"Yeah, the ones that suck the life from our plants, infecting them with viruses at the same time. There's a strong resemblance between the mutated humans and those bugs."

I knew my arched eyebrows gave away my disbelief. I dreamt that shit. It wasn't real.

"We're talking parasitic feeding, Evie. Resilient defenses. And they look like them."

My curiosity piqued. I remembered the initial medical reports speculating that the nymph virus was designed to attack victims with low testosterone. The virus targeted human women, and a group of Muslim extremists topped the list of suspects.

His downcast eyes reflected the worry I felt. "No one knows if the virus was targeted at women intentionally."

I fought a hard swallow.

"Or if part of the plan involved mutated women spreading the infection to men," he said.

I tensed against a shiver as I replayed the frantic phone call from my brother-in-law announcing my sister's infection the day after their children passed. That night, he put a bullet in my sister's head and one in his own. I should've expected it. His was the typical response. Those early reports claimed mutated women—nymphs, they called them—attacked their own husbands, fathers, brothers.

"Do they know how the infection spread from women to men?" My voice was thready.

He nodded. "An infected woman changes, mutates...whatever you want to call it. And because of this mutation, she has these altered mouthparts." He wiggled his fingers in front of his mouth and dropped his hand. "Are you sure you want to hear this?"

"I can handle it." Perspiration formed on my spine.

"Okay, before the Internet went down, I watched a home video of this woman in bed. She looked like she had the flu. You know, sweaty, face all sunken in, lethargic, that kind of thing. Then a man knelt next to her and wiped her face."

He narrowed his eyes at me, waited for me to tune him out or tell him I'd heard enough. "This foot long tubelike thing shoots out her mouth. You could see the pointed end. But the man just fucking sat there. Even when it stabbed him in his chest. The camera was jerking around, darting out of the room, but you could still see that tube stuck in the man's chest. It was like a straw sucking up his...juices." His lips pinched in a line, eyes locked on mine.

Maybe he expected a shocked reaction. But I'd seen it before. In my nightmares. "The infection is transmitted during this feeding?"

"Yeah. The nymph injects some kind of wax-like compound that turns man into aphid."

"Have you seen this in person? The mutated mouth?"

"Not close up. They're impossible to run from because they move too damn fast." He paused as if replaying a specific memory. "You can't see them move. A fucking feat so terrifying, it feels like a trick on the eyes. I've kept my distance."

I covered my mouth with my hands. To think he'd been worried about *my* safety when he left me alone to take these day trips. "Jesus, Joel. What the fuck were you thinking?"

"I've only crossed paths with one a couple times and not until recently. I heard the rainy season kept them at bay. Water may be a weakness worth investigating."

I sagged against the headboard. Insectile humanoids. No women. Joel seemed so convinced. How did I avoid the infection? Just staying secluded? Maybe there were other mothers holed up like me. But my A's...the virus had been in the house.

His bright eyes roamed my face. "It's just you and I left in Grain Valley. Maybe in all of Kansas City. It's so desolate out there." A shadow passed over his face. He lowered his head. "I need you, Ba-y. I need you to help me figure this thing out."

Guilt squeezed my chest. I'd abandoned him and he didn't want to deal with it all alone anymore. "Okay. Help me take a shower and tell me more."

I swung my legs over the side of the bed. From the corner of my eye, I caught him staring at a rose etched hair-clip on my night stand. Annie's clip.

He lifted me and ducked his head, but not before I glimpsed the wetness in his eyes. My lips gravitated to his neck as he carried me away from the bed, the glass doors, and the lingering handprint.

Over the next two weeks, my insomnia persisted, but I ate everything Joel put in front of me. Day by day, my strength returned. We didn't have much of a plan, but we agreed on two priorities. Stay alive. Seek truth. Those words became our mantra.

He wouldn't let me run his day trips with him. Advertising my survival had too many unknown repercussions.

I held him in a hug. Given the scarcity of survivors, he'd have to travel out of state to gather supplies and information. He'd be gone all day.

When he left, my imagination went feral with visualizations of Joel in an ambush. Joel being gang raped. Joel riddled with bullets. Mutated Joel. To curb these thoughts, I cleaned our guns and took inventory of our ammo and food supply. Our produce was bare. He warned me to stay inside, but the spinach needed harvesting in the greenhouse and I needed to stay busy. His thorough patrol of the town had confirmed we were the only humans left for miles. I grabbed my USP .40 handgun on the way out.

The pool sat a few steps off the back porch. Hydrangeas, rhododendrons and peonies bordered the walk around the pool to the greenhouse. Cyprus mulch laded the air with fond memories. Once upon a good life, I had spent hours making over the various plants.

In the greenhouse, I settled the pistol on the lip of the potter filled with Brusselssprouts and tackled the spinach, green onion, basil. The plants weren't keeping up. Maybe Joel would find more seed.

The hairs rose on the back of my neck. I stilled my movements.

Nothing. No birds. No katydids. No rustling trees.

I stepped out. Two familiar figures stood on the retaining wall on the other side of the pool. Annie wore her sundress with rainbow stitching. Aaron hunched behind her in his Star Wars shirt, an arm wrapped around her leg, the other around a teddy bear named Booey. I took a steeling breath and approached the pool on shaky legs.

Annie's face lit up. "Look Mama. I found him. See?"

The wind caught her dress and she held it in place. Aaron looked up at his sister and giggled.

She ruffled his hair and pinned me with the golden glow of her eyes. "Mama? The water's warm now. Can we swim today?"

My heart jumped to my throat. I stopped a few feet before them. "I don't think so, honey."

She tilted her head and crossed her arms. "You don't have time for us anymore, Mama."

"Course I do, sweetheart." Sobs cut up my words. I wanted to comfort her, but she was just another hallucination.

Annie extended her arm and pointed a finger in my direction. She tugged Aaron to his feet. Their skin and muscle sizzled. Then it melted from their small skeletal frames.

My muscles locked. I opened my mouth to scream. No sound came out.

Their skeletons flaked into dust and evaporated into a gray mist. The vapor gusted through me as if a vacuum inhaled it from behind.

All the sounds of summer exploded at once. Chills invaded, reached into my bones. I covered my ears and turned my head to follow the mist.

A fully mutated aphid crouched six feet away. Its wide body and enlarged back forced it to hump over. The insect-like mouth wormed out. A stylet protruded from a sheath. The mouth clicked. Black fluid leaked out.

Pinpricked pupils dotted its all white eyes. Eyes that measured me in the same manner I measured it. Muscles and blood rippled under green see-through skin. Scraps of a receding hair line and beard outlined its bulbous head.

No, it couldn't be. A heart and arrow tattoo seemed to pump over cartilage and veins on its chest. It was Stan. Flirty fucking Stan who lived two houses down.

It shifted on its double-jointed legs and inched forward. Fuck. The fucking pistol was in the greenhouse. The scissors I used to cut spinach weighted my hand.

The pool sat a knife's throw to my left. Was it a good time to test Joel's water theory? A pitch fork stuck out of the compost pile on my right.

Stay alive.

I whipped the scissors at the aphid. Leapt for the pitch fork. Pinned the handle between my ribs and upper arm. Then I turned to face it.

It plunged into the fork with mouthparts snapping. Hooks for hands clawed at my face and missed me by millimeters. The thing continued attacking as if it didn't feel the tongs impaling its chest and the scissors lodged in its neck.

My pulse raced. I held it squirming at a distance as it robbed my courage. It weighed at least a hundred pounds more than me and struck with the speed of a rattler. I needed skill over strength.

Can we swim today?

I aimed the fork at the pool. It shoved back and redirected with a swinish force. We were three feet from the water's edge. Might as well have been three miles.

A claw flew out. Brushed my hair. Missed my head. I squeezed the fork's handle. Wrenched it from the aphid's chest and raised it over my shoulder.

My heart raced. Black innards dripped from the fork's tongs next to my face. I swung the handle downward, smacking the point that thrust from its gaping maw.

The mouth went limp with a squeal. I hit it again. Exhaustion stole my balance. The aphid hit the ground and so did I. I kicked it in the torso and it rolled over the edge of the pool.

A pincer shot up and closed around my ankle. I scraped my nails along the concrete edge. My fingers lost purchase. A huge breath filled my lungs and I went underwater.

He thrusts his fists against the posts and still insists he sees the ghosts.

Stephen King, *It*

CHAPTER THREE: THERAPY

The noon sun lit up the water with crystal clarity. The aphid sank and pulled me with it. I bent my waist and pried the claw on my ankle. It clamped harder.

Pressure pounded my chest. The aphid body had zero buoyancy, a fucking anchor attached to my leg. It didn't struggle. Didn't pull. Just simply sank.

Panic set in. The need to gasp set my lungs on fire. What was I thinking using the pool as a means to escape that thing?

The aphid's skin pulsed in a pearlescent glimmer. A kaleidoscope of formations came and went, morphing its body. For a few precious seconds, I was captivated by the transformation. Tumors emerged, fungus-like, bubbling on its back and arms. Beads of air clouded the water and clung to my hair floating around me. It was dissolving.

I kicked with my legs and worked at the claw with my hand. Tiny hairs, like razor-sharp spines, bit my palm.

Then the hook went limp, releasing me. The abomination that was my neighbor drifted away, sinking, eyes open and staring. I swam like hell and didn't look back until the front door was barricaded behind me with extra boards and more nails than it needed.

Joel found me that night slouched at the kitchen island, still in my clothes, which were dry and stiff. *Clunk-clunk-clunk* filled the room as his gear hit the floor. I slipped my shredded palm under the counter when he approached.

He glanced at the reinforced front door then turned hawk eyes on me. "Evie?"

I gave him a lazy smile. "Hey."

"What happened today?" Low and steady, his tone alerted me nothing was getting by him.

"There was a situation."

He sat down across the island and raked his fingers through his hair. "Tell me."

The story unraveled. In his dominating way, he stripped every detail from me. Except my A's. I didn't discuss my delusions. Never.

His composure disintegrated as my report went on. His face flushed. Trenches rutted his hair from his fingers pushing through it. But he let me unfold the events without interrupting. The greenhouse. The aphid. The pitchfork. When I told him I was pulled into the pool, he gripped the edge of the counter with white knuckles.

Then I recounted the part about the spiny arm shackled to my leg. He sprang from the stool and kicked it across the room. It bounced off the wall.

"What the fuck?" He paced, keeping his distance from me. Red splotched his face and neck.

He paused before me, his control on a brittle leash. "You went outside. Oh wait…No. Not only did you go outside, you were armed with a pair of scissors? Are you fucking stupid?"

Probably, but I was smart enough to keep my mouth shut while his temper roared.

"Okay. Fine. We're going to make this real clear." He pointed a shaky finger at me. "Absolutely no going outside alone." He dropped his hand to the counter and blinked at me. "Nod your head."

Feeling like a sixteen year old with a bad report card, I nodded.

"And *if*...I repeat...*if* you have to leave this house alone"—he paused—"we're talking about the house on fire here." He played with his goatee, probably considering other scenarios. "If you have to egress alone, under no circumstances do you do so without your shotgun, carbine, side arm and vest."

I nodded again.

He paced a few laps around the island, pausing at the floor-length windows each time to survey the backyard. When it came to me, he was all bark. I wasn't frightened. Just too exhausted for a boiling confrontation. So, I kept quiet. Watched him pace. Waited for the cool down.

He righted the stool and settled on top of it. "Let me see your hand."

I put my hand in his, palm up. Crimson gashes tattooed my skin, wrist to fingertips. I watched his eyes, asked the question that had been plaguing me. "Am I infected now?"

His head snapped up, face soft. "No, B-ay. Since you seem to be immune to the airborne virus, we only have to worry about getting bit now. That...mouth thing has to release a compound. That's how men absorb the infection." He squeezed my arm. "I may not know a lot about what's going on, but on this I'm positive."

"How do you know? I could be carrying it now and not know. What are the symptoms?"

His flinch mirrored my inward cringe. I wanted to withdraw the question. Instead, we sat in silence, reliving our worst memories. The fever. The thinning skin, turning gray then green. Bloody vomit soaking butterfly-printed sheets. Contorted faces. Pupils receding until they weren't there at all. Tiny hands hardening, elongating. "You're right. I'm not infected." I forced my eyes to his. "There's not much left of the aphid. I checked from the deck a few times before the sun went down."

He prodded my hand. "Maybe there's something to that water theory, huh?" He laid my hand on the counter and fetched the medical kit.

"There's something else," I said. "This will sound naive, but I wasn't afraid of it. I tapped into…I don't know what to call it, instincts maybe, that I didn't know I had. I mean, I was worried at first. Then I remembered my self-defense training and figured out how to beat it."

"It's called adrenaline. Grandmas use that shit to lift cars and save little kids." He returned with antiseptic and bandages. "Doesn't matter. Next time, you'll be armed. No more close encounters."

"Yeah…okay." Except that close encounter made me feel alive for the first time in two months.

Although Joel's uneventful day paled in comparison, his productivity lifted our morale. He collected most of the items on our supply list, acquiring the majority from empty homes. All of the gas stations were dry, but he siphoned more gas than we needed from abandoned cars.

"Most of the neighboring cities dropped off the power grid," he said. "Grain Valley will follow soon." Water had shut off two days earlier.

He stood and rummaged through one of the pouches. "I only ran into two men today. And I saw at least half a dozen aphids. I wasn't able to pry anything substantial from the men. They were pretty skittish. Neither had been out of their homes in a while."

Two weeks had passed since I crawled out of my depression. The last broadcast television station went off the air a week earlier. We longed for communication, news, any information that could give us hope.

He glanced up at me then went back to his bag. "I don't think there are many people left. If there are, they've moved on."

Made sense. I remembered a statistic on the problem the Social Security Administration faced concerning the country's population. A smile crept up. There was a problem solved overnight. "The SSA reported something like sixty percent of the U.S. was between ages eighteen and sixty-four. Would that be comparable to the age group that survived this thing?"

He nodded, interest glinting his eyes. "Cut that in half to eliminate women and we're down to thirty percent."

"But a lot of men in that age group died, with all the mutant attacks, crime, accidents, other illnesses. At best, I'd say only fifteen percent of the human race is alive today." It was probably closer to ten percent. And without the ability to reproduce, that number would dwindle.

He stood, hands behind his back. "You're such a nerd."

Well, I was a numbers junkie by profession and currently on disability leave from my big bank job. My employer had called it mental stress. I lost my kids. Mental stress seemed an inaccurate description. Didn't matter. All world markets crashed a week later.

He curled up the corner of his mouth. "I have a surprise for you."

My eyebrows rose.

He dangled a clear bag in front of me. It unrolled and three joints settled to the bottom. "Wanna fly Mexican airlines?"

I wrapped my arms around his neck and whispered against his mouth, "Mr. Delina. You shouldn't have."

"Mmm…I figured we both could use a little escape."

He pulled me against him. Kissed along my jaw. Paused at my ear and wet his lips. His voice rumbled from deep within his chest. "Here's how this is going to go down. We're going to light up the ganja in the sun room. Then you're going to ride me before we hit the second spliff. And when we are good and ripped, I'm going to bend you over the side of the bed and take you from behind until you scream for me."

Just like him to tell me how it was going to be. He knew what that did to me. A forgotten sensation resurrected in my womb. I squeezed my thighs together and grabbed a six pack of beer from the counter. "Why are we still talking?"

In the sun room, we reclined on the couch. He exhaled and passed the bud.

I twisted the joint back and forth between my finger and thumb. "Where'd you get this, anyway?"

"You know that punk kid who always parked his beater on the street at the bottom of the hill?" He tilted his head toward the street. "Beater's glove box."

He brushed a stray hair from my face. "It's a damn fine thing to see some of your vices back."

I squashed the roach in the ashtray and wrinkled my nose at him. "Are we talking about the nicotine addiction or the sex addiction?"

"You know damn well it was the pack-a-day I didn't like."

I straddled his waist and planted my hands on the back of the couch on either side of his head.

His mouth caught mine and his arousal nudged my belly. "I'm sorry I yelled at you today."

I ran my thumb across his lips. "I know."

"You used to stand up for yourself when I lost my temper like that."

I shrugged. "I know." I didn't blame him for losing it. He carried enough guilt leaving me alone, each time outlining do's and don'ts. I disobeyed him and I paid for it.

His fingers pressed into my waist. His hips ground against mine. "I guess I'll sleep better when all your vices are back. Though, I think I can wait for your temper to return."

"Then let's just focus on one nasty habit at a time, shall we?" I twisted his nipples. His back arched.

He ripped off my nightshirt and followed through on his promises. I screamed for him several times and rediscovered the part of me I'd buried. Did it mean I was moving forward? Had I finally conquered myself, my grief? Where were the tears? Maybe they'd never come.

After, we held each other and lapped up the afterglow of sex, smoke and tender memories of the very good life we once shared. We kept our conversations light, aware of the pressing decisions we faced and danger that awaited us outside.

And neither of us gave voice to the question that hovered between us, the one that screamed to be answered. Why had I survived?

April is the cruellest month.

T. S. Eliot

Chapter Four: April Fool

Scissors in hand, I stared at my reflection over the vanity, at the long hair Joel favored. I sectioned out a chunk and whacked off ten inches. The tresses hit the floor. No retreat. Much like the devastation of humanity.

Looking back, we should've seen it coming. Escalating religious unrest. Ethnic conflict. Political struggle. We should've known. It was happening globally in every city, every country.

I brushed out the next section. Chopped another ten inches.

A growing bravado from Muslim extremists had intensified the wars with…well, anyone who wasn't Muslim. The U.S. spent years attacking the source. But when the war arrived on U.S. soil on April first, everything changed. I tried to put up a wall around my remembrance of the day the virus hit. An ugly ball of grief swelled in my throat and my memories pierced through.

I sat in the boardroom at work. Grain Valley Elementary flashed on my cell phone. The school's nurse. Annie and Aaron had high fevers. I called Joel and left to pick up the kids.

Annie and Aaron died ten hours later.

I yanked the comb through a tangled knot. Gave up. Cut an angle to frame my face. The next section dropped in my eyes.

Those final ten hours replayed in my head every day since. Tucked together in Annie's bed, my A's held on to each other through bouts of fevers and chills. Joel and I held on to them. We sang their favorite songs with them. When their voices ebbed, we read to them. They dozed in and out of consciousness and I told them, "When you feel better, we'll go to the park. We'll slide down that big slide you love."

Two little heads bobbed in agreement.

"We'll go to the zoo. You know we just got a new polar bear? We'll go visit him."

That earned me pallid smiles. I kissed them all over their tiny faces and hands. "Mommy loves you so much."

When Aaron exhaled his final breath, Annie touched his cheek. "Mama? Where did my brother go?"

I shook my head. The weight of the house pressed down the ceiling and crushed my chest. The walls closed in. Squeezed my shoulders. Cut my breaths.

"Don't worry, Mama. I'll find him." The curve of Annie's mouth slacked. The rise and fall of her torso slowed. Stopped.

I extended the scissors open. The sharp end sliced my wrist. Blood dripped down my arm and pooled in the bend at my elbow. I hadn't shed a single tear in my grief. Joel always teased that I was born without tear ducts. Even through my children's deaths, even while in the deep well of despair I'd receded into, my eyes remained dry.

We never impressed a religious opinion on our A's. They asked numerous questions about creation and death, to which we would shrug our shoulders and ask them what they thought. In our worst nightmare, we weren't prepared for our dying daughter's inquiry.

Where did my brother go?

I stabbed the scissors' edge deeper into my wrist. Would bleeding be a proxy to crying? The tip felt cold and unforgiving against my skin. I pressed harder. Crimson welled. I waited to bleed out, to feel peace as my life soaked into the carpet.

"It's shorter than mine now."

I jumped. Joel leaned around the door frame. I followed his gaze to my wrist. The scissors hovered over the unblemished skin. I blinked, shook off the fantasy and set the scissors down.

"Yeah." I cleared my throat. "I attempted the shag style teen boys were wearing. Think I can pass as one?"

He stared at my chest. A smirk plastered his face.

I flattened my palms on my breasts. "I can make these less noticeable. Otherwise, what do you think?"

He kissed me. "I think your body armor and weapons will help."

I returned the kiss with a love that matched my hate for the world.

"Come on." He led me to the den.

I nestled into one end of the couch. The room touted two stories of floor to ceiling windows and opened to the deck and sun room. The reflection from the pool water rippled along the khaki walls. Behind us, a staircase led to the open balcony of the top floor. The floor once occupied by a seven year old girl adept at painting flowers and a six year boy who proudly conquered *Lego Star Wars* on the Xbox. Having our bedroom on the main level made it a little easier to ignore the rooms upstairs.

He knelt over me, took my mouth with his and rescued my thoughts. I reveled in the feel of his weight on me.

We came up for air. Good to know I could still throb from only a kiss.

His voice was husky. "What were you obsessing about in the bathroom?"

He knew too well how my anxiety funneled south, bottlenecking between my legs.

I locked my thighs around his hips. "The virus."

His eyes darted to the top of the stairs. He tensed, seemed to be engaged in some kind of internal war. His jaw clenched, relaxed, then he looked at me, heavy-lidded, resolve in place. "The virus you survived." His lips moved down my neck.

The virus that was created by a Muslim insurgency and released in Denver International. The virus that killed or mutated victims within a few hours of exposure.

His mouth hovered over my breast and dampened my shirt. I exhaled, "Yeah, that's the one."

We tossed our clothes on the floor. Guns followed. A sheen of sweat stuck my back to the leather couch. His mouth found mine, his muscles flexing around me. Our kissing deepened. We began to share breaths.

"I'm the luckiest man on the planet," he murmured.

"Uh huh."

"I'm the only man who gets to make love to his wife."

I sighed. We couldn't assume I was the only woman. And he told me women didn't mutate immediately after exposure. Maybe some recovered from the sickness.

He pulled back. "Where are you?"

"Why do they call them nymphs?"

He perched his chin on his fist. "A nymph is a smaller immature version of an adult bug. Like a baby bug."

This implied nymphs would grow into aphids. Which meant aphids weren't just male. "What do you know about them?"

He traced a finger over my ribs. "I don't know, Ba-y. Haven't seen one since those first couple weeks. I think they all died. In those videos I watched online, they looked sick, but not scary—at least when they weren't attacking. Not scary like an aphid."

I thought about the alabaster eyes that stared back at me when the aphid dragged me to the bottom of the pool. "But they attacked people. Turned their victims into monsters."

"Yeah, but in those first few days, everyone was doing whatever was needed to keep their families safe. Honestly, Evie, I don't know what I would've done if you woke up next to me with eggs for eyes. Which probably means most husbands, boyfriends, didn't survive."

Didn't survive. He meant mutated. Unlike all the children and elderly, who died because they were too weak to make the transition.

Fingers moved down, explored my hip, kneaded and circled their way to my inner thigh. His body hummed against mine. Worry lines vanished from his forehead and the heat in his eyes burned out the remainder of my anxiety. The moment he filled me and our bodies slapped together, the storm of pleasure was all I cared about.

Thump.

The muffled echo from the basement stole the air around us. Neither of us moved. Or breathed.

Thump. Thump. Thump.

The walls vibrated. Then the shatter of glass. The basement window.

I gasped. "Joel?"

He jumped off me, gathered the guns. I followed at his heels, my pulse a hot beat in my ears. In our bedroom, he dressed, strapped on his holster and hooked mags on his belt.

I pulled on my clothes with trembling fingers. "Where are you—"

"Shh." He shoved my carbine against my chest. "Stay here."

"No."

He narrowed his eyes at me, jaw set. "Wait. Here."

Scratch. Scratch. Thump. The basement door.

"Fuck you."

"Dammit, Evie." An impatient exhale. "Don't forget your fucking vest." He jerked his head to my bullet proof vest slouched in the corner and bolted from the room.

I lugged on the vest and carbine, and found him squatting at the top of the basement stairs. If the door at the bottom remained closed, we couldn't tell. Sandbags stacked to the ceiling and three stairs deep. The true barricade. The painstaking task took him about a week of collecting and hauling. Another activity I left him to do alone.

The scratching grew more persistent.

"Whatever it is, it can't get in," I whispered.

"It's already in. It's already in our fucking house." Deep creases marred his brow.

"Fine. But it can't get to us."

The scratching stopped. The distant sound of waves broke through the sudden blanket of silence. Like the brushing of water along the shore at low tide. But it wasn't water. It was sand. The steady flow of sand pouring out of our sandbag wall.

Let us not look back in anger, nor forward in fear, but around in awareness.

James Thurber

CHAPTER FIVE: DO NOT LOOK BACK

An orange glow spread over the horizon and dimmed into the violet sky above. Joel and I crept down the hill along our house to the backyard, where the walk-out basement was exposed.

His fist popped up and his eyes bored into me. I nodded. No sound. We edged though the dark and I gathered my courage. Did we make the right decision? We could have waited inside for the sandbag wall to empty and killed the bastards as they came through. Maybe it wasn't too late to turn back.

We rounded the final corner and I matched his steps to the daylight windows that dressed the basement's foundation. June bugs tapped off the wide lens of my flashlight like popcorn. Shards crunched under our boots as we neared the broken window, under the cover of the deck forty feet above.

His back stiffened. Then he sucked in a breath and let out a shrill whistle. I shrunk into myself. My eyes darted behind us, expecting the backyard shadows to solidify and attack.

He shouted into the hole, "Hello."

A toad croaked a mating song from the thick sedge of the surrounding woods.

"Come out," he yelled.

Katydids responded in vibrato from the trees above.

"Come out now, or I'll burn the fucker down."

Uh huh. Like I'd let him do that. Several minutes passed. The darkness within held still. The creatures of summer nights chirped around us.

He caught my eyes. "Remember the plan?"

Yeah. The plan I didn't agree with. The plan that sent him in after the threat if it didn't come to us. The plan that left me outside standing watch. I handed him the flashlight. I lost the argument in the house. Further obstinacy would gain me nothing.

He accepted the light and vanished through the toothy window, fading into the shadows.

I scanned the pool area. This was the part of the plan I hated most. If he didn't return after a few minutes, I was to run. Drive away. Don't look back.

A crash echoed across the basement's tile floor. I was never very good at following orders.

I stepped over the window ledge and looked for his light. Pitch black. "Joel?" One heartbeat. Two.

Why didn't we bring two flashlights? Even in our haste, we should've planned better. I inhaled a shaky breath. The bulk of the unfamiliar vest hampered my movement as I sidled along one wall, tapping one foot in front of the other. The basement's musty aroma carried a hint of bitterness. Metallic. Blood.

My mouth formed Joel's name. Only a soundless gasp escaped. My boot kicked something. Metal clanked through the dark.

His flashlight. The source of the crash.

My muscles tightened as it rolled to a stop. I marshaled my breathing and waited for quiet to settle through the room.

A rustling sound crept from the next room. The room where the stairs were.

"Joel?"

A man-sized silhouette illuminated the doorway. How was it glowing? Hunched over, it ran a claw across its mouth. Black blood pumped under flickering skin that stretched like the dorsal of a well-fed tick. Its hunger was so palpable, the strength of it seemed to fuel the glow.

Its head cocked right. Then left. Could it see me? I tightened my grip on the carbine. Lifted the stock to my jaw. Dammit, where was Joel? If I started spraying ammo, I could hit him with stray bullets. The gun rattled in my grasp.

The aphid crouched forward on its hind legs with claws outstretched.

My finger slipped with sweat next to the trigger. The thing prowled closer. I waited.

A few feet away, the aphid extended its jaws and spat a ribbon of matter down its torso. The outline of its body quavered. Then it swiped its forearms and emitted a high-pitched buzz. The pitch was dizzying. I wavered, disoriented.

It lunged with hunting weapons gripping my body. I kicked at its legs, landed on my back and the tile bit my head. The damn vest made it impossible to move. The bug took advantage of my awkward rolling and struck out its cutting mandible, flinging dribble on my cheek like warm maple syrup. The mouth's keen tip lanced my vest and sliced it open, inch by inch.

Somehow while falling I'd managed to position the barrel of the carbine under its jaw. My finger made a final lap around the trigger guard. I plunged and squeezed. The gun's recoil ricocheted through my ribs and the lifeless body crumbled atop me.

I lay on my back, numb and blinking through dregs of gore that pooled in my eyes. "Joel." It was a choking scream. Please answer. Please be okay.

The slow leak of the aphid's blood trickled over my throat to my nape, soaking my scalp, fingering its way to my back through the vest. Just blood. It wouldn't infect me.

I shoved at the body, rolled it off with a grunt. "Joel." Louder that time.

"Evie?" His footsteps sped up and grew nearer.

The worst of my dread seeped from my muscles. I swiped my eyes with the back of my hand.

"Evie." His hands searched my body. "Evie, fuck…thank God you're okay. I'm sorry. I dropped the damn flashlight. Then the fucker hit me. Knocked me out. Evie, I'm so sorry."

The intent in his voice, the depth of his love, he was my existence. It hurt to hear it, to feel it, knowing one bite could steal it all away. "Was there just one?"

He turned his head, eyes knifing the shadowed corpse at my side. "Yeah."

"We're leaving." I cupped his jaw, captured his gaze. "We're packing and we're going to my dad's." My father's home at Pomme de Terre Lake was a three hour drive. It was isolated. On a lake. Easier to defend. Safer.

His hand reached for mine and he pulled me to my feet.

We wouldn't leave without securing the house we worked so hard to make our home. We hoped to return someday. Neither of us spoke as we labored through the night, packing and boarding up vulnerable entry points.

In the early morning, I stood at the kitchen window and watched the rain splash on the surface of the pool. Joel leaned a piece of plywood against the wall and waited for me to move. Only one window left to board up.

I stepped out of the way. "What still needs to be loaded in the Rubicon?"

He lifted the board and set it in place. "Did you get the last of the winter clothes?"

"Yeah. Just the clothes from our closet."

His eyes darted to the top of the stairs. We stored most of our seasonal clothing in the upstairs attic, but neither of us would go up there.

"You know we'll need to say good-bye to their rooms," I said. "To their things."

He looked away and screwed the board in place. A chill raced down my spine. I knew if I didn't go up there, I'd never have closure.

He sank the last screw and leaned against the board. "I know." Dark circles bruised his eyes. We didn't talk about the previous night. Just like we never talked about that final night with our A's. When Annie took her last breath, somehow I found my feet and walked out. I slid into our bed and into my abyss for two months. I shouldn't have left him to deal with their bodies alone. I knew the mortuaries turned him away. Too many dead bodies. Too much fear of contagion. But I stayed in bed, lured by the dark edges of my depression.

My throat tightened. I backed away from his downcast eyes. His voice echoed on a distant plane. "Don't do this. Don't sink back to that place again."

He cremated our babies in the backyard. I remembered the vista from my bed and the smoke that hovered over the deck for hours like a Thanatos taunting. An embodiment of death.

My heart pummeled at my rib cage as if it wanted out. The throwing knives Joel gave me a few years earlier could quiet it. I fantasized piercing the thumping thing in my chest with the six inches of high carbon steel. With the right angle of the blade between two ribs, I would push hard and fast on the handle.

"Evie. Stop this goddammit. We grieved in different ways. And doing it alone was our way." He gripped my shoulders and forced me to look at him.

I pushed a syllable past the lump in my throat. "'kay." I hated that my voice sounded so weak.

He tugged me to his chest and rested his lips on the top of my head. "So you're going to pull your shit together. Then we're going to go up there and say good-bye. Then Evie?" He fastened me with his eyes, held me there. "We are *not* going to look back."

His arms dropped and he stalked out of the room.

I clutched the railing at the bottom of the stairs and steeled myself for the rooms above. Remembered images flooded in. Hand painted grass stretched to a cotton cloud sky and brightened the walls in Annie's room. Sparkling butterflies dangled from the ceiling and her four post bed animated the room with grace and charm, mirroring her spirit. Aaron's room was a dark contrast, with the walls and ceiling painted black. The top half of a crater covered moon peeked up from the floor and devoured an entire wall. Glow-in-the-dark paint glazed the surfaces, illuminating it at night.

Viewing their rooms for real turned my stomach over in violent waves. I rubbed a bead of sweat from my forehead and jumped when Joel touched my back.

"Are you ready?" His voice was thready.

I interlaced my fingers with his and squeezed. We looked up and began our ascent. I focused on cheerful memories like the A's garland-draped balcony at Christmas. They would hide on the landing and spy on Santa below, who was Joel and two pillows stuffed in a Santa suit.

We reached the crest and he turned me to Annie's room. With the windows boarded up from the outside, the room harbored unfamiliar shadows. He must have boarded those weeks earlier. He whispered next to my ear, "It's okay."

I drew on his strength and forced my feet to step into the room. The bed sprawled in the center. Stripped down, the naked mattress served as a heart-breaking reminder of its eternal vacancy. I opened the closet and ran my fingers along the hems of her dresses. Ruffles and lace and ribbons of all colors. Her favorite doll sat on a shelf and stared at nothing.

The air around me squeezed my chest. I wheezed and backed away from the closet. His hands tightened on my arms. "You have to breathe, Ba-y. Deep breaths."

I took his advice then wrestled away from him. "Joel, you're not just up here for me. We do this together. I'll keep my shit tight, okay?"

He nodded once and reached for my hand.

In Aaron's room, I struggled with a fear of confinement. The black walls caved in. Unexposed to light for weeks, the galaxy no longer glowed. He handed me the Maglite from a pouch on his riggers belt. I walked to the bed and flashed the beam over the bedding. I didn't find what I looked for.

He stepped behind me and said, as if strangled, "Booey isn't here."

I faced him. Though I knew the answer, I asked, "Where's the bear?"

"He's...he's with...oh God Evie..." He buried his face in his hands and slid down the wall.

I dropped to my knees and held on to him. Pressed into the curve of his shoulder, I absorbed the vibrations of his sobs. Heartache slammed into me like a fighting bull.

I didn't know how long we clung to the shadows that darkened that room. "I'm glad Booey is with Aaron. He loved that bear."

"I know, Evie. Christ, I know."

We stood, helping each other find footing. Then we made our final descent from the top floor and never looked back.

In the garage, Joel and I stared at the Rubicon. Annie and Aaron called it the jumper jeep. With a five inch lift kit and mud terrain radials, the kids rode in it like a ride in an amusement park, bouncing and giggling.

With the packing complete and the house locked up, I looked to Joel.

He lifted the two A.L.I.C.E. packs in front of him, shoved one of them at me. "Whatever you do, don't lose this."

Expecting about thirty pounds of weight, I accepted the pack and wasn't surprised.

He locked his eyes with mine. "It contains all your basic survival stuff. If anything happens to me, if we get separated…or worse, you grab it. Okay?"

I threw it over my back. My five-foot six frame held it ineptly, so I straightened. "Okay, I get it. Just like your life insurance policy."

He smiled. "Exactly."

After loading the packs, we donned our armored vests and raised the garage doors. In the jeep, I plugged my MP3 player into the stereo's aux jack and set up my punk rock playlist.

He backed out of the garage and locked up. When he jumped back in, *Theme From a NOFX Album* thumped through the speakers. The song's catchy beat had a way of pounding away my fraying nerves. I needed its cheer.

He rolled the jeep to the end of the driveway and stopped. I hadn't left the house since I brought my A's home. Their last day of school.

Two months of isolation. I didn't know what to expect. Twice, I fought an aphid and won. What if I'd burned through my luck?

He chewed his bottom lip, his eyelids half closed as he slid on his driving gloves. He taught me everything I knew about self-defense. Yet he fouled up his first close-encounter against a bug. Would his luck be better next time? And the time after that? I concealed my trembling fingers under my thighs and looked back at the boarded up house. The house we raised our babies in.

"Stay alive. Seek truth." I forced the mantra passed my lips.

"And do not look back."

We were doing this. We'd be fine. Yeah, we were fine. Just fine.

The chorus clapped in. He blinked then joined the vocals. With a seemingly forced smile, he raised his voice, singing.

I wanted to share in the optimism that peeked around the shadows on his face. But to be honest, it gave me the creeps. As he backed into the street and coasted down the hill, my gut rolled with dread.

Death is as sure for that which is born, as birth is for that which is dead.
Therefore grieve not for what is inevitable.

Bhagavad-Gita

CHAPTER SIX: GLOW OF THE ETERNAL PRESENT

I nudged up the bill of my baseball cap and dropped my chin to let the sunglasses slide down my nose.

Overgrown landscapes swallowed the monotony of patios and sidewalks. Porches offered withered flower pots and morning newspapers that decried the end of news. Other homes crumbled, burned from pillage and rioting.

Choking sewers and decaying crops replaced the usual summer perfume of cut grass and burgers on the barbecues. And beneath the miasma of abandonment, lurked the rot of the dead.

Nothing stirred beyond a tattered flag, a waving screen door, and the drift of a child's swing. Nothing lived.

Joel slowed under a darkened stop light and dodged a large furry lump baking into the asphalt.

"A dog?" I asked.

"Or coyote. There used to be a lot strays. Now, it's a rare thing to see something walking around on four legs."

Because aphids fed on all mammals. But only the lucky human genome was susceptible to mutation.

A crow perched on the exposed rib cage, beak buried in the bowels. An overturned skateboard teetered on the curb beside it.

Wreckage barricaded the road ahead. He rolled over the curb, cut through a yard. From within the warped metal, protruded a disembodied arm, a booted leg. A shredded torso folded over a car door. I shuddered, tensing more when his hand squeezed my knee.

In our bedroom community, everyone knew and trusted each other. Yet the neighbors who hadn't perished in their homes or on their front lawns seemed to have slipped into the night. I thought about Jan, the Pump 'N Go brute, who sold me smokes with a grunt and a bothered glare. I bet she used an insectile mouth to take out her angst on an unsuspecting customer.

Then there was Ted, the baker at the Piggly Wiggly. His kind smile and crusty Italian loaves made listening to his tales about nineteen grandchildren worthwhile. He probably mutated then fed from the family he adored.

I smiled, remembering the kid at the corner McCoffee. He could barely keep his dick in his pants long enough to steam my espresso before skittering to the parking lot to steam his windows with the girl *du jour*. I didn't have to do too much imagining to guess his demise.

"Evie, keep your face covered. Just because we haven't seen anyone, doesn't mean we won't."

His distraction wouldn't work. The brick building, the playground, and the school buses filled my horizon. The "Home of the Grain Valley Eagles" sign swung on one end, a haunting reminder of what must have occurred there.

I traced a finger along the stitching on my forearm sheaths. It was the first time I'd worn them outside of training. Joel gave me six knives. I wore two on each arm. Each had a black six inch blade of 1050 high carbon steel with a paracord wrapped handle. When he gave them to me, I read *The Art of Throwing*. Then he drilled me in the same way he did all his training. Merciless repetition. But I looked forward to the drills and to the rush of power from every throw. Within a few months, I was flinging them with confidence. Each time the blade slipped from my grasp, down that horizontal plane, I felt invulnerable. My small size no longer significant.

I flexed my forearms to test the straps. They felt like they belonged there.

Joel hissed. I snapped my head up from the knives in time to see an aphid lurching into the road. He jerked the wheel to avoid hitting it and regained control of the jeep long enough to throw us into the path of three more. The brakes squealed as we bowled into them.

Given the height of our Rubicon, we bounced over two of the three, jarring my body against the seat belt. But the hard brake caused the jeep to take a slight nose dive and send the third one up the ramp of the hood. Just as quickly as it cracked our windshield, the aphid regained its bearing and glared at us through the crunched glass.

Black blood bubbled from its head wound, but it didn't seem to notice. It crouched on the hood, its humped body vibrating in sync with its buzzing.

The aphid orbs fixed on me, unmoving. Its hunger dripped in shoestring spittle from the pointed mouth that writhed in its jowls. But under the hunger, something else lurked. Something trapped in its milky eyes that didn't blink. There was a knowing.

For the first time, I felt the weight of the knives buckled to my arms. I didn't care if the thing staring back had once been Jan or Ted or the horny coffee boy. It wanted to eat me. I rolled down the window and unsheathed a blade.

"What are you doing? Roll up the fucking window." He thumped the gas pedal to the floor.

The jeep propelled forward and the back of my head hit the seat. The aphid lashed out a claw and smacked the brittle windshield. More spider webs crawled through the glass. It held on, its claw embedded in a splintering hole.

We raced down two blocks, building speed. The aphid reached through the open window. I swiped its forearm and amputated the claw. A spurt of blood filled the car with a metallic rot.

The aphid yanked its maimed appendage tight to its body and hung on to the windshield with its good arm.

It took six blocks of unobstructed roadway to max out our speed. He released the gas and locked up the brakes. His forearm smacked my chest as inertia shot the aphid tumbling through the street before us. He stomped the gas again. The bug screamed as we rolled over it. I rubbernecked to watch it drag its mangled body into the gutter.

We arrived in Hermitage, Missouri three hours later with fewer bumps in the road. The sky opened between soggy clouds as daylight weakened under the segue of dusk. The jeep's knobby tires stirred up dust laden with acidic moisture, scenting the air with the earthy aroma of rain.

Joel sped up when we neared an open pasture. Four aphids grazed on a bull, which was toppled over and turned inside out. The placidness of the feeding seemed unnatural. One of the aphids lifted its head from the carcass and watched us pass.

At the end of the field, a cow pressed against the fence. Its big brown eyes stared at nothing as it bellowed, nudging the post with its head.

My heart flipped over. "Joel, we have to—"

"Where was the cow destined before the virus? In the hands of humans, in the claws of aphids, the food chain hasn't changed."

Except our species lost its position as the top consumer. My heart landed somewhere in the vicinity of my stomach.

"We should stop there and see if there's anything we need." He coasted the jeep into the parking lot of a small grocer station. Pristine panes of glass veneered the exterior. "Doesn't look like anyone's looted this one yet."

I let out a choked laugh. "Yeah, bet we just passed the town looters in that pasture. They're looting other things now."

He frowned as he angled the jeep with the driver side door inches from the entrance. Bent over the steering wheel, he scrutinized the store's small interior. "I'll keep the engine running while I check it out. Ready your—" He glanced at the pistol in my hand. "Good girl. Five minutes, okay?"

I nodded, scanned the bleak horizon through the cracks in the windshield.

The car door latched shut and the wait began. I chewed a nail. Checked the mag. Chambered a round. Back to nail chewing. Come on, Joel.

A motor rent the air, grew louder. Then a lone figure rolled over the hill on a motorcycle. The gun shook in my hand as the bike turned into the parking lot.

Inside the store, a dusty dark clouded the depths. Where was he?

The biker stopped beside me, his eyes bugging under his helmet. Should I point the gun? Would that scare him away?

The features on his weathered face rearranged themselves from strained shock to soft elation. Then his mouth and eyes hardened. Determination.

I raised the gun, trained it on his chest.

He shook his head. "Open the door." His voice muffled through the window.

My other hand joined the one on the gun, cupping the grip, stabilizing the aim.

He showed his empty hands, his smile. "You're...aw, Christ, you're a looker. I haven't seen woman since..." His eyes made hungry promises. "I just want to look. What do want? I'll give you anything. Just let me touch."

I stopped breathing.

Then his arm snapped out and grabbed the door handle.

In a flash of movement, Joel was behind him, swinging the butt of his shotgun. The stock collided with the back of the man's head. His body dropped, eyes rolled to the sky.

Joel jumped behind the wheel and dumped a box of bottled water and packaged junk food in the backseat.

Blood pounded through my veins. "Is he dead?"

He shoved the gear into first and rolled to the edge of the lot, gaze locked on his side mirror.

I holstered the pistol on my thigh. "It's okay, Joel."

"No." A heavy rasp pushed past his teeth. "No, it's fucking not okay."

We faced the road, unmoving. He remained fixated on the mirror. I looked in my own, which reflected the unconscious man sprawled on the gravel.

Thirty seconds passed. I tapped a finger on the carbine. "What are we waiting for?"

As if on cue, the prone man raised his head, rubbed the back of it.

Joel hit the gas, spitting rock in our wake.

"You didn't want to leave him vulnerable," I said, a few minutes later.

"No, though make no mistake. If killing him would've been the only way to neutralize him, I would've done it without hesitation."

The fact that he hadn't just killed him gave me renewed appreciation for the kind of man he was.

A few miles later, we skidded onto a gravel road and made our descent to my father's lake house. Joel had told me my dad stopped answering his phone two days after the outbreak. And I knew if he survived, he would have found a way to contact me. A shiver licked my spine. Was he prowling his property in a mutated form? Could I shoot him like I shot the aphid in our basement?

Joel eyed my fingers plucking a frayed hole in my jeans. "You're worrying."

"Yes."

"Want a hug?" His eyes crinkled.

A laugh bubbled up, came out as a snort.

His hand squeezed my thigh. "There's a pack of smokes in the glove box."

I let him see my face and he returned the smile. Then I exhaled a little of my tension.

A mile north of my father's property, we passed the arched entrance of the Hurlin family's eight hundred acre ranch. I wondered if the infected ranchers were dining on their prize winning stallions.

He pulled the jeep into my father's circle drive. The motion activated light came to life. I grabbed the door handle and remembered what Joel had said, "Side-arm, carbine, shotgun, vest,"like a fucking nursery rhyme.

Already snug in the bullet proof vest, I wrestled out of the seat belt and hooked the carbine over my shoulder by its single point sling. I loved the look of my M4. With a collapsible stock and 14.5 inch barrel, its black metal frame and plastic hand grip made it an easy weapon to use. It was my weapon of choice.

When I secured the USP .40 in my thigh holster, he flashed his white teeth in the flood light's reflection. "Ready?"

Under the weight of my artillery, I puffed out my chest. "You bet."

He clicked his tongue. "No heroics, Evie."

We didn't enter the house. The best way to identify a threat inside was to check for compromised entry points. As we crossed the yard, I remembered the day Joel gave me my first carbine. Before he took me to the range, he ensured that I knew how to handle it tactically. He showed me low ready, muzzle down when not ready to shoot. And high ready, barrel up while looking for or locking on a target and expecting a fire fight.

Carbines in high ready, we crept around the house. I approached the bends and sliced off each piece of the corner as I went. Like slicing a pie. It enabled me to visually clear most of the new view while still remaining covered.

At the second corner, I asked, "Why do I need the side-arm and shotgun, in addition to the carbine?"

He trolled the dense trees through his scope. "Everyone prefers to shoot with a carbine, because you can plow through your ammo and your threat with a more accurate, longer reaching and heavier hitting round. However, let's say you are going along"—he aimed his carbine at the shed and mimed shooting—"Pop, pop, pop, click. Your carbine goes dry. Instead of dropping mag and reloading, to continue to get bullets down range it's easier to immediately draw your side arm."

Made sense.

He looked at me from the corner of his eye. "Your pistol's only good as a last resort concealable close range weapon. Got it?"

"Got it. And the shotgun?"

Duh was written across his face. "Because you can blow a huge ass hole in almost anything at close range."

Duh indeed. We continued to the next corner. The property appeared secure until we rounded the final side.

Squatting along the tree line about fifty yards away waited seven...eight...nine aphids. Under the twilight, they glowed neon green as if they'd developed radioactive herpes. I pressed the butt of the carbine into my shoulder and held its eight pound weight steady. A deep inhale filled my nostrils with the scent of gun oil.

Thirty rounds. Nine targets. If I fired accurately, I could go with the three shot rule. Two in the chest, one in the head.

I looked through the reflex sight of the carbine, exhaled and squeezed the trigger. The first bug squealed and rolled. Twenty-seven rounds. I took down three more aphids. Why wasn't Joel's carbine firing next to me? I squeezed again with a trained exhale.

Despite the queer buzzing in my ears, I slipped into a zone. Five aphids remained and how many rounds? Shit, I lost count. But I didn't let it distract me. The damn things dropped like flies. As if they couldn't see where the gun fire came from.

One mutant remained, hunkered next to its fallen comrades. I wanted a closer look and decided to take it. I swiveled my head to look at Joel behind me.

"Evie. Evie. What the fuck are you shooting at? Give me the gun."

I returned his puzzled expression with one of my own. "There's still one left."

"One what?" He reached for my carbine.

Then it dawned on me. He couldn't see them. I angled the gun out of his reach and took off toward the trees.

Ten feet from the lone survivor, I dropped to low ready and freed the Maglite. When I clicked it on, the bug straightened and looked in my direction. Aggression sprayed in a mist of drool. Its porcelain eyes reflected against my light. That drooling atrocity didn't have night vision. Pupils dilated in the dark to let in light and the tiny aphid pupil didn't dilate.

It ramped to spring and spat more snot. I killed the light. I wanted to knife that one.

I reached for the dagger in my forearm sheath and startled when Joel's pistol popped on my left. The aphid crumpled to the ground. Its neon glow dulled. Without lowering his pistol, Joel released his Maglite. I could see his profile in the light's halo, his eyes searching the nine bodies that lay at our feet. "How did you...I didn't see them—"

"Joel, look at me."

He put his arm across my chest and backed us up without lowering his pistol. Ten paces back, he stopped and met my eyes.

"I'm not fucking helpless. Stop being so overprotective. You gave me all that training. You gave me these knives." I shook my arm at him. "Let me fucking use them."

He blinked at me. "I know you're trained, but you're fucking dangerous." A sigh. "Yet here you are, proving yourself again..." His eyes darted around. I waited while he worked it out.

Eventually, his muscled arm yanked me against his chest, squeezing. His lips moved against my brow. "You're right. But I worry, okay? I'm an overprotective asshole and I fucking worry myself sick about you. I won't take unnecessary risks with you. Everything I do has your safety in mind. *Everything*." The last was a harsh whisper. He leaned back to peer at my face. "Next time, stick with the carbine. Like the pistol, those knives are last resort."

I let it go as we looked back at the carnage. The glow of the last aphid faded. I pointed at it. "Can you see the glow?"

He squinted. "No."

"Huh. I don't get it. They were lit up like a goddamn howitzer. And they can't see in the dark. I'm sure they couldn't see us."

He completed a three-sixty with the Maglite, probing the edge of the immediate yard. "Little pupils. Makes sense."

"Yeah. And the buzzing? Did you hear them?"

He scratched his beard with his flashlight hand. "Yep. Right before I shot the dickless bastard."

"The others buzzed too. Each one had its own tone or pitch. Like they were communicating. "

A horrible thought came to me as I stared at the bodies piled in a sticky black bath. "You don't think...my fa—"

"No. Remember Eugene said he found your dad's Rhino miles from here? And even if your dad turned into...you know he never went anywhere unarmed. He would have ended his life before he mutated."

"Yeah."

"Even if one of these things was someone you knew, after the mutation it's not anymore. It would kill you as sure as you stand there. Don't ever hesitate, okay?"

I didn't want to have this conversation.

"Evie?" He waited for me to look at him. "You shoot to kill. Just like you did tonight. Even if it's me. *Especially* if it's me. Come on. We'll do another patrol around the property and pray for no surprises inside."

The distant purr of a motor interrupted the desolation. The hum came from the direction of Eugene's house, my father's only neighbor within an audible distance.

"The jeep," he said. "Now."

I didn't question him. Concealment was hiding behind things that didn't have a ballistic value, like weeds or car doors. True cover concealed and protected. The engine block.

He swapped out his side arm for his M4 and held it in high ready. "We can't assume it's Eugene. So be ready."

I reloaded and mirrored his stance. Who else could it be?

The final forming of a person's character lies in their own hands.

Anne Frank

CHAPTER SEVEN: DIGIT RATIO

The motor rumbled from behind the grove. I shifted my weight from one foot to the other and flexed my fingers, loosening my grip on the carbine. Wind blustered through the canopy. An owl screeched.

Through the scope, two pairs of headlights emerged from the hill and hovered over the gravel road, slowing and bobbing at me. I filled my scope with the first driver. From the corner of my eye, Joel lowered his barrel and stepped around the bumper. The ATV skidded to a stop and a man leapt from it, grabbing Joel by the vest, swinging him around, laughing. Eugene. Then he saw me, set Joel down and whispered my name.

I clicked the safety on and lunged into his arms. He held me tight. A welcome home. Then he released me. "Aw, thank the Lord you're safe. Y'all remember my boy, Steve?"

"Of course." I extended my hand to the man on the second ATV.

Steve's eyes were hidden behind a veil of black shaggy hair. He squeezed my hand. "Hey Evie. It's been a while." Then he smiled. "Damn, it's good to see a friendly face."

"Yeah." I glanced at Joel. "We've been lonely too."

Joel reached around me and shook Steve's hand.

"Now what in tarnation was all that racket up here?" Eugene laughed, low and hearty. "Sounded like a pack of basset hounds on the Fourth of July." He rocked back on his heels and rubbed the bowling ball belly that hung between his suspenders. He looked just the way I remembered. Greasy dark hair encircled a bald spot. A wiry beard framed full ruddy cheeks.

"Well Eugene," Joel said. "Evie cleaned house. Come on, I'll show you." He glanced back at me with razor eyes. So, his mollycoddling wasn't going to disappear overnight. I set my jaw, jut out my hip and strummed my fingers on the carbine. He went on his way.

Steve stayed.

"Have there been a lot of attacks here?" I asked.

He shrugged. "Guess so, but we've been pretty isolated." He leaned against the jeep and shoved his hands in his pockets. "I was in St. Louis when the outbreak hit. Saw a lot of shit I'd like to forget."

I looked him in the eye. "I'm sorry."

"We're all survivors." He sniffed. "I know you had little ones."

I flinched and tried to cover it with a cough. Then I grabbed the cigarettes from the glove box and offered one to Steve.

We savored the nicotine in silence until Steve broke it. "How'd you kill those bastards in the dark anyway?"

"This"—I patted the carbine—"and the glowing skin helps."

He arched his brows.

I took a final drag to settle my guts. The cherry flared and dulled. I thought about the aphids' brief glow before they died. "Have you ever seen one in the dark?"

Steve looked away and muttered, "Yeah, my girlfriend."

Wilted shoulders, tucked chin, and bruised eyes. I should've let it go, but asked, "She didn't glow?"

"No. Nothing like that. When she got sick…" His eyes dropped. He kicked at the loose grit that dusted the driveway. "I would've noticed something like that."

Eugene thundered around the corner, "Gah damn, Evie girl. You're tougher than woodpecker lips. Just like your ol' man."

Just like my father. I shuddered at the thought of finding his body in the light of day. I forced a smile for Eugene.

Spread out, we called "all-clear" from each room. Then we unloaded the supplies from the jeep. That done, Eugene and Steve loitered by the front door. A kind of reluctant good-bye. I gave Joel a short nod.

"Would you fellows like to stay?"

Their lips floated up in relief.

I cleaned weapons while they secured the house. I dissembled the carbine and wiped down the bolt assembly. Joel's voice was like a jingle in my head. *Take care of your gun and it will take care of you.* I asked him once why he took my training to such extremes. Martial arts. Tactical drills. Knife throwing. Target Shooting. He responded, "I only need to be right once to justify the preparation."

Hammering from the other room lowered my blood pressure as I pushed a bore brush into the carbine's barrel headspace. I imagined the kind of booby traps and homemade security devices they'd install. In addition to gun dealing, Joel was a security consultant for the federal government. While it lent a certain practicality to our situation, it made him paranoid.

An hour later, the four of us settled in the family room with a few bottles of my dad's homegrown wine. My dad claimed to have made the best in the county. That night, I agreed.

Eugene shared what he knew of Hermitage and the surrounding area. The town collapsed then quieted within two weeks of the outbreak. Joel and I told them everything we knew and everything we speculated. Our friends couldn't validate or deny any of it. We were the first survivors they'd seen in weeks.

"What about Evie?" Eugene asked.

When Joel narrowed his eyes, Eugene said, "Why ain't she turned into one of them things?"

"Her immunity," Joel said, "we suspect, has something to do with testosterone."

Excess testosterone would explain my sex drive.

"Oh, right." Steve jumped up with unexpected excitement. "I have an idea. Let's try something." He knelt before me, and held up his hand with fingers together and pointing to the ceiling. "Do this."

Curious, I mimicked him. He traced the tips from index finger to ring finger. "No way. Do you see this?"

"Um...no?"

He sat back on his ankles. "Ever heard of digit ratio?"

I shook my head and Eugene said, "Ol' Steve here is just a well o' useless information, aren't ya, boy?"

"This one might come in handy, Pop." Then Steve said to me, "I heard this theory at school. There's a correlation between testosterone in your mother's womb and the length of your ring finger compared to your index finger." He turned to Joel and Eugene. "Are your ring fingers longer or shorter than your index fingers?"

They examined their hands and said in chorus, "Longer."

Steve returned to me, eyes tapered under his black mop. "Your ring finger is longer too, Evie. Thing is, girls' fingers are supposed to be the same length. The study claimed only men have longer ring fingers. Higher testosterone."

I flipped my hand to and fro in front of me, stretching the fingers in an attempt to modify their length. "What are you suggesting, Steve? That I'm not a woman?"

He choked on a laugh. His cheeks reddened against a pale complexion. "Uh no. Um...I think it could just mean you have high testosterone for a girl. Could explain why you survived."

I met Joel's eyes.

Then I dropped my hand and stood. "Okee dokee. I think I've had all the fun I can stand tonight." I turned to Steve, whose face slacked with a culpable look. "Hey man, thanks for the insight on the finger theory. It's the closest thing I've had to an explanation."

Curled around a pillow in my father's overstuffed bed, I thought about other known side effects of high testosterone. Years prior, I had laser hair removal on my entire body. I had the money. Why not? I didn't have excessive hair then, but too late to prove it. What about other symptoms like increased energy, aggression, muscle mass, extreme emotions? Anger. Anxiety. Yeah, all those rang true.

Muffled laughter bounced down the hall from the living room. It wasn't long before my eyelids drooped.

I swayed in the center of the Hurlin Ranch corral. The rot of the stallions surrounded me. My stomach cramped and I plugged my nose. The taste of decay was like rancid milk on my tongue. A breeze drifted from a pathway down the hill. And the hum of Annie's voice.

I lifted my chin and climbed two bodies. Offal slipped between my fingers. The leathery hide tore away from the bones underneath. I rolled off the last horse. Saliva thickened. I left the contents of my stomach in the dirt. Annie's song...

The lake before me, I lunged down the path. Prickly locust trees canopied the trail. I froze at a small foot bridge that stretched over a shallow ravine. Near the bridge, a man's pale body lay on the rocky bed. Loose brush covered his head. Annie's voice grew louder.

I scooted into the ravine. Bent over the body. Pulled away the foliage. A scream stuck in my throat. Large yellow-green eyes stared at me from my father's taut face.

A red ropelike shape wormed away from his body. I yanked at the remaining underbrush that clung to him.

I fell back, hand over my mouth. My father's bowels crawled from a gaping hole in his stomach. I followed the intestines up the ravine to the shade under the bridge. A tiny foot poked out from the shadow and wiggled in pink mary-janes with a red jeweled buckle.

The air felt thin. I gulped for more. Annie sat in a puddle of innards. Bracelets of dark viscera wrapped her wrists. She drew circles in the blood. Six lines spread out from every circle.

R-E-D, Red. R-E-D, Red.

That spells Red. That spells Red.

Ouchies are Red. Ladybugs are too.

R-E-D. R-E-D.

She sang to the tune of Frere Jacques and blinked glassy alabaster eyes.

I shook my head. Scrambled to my feet. Slipped on blood-slick pebbles. Landed on my back. My back teeth ground together. I tried to sit up, but failed. Tried to wake up, but failed as well.

The entrails slithered and twined over my neck. They constricted. I clawed at my throat, my shrieks shallow.

The sacrifices of God are a broken spirit;
a broken and contrite heart,
O God, you will not despise.

The Holy Bible, Psalm 51:17

CHAPTER EIGHT: CONTRITION

I jerked against the hands restraining my feet and wrists. Joel lay across my body and pinned me to the mattress. His cheek rested against mine. "Evie. Evie. Wake up. Shh. It's okay. It's okay."

Steve hovered above my head holding down my arms. His spooked eyes met mine and he averted them. Eugene struggled to catch his breath at my feet. Joel's face floated inches from mine, his eyes dark.

What had I done in my sleep to put those looks on their faces? My throat scratched. "You can let go of me now."

Joel sat up and caught my wrists in his hands. He held them in front of me. Fresh blood dirtied the nail beds. When he released me, I touched my throat. Traced deep scratches in the skin. My shirt stuck to my chest, warm and wet with bile. The slaughterhouse stench burrowed in my taste buds.

My father's eyes, open and waiting, fractured something inside me. Pain seared behind my forehead. Common-sense splintered away. I looked at Eugene. "Do you know how to get to the ravine at ol' Paul Hurlin's place?"

"I know it. Empties into the lake at marker L2. Good walleye catchin' there."

"Will you take me? I won't find it on my own."

We left for the ranch in my father's boat before dawn. By the time the sun crested the skyline, we found my father.

Rigor mortis came and went weeks earlier. Sun-broiled skin hung on his body, stretched by the inflation of abdominal gases.

We rolled his body onto a gas soaked wood pile. Despite the decomposition, I knew it was him. His St. Francis medal still hung from his neck.

I stood over him, my muscles straining under the weight of my artillery and vest. My eyes burned and I willed the tears to come. But they wouldn't. Just emptiness bubbling from my chest, forming a lump in my throat.

He told me once if forced to choose between his family and his god, God wins. My mother left before my sixth birthday. I never blamed him for putting her second to his god. After all, she left me too.

Eugene's big hand squeezed my shoulder. "You gonna say somethin', Evie girl?"

"I'm not a priest. He'd consider it blasphemous."

He blew out a breath. "Your dad was a stubborn son o'bitch. But he loved you."

I gave him a small smile, a bitter taste on my tongue. I wanted to feel grief. But hate consumed me. Hate for the religion that stole him from me.

In Catholic school, I questioned everything. My insubordination was dealt with by way of large doses of quality time with Father Mike Kempker and his flock of narrow minded nuns. Countless prayer candles were lit on my behalf. But the disconnect between my father and I didn't ignite until high school. At eighteen, I received an ultimatum: participate in his Vatican regimen or face banishment. I chose the latter.

After my A's were born, we began visiting my father at the lake. He never turned us away.

I couldn't unearth his religious holdfast, but I glimpsed the contrition behind his weary eyes. It was enough. During those visits, we spent most of our time with Eugene. My time with him brought me the closest I would ever get to the paternal relationship I longed for.

Eugene's hug brought me back to my father's disfigured face. Petrified in peace. His woolly beard, made thicker by all the blood, hid his Aryan features. Everyone always said I looked like him. I knew it was our eyes.

I spun the thumb-wheel on my father's zippo. *"Vater, ich hoffe euer Gott ist alles was sie wollen"*. I flicked the lighter into the pyre. "Good-bye, dad."

Eugene steered my father's Sea Ray deck boat away from Hurlin's ravine. The plume of smoke shrunk behind the tree line. We breached the open water and Joel joined me in the back seat. He kissed my brow. "What did you say to your father back there? In German?"

I rested my head on his shoulder. "I told him I hoped his god was everything he wanted. Or at least I hope that's what I said." I let out a small chuckle. "My German's a little rusty. If he heard me, I hope he appreciated the attempt in his parents' tongue."

Joel raised his eyebrows.

"I know. I still don't believe in afterlife. But after following this visionary nightmare thing today, I have to wonder if there isn't something."

He wrapped his arms around me. "Of course there's *something*. Look around us. The forest, the wind, the lake, the stars…you and me. That *something* is the very energy that connects us." He rested his lips on my temple. "Everything happens for a reason, you know."

On the way back, the stillness around us hovered like a miasma. Besides the plant life on the shore and wake behind our boat, life was scarce. There were no other water crafts on the lake to rough the water, no squawking in the trees by ruffled birds, no squirrels scurrying dry leaves. The silence lay like a dead thing between us. We exchanged uneasy looks.

Eugene docked in the boat house.

Joel hopped out. "Stay here while I clear the property."

When I caught up with him on the shore, we bandied glares. Then he glanced at the boat, where Eugene and Steve waited. "At least someone listens."

We set off up the path toward the house, scrutinizing everything within the periphery. The small vineyard, the lawn around the house, the circle drive, the woods fringing all sides. No tracks in the dirt. No suspicious noises. The property was free of threats.

Halfway to the house, twigs cracked around us. Foliage rustled. A growling hum erupted and entered my chest. Aphids swarmed out of the surrounding grove from every direction.

Drool stretched from disfigured mouths. Claws snapped in our direction. At least a dozen blocked our path to the house. Their numbers grew.

"Back in the boat," Joel shouted.

I raised the carbine, pelleted the nearest two as I retreated. They didn't slow.

Joel did the same, running with me, screaming between trigger pulls. "Start the boat."

The motor rattled, drowning out Eugene's shouts. More rounds fired. More unsuccessful hits. We had to get out of there. I spun toward the dock.

A sea of green bodies swallowed the entrance to the ramp.

Cheek against the stock, I exhaled and squeezed. Empty brass sprayed around me. The aphids in my scope ducked and darted. Most I tapped just jerked under the volley and continued chasing.

Pop, pop...pop, click. I hit the mag release. Tilted the carbine. Knocked the mag loose. Only four aphids down. All head shots, just like the one that broke into our home. Was that the only way to kill them? Destroy the brain?

"Aim for the head," I yelled.

He grunted, fired off continuous rounds.

They were quicker in daylight. They could see us, dodge our bullets. And a head shot was the most difficult, especially on a moving target. That boat looked farther and farther out of reach.

I reloaded. The decibels of repeating trigger pulls rang my ears. Gunpowder chased my inhales. Carbine in high ready. Exhale. Squeeze.

His empty mag dropped at my feet. "Jesus...fuck...what've you got?"

Two M4 mags. Plus the twelve rounds in my USP. "Seventy-five." Only a fourth of our predators were down. Some were dragging themselves back up. Maybe thirty, forty still alive.

"Make 'em count." He clicked his mag in place.

The carbine tapped my shoulder, buffered by my vest. The barrel was hot. Clinking echoed around us as our missed shots ricocheted off the house, the shed, the Rubicon. Christ, their daylight reflexes. Seventy-five rounds should've been enough, but only one in ten bullets found its target.

The bugs forged ever closer. He screamed, "I'm out."

I was down to the pistol. Five aphids remained, moving in from the tree line. I had about that left in .40 caliber rounds. I took a step toward the survivors. He grabbed my vest and tugged me back to his side.

"*Joel.*"

His jaw clenched. I was a better shot. He let go of my vest.

I swiveled back to the fast approaching aggressors and swallowed. Twenty yards. The pistol felt awkward in my hand. I adjusted my grip. It was not the time to be a candy-ass.

I bared my teeth and charged. The bug nearest to me lunged. I sidestepped its claws and Joel pistol whipped it. Its head dropped back. Orbs pointed to the sky. I shoved the barrel into its chest and filled it with lead. It fell against me and slid to the ground. I resisted the chance for a double tap and blinked through the spray of bug guts plastering my face. Joel beat another aphid with dull thuds.

Double jointed legs shot out of the bloody pile before me and knocked me off my feet. Shit, I hadn't shot its head. Joel wailed my name. I unsheathed a knife from my forearm and sunk it in the bug's eye. It sagged to the ground.

I climbed to my knees. Met two more. Plucked the blade. Plunged it into an eye socket above me. A sticky discharge clotted my fingers. It, too, fell on me. I shrugged it off. Drew the pistol. Aimed for the eye of the other one. Fired.

It screamed. Dark matter burst from its head. Its eye socket stared, hollow and leaking.

The remaining two hovered over Joel. He dodged them with nimble Jujitsu rolls and redirected their force with a swift arm. But his jabs waned. His kicks slowed.

"Hey," I screamed.

The aphids ignored me. Joel jumped on one's back. It shook and knocked him free.

I holstered the pistol. Gripped a blade in each hand. Lanced my left bicep, quick and deep. Enough to lace the air. A gush of fire burned through my shoulder. The blood welled. The aphids turned.

Man must evolve for all human conflict
a methodwhich rejects revenge, aggression and retaliation.
The foundation of such a method is love.

Martin Luther King, Jr.

CHAPTER NINE: UNTIL YOU HATE ME

The final two aphids sprinted toward me and stabbed the air with speared mouthparts. I dodged. Thrust the daggers at their eyes. Missed.

One crouched to spring when the second lost its footing in a mole hole. I whipped a knife at the crouching aphid's head. Spun to my left. Sliced off the mandible of the stumbling second.

The second fell back and spewed a black parade of blood and fleshy bits. I finished it with the blade lodged between its eyes. I twisted around. The handle of the knife protruded from the first one's face, mangled as it was. Its body twitched and sighed.

The strength left my legs and I fell upon my knees. Fire raged from the wound on my arm. I squeezed it to make it stop, but touching it set my teeth against each other and I bottled a scream. At least the arm slicing worked. They couldn't resist the blood, but—fuck—the pain.

Joel dropped in front of me, his chest bare and his T-shirt in hand. He ripped it in strips and dressed my arm. His silence stung.

"It's okay, Joel. Really. I mean…there were only a few close calls." I smiled. Tried to make it reach my eyes. "I think I did all right."

His voice shook. "You did better than all right. You fucking moved like them. You matched their speed. I don't get it." He brushed the hair from his face. "Christ, I don't know if I *want* to get it."

I leaned back, wrinkled my nose. "What do you mean?"

Eugene and Steve approached from the dock. Why hadn't they covered us from the boat? They were both armed.

Joel glanced at a nearby pile of bodies and looked back at me. "What did you see? I can't even track them with my eyes. They move like a blur. And you did too."

I shoved to my feet. "What do you mean a blur? They moved..." Normal. Did he think...? "I'm not like them. I'm nothing like them." My skin would be green. I wouldn't be able to see in the dark. And my mouth...

He hugged me, buried his face in my neck. "It's okay. It's going to be okay."

Were his words for me or himself?

I stood on my father's deck under the weeping arms of the willow trees, and waited for the rest of the house to wake. Another sip of coffee roused my senses. I leaned on the cedar railing and closed my eyes while the breeze from the lake took me through a memory.

The richness of Colorado mountain mahogany after the rain hung on my inhale. I felt the corners of my mouth tug up at the chimes of children's laughter saturating the air. Fronds, laden with drizzle, trickled a grateful melody. A nearby stream joined in as water pushed over mountain moraine.

Joel picked through kindling. Annie and Aaron romped through tufted hairgrass and foxtail barley and rolled down a gentle swell in the forest floor, energized by their first camping trip. Beyond their playground, aspen trails snaked through far-reaching hills and valleys. I propped a branch under the tent roof and waterfalls of rain cascaded down the sides.

"Mama, look," Aaron called. A giant swallowtail hopped from his arm to his tousled locks, antennae pulsing like radar. Powdered wings in bands of black and yellow spread the width of his head, beating in step with his giggles.

The smell of peat and standing water choked out the mountain mahogany. Wetland smog of death and decay settled over me. I opened my eyes, burning but dry. Always dry. I blinked at the lake. Smooth as glass, the surface didn't move.

Neither did the bodies piled up in the field below. Two days passed since we returned from Hurlin's ravine and killed twenty-three aphids. None of us wanted to touch them. But the cloud of rot crept closer, grew stronger. It was time to dump them in the lake.

After breakfast, we gathered around the nine aphids that attacked the first night. Steve parted his lips and tightened an arm against his gut. Eugene squatted next to one and slurped coffee from a travel mug. "Damn. That there's a lard bucket full of armpits." He fanned his nose.

"An astute observation," I said.

"Beauty *and* brains, Evie girl." He puckered his lips and mimed hair fluffing.

We laughed. Even Steve looked a little less sick. Joel rolled a wheelbarrow next to the first pile. Then Joel and Steve hauled while Eugene and I stood guard.

One by one they carted them to the far side of the shoreline, each body more spoiled than the last. The ground was too hard to dig holes. Burning them would attract attention. So, they dumped them as far away from the boat house, and our swimming spot, as they could manage, and watched the alien bodies dissolve in the water.

Eugene lent assistance as the morning wore on. Two hours later and only one breakfast lost—Steve looked the better for it—I plopped next to Eugene on the dock. Rough breaths pushed through his mouth.

I patted his sweat soaked back. "You okay?"

"It's hotter'n a taste bud in a pepper eating contest." He dabbed at his forehead with a rag then used it to blot each armpit.

I nodded. "Those bastards are heavy too, huh? I found that out the hard way." I told him about my encounter with the aphid by the pool.

Eugene whistled. "Ain't that something? Not surprisin' though seein' how you move like 'em."

Oh hell. I didn't like the undercurrent of his tone. Every time he smiled and met my eyes, was he looking for tiny pupils? He always took his meals with me. Was he making sure I hadn't switched to a liquid diet?

My expression must have betrayed me because he said, "But don't you worry 'bout that, Evie girl. I reckon the Lord's got big plans for you. Your ol' man would be proud." He rested a hand on my leg, fingers squeezing my inner thigh.

"Thanks, Eugene." I wiggled away from the touch. "Now let's go cool down and wash off the bug sludge."

We joined Steve and Joel at the end of the dock. They were down to their briefs. Droplets of sweat glimmered on their backs. I stripped off my vest and weapons at the edge. Then I plunged into the water. Damn, it felt good.

A shampoo bottle and a bar of soap sat on the dock's edge. We bathed there. We hauled drinking water from there. I tried not to think about that.

Under the murky water, I stripped off my clothes and tossed them next to my boots and weapons.

Joel sprawled on a life vest and floated over to me. "I've been thinking."

My fingers shot to his temples and I massaged with feigned concern. "Don't hurt yourself."

He grunted. "You're not as cute as you think you are."

A wiry hair curled away from his sideburns, begging to be yanked. I obliged.

"Ow." He slapped a hand over the hurt. "Listen, witch." The water rippled as he heaved me flush against him. "I need you to clear your calendar for the next few weeks."

"Hmm. That'll be tough. Who's gonna reorganize the sock drawers and buff the handguns to award-winning shine?"

"My point. We need to keep busy. So we're going to start training again."

I widened my eyes. "Really? Just like old times?"

He flashed me one of his glad-you-approve grins. "We'll start with a refresher on knife throwing since you seem so intent on cleaving bugs. Then we'll brush up on your hand-to-hand techniques. And once I'm satisfied"—his grin widened—"I'll drill you on swat scenarios until you hate me."

I looped my arms around his neck. "Oh, Mr. Delina, I could never hate you." I brushed my lips along his whiskered cheek. "But why the renewed interest? If you haven't noticed, I'm kind of already kicking ass."

His hands circled my waist, letting the life vest float out from under him. "Yeah, and good thing it's not getting to your head." He palmed my backside, dipping into the cleavage. "But practice will make you better. And after watching you dance with those bugs, it's like you…"

I held him with tapered eyes and he said in his Mr. Miyagi voice, "Lesson not just karate. Lesson for whole life."

Good God, he was backpedaling behind a 1980's movie impression.

He bit his lip, but a smile broke through anyway.

I returned the smile. I didn't want to hear about my alleged super-human speed or some sermon about everything having purpose. "Fine. But I'm not waxing—"

Strong lips claimed mine. His fingers stretched under my rear and spread between my thighs while his other hand paddled. I clung to his chest and ground my pelvis against his. A groan erupted from his throat.

The water behind us sloshed as Eugene and Steve treaded, watching.

His lips moved over mine. "Can you fellows give us some privacy?"

When splashing sounded their exit, I relaxed my shoulders and kissed him back. I let my enthusiasm about the training build in that kiss, drowning him in licks and nibbles while he kicked his legs to keep us afloat.

Over the weeks that followed, our aphid infestation grew. We blew through at least one magazine a day to keep them at bay. With our ammunition dwindling, Eugene and Steve volunteered to gather more.

When they left, I knew they'd be gone awhile, traveling far to make the venture profitable. I also knew they might not return. I couldn't think about the latter. Instead, I imagined the myriad of ways Joel and I could enjoy that time alone.

But he kept us on a regimen. Knife throwing for two hours. Jujitsu or Muay Thai until lunch. Kung Fu or Eskrima between lunch and dinner. My joints creaked, my muscles hurt to touch and Joel was inexorable.

Two weeks later—Eugene and Steve still gone—I lay on my back on the basement floor, massaging a sore calf. Joel stood over me, laughing and beating me with Aristotle. "We cannot learn without pain."

He raised an ankle to hismuscled ass, stretching his quadriceps. A taunting reminder of the kick I just absorbed. My knee popped as I stood and limped to the door.

Still laughing, he said, "Evie, come on. Use your aphid speed."

"Apparently it just works on aphids. Not assholes." Damn, I was a poor loser. But still.

"There's that temper, which reminds me"—I continued toward the exit to escape the impending lecture—"forget everything I've ever said about your anger."

I stopped before the stairs, but didn't turn around.

"Go ahead," he said. "Explode. But when you do, pay close attention to it."

I blew out a breath and faced him.

"Figure out what it was that pissed you off. Was it anxiety, impatience,"—he cleared his throat—"humility? Take notes."

I crossed my arms. "Why?"

He dropped his leg. "Because if you understand the foundation of your anger, you might be able to promote it in others." A pause. "Think about it. On one side you've got an ill-tempered fighter blinded by her rage. On the other, an alert opponent in control of his own disposition. Who's going to win?"

I shrugged and plastered on my best I-don't-give-a-rat's-ass expression.

"Just more tools for your toolbox."

Anger made a pretty sharp tool, but... "Okay, asshat."

We spent the next couple hours walking through Chi Sao rolling hand forms. His relentless barking gave me plenty of opportunities to note the signals of my anger. *Control your speed. Sloppy. Watch your timing. Focus. Hit me. Fook sau. Again.*

Then he mounted a plank of wood marked with targets on the wall. I spun my first blade from twenty feet away. It nailed the edge of the inner ring with a thunk.

He tapped my foot with his to adjust my stance. "Good. Now alternate between no spin, half spin and multi spin. And vary your distances."

I nodded and wiped my forehead on my arm.

"Remember. This is like all your other training. When you apply it, it's got to come natural. And you'll only get there through repetition." He grinned. "Hate me yet?"

I smirked and flung another blade. The silent whirl, as it flipped end-over-end toward the eye of the target, lifted my chin. Several bulls-eyes later, I said, "Really, I've got this."

He unbolted the basement door and lifted his carbine. "Let's find out."

Under the weight of my knives and the thick midnight sky, I followed him outside. Our boots scraped over the gravel trail to the lake. A fog shrouded the surrounding grove. The ground cover stirred within.

The last time I fought aphids was on the very trail we walked. I remembered their claws on me. And the blood, dark and oleaginous, leaking from their wounds. A twinge festered in the pit of my stomach. A birdcall floated through the walnut boughs. The shadows below grew louder. So did my heartbeat.

"The plan?" I whispered as we crossed the dock.

"When they hit the ramp, aim between the eyes. Since you can see them better than I can, I'll be relying on your eyes until they're close enough."

We stopped with our backs at the edge. I wore four knives. He handed me six more from the pouch on his hip.

"And when we're out of knives and ammo?"

He thrust his chin to the cove behind us. "We swim."

The ashen moon's double lay motionless on the black water. The humidity clung in beads on my upper lip. Beside me, his carbine trained on the ramp. Then the grove lit up with a glow only I could see.

"Show time," I whispered into the dark.

The aphids emerged. Numbers in the twenties, they boarded the ramp. I snapped down my arm and released the knife at shoulder height. It traveled through the air in a vertical spin and plunked as it broke the water's surface.

Dammit to hell. "Can you see them yet?"

"No."

I waited until the first one skittered past the final boat slip. Flicked the knife. The aphid dropped, as did the next. My remaining knives found their targets. Aphids toppled upon each other. Some rolled from the ramp and bubbled in the lake. Others slipped by, climbing over the fallen and thrashing under Joel's volley.

The last three survivors inched within a few yards, oblivious to the lead peppering their glowing frames. Faces shredded from grazed bullets, limbs missing, heads hanging by sinews, they moved ever closer. Joel's night vision was worse than I thought.

He met my eyes. We stepped back and dropped off the dock. The water washed over my head, drowning me with dread. I propelled to the surface and wished I'd retained a blade.

The *pop, pop, pop* of his carbine echoed across the cove. The remaining aphids tumbled into the water.

"Fuck." I kicked away from the dock. The drum of my heart pounded in my ears. "Now they're fucking in here." My voice hitched. "With us."

My arms beat the water. He glided up to me, holding the carbine above his head. "Calm down, Evie."

Something brushed my foot. I clamped my jaw. Bagged a scream. "Why the fuck did you shoot them? You knew they'd fall in." Did something else just bump my leg? "Goddammit. They don't die right away."

"Evie, stop. After your fight in our pool, I had to push you past this fear."

I arced my legs out. Searched the depths. "You don't need to push. I'm not a fucking daffodil. I just—"

Tiny bubbles fizzed on the water's surface before me. I jerked backwards and swam with determined strokes, shouting, "Next time you decide I need a lesson, discuss it with me first."

I reached the opposite end of the dock, plucked my knives from mangled heads, and returned to the house.

Three days later, Eugene and Steve arrived in two trucks filled with generators, water barrels, batteries, ammo and enough non-perishable food to last a year. Joel stood guard while we moved everything to the basement.

"Went to Arkansas, Alabama, Oklahoma and Texas," Steve said as I rummaged in the truck. "Ain't no other women."

I pulled out a bad-ass looking shotgun from the cab. "Shit. Is this what I think it is?"

"AA-12? Damn straight."

I crept toward the tree line, scanning through the scope. The Auto Assault-12—fully automatic, gas operated, twelve gauge—was by and far the deadliest shotgun on the planet. I watched a video about it once. Scared the piss out of me. I was thankful at the time that it was only in the hands of the military. Because of its low recoil, its unmistakable twenty shell drum could shred a body from two hundred yards.

Steve tugged it from my grasp and winked. "I might let you play with it later."

Something about that wink seemed…off. Then I realized his hand was on his groin and I turned away. I could feel the probe of his gaze, knew his eyes had dropped to my ass. What the fuck? I returned to the truck with a wooden walk. By the time I reached it, Steve was gone. Heat flushed my face. Damn overactive imagination.

A box sat in the front seat filled with various pulleys and nylon rope. Eugene poked his head in the other side.

"Hey Eugene, what's all this—"

"Ah just some extras we might need. Can you help me with this barrel over here, Evie girl?"

I gave the box one last glance and followed him to the other truck.

That night, I slumped into bed, too fatigued to remove more than my shorts. "You pommeled me with swat scenarios for a week. I officially hate you."

My yawn turned into a full body stretch. Joel's hand froze on his boot laces, his eyes traveling up my bare legs, pausing on the small swath of silk blocking his view.

I stretched my arms over my head, letting my knees fall out to the mattress. The hem of my tee climbed up my ribs, slow and subtle. "What's the plan for tomorrow?"

"Target shooting." His eyes remained fixed on my panties, but his hands sped up, tearing at the laces, tugging off the boots. His pants dropped. Boxers followed. When he reached behind his head to yank off the shirt, his biceps flexed in the muted light. "Your precision with the pistol is..."

"Unequivocal?"

His laugh consumed his beautiful face. "The only thing unequivocal is the barrage of .40 caliber holes in our jeep."

"Fine. Send me the bill. I like the carbine." I also liked the view, muscle after perfectly designed muscle. If there were a God, He knew how to architect a body.

He slid under the covers and wrapped all that muscle around me. "Still mad at me for shooting the bugs into the water with us?"

"Definitely."

"Good." Lids lifting, his gaze heated. "You're fucking sexy when you're mad. And you have ten seconds to get out of those clothes."

My breath caught. He was domineering and handsome and oh, how that made me want him. "I should make you beg." I shed my clothes in five.

He groaned and the sound jolted the place already throbbing below my waist. He raised the sheet, eyes dark with lust. "Come here. I want to test a theory."

I rolled against him, drawing in his comforting scent of Cavendish tobacco. "If this theory involves you and me naked in bed, you have my full attention."

His hard body tucked against my soft one. "I've noticed a pattern." He coiled his arms around my waist and nuzzled my neck. "When we sleep like this, skin to skin, you don't wake with night terrors."

Huh. Was that right? When his tongue slipped between my lips, I forgot what we were testing.

Over the next few days, Joel rigged a system to convert lake water to drinking water. As the sky blushed with dawn's sun, we stood around a tiered drum layered with gravel, sand and charcoal, each layer separated by thin cloth.

Joel didn't even try to hide his proud grin. "I'm gonna go help Steve bring down that last barrel." He looked at me, opened his mouth, shut it. Then he grabbed my chin and planted a kiss on my lips. "High ready while I'm gone." He nodded to my carbine. "Finger next to the trigger, okay?"

"Roger that."

He kissed me again and took off.

Eugene bent over the siphon, watching the water pump into a barrel strapped to a refrigerator dolly. While we waited, he cheered me with far-fetched narrations about the monstrous fish he and my father caught in the very cove we pumped from.

"Hey Evie," Steve yelled from the house. "Can you come in a minute?"

Eugene nodded. "Go ahead." He tapped a finger on the sidearm holstered at his hip. "I'll be fine."

"Okay, be right back."

I flew up the ramp and stumbled into the dark basement. As I waited for my vision to adjust, a muffled moan tingled across my skin. I turned. "Joel?"

Steve stepped out of the shadows, his smile distorted from its usual easy lift. Then his arms rose. The last thing I saw was the butt of his shotgun swinging toward my face.

Well, I can kill too because now I have hate!
How many can I kill, Chino? How many?!
And still have one bullet left for me?

Arthur Laurents, *West Side Story*

CHAPTER TEN: END OF MY ROPE

Pied light penetrated my swollen lids. I cracked them open.

Steve knelt over me. "Good morning, beautiful."

I groaned. Needles pulsated in my head. "What are you doing?" I tugged my arms. They were tied at my back. My ankles and knees were bound as well.

He cupped my jaw. "Shhh. Soon." His smile threatened, hinted at something cruel, and he knew it.

When he dropped his hand, I arched my back and tilted my head. Joel lay hog-tied in the corner, his eyes pitch-black and penetrating, his mouth a pinched line.

Was this another fucking nightmare? "Are you okay?" I whispered.

He blinked and sucked in his cheeks.

"Joel?"

His lashes lowered and his chest shuddered through a ragged breath.

"Joel? Why aren't you talking?"

"Because"—Steve paced a circle around me—"he understands the rules."

A deep inhale helped me squash the emotion from my voice. "What are the rules?"

"Each sound he makes will be paid in blood." A frightening grin wrenched his lips. "That would be your blood."

I'd bet our ration of ammo that every sound he didn't make would also be paid in the same. I rolled my head, forced my gaze to the unknown across the room. Eugene was on a ladder, drilling something into the ceiling. Several pulleys were screwed into the joists with rope laced through them.

"Eugene." My shout inflamed the pain in my head.

Steve stood over me, framed in halos of fluorescent bulbs. "He's busy. What do you need?"

"I want to talk to my husband. Let me go over there."

"No fucking way."

How the hell did they take down Joel? Mother fuckers had the advantage of surprise. He trusted them and they used it against us.

I lay on my side and waited for Steve's hovering shadow to float away.

Joel's eyes burned into mine and I furrowed my brows, let him read the question there. What was the plan?

His gaze jerked between me and the clatter on the other side of the room. His lips formed words, soundless and careful. "Your. Pack. In. Boat. Go."

I shook my throbbing head and whispered, "I'm not going anywhere without you."

A vein bulged on his forehead. "Promise," he mouthed.

Even if I could escape, I'd never leave him. I thrust my chin left to right.

The muscles in his chest and arms pumped up for a fight. "Promise. Me." His moving lips were mute, but I felt the venom of his demand in my gut.

The squeak of sneakers on concrete pierced the silence. Footsteps approached. Hands curled into my bound arms, lifting me.

Joel tried to get up, eyes wild. Then I was bent over Steve's shoulder, watching his back and legs move over the concrete. I arched to look at Joel, captured his gaze, and mouthed, "I promise."

He closed his eyes and sagged against the wall.

Steve bent and my back hit cement. A smile slithered across his face and kicked up my pulse. "Hey Pop, 'bout ready?"

"All set." Eugene strutted over to me, hiking his trousers over his gut. "Oh, Evie girl. Steve and I's been real lonely, like. Seeing how you're the last woman left, it's your job to help us out with that."

A hot acid burn made its way to the back of my throat. "What? Eugene, no. Don't you fucking do this. I'll fucking—"

Steve shoved a rag in my mouth. I bit his finger and tried to head butt him. He sat on me and tied a gag around my head. That done, he raised the AA-12 and aimed it at Joel.

Eugene knelt next to me, fisting a large hunting knife. I bit down on the rag and dug my nails into my palms, but the heave of my chest betrayed me.

"Now you're gonna hold real still for me while I cut away your clothes."

"Or else," Steve said, "I'll introduce Joel to this shotgun you fancy so much."

Piece by piece was cut away. Eugene kept his eyes on the knife, careful not to nick me despite my squirming and moaning. Finally, the last scrap of clothing was removed and I lay bare on the cold floor.

Eugene collected the rope hanging from the pulleys. Used it to replace the ties on my wrist. Then he yanked hard on another rope and slid me into place. I hung from a pulley system designed to lift me up and down. I twisted my arms and pulled as hard as I could against the binds. There was no give.

I thought about my life leading to that moment, about my father. When he pulled the trigger on himself, was he sorry he never hugged me? Never told me he loved me? If he were there, would he have given me those comforts knowing I so desperately needed it?

"Pop, let me do the honors, huh?"

"Go ahead, boy."

Steve tossed him the AA-12 and squatted before me. His eyes seared every inch of my skin. "Fucking beautiful. I've been watching you, you know. When you and Joel thought you were stealing away those private moments. When you thought you were bathing under his eyes only." He wet his lips and pulled a blade from his boot. "But I've longed to see you close up. Like this."

He traced the inside of my thigh with the blunt edge of the blade. I tried to stifle the brutal shaking in my muscles and failed. He cut away the ties at my knees and ankles.

I kicked out a leg. He was expecting it and dodged. "Now, now. There's only one reason we're keeping Joel alive."

Eugene stepped over to Joel and kicked him in the side. I writhed against the rope, my face boiling.

Steve squeezed my chin. "So you'll be cooperatin' from here on out, 'kay?"

My teeth gnawed the gag when his cold hand gripped my waist, burned my skin. The moment he cupped my bared sex, it occurred to me that I'd half-fooled myself into thinking they wouldn't go through with it. But, oh God, it was happening. Panic ripped through me, ramping my pulse and catapulting my stomach to my throat. I jammed my eyes shut.

Time passed like the stages of grief. I kept my eyes closed, pretending it wasn't happening. Then the nauseating pain became difficult to ignore. It fueled a hatred so deep, my bones thrummed with it.

When I opened my eyes, I sought out those of the men hurting me. Neither would meet my glare. That was when I looked to Joel. If I could wash away one memory from my life to date, it would be the suffering in his eyes while I was raped in front of him.

After that, I hid behind closed lids, certain Joel and I would die. I didn't want to watch it happen. The realization crushed my heart in a suffocating ache.

When I eventually dragged my eyes open again, daylight's glow no longer outlined the basement's exterior door. By then, my body sagged, numb in most places. A dull throb in others. I knew the tissues between my legs were ripped from the dry penetration, the sandpaper scraping of meat on meat. At least, until blood and semen wet me there.

I hung from the ceiling by my wrists, knees cut and bruised from dragging on the floor. Each time I struggled to stand on wobbly legs, I was knocked down with a kick, a fist, the butt of a gun.

Steve sat back on his ankles. "I won't listen to his sniveling another goddamn minute." He pushed me away and aimed the shotgun at Joel.

A guttural sound barreled in my chest.

"Nah, got a better idea," Eugene said. "Take him outside."

They hauled Joel through the door, one on each arm. No, no, no. The image of Joel bound amongst aphids rammed my heart against my ribs.

The door shut and I worked at the knots on my wrists. Tied with precision, the heavy nylon rope destroyed my hope for an easy escape. I took two forced breaths to battle my panic. My forearm sheathes were thrown on a shelf a body's length away.

Stretching mine as long as I could, I reached for the knives with my feet. The rope gnawed and shredded my wrists. The distance was too convenient, the dumb asses. Then I realized. Three inches too short. I needed air.

I pushed off, tucked my knees to keep them from dragging, and swung. The rope around my wrists burned. My hands went numb. Once I had momentum, I bent at my waist keeping my legs in front of me, demanding more strength than my upper body could offer.

On the final thrust, I kicked my feet at the shelf. A blade clinked to the floor. I swept it with my foot. The handle lay at my toes.

Should be just like plucking dandelions with my bare feet while lying in the grass with the A's, right? I wrapped my toes around the handle. My muscles quivered as I raised the blade to my fists in front of me. A brief sigh of relief.

The backyard woke with the sounds of screams. I cut my arms free and lunged for the door.

I reached for the handle and heard voices on the other side. Fuck. I twirled around. No guns in sight. I ran back where they left me and stood in front of the rope, hands and knife behind my head. Dread attacked my body in violent shakes.

The door opened and Joel's screams grew louder. Then silence. Steve's smile waved through my dizziness, the AA-12 strapped to his back. "Hey gorgeous, you ready for more?"

Eugene slammed the door behind them. My stomach lurched. They swaggered closer, naked and erect. I stood unresponsive until they were an arm's length away.

With a downward swipe, I split Steve from sternum to groin. His skin peeled from the blade and gave way to an avalanche of bowels. Eugene yanked me back by my hair but I was already circling the knife up. I caught him in the throat. His jugular erupted in a red monsoon and he dropped next to his son. Steve writhed. Eugene gargled.

Satisfaction tingled through me as I appreciated the damage. But I wasn't satisfied. The AA-12 lay next to them. I scooped it up, squeezed the trigger. Again. And again. And again.

Cradling the gun to my chest, I shuffled over the splattered concrete, toward the silence on the other side of the door. It creaked open.

I opened my mouth, but my cry was trapped with my breath. I tried to take a step, refusing to understand what I saw. I collapsed to my knees. Reached out my hand. I began to crawl.

I desired my dust to be mingled with yours
Forever and forever and forever.
Why should I climb the look out?

Li Po

CHAPTER ELEVEN: THE LETTER

I woke on my father's boat. The rhythm of side to side rocking quickened the nausea in my gut. I sat up and retched water and bile over the side. Every day had been much of the same. Wake. Puke. Pass out. I didn't know how many days passed on that boat, anchored in the center of the lake. My memories were full of holes. I remembered my hand on the basement door. The flame creeping down the match, burning my finger. The heat on my back. The crash as my father's home collapsed. Gasoline and charred meat soaking into my pores, invading like cancer. And I remembered Joel's lifeless eyes.

When Annie was five, she asked me why I never cried. I told her then I had nothing to cry about. But she knew there were times when it would've been appropriate. Like when Joel and I fought. Like when our dog was hit by a car. Like losing the man I loved, my whole world.

Fire spread in my cheeks. Tingling sparked through my arms and fingers. I failed Joel. My eyes blurred as I lost my grip on consciousness.

My hand slipped around the knob. The door opened. A breeze greeted me. Metallic. Familiar.

Clank.

Joel bucked against the pole. My voice wouldn't work. Neither would my legs. I floated away from myself. My limbs moved mechanically.

Clank. Clank.

I gripped the cold chain to stop the banging. My blade touched Joel's forehead. The bead of blood grew. His eyes glazed. The pain was too much. I pushed hard and fast.

I woke again.

Aaron was sitting in the captain's chair. He stood—solid but airy—and drifted toward me, one hand behind his back. Booey hung by a paw from his belt loop. He lingered close enough to touch and looked down at me with yellow-green eyes, outlined in a brilliant ring of emerald.

His hand appeared from behind his back and his fist opened. A ladybug perched on his palm, peaceful and unafraid. He brought it to his face for closer inspection. It lifted red wings as if to stretch then tucked them back to its body.

Puckering his lips, he blew on it until it took flight. It danced between us then flew over my head. Aaron extended a tiny finger and pointed behind me. His voice was harmonious. "Follow them, Mommy."

Over my shoulder, swarms of ladybugs fluttered around the bow and over the water that stretched to the eastern shore. They winked in and out like beacons toward the undeveloped savannahs rich with Mead's milkweed and other native grasses. It was a dreamlike landscape. Maybe I was dreaming.

The ladybugs hovered as if waiting for me to respond. The pack lay next to me, unopened. I turned back. Aaron was gone.

Grief consumed me, ripping and pulling. I yanked at my hair. Buckled over, hugging myself, rocking on my knees. "Where did my brother go? Where did my brother go?" Then I snapped.

I grabbed the first thing in reach, the pack Joel left me, and heaved it across the boat. Despite its weight and the little strength I had left, it flew through the air and propelled over the side, hitting the water with a splash.

Darkness tried to steal my vision again. The spotted beetles pestered. I swatted at them and screamed, "Leave me the fuck alone."

The pack burped. I moved to the edge and watched it sink.

Whatever you do, don't lose this.

The last of the air escaped and water rolled over the insurance policy I'd hoped to never use. Shit. I dropped to my knees and lugged it back onto the boat. The swarm settled around me.

A.L.I.C.E. All-purpose Lightweight Individual Carrying Equipment. The durable olive-drab rucksack was designed to haul basic survival supplies for the U.S. Army. I eyed it with contempt. He had it all planned out. The boat, a deliberate choice assuming it was aphids I was escaping. And the pack. I bet it contained everything needed to survive. What made me sick was the realization that his pack wasn't there. His attention centered on my survival and mine alone. I loosened the cover straps with a thousand pound heart.

A cortege of soggy contents poured into my lap. Sleeping roll. Individually wrapped MREs. Camel Back water hydration system. Solar flashlight. Otis gun cleaning kit. Water filter system. First aid kit. Spare mags and throwing knives. Waterproof matches. Waterproof pouch.

I tipped over the waterproof pouch on the boat's vinyl seat. My cigarettes fell out. Then my music player, wrapped with headphones and a solar charger. I thought I'd lost it. I pressed the power button and my spirit lifted a little as my punk rock playlist loaded up. I tilted the pouch and a sundry of batteries rolled out. I held up a package of lithium button cell batteries. What would I use these for? Unless...

I tapped out the remaining item. My bullet. My little pleasure toy. My shoulders slumped. Of course he did. He knew me better than I knew myself.

When I repacked the waterproof pouch, I felt a piece of paper folded in the bottom. I opened it with trembling fingers.

Ba-y,

If you're reading this, then our paths have parted. You have the tools to travel yours, with or without me. Remember our mantra. If you think about giving up, remember your promise. Keep breathing. Find your tear ducts if you need them. Stay hydrated.

I'm so grateful you shared your life with me. Fuck, I wanted to scream at the top of my lungs when you rose from that bed and strong-armed your grief. I wanted to scream with pride because I knew what it cost you. And I wanted to scream in fear because I'm a selfish bastard and I didn't want to share you with the world. You're special, Evie. You survived for a reason. I know you'll figure this thing out and provide hope for those left.

There's a community of scientists making progress on a reversal for the nymph virus. They're searching for human women. I didn't know how to tell you. I couldn't. I was scared, so damn insecure about others finding you, taking you from me. But, I have faith in you. Should your path lead you to Reykjavik, some call them the Shard.

No matter where your feet take you, wrap yourself in the gift Annie and Aaron gave you. Wear their unconditional love like armor. Let it keep you warm and protect you. No one can take it away.

And when the time is right, listen to the song and remember I love you.

Joel

The letter crumbled in my curling fists. Then I read it another five times, trying to decipher when he wrote it.

Find my tear ducts? Fuck if I could. I loosened a dagger from the sheath on my arm. The tip glinted. The paracord handle stained red. Was it Joel's blood? What had I done?

My throat burned as I tested the keen edge with my finger. I couldn't carry the weight of his final breaths, the memory of his eyes. I didn't want to know what happened to him, certain it would destroy me.

I flicked the dagger into the bench that wrapped the bow. The bow pointed east, like the needle on a compass. I didn't want to know about the Shard. Our cruel gluttonous race didn't deserve saving. I'd mind his mantra, but Iceland was out.

Listen to the Song? Joel's notions of love and following the heart had always been too abstract for me. In matters of intimacy, I relied on sensory data. Like the tremolo of a racing pulse. The quavering hum below the belly. The serenade of laughter. Joel called it the song. But why include it in the letter?

I contemplated a life alone. Would my need for touch, for sex, force me to seek comfort in another man's arms?

My guts rebelled, sent me dry heaving over the side of the boat. The ladybugs were restless as I hung there, spitting from a dry mouth. They crawled in my hair and slipped under my clothes. Most of them were still flittering toward the eastern shore.

I didn't want to leave the boat. I didn't want to face what prowled on land. Not without Joel.

The first aid kit soothed some of my sores. I cleaned and patched with detachment. My torn wrists. My battered eyes and lips. But when I reached the mangled flesh between my thighs, I couldn't fight the violent tremors.

To avoid another bout of dry heaves, I choked down water, tuna and a handful of crackers. So much for my vegetarianism. Piece by piece, what made me *me* was being stripped away. What would be left?

I repacked, returning the letter safely to the waterproof pouch. The motor purred as I guided the boat to the eastern shore. There, I disembarked it for the last time, humping the pack, the pistol, the carbine and the AA-12.

I slipped into the concealment of the woods where the ladybugs dispersed at the tree line. They were leaving me? I didn't know where I was going. When I stumbled upon a quiet creek, I let it lead me through the thick brush. On edge with misanthropy, I moved quickly. Joel's moaning reechoed until I wanted to stab my ears to make it go away. So I chanted. Stay alive. Seek truth. Do not look back.

I treaded all day through the forest along the creek, keeping my senses alert to buzzing or blood in the air. I didn't pause once, knowing if I did, the abyss would find me. My back and shoulders ached from hours of hanging on a pulley. The weight of my burden magnified the throbbing. My arm sheathes rubbed against the bandages on my wrists. But it was nothing compared to the pain of Joel's absence.

Where would I go? The provisions in my pack wouldn't last forever. I followed my feet and ache in my chest as if both were pushing me as fast as possible away from the place of painful memories.

When the treetop spray of daylight retreated behind the big oaks, I looked for a spot to make camp. A short time later, the dense woods opened into a glade. I let my head roll back. Full and glorious, the moon kept me company. It didn't care that I was a woman or judge my godlessness. Didn't try to plug the gaps in my memories or question my sanity. The moon was simply there, sharing its light.

The ripe odor of sweat overpowered the clay and mud that clung to my boots. My tank top dripped under the rucksack. I removed it and my fatigues and hissed at the sight of my bony hips, which bore open sores from the rubbing pack. Then, under the protection of a large American elm, I unfurled my bed roll and listened.

Nothing. Not the singing crickets. Not the warble of a bat. Not even the wind brushing the leaves. I knew very little about biology and life science. Maybe the ecosystem was somehow impacted by the virus? Or by the introduction of a mutated species?

I closed my eyes and focused on the single sense. I wanted to hear something besides the pounding of my own heart.

Then I did. A rustling. Soft footsteps across the ground cover. Wet heavy breaths. The breathing grew louder. I sighted the carbine in the direction of the disturbance.

A pair of large brown eyes glistened in the moonlight through the brush, no more than six feet away. Propped on one knee, I inhaled and slid my finger next to the trigger.

The woods are lovely, dark and deep.
But I have promises to keep, and miles to go before I sleep.

Robert Frost

CHAPTER TWELVE: DARWIN

Whatever was in the bushes didn't give a shit about discretion. Its breathing alternated between sniffs and muffled huffs. The leafy underbrush thrashed. I steadied the carbine. My fingers ached with tension. I waited.

A dark football shape rolled out of the brush. I strained my eyes, tried to make sense of it. Covered in green and brown feathers, a long neck flopped to the side. A dead duck. No visible wounds. No odor. Realizing I'd dropped the barrel, I raised the carbine back to the breathing shadow.

Two tan paws slid out along the ground. A dark wet nose settled between them, eyebrows twitching and brown eyes shifting upward.

I sat back and squeezed the carbine to my chest as it was the only thing I could hug. I didn't know whether to laugh or cry. The dog's tail swished somewhere behind it in the brush, rustling the ground litter. Relief poured out of me in a long deep breath.

It inched forward and nudged the duck.

A gift? If I moved to pick it up, would I scare it?

Another nudge. Then it scooped up the duck in its mouth and flipped it to me. A smile took hold of my lips as I pulled the offering into my lap.

The dog watched me with puppy dog eyes, crawling ever closer on its belly.

"Hi."

It lifted its head and barked once. Then it rose and sat before me, panting. A German shepherd. Larger than me, he bore a muscular and well-fed frame. Golden tan markings outlined the black on his back, tail and muzzle. Large pointed ears defied gravity, flicking back and forth.

I extended my hand. He pressed the top of his head to my palm so I could scratch between his ears. I held up the duck. "Dinner?"

The dog followed at my heels. I kindled a small flame and cleaned the duck. My anticipation for a fresh meal overruled my worry about attracting threats with a fire. He watched while I cooked the bird on a spit. A thick pink tongue hung from the side of his lips, which seemed to curl in a smile that matched my own.

Where did he come from? I hadn't seen a dog since the outbreak. Though humans were the only species that could contract the virus, aphids fed on all mammals. How had he escaped them for so long?

I knew the breed was intelligent. Opa, my grandpa, held membership in the Vereinfür Deutsche Schäferhunde, the German Shepherd Dog Club of Germany. He bred and trained dogs for a living using Schutzhund style training. A style that focused on tracking, obedience and protection.

We picked over the duck and the dog lapped up water from my camel back. Then I extinguished the fire and crawled onto my bed roll. The dog settled on the other side of the clearing, watching me. Alone in the woods all day, my senses were strung out from patrol. But as I watched the dog watch me, my muscles began to relax. My vigilance eased little by little, comforted by his keen stare. He looked at me as if waiting for instruction. Had he been trained? Opa taught me a few Schutzhund commands. I tried to remember some as I fought the increasing weight on my eyelids.

A howl pierced the haze. Darkness pinned me down. A string of whines rang out, high-pitched and relentless. I jerked up, landed on the balls of my feet, the carbine in high ready.

My eyes adjusted. A fog hung over the glade and clung to my skin. Moonlight thickened the haze into a squatting cumulonimbus.

The dog stood a few feet away, nose pointed at the tree line, haunches up. His withers spiked in golden tufts. His whine deepened into a throaty growl.

I trained the carbine on his point. Through the scope, through the fog, through the shadows of the raving sweetgums, a silhouette flickered. A tennis court length away, the distance was nothing for the carbine and scope. But spirally stems and broad leaves concealed the kill shot. I inched into the clearing.

The hunched-back figure pulsed, varying its illumination. Alien vocal cords filled the air with a screech as it sprang forward with the strength of its mutated legs. The dog spooked and darted into the woods. The bending and snapping of woody hurdles narrated his parting. The crackling faded and eventually died. He was gone.

I couldn't stop my disappointment from distracting me. A swell of heat spread inside me, simmered into convulsions that made my hands tremble. Losing the dog resonated a hollow thud in my head, muting all other sounds. Screw the kill shot. I lowered the carbine a few inches, moving the sight to the shoulder. Was that one alone? I scanned the area with a hunter's calm. Alone indeed. Exhale. Squeeze.

The thing thrashed backwards against the impact, buzzing and snarling. Its arm hung by mangled sinews. I sighted its other shoulder and repeated the shot. It fell down, but quickly regained its footing. Gristle and bone coruscated under black blood pumping from the crater that was its arm.

The aphid crept closer. The torso seemed to float on its double-jointed legs. I sighted between its eyes. Twenty yards. I knew where the kill shot was. But I knew little else about its defenses. Fifteen yards. Could it regrow limbs? Did it need its organs? Joel had won the arguments against capturing and experimenting on one. Ten yards. I lowered my scope, settled on its knee. Time to test some theories. I squeezed the trigger. It squealed and dropped. Then it leveraged its bloody stump and rose on one leg.

Its remaining arm lolled by a string of muscle. I shot it off. The aphid spun around. A pit blossomed on its side. It landed on its back. I closed the distance. Three yards. I aimed at its good leg. A sting of snapping rubber bands rippled through my gut. What the hell was going on with me? I pulled the trigger.

The aphid's torso lay in a welter of life and limbs. It stretched its jowls. Fleshy bits wormed in the mouth, arranging themselves around the tusk-like tube. The meaty fingers melded to form a sheath for the spear. Perhaps a casing for air-tight suction.

Carbine on my sling, I released a dagger from my forearm sheath and swiped. The aphid's remaining weapon plopped in the goulash.

I picked up an amputated arm. The aphid's orbs followed my movements as I flipped the arm back and forth, stretching the pincers and clamping them shut. Rows of sharp barbs jetted in one direction on the forearm. Tiny hairs furred the thin green skin.

Its chest heaved. Sputters purled from its throat. It choked. Something like static pinched my insides. I tossed the arm and kicked its torso, rolling it on its side. Then I crouched next to it.

Blood coursed from the shredded mouth and with it the aroma of rot. I flicked the dagger in front of its face. Its eyes stared. No blinking. No expression. I rubbed my stomach. A vibration sparked under my hand. I gripped the carbine, sat back and rested it over my knees. Would it regrow new limbs or would it bleed out? How long would it take?

The tiny aphid pupil didn't move. A hum churned inside me. I wiped my palms on my jeans. The hum I felt should've been the twinge of mercy. But it wasn't. I waited.

I opened my eyes against the light penetrating the forest canopy. Blood and decay tainted the warm breeze caressing my shoulder. Shit. I flipped over and met face-to-face with the still breathing aphid. Its wounds had soldered sometime during the night. Black leaking holes were dried and closed. No regrowth. At least not yet.

The aphid's hanging jaw twitched. I should experiment more, remove some organs, and try to bleed it out. My stomach groaned. Food first. Then weapon cleaning. Then I'd deal with the aphid—

A twig snapped in the scrub across the glade. I lifted the carbine. A blur of tan and black splayed the fronds. I gulped a breath and dropped the gun on its sling.

The dog bounded toward me, tail to the sky, tongue flapping. My knees hit the grass and he licked my hand. I stroked the top of his head, relishing the silken warmth of his coat. A prickle broke out on my spine. Then a strangled buzz from the aphid behind me. The dog scrambled backwards.

"Oh no, wait." I lunged after him, palm out. When he nudged my hand, I led him away from the bug, scratching and rubbing his ears as we walked.

How was it that he and I survived when so many hadn't? Was it genetic or environmental? Did some kind of Peter Parker freak exposure make us *super*? Maybe I watched too many movies. Whatever the reason—survival of the fittest, natural selection—the dog and I survived. The knot of loneliness in my gut loosened, cracked, and the sharp edges fell away.

"I'll call you Darwin." A symbol of his unfavorable survival against nature.

He barked and lathered my cheek.

We shared an MRE and I cleaned the carbine and daggers. That done, I perched beside the mutilated aphid, dagger in fist. Then I took a steadying breath and sawed through its neck. It took longer than expected. My stomach twisted and burned. What was happening to me? I wanted to do it. When the neck snapped and the head rolled off, the eyes went flat. The tension in my guts uncoiled.

I dragged the head into my lap and scored the skin to peel it from the bone. With another knife wedged as a chisel, I pounded it under the top of the skull and pried it off. The pinkish gray brain had two halves and filled the bulbous cranium. I scooped them out and scraped off the membrane covering, revealing a tofu texture. I didn't know what an insect brain looked like, but I suspected it was very different from the human-like brain in my lap. Did it mean they still had emotions? Memories? Christ, what if they were still human, trapped in these bodies?

My mouth went dry. I couldn't think like that. They showed no anger, no remorse. An aphid wouldn't hesitate to kill me. Which was why I had to kill them first. I tossed the brain onto the heap of limbs. Then I washed my hands with my camel back and joined Darwin at the tree line.

We plowed east through Missouri's Ozark Mountains. I followed Darwin up and down rugged slopes, his paws hooking around boulders and loose rock with ease. I chased him along the river way, wheezing, my calves burning. Often, he sprinted too far ahead and disappeared into the bush. Minutes felt like hours until he returned, bearing fresh water fowl.

A week passed and I grew dependent on his low growl, his aphid alarm. He sensed them before I did. For fear of losing him again, I'd herd Darwin in the opposite direction of the threat. I knew I was just tarrying until our peacetime lifted. The buzz of aphid hunger vibrated the air. I couldn't run from the aphids forever. I needed to test the dog's reaction to gun fire.

"*Hier*, Darwin." He ran to my side and leaned against my leg. I scratched his head and kissed the bridge of his snout. No doubt he knew more Schutzhund commands than I did. Maybe he'd been a police dog.

"*Fuss.*"

He obeyed, heeling as I walked along the riverbed toward an open field. The field animated with sunflowers, swishing and stretching to the summer sky.

"*In Ordnung.*"

Darwin took to the field, romping through the yellow blooms like an adolescent whitetail, spraying them to and fro in his wake. Then he stopped and looked back at me. He was really enjoying himself, his playfulness contagious. Focus, Evie.

I targeted the carbine on the trunk of a dead cottonwood bridging the river. Exhale. *Pop.*

He pricked his ears, the only thing he moved.

I sighed my relief and tramped to his side."*Sitz.*"

Darwin sat on his haunches.

I raised the AA-12. Sighted it down field. Told him to stay. "*Bleib.*"

Exhale. *Clap. Clap.*

Shotgun still in high ready, I gave Darwin a sidelong glance. His eyes met mine, his body stiff with attention. My lips twitched. Wouldn't it be something if Darwin were there because of Joel's doing? Joel always knew what I needed. My injuries were healing without infection and Darwin kept my mind off them most days. The dog numbed my pain.

I bent and hugged him. "Well done, boy."

With a raised hand, I sheltered my eyes from the sun's glare and scanned the field under the Ozark highlands. The hills tinged blue under the haze of the humidity. "Where to now, Darwin?"

He bounced around me and prodded me to play. We should've only been a few miles from the highway. That meant we'd see civilization soon. Sweat trickled down my spine. We'd find a car and maybe sleep in a soft bed. I gathered my gear and hiked east. "*Fuss.*"

Darwin followed.

The sun dropped below the hillside and sketched shadows on the dam saddled by Highway 65. We climbed the bulwark and gaped up and down the highway. An old pickup truck sat in the southbound lane. Darwin wet his nose with his tongue and resumed panting.

I knew the area, had traveled that highway dozens of times. The lake was only ten miles behind us. But thanks to the August heat, the overgrown woods, the continuous stops to rest my injuries and ease the weight of my gear, it'd been the longest ten miles of my life. With languor setting in, I trudged to the truck while Darwin led the way.

The unlocked doors on the Ranger made entry easy. The missing keys offset my luck. I stripped my gear and chased away images of the truck's prior occupant emerging from the woods and slashing me open with an insectile mouth.

I crawled under the steering column. After a few sweaty minutes of wire tapping, the engine came to life. The needle on the gas gauge swung to *F*. I blew out a breath.

Thank fucking God for my old Chevy. I hated that clunker when I was a kid. Had to hot-wire it to start it. Memories of hunkering under the dash, late for school, fingers trembling over the wires in frigid temperatures. Never imagined I'd be looking back on that with a smile.

Now for a grocery store and uninhabited housing. Sedalia offered the best chance of that. Only an hour north.

But a town of its size could be rife with men. I jolted at the shiver that ran down my spine and gripped the steering wheel. Ugly reminders discolored my wrists. My limbs grew numb. My body labored against heavy breathing. The pain in my chest felt like a heart attack. I knew it wasn't. The sudden sweating, dizziness and accelerated heart rate were telltale symptoms of a panic attack. I needed Joel.

I rolled down the window and gulped fresh air. Then I lit a cigarette. I wasn't prepared to come to grips with my wounds. Facing one of my own species terrified me far more than fighting an army of blood spitting bugs.

The grocery store would wait. Besides, Darwin kept me fed on fowl and fish. I put the truck in first and headed south. South to MO-64. Then east to I-44. East to Fort Leonard Wood.

If my memory was right, Fort Leonard Wood served as a training facility for the U.S. Army military police. Perhaps I could upgrade to a military SUV and gather more artillery and supplies. Beyond that, I didn't know what to expect.

An hour later, I passed a guard building surrounded by a towering fence and rolled over the trampled gate. I kept the truck at a crawl, straining my eyes against the pitch black milieu for signs of life. A light on in a building? A fresh worn track? Movement in the shadows? With only the light from the headlights, an overt assessment was impossible. By what I could see, the base seemed barren.

Then I smelled it. A rot so thick it slid down my throat and met the bile rising there. I choked, buried my nose in the crook of my arm. My foot slid to the brake, my free hand slapping at the window crank. My gag reflex won.

The window half down, I emptied my stomach over both sides of the door. Another choking breath and I retched again.

I wiped my mouth, spun the wheel till it stopped and began a tight three-sixty turn. The headlights illuminated an empty field, a charred building, the entrance to the base, then mountains of…holy fuck. The knot in my gut rushed back to my throat. I held it off, swallowed repeatedly, breathed.

Scatters of arms, legs, gutted torsos, and unrecognizable fleshy parts blotted the horizon, stretching beyond the reach of the headlights. And the faces. Oh God, the faces staring out of the heaps. Men. Women. Aphid. Skin peeling, baked from the sun. Bones exposed, splintered and crushed.

I was out of the truck, moving closer, and realized a person could have too much courage. But I was sure it wasn't courage. It was a train wreck. I couldn't look away.

Bodies strewed the ground, piled where they fell, dismembered or eaten. Tanks and other armored vehicles belched human remains. A post-battle wasteland. Perhaps civilians were seeking shelter at the base and killed out of fear of infection. Maybe aphids overran the command post and the residents used up their ammo.

Decayed hands held shotguns and rifles. Empty eye sockets stared into the beam of the headlights. Mouths froze in silent screams. Human and aphid lay side by side in repose. The scene was peaceful. Could've been a painting if it hadn't been so painful look at it. Did anyone survive? My stomach bottomed out. I whirled, carbine raised and searched the night for a breath of life.

Darwin huffed in the cab, ears up, eyes alert. My muscles relaxed. The rot was ripe. It wasn't a recent battle. Survivors would be gone.

As I drove to the other side of the base, the stench dissipated. Pillaged structures and exsanguinated bodies became fewer and fewer.

Twenty minutes later, I parked in front of a narrow barracks, its two windows and single door untouched. Humping my pack and artillery, I surveyed the perimeter of the building, unable to ignore my exhaustion.

I broke the dead bolt with the butt of the carbine and swept the single room building with the Maglite. Darwin darted in ahead of me and sniffed out every nook. Empty mattresses lay on the bunks. Metal blinds covered the windows. A fucking Ritz Carlton.

I moved a desk in front of the door. With Darwin at my very sore feet, I was certain he would alert me of danger. My head hit the bed and sleep pulled me down.

I sprawled naked in the damp dimness, a stone slab cold against my back. My arms and legs stretched with heavy chains. The aroma of blood burned my nose.

Plip. Plop. Plip. Plip.

Beads tapped my face and trickled down my cheeks. Shallow respiration at my feet broke the rhythm of the dribble.

"Who's there?"

The blanket of darkness lifted, unveiled a hollow cave. I blinked through the drops in my eyes. My vision clouded under a scarlet hue. Dark rain spotted my body. The ceiling was bleeding.

A figure emerged through my blinks. He stood at my feet, staring back through onyx eyes, cloaked in a sable cape. He pushed back the hood. Black curls curtained his Middle Eastern features.

"I am the Drone", he offered with an Arabic accent, emphasizing the D.

I tugged at the chains. "What do you want?"

He leapt upon the alter and straddled my waist. "I think you know." He smirked. Then a spear erupted from his mouth and pierced my chest.

Smoldering pain. I pawed at him, my hands not working right. Screams echoed. My screams. The ceiling erupted in a mud slide of blood. The gore rushed from unseen pores in the walls.

I bucked my hips against the pang of the Drone's sucking mouthparts. I couldn't escape the stabbing spasm in my chest.

"Fuck you." My voice was strangled.

His slurping continued, each pull with the throb of my heart. An obscure shape swelled behind his shoulders. He crooked up the corner of his mouth around the bloody spear and extended immense transparent wings.

I screamed until the burning in my throat overbore the wound in my chest. The light danced away as if in fear. When the darkness curled under my chin, it was warm and wet and very much alive.

Deep into that darkness peering,
long I stood there, wondering, fearing, doubting,
dreaming dreams no mortal ever dared to dream before.

Edgar Allan Poe

Chapter Thirteen: Severed Tongues

Slimy slaps doused my neck. Something slithered over my cheek. Warm puffs filled my ear. I opened my eyes and sucked in air to keep my scream from escaping.

Spittle showered my nose. Darwin's dripping tongue hovered inches away. He licked his chops and recommenced slobbering my face. I wrapped my arms around his neck and buried my face in his fur. "Was I screaming, boy? Did I scare you?"

He leaned into my hug and rolled to his side with a rumbling moan and a playful snap of jaws.

Daylight leaked in around the edges of the window blinds. My senses back online, I bent my arms and legs to test flexibility. The fatigue and stress in my muscles were faint compared to the prior night. I rubbed my chest. No rents in my skin despite the ache.

The Drone.

Wish I could've told Joel about the dream. He would've wrapped me in the strength of his arms and nuzzled my cheek while murmuring reassurances. Then he would've set me on my feet and told me in his stern voice to pull my shit together.

As I sat there, feeling forsaken, panicked even, some intangible timeline forced itself upon me. It was a tug, clawing inside my chest.

I ground myself in the urgency of it, threw on my jeans, black tee, armored vest and cap and removed the desk barricade.

As far as I could see, the base spread out in a barren reminder that even our military couldn't fight this thing. Bodies scattered the ground, tattered by wind and cankered by the heat. I stared at them for long moments, waiting for them to rise.

On the way to the truck, I carried that expectancy with me. But there was no buzzing. No movement. No blood in the air. Only the hot scent of asphalt and the dormant lawn crunching under my feet.

Darwin froze halfway to the truck, his muzzle pointing at three vultures pecking at a thick clutter of decomposed bodies. In a flap of wings, the birds took air, chased away by a scraggly dog. As if my nose had just caught up with my sight, I gagged. The stench overpowered my other senses and caused my steps to falter. Darwin seemed to be effected by it too if his whimpers were anything to go by.

"Darwin." I motioned to the truck, and like always, he obeyed.

It took several circles around the base before I spotted the armory. A single story brick building squatted off the outer road. The lot provided a breeding ground for daylilies. Bursts of orange overran the landscape as evidence of runners sprouted new growth in every direction. The armory's thick steel door and only entry appeared closed and unscathed. It was either once heavily guarded or impossible to plunder.

I drove the truck over the lawn and parked a few feet from the door. Carbine in high ready, I crept to the entrance while Darwin fertilized the lilies. Would it be locked? I reached for the handle.

It cracked open. My hand jerked back. If there were men watching on the cameras, they'd see me going in. The truck felt like a magnet behind me. Ten paces would put me back in that cab.

Minutes passed. The cameras wouldn't be working without electricity, and I blamed the breeze for moving the door. I thought about the ammo I needed and could possibly acquire. I steadied my breathing and summoned my grit. Then I stepped through the door.

The training Joel drilled into me took over. I blurred out of the doorway's halo and swept right, back to the wall. Musk and alcohol lingered in the small foyer. I pressed into the shadows. That was when I realized my folly. Electric lights illuminated the corner. Fuck. A generator powered the building? That meant human occupancy.

I pivoted to the entrance, started to run.

Whoomp-click.

The slide action reverberated through my body. A chambered shell. I planted my feet.

In the doorway, Darwin snarled and bared his teeth.

Without turning around, I mimicked Darwin's growl. "Lower your gun. I'm not looking for trouble."

"Call your dog away or I'll do it for you." A masculine voice, deep and confident.

Darwin's ears pinned flat to his head. His hackles shot up. I wasn't about to do anything to chance his life. "Get. Shoo."

His growl wavered, but his body remained stiff.

Shit. I couldn't remember the command. Maybe *"Geh rein?"*

He slinked inside, head low to the ground, lip pulled back. Boots squeaked behind me.

I shouted, *"Nein. Nein."*

Darwin stopped.

Blood pounded in my ears. I held up my hands for the benefit of the gunman and flexed my fingers when I realized they were trembling. "I'm trying. Give me a minute."

"Not itchin' to destroy such a fine animal but you've got five seconds to find out exactly how much I care."

I took a deep breath. "Darwin. *Geh raus.*"

He backed out of the door and disappeared.

The number of boots squeaking the floor multiplied. "Now drop your gun and turn around."

Until I knew what I was up against, cooperating was my only option. I set down the carbine, my only gun, and turned around.

Five men crowded a dark hallway and aimed guns of varying sizes at the only vital part of me not protected by my vest. My head.

Two of them used free hands to raise pants zippers and clasp belt buckles, faces flushed and sweaty. Didn't take a genius to know what I'd interrupted. An environment stripped of women, much like prison, would be tainted with dominates and their bitches.

The one with the buckle walked by me and closed the door. My muscles trembled.

The bossy one gripped my neck. "Looks like one of Satan's whores just stumbled in our door, boys."

Their laughing carried undertones of something poisonous. Something not unlike insanity. A reminder that, for most, surviving the apocalypse meant surviving attacks by those they trusted. Did these men kill their own mothers, sisters, lovers to save themselves?

Veins bulged in their foreheads. Their eyes were cold and narrowed. I kept my arms behind my back and traced the stitching on my forearm sheath.

The grip on my throat tightened. A lingering lick caressed my cheek. A promise of what was to come. My quivering muscles betrayed me.

Someone said, "Look at her arms."

Another laughed. "Goddamn. Bitch'd cut off a finger using one of those knives."

Then a shout. "Take your knives to the kitchen, woman, and make me some dinner."

More rounds of laughter. More ignorant barbs. But they didn't take the knives. I smiled inwardly with images of serving them their own severed tongues on fine china, their starved mouths flapping as they silently begged for more.

"If you think I'm so inept at throwing knives," I said, "put down your guns and try me."

The stoutest brute roared. "No way am I wasting a fight on a worthless woman."

If you understand the foundation of your anger, you might be able to promote it in others.

"If I don't mind, why should you?" I said.

The brute's face reddened, but confidence blazed in his eyes. He handed his weapons off to his buddies.

I jumped on the distraction, stepped back and brought up my left hand. The inside block knocked the bossy one's arm off my neck. I hit his knee joint with a side kick. He stumbled back. I freed a blade and pierced his lung. He collapsed.

The stout brute's fist hit my chest and gripped my vest. Shouts filled the air. A bullet whizzed by my ear. Then another. I sucked in a breath and trapped his hand and thumb with my left hand. I locked his arm, twisted it and knocked him off balance. With another blade, I struck his forearm. Something stung my thigh. A grazed bullet? I shot a shin kick to the bastard's groin. He clutched his nuts, dropped to his knees, his mouth a huge *O* of surprise. I stomped his calf. His fibula cracked, piercing through a mangled hole in his knee.

The bossy one was on me again. I shifted his body, using it as cover and forcing a wheeze from his damaged lung.

Gunfire riddled the floor and shredded the furniture. His body jiggled under the spray. The entrance was closer. I dropped him and darted for it.

Lead ricocheted everywhere. I ran faster. The sun reflected off the metal door as I swung it open. I squinted against the glare.

Boots and bullets followed me outside. A vibration hit my stomach. I skidded to a stop. Six aphids blocked the walkway.

I spun to the side and let the bastard behind me absorb the first strike. Two mutants covered him, sucking him. His head fell back. His mouth opened, gargled.

The remaining aphids slashed their beaks and stabbed the chests of the final two. The assholes hadn't even unlocked their stances or lifted their weapons. Maybe Joel was right. Maybe the bugs did move fast despite my inability to see it.

The feeding paroxysm allowed me to pass unnoticed a few moments. They were sucking with vigor, torsos heaving, bulbous heads bobbing with each pull and swallow. I crept backwards toward the door, toward the carbine.

A pair of alabaster eyes met mine. Its mouth retreated, making a sucking sound when it pulled free from flesh. I grabbed the door handle and pulled hard. The damn thing wouldn't latch, the lock disintegrated by gunfire.

I backed up and grabbed the carbine. The door rattled. The buzzing grew in intensity. Then the door crashed open.

Only one aphid entered. It maneuvered through the room, its tiny pupils never leaving me. It hovered within reach, studied me. Curiosity kept me from squeezing the trigger.

The man on the floor moaned. The aphid cocked its head. Blood dripped from its jowls. Why wasn't it going for the easy fodder? Was it sated? Or did it want a challenge?

It spread its pincers and thrust its chest forward. An alien pitch rattled through me. My spine tingled. Was it trying to unsettle me? Its jaw snapped between vibrational effects. Then it lunged toward my neck.

Pop.

A 5.56 round ruptured its eye. A kaleidoscope of matter poured from the cavity. The aphid dropped at my feet.

With the carbine still level, I walked back outside. Five trigger pulls. Five kills. Either I was getting better at it or the aphids were easier to kill during dinner time. Of course, knowing where the kill shot was helped.

Three human bodies contorted and sloshed in a dark bath. I knelt over one, blood soaking my jeans. His eyes glazed over, irises blanching, face twisted in pain. I wasn't sorry about that.

His jaw hinged open. A gurgling scream erupted. Inhuman bits writhed in his throat. Christ, the beginning stages of mutation happened quickly.

I unsheathed a knife. Pressed the tip under his ear. Dipped the edge and sliced his throat. Then, sitting in the cesspool feeling strangely alive as blood and death clung to me, I watched his life slip away.

Early news reports said it took a couple hours to fully mutate after a bite. He bled out in less than a minute. Not surprising considering the donation he'd given the aphid. I stood. Then I sliced two more throats.

A rustling whisper came from the armory. I followed it. The stout brute crawled on his belly, a useless leg dragging behind him.

I crouched in front of him. "So easily submitted by a subordinate woman. What were you planning had you found my skills wanting?"

He hissed, "Ssstupid slut. You nasty whores brought this evil upon us." Blood and saliva congealed on his chin. "I would have delivered you to Satan after ssspreading your filthy le…ahgg…argggggh—"

I sliced out his tongue.

After great pain, a formal feeling comes.
The Nerves sit ceremonious, like tombs.

Emily Dickinson

CHAPTER FOURTEEN: SPOTTED WING

I woke with my neck crooked at an uncomfortable angle. The military Humvee I upgraded to at Fort Leonard Wood made it easy to maneuver cluttered roadways and steep embankments. But the spartan interior was miserable to sleep in.

For three days, I just drove. No destination in mind. But always heading east. I didn't know why and that scared me more than the hungry creatures that sniffed around my truck while I slept. Was the numbness a way of protecting myself against an emotional avalanche? If I forced myself to care, would the pain of recent events be too excruciating to bear?

Eventually, farmland turned to parking lots and the interstates became crowded with wreckage. The twisted remains of panicked evacuations forced me off road more often than not.

A jet had pulverized a portion of the highway. A helicopter stuck out of a skyscraper. Bridges gave way to gaping holes filled with freight trains reduced to chewed-up metal and soot. And the bodies. They slouched over steering wheels, splattered in boutique windows and hung from water towers. Dismembered flesh painted the concrete and blistered in the sun, evidence that death in the city came by human hands. Aphids didn't leave human bodies behind.

I rested in a pasture along I-64 just outside Shelbyville, Kentucky, tucked behind a dilapidated barn. The glaucous blue moors rolled velvety ripples in all directions.

Under the Humvee's .50 cal mounted turret, I stroked a hand along the black and tan coat that warmed my feet. My lips twitched at the memory of finding Darwin hiding under a parked car in the armory lot. I carried no regrets from Leonard Wood. The venture had been profitable.

Darwin dozed amongst the hand grenades, shoulder fire rockets, flash bangs, flares, smoke grenades, ammo, a portable siphon and diesel fuel. I had also acquired another bullet proof vest and sundry supplies at the commissary including boots, socks, maps, water, smokes, commercial food and medicine. I even found a battery hand drill with carbide drill bits for lock picking.

A rumble skipped over the hill. There hadn't been a lot of traffic on that stretch of highway, but it wasn't dead either. My body went taut with anticipation.

Moments later, a van roared by. The brake lights illuminated. It swerved off the road about hundred yards ahead. I grabbed binoculars and slipped into the driver's seat with the AA-12 in my lap.

Three burly men climbed out, shirtless and grimy. Ages ranged thirties to forties, my guess. They walked around a T-boned Escalade in the left lane, packing the standard artillery. Pistols in shoulder and hip holsters. Rifles strapped to their backs. Bulges around their ankles and thighs meant concealed weapons.

A low growl erupted next to me.

"*Platz.*" My voice was firm. Darwin lay on the floorboard but his hackles didn't relax.

They rummaged through a few more SUVs, unable to start or move any of them. Finally, they drove away in the van they came in. I rolled back my shoulders, tried to release the knots there. Then I patted my thigh. Darwin's head dropped in my lap.

Since Leonard Wood, I had managed to dodge man and aphid. Same could be said about ladybugs, ghost children and other phantasms. Did I miss the visits from my A's? Most days, the vacant cavity of my existence was too much to bear. Still, amidst the void, something tugged. Kept me moving.

A U.S. map of the east coast sprawled on the drivetrain. We would reach Appalachia soon. I was okay with that. Maybe the mountain air would give me strength. And help me rebuild.

I arrived at the northwestern edge of Monongahela National Forest in West Virginia the next night. Colorful deciduous trees dappled the steep mountain range and warmed my soul.

Darwin hung his head out of the window. The perfume of fertile soil and fallen pine needles swirled around us. The sound of cheery birds and whirring winged insects made me feel less alone. Though I feared alone was the only way a woman could survive in this new world.

I made camp along an overgrown hiking trail and plopped next to my modest campfire. The crickets chirruped in the dense sedge. Rodents stirred up leafy debris. A sward of mountain oat-grass whistled under the erratic flight of a nighthawk. Could I make a future there, in that place full of life? Would the isolation grant the peace I sought? I ran my fingers over Darwin's back, his body stretched in repose. He seemed to think so.

We spent our first three days content and lazy. I didn't want to stray from the truck until I trusted the absence of threats. So we picked through the nearby bramble and investigated narrow paths and creeks.

The fourth night, I greased the pistol next to the campfire, sheltered by a wall of saplings and rocks. Something stirred near the

Humvee. Darwin sprawled next to me, undeterred. I went back to the pistol.

Footsteps scraped, soft but sure. Darwin didn't move. I strapped on the carbine and approached the truck.

The forest chatter died and through the silence, I felt her presence. She fluttered within me, surged through my veins.

"Annie?"

A melodious twitter echoed back. I followed it into the thicket. Thorns and stems reached, tearing my legs. Ferns slapped my face. But my clambering was nothing to the sound of my heartbeat.

Annie perched on a slope crowded with sugar maples and American beech. Leaf litter clung to the hem of her dress. She clapped when she saw me. Then she ran, the gold in her hair like metallic ribbons in the moonlight.

I followed her. We sloshed in bogs and waded through streams. I hauled myself over a dead tree, my lungs burning. On and on we went.

My back ached under the weight of the carbine and the speed at which we moved. I was always too far behind. Never able to catch up. Then I smacked into wet rock wall carpeted with lichen and clubmosses and fell on my back.

She stood on the bluff above me. I gulped heavy breaths and contemplated defeat. My ghost didn't need to climb. She could simply float. My chest ached. Not from exhaustion, but desperation. She curled rosy lips and twirled her skirts. I longed to be with her. To hold her.

I dug in a toe and began the climb, using the roots as rungs. When I reached the crest, she spread out her arms, imitated an airplane, and zoomed down the other side. I wrestled for breaths, my shoulders drooping.

She sang with soprano as she ran.

Ladybird ladybird fly away home
Your house is on fire and your children are gone

I caught up with her in a clearing. She stood in front of a fire surrounded by a shallow stone hearth. Fire? Was that part of the delusion?

Her eyes glittered as I drew near. She continued her ballad.

All except one and that's Little Ann

For she has crept under the warming pan

I extended my arms to embrace her small frame. Her delicate chin lifted. The freckles on her nose sparkled in the firelight. Then she melted into a shroud of mist between my fingers.

"No. Please. No." Hugging her was like hugging a draft or a gleam of moonlight. My hands had never felt so empty. I squeezed them into fists while my hope of ever holding her again caught fire and burned its way to my heart.

Her silhouette solidified on the stone hearth. The flame danced inches behind her. Then the blaze intensified and transformed into something like a clawed hand. It crackled above her. I reached for her again. The hand smashed down and dragged her into its fiery pith. I dove after her.

My face and arms stung as I lay in the dirt. The heat from the fire fueled the pain, evidence that my chase with Annie wasn't a dream.

A deep voice drifted down. "Half-wit."

I flinched and opened my eyes. The voice's owner stooped over me. Long black hair hung in sheets around his dark face. On the other side of the fire, an elder man with silver braids perched on a log. Darwin rested at his feet.

The elder said, "Leave her be, Badger."

Badger straightened but stayed at my side. "She's covered in burns. What if she tries to throw herself into the fire again?"

The elder stood and approached. I trembled with trepidation and chill from the burns. I couldn't feel the weight of the carbine. It was nowhere in sight.

He crouched in front of me. Dark senescent skin announced his Native American heritage. Black and red feathers twisted through leather accessories in his hair and clothing. "Do you chase ghosts or do they chase you?"

My shoulders bunched at the intimation. "Depends on the ghost."

A toothless smile crossed his wizened face. "I suppose what is true in our world is also true in the spirit world. The children are our guides. They preserve the truth."

I must have been hallucinating. How else would he know anything about children who haunt me? I moved my head a few inches. The carbine leaned against a black cherry tree several yards away.

His voice soothed. "You don't need gunpowder here, woman. We are a peaceful people."

I kept my eyes on the gun.

"I have herbal medicines for your burns. Can you stand?"

I lifted my upper body. My sagacious pup stood in anticipation. His instincts hadn't misguided me yet. If he trusted them then I should.

Badger helped me to my feet. My skin burned under his touch but I didn't react. I asked the elder, "What do you want?"

"A nation is as strong as the hearts of its women. Its warriors may be brave and many, but when the blood of its women spills upon the earth, the battle is lost."

Darwin remained still as if waiting for me to follow his trust. I wasn't going to let the old man deflect my question. "What do *you* want?"

He sighed. "The great Chief Seattle spoke of the end of living and the beginning of survival. This is not want. This is hope. Come."

I lunged for the carbine. Tension unfurled inside me when I gripped it. Behind me, the two men waited, unmoved. Maybe I was paranoid, but I wasn't inclined to drop my guard. I stood, shoulders back, and nodded.

They guided me through the woods and ended the hike at a stream, bordered by a few lean-to'sfashioned from dead branches and spruce needles. I followed the elder to his lean-to in the heart of the camp with Darwin at my side. He pointed to a sanguine wool blanket as he rummaged through his baskets of dried herbs and ointments.

I settled on the blanket, the carbine on my knees."What's your name?"

He found what he was looking for and squatted before me. His eyes flicked to the gun and back to me. "My people call me Owota la Akicita."

I blinked. "Oh…wha—"

"Call me Akicita."

"Ah-kee-chee-tah. I'm Evie. So what does it mean, your name?"

He opened a small jar and plunged two fingers in it. "Honest peacekeeper." He held up the fingers caked in salve. "This will burn."

I nodded and sensed someone behind me.

"Lean against Badger." He slavered my face with the minty smelling anodyne. I jerked back at the stinging sensation. Badger pressed against my back. I closed my eyes and let the man rub my face and arms.

Palliative humming rumbled from his chest as he worked. My burns began to numb. Drowsiness settled on me like a heavy blanket. Then I could no longer fight the weight of my eyelids.

"Good Morning, Half-wit."

I rubbed my eyes against the twilight.

"No. No. Don't rub." Concern coated the soft voice.

I dropped my hands and smiled. "Hence, Half-wit?"

He laughed and knelt at my side. "Yes, very. And you must be feeling better." His inquisitive brown eyes pierced mine. "So who are you?"

"Um—"

"Oh wait. It's Evie, right? Akicita told me."

A boyish smile stretched under sharp cheekbones. His thick hair draped his shoulders and back. My fingertips tingled to touch his dark skin which looked like it had been sanded to a smooth perfection.

"You talk in your sleep, you know?" he said. "Where are you from? What's your dog's name? We haven't seen any dogs since the reservation. Where are you headed? Are there any…"

Jesus. Fuck. My mouth hung open in several failed attempts to interrupt. I couldn't get a word in.

"…the mountains. Why the hell did you throw yourself into the fire? For the love of the Great Mystery, what were you thinking? I—"

"Badger, give it a rest."

I turned to mark the new voice. His features and mannerisms weren't unlike Badger. They could have been twins. Only the stranger seemed older.

"Hey. I'm Naalnish. Don't mind my brother. We told him to watch over you, not talk you to death."

No shit. "He's fine."

He whacked Badger on the back of his head. "Get out of here. Let her eat in peace." He slid a bowl before me and Badger grumbled his way out.

"Naalnish you said?"

He smiled. "A Navajo name."

"You're Navajo?"

He shook his head. "We're Lakota. From North Dakota. Our father was Navajo."

He guessed my next question. "We left the Dakotas after the outbreak. The bugs like our semi-arid climate and chased us out."

"Only three of you?"

"Four actually. Lone Eagle left this morning to retrieve your things. There were dozens of us at first. The journey has been long."

"I'm sorry."

His smile was warm. "Eat." He nodded to the bowl. "It's pemmican. The fat and protein will help you heal." With that, he left.

Besides a variety of berries and chewy meat, most of the concoction was unrecognizable. But it filled my belly and boosted my energy. I slurped up the last bite, strapped on the knives, I ventured out in search of Darwin.

I found the men near a fresh-running stream. Naalnish waved when he saw me and laughed at Darwin when he pounced a trout in the shallow water. Akicita and Badger met me half way.

The elder prodded my face. "It heals. The energy flows strongly through you."

"What energy—"

"Come on," Badger grabbed my hand. "We have a million questions."

Akicita rested his skeletal fingers over ours, freezing Badger's forward motion. "No questions, Badger. We'll talk about the weather or the abundance of rabbit in this region. Or that incredible dog of yours."

I smiled and followed them to the river.

We were gathered around the stone hearth when Lone Eagle returned with my gear. He appeared from the footpath and his eyes greeted mine.

For a moment, he stood there, staring at me. I stared right back. He wasn't what I expected. Not a clone of Naalnish and Badger. His bronze skin and strong facial features hinted Native American blood, but his stunning eyes and short wavy russet hair suggested another heritage. He was exquisite.

I swallowed against a reflex of guilt. Gawking at another man felt like cheating. Still, I couldn't look away.

His thumb tapped the limb of his bow, the string sawing back and forth on his muscled thigh. And his eyes…something swirled in their coppery depths, as if he was seeing me. Inside me. Then his mouth dipped in a frown. His mouth was distracting. I swallowed again.

Silence rippled through the camp as he approached. The air seemed to follow him.

"I moved the Humvee further into the mountains. It's still miles away." Despite his stolid tone, a few words were traced with a southern drawl.

"How did you—"

"I'm a tracker. Where do you want your things?"

Ah. No doubt I left a screaming spoor in my chase with Annie. "I'll take them. I'm not sure where I'm staying."

His brows gathered. Contempt? Or was it curiosity? Before I decided, he marched toward the lean-to's with my things.

Badger joined me. "Don't worry about him. He's kind of a loner. Hasn't been with us long this time. Found us after the outbreak. His mother was one of us."

Without replying, I took off after my things and the peculiar man who conveyed them.

I found him settling my supplies in the last shelter at the far end of camp. None of my weaponry made the trip, not that I expected it considering their attitude toward guns. I said to his back, "Lone Eagle, is it?"

When he turned, I melted a little. The man was as hot as the Appalachian sun.

"My mother called me Lone Eagle. It's Jesse actually. Jesse Beckett."

"Okay, Jesse. Thank you for collecting my gear."

His body tensed and his eyes glowed. "The arsenal you are transporting...you don't even know what you're about. I'm surprised you haven't blown off any limbs. And where did you get an AA-12? You realize if you actually saw real combat, that shotgun would be taken from you and used against you."

Heat rushed to my face. "Would you offer me the same judgment if I sported a dick? Fuck you."

He winced. Then stepped around me, leaving me fuming through a vehement grinding of teeth.

I paced in front of the shelter. Who the hell did he think he was? I pressed my hands to my cheeks to cool the blaze there. My lungs labored to suck in air. If I actually saw real combat? I wanted to box his ears. And shove my boot up his ass. I turned on my heels to go after him.

Badger hailed, "Where are you going, Evie?"

I took a deep breath. "I need a cigarette."

He lit and handed me a hand-rolled. The first drag rolled across my palate. Some of the strain released from my shoulders. I pointed to the shelter where my gear resided. "Whose lean-to is that?"

"Uh...that's Lone Eagle's. He doesn't sleep there much. He stays out there." He gestured to the surrounding woodland. "He put your stuff there? It's yours now. I don't think he's in the habit of hanging around people. He grew up with us. You know, on the reservation? All our families were close. But then his parents split. He left for Texas with his old man. Came back in the summers sometimes. I guess he was some sort of football champion in high school. Heard he got a big school scholarship. But something happened. He didn't go. Then he disappeared. That is until a few months ago. He found us after the outbreak..."

I tuned him out, counted to ten. Then counted again. Eventually, he took a breath.

"Did you ask him what happened? What he's been doing?"

He laughed. "Of course. He told me the Lakota don't ask questions and scolded me for talking too much. Now I just leave him alone."

A fucking understatement.

"What's that?"

Shit. I said that out loud? "You do talk a lot."

He held out his hand, his face split in a grin. "Then come back to the campfire and you can do all the talking. We don't know anything about you."

I considered his offer. I wouldn't be able to avoid their questions for long. And I didn't feel an urgency to run off just yet. They were nice. Decent people. Most of them.

Maybe I could answer a few questions. Recount some impersonal aspects without picking at unhealed sores. I accepted his hand and followed him to the hearth.

The Lakota were all there, listening to Akicita unravel a captivating tale about an encounter with a grizzly. Jesse sat on the far side, his expression cryptic. His vivid copper eyes followed me until the bonfire's blaze blocked his view.

Badger pulled me down next to him and prodded me with questions. So I began my story with the aphid by the pool. Then I detailed my other aphid encounters, brushing over particulars about my personal life. They hooted at the narration of the night I met Darwin.

My talkative friend couldn't resist questions about marriage and children.

"Like you," I said, "I also lost everyone I loved and cared for."

Akicita followed my noncommittal response with the Lakota story. His eyes sparkled and his soothing voice curled around me in a warm embrace. When he finished, I said, "Tell us another one."

He cast me dark eyes underscored with years of knowledge. "I have many more, but first"—the corners of his mouth creased—"I give you a Lakota name. We will call you Spotted Wing."

"Spotted Wing?"

Naalnish ran his hand through my hair. Two ladybugs clung to his finger. "They like you."

My lids drifted closed. The journey there had been a lonely one. And lingering at the edges of my mind was a sad resolution that my future held more of the same.

I had a myriad of questions for them but I remembered Badger's warning. The Lakota didn't ask questions. I found a kind of safety in that. They offered possibilities. A new name. A new life. In the Allegheny Mountains among gentle men. As far as options went, I couldn't come up with a reason against staying.

Jesse stood, hurled a clod of dirt into the fire. Then he pinned me with a glare and disappeared through the timber.

Okay. There was one.

Let everything you do be your religion
and everything you say be your prayer.

Lakota Sioux

CHAPTER FIFTEEN: LA VIDA LAKOTA

The following weeks flew by as we readied for winter. I learned to make clothes, weapons, food and medicine from the mountain plants and animals. When the first snow forced us downstream, we settled into an abandoned one room cabin.

Idleness and seclusion narrowed the world to that little room where hibernation imposed itself on me, shoving me into a painful awakening. Stripped of distractions, I was left with an abundance of introspection. Those final hours with my dying children. My forsaking Joel to escape within myself for two months after. The dark basement at my father's house. My knife in Joel's head.

With Akicita watching over me, I slept to escape my self-scrutiny, my loathing, and my mistakes. Only, sleep forced me to face my nightmares.

Akicita administrated sleep aids on the worst days. He told me a restful body would germinate a conscious mind. I just wanted numbness and accepted his antidotes with abandon.

And so, I slept. In and out of consciousness, days turned to weeks until four months had passed. Time nurtured my trust in the Lakota, my worry about the aphids and crazed men forgotten. I knew the bugs were still out there in our isolated woods. I could hear my companions fighting them.

I would never be able to repay them for their protection, for the time they gave me to nurse the bruise inside of me. But I accepted the gift with a healing heart. And there, in the tiny cabin under Akicita's care, I slept until spring.

A web spread through the darkness. I balanced on a gossamer thread. Gloom rose from the abyss. It licked the bottoms of my feet, teasing. One slip and I would spiral. I stretched out my arms, focused on keeping my feet stuck to the thread. For within the gloom, flickered memories. Memories of my final hours with Joel. Memories I didn't want.

The abyss surfaced in smoky tendrils. Then it solidified, curled like fingers and plucked the thread. My balance wavered. A laugh erupted, intoned with Arabic notes. It came from everywhere. From nowhere. The thread bounced. My heart pounded in my throat. My feet slipped.

A sweet haze of citrus smoke and minty anodyne caught me, floated me forward. Then a figure appeared. A red shadow. He held out his hand. Sedative humming slowed my pulse. I reached for him.

I woke from the dark. Birds chirped the song of spring. Akicita sat at my side, haloed by dawn's illumination from the window behind him. I covered a yawn and accepted the hickory coffee he placed in my hands.

"Hihanni waste," he said.

"Good Morning."

His dark eyes swept over my face, asking the question he didn't verbalize.

I shook my head. Another empty dream. Much like my memory of the prior months.

"You fight inner places, Spotted Wing."

"Maybe."

He closed his eyes. He wouldn't belabor what we both knew. I couldn't control what I saw when I slept. Nor could I fight the sleep that stole most of my winter.

"To rest is to heal." He turned away to scrape resin from his pipe.

I was tired of resting. And while the nightmares were mild—thanks to his hallucinogenic teas and herbal pipe—I was tired of them too. Akicita believed my dreams were visions. But how could I follow what I didn't understand? And let's not forget the vibrations that crawled through my guts every time an aphid neared. Nothing felt familiar. Not my dreams, nor my visions, nor my body.

"No more sleep aids, Akicita." No more hiding.

His ears twitched under thick silver braids. I couldn't see his face but his voice told me the smile was there. "The heart wakes."

The density of his words soothed me even if I didn't understand them. Just like his presence. He never left my side through the winter, pushing daily exercise and filling my belly. The others hunted and guarded. But they always checked in, their eyes filled with expectation. What they expected, I didn't know.

The shuffling of feet slipped under the door and rustled across the cabin floor. Darwin's nails scraped along the porch.

"They're waiting for me," I said.

Akicita didn't respond.

"What if I can't fight the nightmares? And I still don't know what I am."

Without turning around, he said, "Just be."

I wiggled fingers and toes, the parts of me still familiar. Several breaths in and out. My worry loosened little by little. Then I gathered my gear and emerged from hibernation.

I recovered my strength in the weeks that passed since my winter slumber. As I bent over a net of springing fish, struggling to stand in the river rapids, I wondered what kind of vitamins Akicita had been putting in my food.

"Naalnish. Hurry. I can't hold it," I shouted across the stream. Naalnish bounded through the current with grace. He released me from my burden and I fell with a splash in the shallow bank, laughing.

Badger yanked me out of the cold water. "Evie, when will you learn?"

I wiped wet hair out of my face and snorted.

He pulled me into a hug. "We depend on each other. This is how we survive. It's a Lakota rule."

"Mm. I'll remember that when you remember the Lakota rule on guarding your tongue." His heart thudded against my cheek, warming me despite my sodden clothes. "Besides, you loafers were still asleep and I was hungry."

Akicita emerged from the cabin. Darwin dashed to my side, his tail whipping my leg.

"We'll see who's loafing"—Badger's lips twitched against my crown—"when you go hunting with us today."

I stepped back and knew my eyebrows shot up my forehead. "Oh, I finally get to play with the cool kids?"

He grinned and pulled me back to his chest. "Patience is a strength to carry through life. Your mind needed time. Your heart needed healing." He poked a finger in my rib. "And we were hungry. Your clambering would've scared away the quarry."

"Clambering? Oh, please. I can shoot from—"

"No guns." He held my arms up, sheathed in blades. "It's time we see how you use these."

I let out a dramatic sigh. He ignored it and pushed me toward the cabin.

Akicita waited on the porch, wrapped in red and black wool. His lips spread across his face, deepening the wrinkles in his cheeks. He reached out a shaky hand and lifted my chin. His voice was as salving as the smoke drifting from his pipe. "We hunt many things.

The Lakota show you the hunt for feather and fur. You show the Lakota the hunt for truth. Together, we will learn."

I understood his proverbs as well as I understood the complexity of his gaze. But the hope in his eyes empowered me, made me want to succeed. No matter the road or the expectation.

"I won't disappoint you."

"No, Spotted Wing. You certainly won't." Then he followed Badger back to the snow-fed stream.

The thawing banks gurgled as it drank up the melting snow. Barren of leaves, the forest hid little between glistening trunks and skeletal thickets. I shivered and reached for the door to shed the wet clothes.

The hairs on my nape prickled, had me looking over my shoulder with the sensation of being watched. A shadow darted between the trees, moving toward me. I released a dagger from my arm sheath.

The figure floated closer, gliding with the finesse of a predator who knew its prey wouldn't run. Then his copper eyes glinted. I crossed my arms, the dagger's hilt warm in my fist.

His bow hugged his back, tomahawk on his hip. He closed the distance between us, his gait slow and lethal, his stare never leaving mine.

Our interactions were few, yet I was certain he watched me. I pushed back my shoulders and pretended he didn't unnerve me. And why did he unnerve me? Was it his sinful beauty? His bed ruffled hair? The flex of his muscles when he flung arrows from the bow? Perhaps it was the flame in his eyes as he looked at me. Like he was doing at that moment. A throb sang below my waist. Jesus, stop looking at me.

His scowl deepened as he stepped onto the porch. "You're hunting today."

"Word travels fast."

"One only needs to open their eyes."

I followed his gaze to the stream. The others stood over a myriad of bows and knives wearing grins even wider than usual. Badger's hands waved in the air, illustrating whatever was spewing from his overworked jaws. I smiled, but it fell away when I looked back at Jesse. There was something in his eyes so unlike the frown on his face.

I held his stare, an effort that made me squirm. "You coming?"

The fire in his eyes turned into an inferno. Quiet wrapped around us, tempered by the dripping snow.

"Because I really savor all our tender interactions." My sarcasm was obvious, right?

His brows collected in a frown. "Wouldn't miss a show of you lopping off a limb." A smirk defiled his gorgeous face. Then he vanished inside the cabin.

What a dick.

We broke our fast with a quasi-succotash of corn, pine nuts and fish, washed down with hickory coffee. Then Badger and Naalnish mounted the trail, each carrying a tomahawk and a bow. The latter man packed a six-foot longbow. I felt naked with only the blades on my arms.

Darwin ran to our side. I patted his head. "I'm sorry, boy. You're staying with Akicita. *Bleib.*"

"Even though you taught us those commands," Badger said, "he still listens better to you."

"Then maybe I'll start using the commands on you," I replied, but my attention focused on the barren tree line.

He leaned in. "Don't worry. He's near. He doesn't let you out of his sight."

I narrowed my eyes. "Jesse? That's…it's weird."

He shrugged and gave me a lopsided smile. Then the hike began. Single file, Badger cleared the path with a long stick and Naalnish erased the trail in our wake. A few miles up the mountain, I slowed to walk next to Naalnish. "Why cover our tracks?"

"We are trackers. So we understand what it is to be tracked. We do not want to tempt our enemy."

The Lakota believed all things were woven together in a network of life and energy. Meaning killing aphids could break the fragile threads that connected us. Oh, they killed when they needed to. But they went to great efforts to protect the web they held dear. "So cover our scent, aphids stay away, the web remains balanced?"

He knew I asked to satisfy curiosity, not because I shared their beliefs. He resettled a bed of leaves and nodded. "The web of life catches dreams, you know."

I remembered the trinkets sold in the old west souvenir shops. Willow hoops and horse hair made to look like a web, fringed with feathers and beads.

"Maybe there are dreams that shouldn't be caught," I said.

"Use the threads to trap the good, Spotted Wing. Lead the bad to the center, let it fall through the hole."

I didn't know what my face held, but if his laugh was anything to go by, I was sure it revealed my doubt. With a gentle hand on my back, he moved me in front of him and reformed the line.

We climbed higher and higher, tramping on until dusk. We made camp near a small gorge. The array of balsam firs hid the moon and emitted a soothing evergreen tang. I reclined on my bed roll and chewed on dried venison. The brothers settled in, bracketing my sides. Their earthy musk enveloped my senses, but no part of them touched me. They wouldn't, unless I asked. I cherished that trust.

Naalnish murmured through the silence. "We hunt here before daybreak."

I raised my head. "And what do we hunt?"

"We hunt what is offered. No more."

I often thought his obtuseness was intentional. Then he laughed and I was certain.

"The mountain cradles much life, Spotted Wing. It would be a great gift to see the whitetail deer, the raccoon or weasel, the cottontail rabbit, and maybe the cave bat. I hope for wild boar or black bear. Whatever we find, we use without waste."

My jaw dropped. "You eat bear?"

"Sometimes you eat the bear. Sometimes the bear eats you."

The men chuckled. I fell back on my bed roll with a sigh. That was when I felt it. A shift in the air, in my gut. Something flickered out of the corner of my eye. A neon shape crouched on two legs below a mountain ash twenty yards away.

"We have a visitor." I gripped a knife in each fist and rolled to the balls of my feet. Four more crept in.

Badger snuffed out the fire and squatted next to me.

"Can you see them?" I whispered through the dark. The flickers moved closer.

"No. I hear them," he said.

Only a few yards separated us from them. But they were as night blind as my companions.

"There are five," I said. "They're close now."

Badger's face hovered inches from mine, his eyes wide and calculating. I knew what he planned. Save the damsel. But he'd never seen this damsel fight, didn't know I wouldn't need saving.

I turned away from him, lunged at the aphid vaulting toward our huddle, and collided with it in midair. We rolled into a boulder. Its eyes stared without seeing. An easy plunge. I regained the blade. The hole that was its eye spouted black blood.

I pivoted. The others inched toward my friends. I ran toward their glow, took down the next three as easy as the first.

The last one danced around me. I grabbed it, pulled its chest to mine, and tucked my head under the flex of its mandible. The aphid's oily body slipped free. It shook its head, chin thick with spit.

I fell back, heaved a dagger. The aphid bent with a blur. The knife crashed through the brush. I flung the next two. Missed the kill shot. What the fuck was wrong with me?

One blade left. "Um guys? Now would be a good time to run."

I jumped on the thing's chest. Raised the knife. Focused all my strength in that swing. The blade's momentum ceased. A hit. I slid off the torso, landed beneath it, looked up.

My final blade protruded from its jaw, just above two others in its neck.

The aphid mounted me. I dodged the mouth and angled my body to reach one of the protruding knives.

When Badger jumped on its back, I screamed, "Goddammit. You're supposed to be running."

The aphid bucked, crashed Badger into a tree and pinned me to the packed dirt.

Fuck. Had my training waned that much during those restful winter months? Instead of killing it, I needed follow my own advice and fucking run. I dodged its strikes, tried to wiggle free. Just needed my leg—

A shrill ripped from its throat. It crumpled on top of me.

A couple pounding breaths later, I pushed it off. A tomahawk jutted from the back of its head, the blade buried to the hilt. The ax's owner bent down, copper eyes inches away. The lines around Jesse's mouth creased with tenderness. With his scowl lifted, his beautiful face radiated. "You all right?"

I blinked through the grime caking my eyes. "Yes." Ugh, that sounded weak. I coughed, raised my chin. "Yes." There. Much better.

He wiped the blood from my cheeks and smeared it over his own. "*Wanunhecun.* I misjudged you." Then he freed his tomahawk from the aphid skull and stalked into the forest.

My whole body seemed to revolt at my refusal to run after him, but I collected my knives and dealt with it. I still didn't trust him.

I woke the next morning to Badger chattering on about the prior night. The same noise I fell asleep to. Apparently, not disheartened by my attack on the web of life.

I moaned and gave him a glower he couldn't misinterpret. "What about the hunt we came for?"

Naalnish eyed me. "There's a bend in the gorge. We'll guard while you dip. Then we're heading back."

I held my arms in front of me. Dried blood and dirt left only a few patches of visible skin. "No hunt."

"Another day." Worry lines fanned from his dark eyes.

The aphid battle must have spoiled Naalnish's hunting spirit. "Okay."

I scrubbed my skin until my goose pimples were red and sore. The protection of towering gorge walls and my trust in Badger and Naalnish accorded me comfort in my nudity. Still, the feeling of being watched was an electric current licking my skin.

"What does *wanunhecun* mean?" My voice bounced between the walls.

Badger responded from around the corner, "The Lakota do not have a word for *sorry*. In the case of an accident, *mistake* or *wanunhecun* is sufficient."

So Jesse admitted fault? I cupped water over one arm until the rust-tinged rivulets turned clear. Knowing Jesse was somewhere close filled me with warmth. And that feeling irritated the piss out of me. I was entirely too curious about the man behind those fire brimmed eyes.

I squatted, giving my hair a final rinse. I wanted to ignore the attraction, but the slumbering need in my womb had awoken. The part of me that longed to heal wanted to hear the song again. I wanted what I had with Joel. Not just the sexual assuagement. I craved the emotional connection.

"Evie?" Badger bellowed. "Everything okay?"

"On my way." I dressed and buckled on the blades, slamming the door on thoughts about Jesse and his apology.

On the hike back, the brothers stopped to celebrate the victory of our fight by chanting a meditative song to the Great Mystery. I sneaked away to go to the bathroom, taking my time among the red and purple blooms of the rhododendron.

From the thrall of the scenery came a whisper without voice. I spun, tripped. The summons burrowed in my chest and festered in my gut.

I followed the pull, let it guide my feet. A short hike later, I stood before a wall of exposed sandstone. A paltry shanty nestled in its shade. The air shuddered around me. A bird took flight somewhere to my right. I crept closer.

An eerie stillness enshrouded the structure. The walls seemed to bulge with an ominous warning humming from within. And there, on the porch drenched in darkness, a small figure appeared. Eyes and expression hid behind shadows. An arm stretched up, waved.

My pulse quickened. The child's body changed density, somewhere between real and not, and floated through the open doorway.

The children are our guides. They preserve the truth.

Shit. It could be Aaron or Annie. I had to follow. I shook out tired muscles, steeled my spine, and approached the porch.

The hair on my arms stood on end. A furry bundle darkened a step. I picked it up and turned it over. Aaron's Booey, soggy with blood. I clutched it to my chest. Why would he leave it there?

Tree branches groaned. Two more steps and I reached the threshold.

A shriek snapped through the silence. The pitch of the voice froze me. A woman?

Her moaning seeped from the walls and ripped down my spine. It couldn't be. I squeezed the bear. Oh God, a woman. I forced my feet inside.

So I wait for you like a lonely house
till you will see me again and live in me.
Till then my windows ache.

Pablo Neruda

CHAPTER SIXTEEN: TEA LEAVES

I choked on the stench of mildew and stagnant water. Green-black mold carpeted the cabin's walls. Behind another door, a woman cried. Dread clotted inside me. But I kept my feet moving, the groan of battered boards announcing each step.

A bloody handprint dripped on the door, tiny and low. Aaron's? Couldn't be real. The wailing on the other side weakened to a whimper. With the tip of the dagger, I nudged the door open.

The woman leapt back, hands blocking her face. Black strands straggled from her balding scalp. Rags matted her cadaverous frame. She dropped her hands, patting the bed behind her.

Her lips were pinched. Her features were human, all but the tiny pupils staring back. Then she opened her mouth. A howl escaped and insectile mouthparts writhed in her throat.

She jumped on the bed, crouched, arms outstretched. Her legs folded over lumps in the sheets. The lumps took shape, forming images I tried to reject. She shifted. A small rotting head rolled off the bed, thudded to the floor. She hovered over the bodies of three dead children.

Heart banging against my ribs, I clutched the bear tighter. The decay in the air was long gone, yet the heads on the bed retained pristine faces. My A's. I knew my mind was twisting reality. Still, I inched closer. I had to be sure. The bed shook under her growing agitation. Her shrills rattled the ramshackle roof.

"Evie." A Texan drawl next to my ear. "No sudden movements." An arm snaked around me and pulled my back against a solid chest.

I reached toward the bed, Booey in one hand. "I need to—"

"No. She's really pissed. We're gonna back up nice and easy, like."

The woman bent over the bodies and stroked the head of one. Clumps of curls fell away in her fingers. The skull wobbled under her touch, no longer bearing a familiar face. Gray skin stretched over cheek bones and sunk into an overextended jaw and hollow eyes.

"Okay, Jesse."

His arm tightened around me. He walked us backwards and out of the shack. She didn't follow. I doubt she moved from that bed. Jesse led me to the safety of the forest canopy and stepped back, but not away.

I held out the cold wet thing in my hands. An opossum carcass. I dropped it. My knees followed. Then I wrung out my stomach until nothing was left. What was wrong with me? It wasn't a vision. It was fucking delusion.

Jesse knelt at my side. I dragged my sleeve along my mouth. "You saw that?" Tell me I didn't hallucinate the whole thing.

"The nymph? Yes." Ruts formed between his brows. "And I felt it. The same pain that haunts you."

"I don't know what…" I did know the nymph's despair. To have children and dreams…then only emptiness.

He offered a sweatshirt from his pack, gestured to the blood and bile soaking mine. I gave him my back and switched shirts. His voice carried over my shoulder. "All living things share the same air. We are of one blood."

I faced him. He stared at the shack, swallowed. "Even the mourning nymph."

His gaze grabbed mine. He reached for my hands and interlaced our fingers. His eyes, whiskey warm, searched my face. "The Lakota believe the Great Mystery has two halves. Sometimes, the evil half shows us more than the good half." His thumb caressed the back of my hand, stroked between my fingers. "I know you had children." He squeezed my hands when I tried to pull them away.

"What? How, Jesse?" I never mentioned them. Never.

"You'll save her, Evie. She is your path."

I jerked my hands. His grip tightened.

How the hell could he think the nymph could be saved? Her mind was gone, her body half-dead. And what did I have to do with it? I didn't even want her saved, did I? Our rotten race deserved what it got. Something pinched in my chest.

The nymph's cries chased the wind, brushing the hair from my face and chilling the air. Jesse held on to my hands, the certainty in his eyes elaborating what his words did not. I came to that forest, to that foothill, to that cabin. I couldn't deny the tug. The same force that pulled me east, to the ocean, and beyond.

Jesse tipped his brow to mine and a heavy silence mantled us. Our breaths melded. The charged current between us made me want to pull him closer. I needed Joel in the worst way.

I untangled our hands and stood. "I'm ready to leave."

He let me go.

The Drone's face floated above me, a brass knuckle dagger in his hand. "Are you pristine, Eveline?" His accent rolled the "p" like a "b."

I spat in his face. His tongue darted out, reaching for the drops of saliva. Then he turned his head and sliced the abdomen of the nymph tied down beside me. Through the fountain of blood, he plunged his hand into her womb, sinking his arm to the elbow. Her wails filled the room.

His shoulders wrenched and his arm reappeared. From his hand, dangled a fetus by its leg. It echoed its mother's cries. The Drone snarled at it, revealing sizeable incisors. Then he tossed it over his shoulder.

The crack of bones against the wall silenced its cry. I raised my head, baring my own teeth. Another swipe of steel and the nymph's head thumped to the floor.

The Drone's onyx eyes flashed as he licked the gore from his dagger. Then he smacked his lips and purred, "If you are without an evil-doer's scion, Eveline, you shall become my queen. Together we will populate the world with Allah's chosen. My chosen."

Consciousness came in a dance of shadows pierced by splotches of light. Akicita wiped my brow with a soft tanned skin.

"These aren't visions." My voice was raspy. "They're nightmares."

"Time finds truth," he said.

"It's been six months, Akicita." Six months since my encounter with the nymph in the cabin. And that much again since I left my father's home. In a year's time, the enigma surrounding my survival, my arcane abilities, and my damn nightmares remained unsolved. What would I find if I followed the tug inside me? Did the answers lie beyond the Appalachians I called home? Beyond the people I called family?

A twisty Red Spruce sheltered our summer sleeping spot, where we'd moved further up the mountain. The hunting had been sparser at that elevation. But so had the aphids.

Akicita puffed on his pipe. "I'll tell you a story about a widowed Lakota woman."

I propped up on an elbow. The fire crackled in the stone hearth, spitting embers into the autumn breeze.

"The Lakota widow was in the midst of great famine when she fell sick with pneumonia. As she lay dying, she strengthened her mind through thaumaturgy and entered the spirit world as a spirit walker."

Another puff from his pipe. "The first day, a raven visited her, with wings as blue as midnight. From his talon, he dropped leaves from a creosote bush. The second day, he brought pleurisy root. The third day, he left wormwood. The fourth day, he returned, talons empty, and found her sicker yet. He asked her if she boiled his gifts and drank them in tea. She shook her head. Then she exhaled her last breath."

He reflected a moment. "A gift ignored is a gift without utility."

I lay back on my blanket. The stars, like tiny pupils, winked at me, called to me. Akicita considered my othersense a gift. It was Annie who led me to the Lakota. And Aaron who lured me to the nymph cabin. And the string inside me, always tugging east? I didn't want it. But it was there, insistent. My tea leaves were clear.

"We're coming with you." Naalnish paced behind me.

The ache in my chest swelled. They weren't trying to stop me. No, they understood this thing, even if I didn't. They called it a vision quest. I pressed my fingers to my breastbone, against the burden I bore there.

Leaving them behind was the last thing I wanted. But they were happy there. They belonged in the mountains, amongst the unity of nature and the safety of isolation. Images of them climbing over twisted metal and wielding guns to protect me instilled a new breed of terror deep in my gut.

Besides, the fucked-up-ness that was going on with my body and memories, I didn't want that shit to touch them. Their harmony was the last beautiful thing left on the planet. It was my journey, my burden. So, for the umpteenth time, "No. You're not."

Next to our beds, the stream had widened as summer trickled to fall. Jesse sat on the opposite shore. Nightfall hid his eyes, but I knew they were on me. They always were.

"Boston's far," Badger said. "A lot could go wrong between here and there."

"Not considering the danger traveling overseas and whatever awaits you there," Naalnish said.

Which was why I refused to let them join me.

"Leave her be," Akicita said from his bed roll.

Jesse leaned against a tree, his bow at one side. Always near, yet so far away.

I stretched on my side, the rabbit skin bedding soft against my face.

Badger settled in behind me and I froze, waiting for the contact that would follow. When my outbursts woke the camp night after night, we confirmed Joel's suspicions. Contact while sleeping, bare skin against mine, quelled my nightmares. Naalnish and Badger slept against me, shirtless—as Badger was doing at that moment—with a bare arm around my waist, under my clothes.

They never abused my trust. Maybe I owed them the intimacy, but my guilt was exceeded by my fear of loving them, then losing them.

He whispered at my ear, "You watch him the way he watches you."

I grunted. Jesse was another story. I wanted to unearth the man who watched me. The man who revealed his humanity six months earlier in the throes of a heartbroken nymph. His frown never returned after that day. But a smile didn't replace it. His mouth remained a pinched slit, as if to trap the sentiment his eyes betrayed.

"Who's going to help you chase away the bad dreams?" Badger asked.

"If there's no one around to hear them, does it matter?"

His forehead dropped to my shoulder and his arm tightened around my waist. I knew my decision to go alone would be the hardest on him. In the morning, my last morning with the Lakota, would I be able to stand by that decision?

Naalnish said, "I mapped what should be the safest route to Boston. And I checked the Humvee." The corners of his mouth fell, lengthening his narrow face. "It still runs."

I gave him a small smile.

"You still haven't told us how you're getting to Europe."

I'd been avoiding that question. We hadn't seen a plane overhead since the outbreak. But Jesse assured us transatlantic exports still ran by ship from Boston. How he knew, he wouldn't say. Assuming security wasn't an issue, maybe I could board as a disguised passenger. Although, when I played out that scenario in my head, it ended in a violent pornography. Just a moment's recognition and I would be a woman trapped on a ship full of men. "I'm still working on that."

Jesse lowered his head and pushed a hand through the thick waves of his hair. Then he rose and waded across the stream. My pulse kicked up as he neared. He pulled a notepad from his pack and handed it to Naalnish. "She can smuggle inside a container on a cargo ship."

He crouched before me and said to Naalnish, "The average transatlantic containership travels at twenty-five knots per hour. We can't predict the arrival port, but the trip should be about five thousand kilometers. At that rate, she'd be five to six days in that crate." He gestured to the notepad. "The specs are all there."

I stifled the urge to jump up and grab the pad. Patience.

"These containers aren't airtight," Naalnish said. "With the appropriate ration of food and water, the trip would be tolerable." He traced the paper. "But the location here…how exactly does she get in one on the upper deck near the forecastle and away from the crew quarters?"

Jesse's eyes burned into mine. "That'll be up to Evie." His face held no expression, but I understood his intent. He was Lakota by blood, but he was also every bit the killer I was. He knew I'd do what was needed to board a ship unnoticed.

Naalnish stood and handed me the notepad. "This may be your best option, Spotted Wing."

A sketched blueprint detailed the compartments and containers on a cargo ship. *20x8x8 feet* labeled one of the cubes. More than big enough for a stowaway.

I held up the sketch. "How do you know about cargo ships, Jesse?"

He leaned in, the red in his hair like cinders in the firelight. "Sleep well, Evie, for it may be your last night to do so." He used that mocking tone that aroused me even as it pissed me off. His eyes flicked to Badger behind me and for a moment, I glimpsed pain their depths. Then he stood and walked into the forest.

The next morning, Darwin lay at my feet, his body motionless except the swish of his tail. I pulled a leather strap from my pack and squatted before him. I trailed a finger over his name seared on the surface, memorizing the grooves.

My throat tightened against a swallow as I tied the collar around his neck. I wanted to take him with me so badly my chest hurt. But sneaking him aboard a ship would've been impossible.

I clutched the collar with both hands and pressed my cheek against his furry one. "You protect them, boy. Just like you did me."

The Lakota waited by the Humvee. Jesse wasn't among them. I stepped through the line, hugging each one. There was no more pleading to join me, no nagging about dangers. Each embrace gave me encouragement. Each one harder to step away from. At the end of the line, I ran my hand over my hair, which had grown to mid-back. Three braids, one given by each man, each tied with a feather.

Shoulders bunched, I turned away, gasping for air, fighting the need to change my mind.

I lifted my chin and inhaled the mountain yews. The trees mottled the ridges with hues of maroon and amber and scattered their leaves to loam and wind.

My hair, and the feathers tied there, lifted with the easterly current, pulling me with it. East, where dawn illuminated the pulsating life of the forest. All life but one. I turned back to them. "Where is he?"

Badger shook his head.

Akicita stepped before me and held up a turquoise rock dangling from a tan leather string.

I reached to touch it. "Is that—"

He nodded and waited for me to lower my head. When it settled against my chest, I stroked the smooth surface. Turquoise formed naturally in arid desert climates. Stumbling across that stone in the mountains of West Virginia was as mysterious as the man who found it.

"Lone Eagle wanted you to have it," Akicita said. "It can strengthen one's capacity to love and connect with others." He pressed his wizened lips against my forehead.

I squeezed the rock in my palm. "You've taught me so much." To hunt. To heal. The web of life. "The circle."

"Mm."

It'd been Fall when I stumbled into their camp. It was Fall again. Everything was a circle. The seasons. The cycle of the moon. The wind when it swirled. Would the circle bring me back to them? The odds of that compounded the ache in my chest. I swallowed. "But I gave nothing in return."

He winked a farsighted brown eye. "You taught us the hunt for truth." His hand rested on my crown, stilling my shaking head. "When you were born, your soul entered here, through the skull's soft spot. The truth is *in* you, Spotted Wing. You showed us how to find it."

The meaning of his words caught the breeze, drifted away. "What truth?"

"I look at you and I understand what I see. I see hope in the shape of the spirit. And when you finish this quest, her shape will transcend."

"Her?"

"Go forward." He released me, a tear escaping down his cheek, though his eyes were dry.

Oh, Akicita. Promises I couldn't keep piled up in my throat. I choked on them and stepped away. Then I gave the tree line a final sweep for Jesse and climbed into the Humvee. The emptiness inside me expanded as the tires crunched the gravel, sounding my good-bye.

For two weeks, I followed Naalnish's route to Boston. After an isolated year in the mountains, curiosity had me stopping several days in larger cities to do some scouting. I wasn't sure if I'd see factions of dystopian governments under the control of tyrants. Or if there'd just be small clans of men working together, rebuilding and protecting each other. But I didn't see shit. Wasn't it human nature for people to stick together and leverage the strength in numbers thing? Perhaps the decreasing ratio of man to aphid was to blame for the lack of organization.

I reached Boston's harbor at dusk and hid the truck in an empty garage. Then I pulled out my cloak. Made from gray fox hides, the Lakota crafted it to fit my frame and conceal my gear. The hood draped large enough on my head to conceal my face.

Humping enough artillery to satisfy Joel, I picked my way along crumbling sidewalks to the wharf. A welded steel wall of vessels lined the docks, moaning as they rocked against the tide. Only one ship crawled with life.

I watched the activity from the rooftop of an abandoned bait shop. At least twenty crew members loaded crates, greased and tightened mechanical parts and guarded the ramps. These weren't the typical guards who once patrolled our harbors. These enforcements carried machine guns and reeked of malice.

An hour into my watch, two crew members scuffled on the ramp. They stood toe-to-toe, blades at each other's throats, shouting. The closest guard turned toward the brawl, raised his gun and shot both of them.

Heart racing, I climbed off the roof and crept across the pier. Smuggling inside a crate before it was loaded would be safer, right? But, as I neared the container yard, I knew it wouldn't be easier.

Shipping containers stacked three high and five deep in a labyrinth of aisles. A fork lift hauled away crates at random to load on the ship. How the hell would I determine which ones were going? I tugged on the doors of the crates I passed. All locked.

The scuffing of feet crept around the corner, followed by the waft of cigarette smoke. Shit, shit, shit. I pressed my body between two crates, and held my breath.

Still round the corner there may wait,
A new road or a secret gate.

J. R. R. Tolkien

CHAPTER SEVENTEEN: 20x8x8

"It's the fucking sea pirates, man. They're shutting down the exports—"

A succession of coughs rent the air and thickened the phlegm-caked voice.

"Christ, smoke another one," a second man said.

The scrape of feet paused at my alcove. My lungs screamed for oxygen.

"I think I will." A lighter sparked. "Besides, with fucking weather blowing across the Atlantic like it's been, this'll be the last ship outta here till summer."

"What are they exporting now anyway? Last five trips were mostly grain, but there ain't any farmers left to harvest the stuff."

"Grain ain't why these ships are still running, my friend. Weapons are the passport. But if you still want passage to Europe, I'll get you on. You'll have to pay your way in sweat." The man coughed. Their boots crunched on the gravel and began to fade. "Gotta warn you, though. The few passengers crazy enough to travel..." His voice ebbed into the night.

After a long silence, I snuck back to the Humvee.

For the next week, I watched the sailors ready the ship. Day and night, they shot, stabbed and mutilated trespassers—aphids and men trying to board the ship. At the end of their shifts, they flitted off to a dingy pub, the wharf's only establishment. The youngest man always split from the ragtag gang and traversed in the opposite direction. That was when my plan hatched. I followed him.

His stroll took us through the seaport's barren streets, his red *Pet Shop Boys* T-shirt like a tail light in the gloom. The dilapidated buildings sat empty, ghosts of what was once the center of commerce. He veered off into a grotto and entered a boarded up retail shop.

In the back, I found a window with an exposed corner. Inside was a bare one room shop with a mattress in the center. Next to the mattress, a meaty, bald man waited.

The Pet Shop boy I'd followed accepted a firearm from Baldy, examined it and leaned it against the bed with a nod. Then his hands went to his waistband. A couple of tugs and his jeans and briefs fell to his ankles. What the—

Baldy grabbed Pet Shop boy's nape and shoved him to his knees on the mattress. Then he freed a revolting purple erection and mounted him.

Something dark and loathsome tunneled its way to my womb. The something that was born in my father's basement. I raised the carbine, but couldn't move, my eyes glued to the spectacle. The pounding hips, the fisting of hair, both mouths wide open. I felt it in my thighs as if old bruises had resurfaced.

Pet Shop boy moaned. His eyes rolled back in his head. Was that what survival looked like? Trading sex for weapons, food…safe passage on a boat?

I lowered the carbine and watched the very thing I'd planned play out before me. The men collapsed on the mattress in a tangle of sweat and limbs. A few panting breaths later, Baldy collected himself and left.

My breath rushed out in a whoosh. Could I seduce Pet Shop boy in exchange for his assistance? What if more men visited? What if I threw up during the first intimate touch?

Turn around. Go back to the Lakota. Why wouldn't my feet move?

The hunger to go east chewed at me. I had to find out what my dreams meant, what my children were telling me, who the Drone was.

For twenty minutes I stood there, fighting it, knowing the need for truth was forcing me to take impossible risks.

Vertebra by vertebra, my backbone girded for action. I tucked my weapons under the cloak and edged to the front. Then, with the pistol aimed under the folds of fur, I tapped on the door with my free hand.

It cracked open. A shotgun barrel and two wide eyes peered out. "Whatever you want, I don't have anything. Please leave." His British accent was as shaky as the gun's barrel.

I slid back my hood enough for him to see my face.

He gasped, lowering the gun as he covered his mouth. Then he looked up and down the street and ushered me inside.

That was too easy, the kind of naiveté that was fatal. The next few minutes were even easier. I stuck to the truth about crossing the Atlantic, the dangers associated with boarding the ship and my need for help.

When I finished laying out my cards, I winked at him. "Got a name, Pet Shop boy?"

He looked down at his shirt and grinned. "Ian." Squared shoulders and a raised chin joined his smile. "I'd be happy to sneak you aboard. I'll keep you safe, I swear it. Anything you need. Anything."

He would do that without anything in return? I didn't think so. The more we talked, the more he smiled. His body hovered closer. His gaze grew bolder. When a yawn broke his smile, he said, "Stay the night. Share the mattress with me?" A tide of red washed over his cheeks.

To think this shy boy was groaning under another man an hour earlier. I should've been repulsed, but he was surviving. Same as me.

"I'll stay the night." I speared him with a look that could not be misunderstood. "To sleep."

When he nodded, I joined him on the mattress.

He pulled blanket over us. "It's been so lonely. Fate brought you to me. Can you feel this?" His hand swept from his chest to mine.

No, but I hummed in agreement and hid my annoyance with his easily duped heart. Worse was knowing I'd break it once I exhausted his usefulness.

He touched my cheek. I gripped a dagger hilt under my cloak, but forced myself to keep it sheathed. His finger trailed along my jaw and down my neck, searing my skin with every stroke.

I rubbed my wrists. No ropes. *I* controlled what was happening. "How long is the voyage?"

"Six days. I can stow you undetected. If I lock the crate like all the others, no one will know."

Six days. What would keep him from second-guessing our arrangement during that time away from me? Would a tease be enough to keep the boy tight-lipped? When his finger tugged at the clasp under my neck and his eyes begged mine, I knew I would make him a promise I wouldn't keep.

He bent over me with blue eyes sparkling and scrawny legs twisting in the blankets. "You're so lovely. I want you. Please."

With a hand on his chest, I put distance between us. "I'm nervous about the journey, Ian. We need to plan it out. Then, when we arrive safely, you'll have me." I held his gaze, despite the burning need to look away.

"Eh, o-okay." He shut his eyes, opened them. "We'll have such a blissful life together in England. We'll live in my childhood home. You'll see."

I needed his allegiance until I reached my destination. So I nodded.

He wrapped his arms around me and dragged stiff lips over mine. I lay still, mouth closed, and tried to ignore the heavy breaths pushing over my face. Eventually, he read my resistance and settled on his side, folding himself around me.

For the next four nights, we plotted my ingress onto the ship, and each night I deflected his advances with the same promise. He adopted restraint with large hopeful eyes and flushed cheeks and my guilt over it grew like an ugly thing in my gut. So, in the dead of night, I held him the way his mother might have and wished I had more to offer than an empty pledge.

Ian and I slipped through the wharf and crouched behind a forklift next to the ramp. He scanned the jetty and the ship then turned to me, eyes flashing under the moonlight. "You know where to go?"

I nodded. "Where's the guard?"

He pointed above board, port side. The guard stumbled under the illumination of a red light, and glanced around him before tipping back a flask in his shaking hand. The vacant ship and the guard's insobriety were just as Ian predicted.

"Ready?" Ian's voice hitched. Whether it was excitement or nervousness, I wasn't sure.

When I nodded again, he gripped my nape and kissed me. In that flickering moment, I imagined he was Jesse and there was nothing else around us. I returned the kiss with equal passion. My tongue matched his and the heat from it filled my chest and traveled lower. When the vee at my thighs began to pulse, I pulled away. Ian reached for me again, his breathing heavy.

I stepped back. "Six days."

"Six days." He walked up the ramp to the ship and approached the guard, waving a flask and a pack of cards.

The guard turned his back on my hiding place. I ran on tiptoes up the ramp. Hugging the bulkhead, I stole through the main passageway. The port side ladder rattled under my boots, a knife's throw from where Ian shared his flask with the guard.

I froze. Don't look at them. Keep moving. Quiet, quiet. I steadied my breathing and climbed.

The swish of the tide and the groan of steel muted my footsteps along the upper deck. Crate after crate, the doors were sealed and locked. All but the one Ian had unlocked. The white cube on the end fit the description. Closer. Closer. The label came into focus. *Canpotex, #526.* Relief rushed through me as I closed the distance and squeezed inside.

Carbine in my lap, I leaned my head against the cold metal wall and waited. Sometime later, Ian slid the lock on the container into place. No turning back. The rest was up to him.

For six days, I avoided deep sleep and the night terrors it could bring. Exhaustion took its toll. I grew restless, trapped in a metal crate with my own waste. In a couple days, my depleted supply of MREs would introduce a new level of torment.

A stampede of pounding feet and irate shouting passed under my hiding place and dwindled toward the anchor-windlass room. The crew members were brawling again.

The frost soaked through my hair. My eyes ached from the abiding strain to see amid the black. I leaned against the container's wall, clicked on the Maglite and unfolded Joel's letter. The flimsy paper was damp. Crumpled from numerous spreading. Creased with clammy hands. I reread his counsels for the hundredth time to remind myself why I left my beloved companions to cross the Atlantic.

I ground my teeth. Why the hell didn't Jesse say good-bye? Was his soul as lost and battered as mine? Even so, it wasn't an excuse to behave like an ass. Screw him.

Two short horn blasts vibrated the crate walls. A breathy mariner announced our arrival in Dover Strait. The scurrying of sailors confirmed the voyage was approaching its end.

Several hours later, the ship halted.

When the door cracked the next morning, Ian rushed me with a pent up fervor. His mouth and hands groped.

I swatted him away. "Ian, please. A bath? And a meal?"

"Yes, of course. It's just…I missed you so much."

"Just a little longer. Go."

Ian distracted the same sloppy sentinel as I crept down the ramp and put two shaky feet on England's shore. I rubbed my chest. Why wasn't I feeling pulled in any one direction? Where was that goddamn tug when I needed it?

The harbor spread layers of parking lots to the white facade of the hovering cliffs. Redolent of brine, the crisp air nipped my nose and watered my eyes. Carbine at the ready, I ran through the pier, darting in and out of alcoves, toward the shadow of the closest bluff. One building to go, I rounded the corner.

A van approached from the other side. Fuck. I jumped out of its path and picked up my pace. Behind me, the van's occupants rushed out in a melee of shouting and chambered rounds. I didn't falter or look back. Until Ian's scream cracked the frigid air.

I looked over my shoulder. The boozer from the ship pulled him out of the van, a blade under his chin. My feet stopped, pivoted.

"Ye were hiding a fit bird?" the guard said to Ian and shoved him to his knees. "I should jolly well think she was worth it."

No, no no. My stomach rolled over in violent waves.

Ian beseeched me with his eyes, whimpering, "I'm sorry. I love y—"

The guard knifed his throat from ear to ear.

In the middle of the journey of our life
I came to myself within a dark wood
where the straight way was lost.

Dante Alighieri

CHAPTER EIGHTEEN: FISH N CHIPS

Ian's lifeless body buckled and fell to the side. I leveled the carbine and squeezed, the guard's chest in my scope. Squeeze. Squeeze. Squeeze. When his body hit the pavement, I continued to squeeze. His jaw tore away. Half of his face lay open. Blood drained from the dozen pockmarks in his chest. The carbine went dry and I realized I squeezed the trigger more times than necessary.

A barrel pressed my temple. Boots thudded out of surrounding buildings.

"You will do exactly as I say. Twitch so much as an eyelash without my asking and you're dead. Nod once if you understand."

I nodded, muscles tensing to enact one of the many hand-to-hand techniques drilled into my mind.

"Good. And you're probably realizing right now that we let you kill the drunk." The man behind the shotgun scowled under matted hair and slid wild eyes over the mob. "If he would've been doing his job rather than getting sloshed, he would've caught her sneaking past him. Piece of shit had it coming."

The mob nodded their heads and whooped.

He shoved the barrel harder against my head and sharpened his voice. "Now drop the rifle, the coat and whatever you're hiding under it." He threw my pack and kicked away my falling weapons. "On your back. Hands above your head."

The memory of cold hands around my wrists crippled my courage. I could endure it so long as he didn't tie me.

The concrete chilled my spine and scratched my knuckles as I lay down and raised my hands over my head. If I could get him in a Jujitsu closed guard position, I could overpower him and use his body as cover against his cohorts who crowded around spouting vulgarities.

He knelt above me and raised my chin with my own dagger. "God has destroyed our women and children. What are you? A demon disguised as a beauty to tempt us?" He spat in my face. "I will not be fooled so easily."

A motorcycle rumbled in the distance. My shirt ripped under his hand. I pulled away. Too slow. He plunged my blade under my collar bone.

A fog of pain blotted my vision. I thrashed beneath the steel, pinned to the pavement. Blade still buried, he lanced my chest along my sternum. Skin peeled away from the carving edge. My chest erupted in fire. I fought to retain consciousness and clutched his arm. The echoed thump in my ears drowned out my screams.

He rounded the blade under my breast. Realization of his intent smacked me. I reached through the blaze of pain and gathered my last shred of strength. I held his wrist, kept him from completing the mastectomy.

Something whistled through the air. With a jolt, he straightened his back. A gasp sputtered from his slack lips. His eyes went flat and he slumped to the side.

Screams and gun fire erupted around me. Pain seared through my chest, shutting down my senses. Blood gushed between my fingers to the march of my pulse. I fumbled for my weapons, vision wavering and recovered the dagger from the limp hand beside me.

Chills racked my body. I found my cloak, seeking its warmth as my vision cleared. That was when I saw it. An arrow projected from the butcher's back.

The shouting and guns fell silent. I blinked away frozen tears. The parking lot littered with dead bodies, harpooned with black and red feathered arrows.

My protector ran toward me, copper eyes intensifying with each step. Several blocks away, a rout of stomping and yelling pursued. The remaining crew.

"They're coming, Evie." His southern drawl sharp. "I can hold 'em. You need to go."

He followed me? He was on the ship? Darkness washed over me. I slapped the concrete to break my fall. Saliva thickened. I stammered, "Just need"—Ignore the pain. Deep breaths—"a minute." Bile rose. I swallowed and counted to three in time with my inhales.

Daylight rushed back. Jesse bent over me, tried to open my cloak. "Evie? How bad?"

An upwelling of emotion took hold of me and the familiarity of his beautiful face filled my empty spaces with an overwhelming sense of peace. I wasn't alone. "I missed you."

He swallowed, reached a hand inside my cloak. "Let me see it, Evie."

I pulled away and staggered to my feet. The fire spread through my insides. "I'm fine."

He gestured to his motorcycle. "Can you ride?"

Dizziness warred with the throbbing throughout my chest. I nodded.

His eyes widened, flooded with warmth. Then they narrowed just as quick. "Go. Get the hell out of here."

The pound of feet grew louder.

"Go now."

I couldn't leave him was my first thought, but his fierce expression sent me stumbling backward. The agony sloughing my chest decided it. I'd lost a lot of blood, but as I sped away, the loss had less to do with the wound and everything to do with the man I left behind.

For several days, I rode up and down the streets of Dover, seeking the man who had followed me. After I raided a pharmacy and acquired bacitracin, my search led me back to the pier. Dozens of bodies spackled the parking lot, polluting the air with decay. But no trace of Jesse. Not even his arrows. Was he eluding me? I couldn't ignore my hunger pangs much longer. Or the green pus that crusted my injury. I had to find food, shelter.

That night, I stood in a desolate street in some small township halfway to London. The derelict building I monitored since sundown showed the first sign of human life since the harbor. Crumbling bricks supported two stories of boarded up windows. Thorny vines braided the structure on all sides. No one came or went for three hours, but candlelight shadows danced through the fluted glass panels in the door.

The stark wind was determined to rob another letter from the pub's only advertisement.

FISH N CH PS SE VED 24/7

The gust dried out my eyes quicker than my tear ducts could crank out moisture to offset it. Sure didn't feel like November. I wiped my nose on my sleeve and blinked again. My stomach rumbled. If I lost my nerve, it would be another hungry night.

I cleared my throat and practiced my masculine one word responses. A few squeaks confirmed that nonverbal communication was my only option. The street remained barren in both directions. No more delaying. I swallowed hard and took a step toward the pub.

Stay Alive.

I readjusted the hood of my cloak, hiding my face in its shadow. Two more steps. I pushed my hands through opposing sleeves and rubbed my sheaths. The weight of the carbine, pistol and pack offered little to ease my nerves. Then I squared my shoulders and engaged my practiced man-walk to the pub.

With a shaky exhale, I jerked open the heavy door. The tables sat empty. Most were shoved to the side and piled with overturned chairs. A kitchen service window revealed a barred backdoor.

A shaggy thick-bodied bartender leaned against the cash register. The pub's only patron sat at the far end of the bar in an ankle length trench coat.

The bartender shot me a rankled glare from under wiry eyebrows.

I followed the unwelcome draft through the door. The patron kept his back to me and his head down. Given my all night surveillance and the empty Bushmills bottle that accompanied him, I knew he'd been there awhile.

The bartender's eyes creased to slits. I focused on my gait and kept a slow pace to the counter. When my boot bumped the leg of the bar stool, I tucked my chin to remain in the shadow of my cowl.

"Wha' ye have?" His skeptical voice exhausted.

I pointed to the chalkboard behind him. He studied my finger. Was he looking for green translucent skin? Formations of pincers? Would he notice the delicate nature of my female hands?

"So it's the stew then. And to wash it down?"

I nodded to the tapped keg.

He grumbled something. "Den' ye talk?"

I touched my throat and shook my head. Then, to avoid further inquiry, I headed to a table in the far corner. The raw gall on my chest flared. I winced and was glad for the concealment of my cloak. I slid out of my pack and carbine sling and settled into the chair with the best vantage of the front door and the backdoor. And of the patron yet to acknowledge my presence.

Thirty minutes later, I threw back my second pint. The bitter hops bounced on my tongue and refreshed my parched throat. Heaven. The bartender brought the stew with my third. He didn't linger. Posing as mute worked better than I hoped.

Unidentifiable chunks floated in the broth. I slurped it down eagerly. Too eager. My tongue swiped the dribble on my lip, my hand catching the stream on my chin. I sucked my fingers clean like a starving thing and sopped up the remaining juice in the bowl with a stale heel of bread. Then I pushed the bowl aside, and considered another.

The patron at the bar raised his head. His honey-hued hair curled at his shoulders, twisting into dread locks and hooking behind his ears. His broad back and shoulders tested the seams of his coat. The nearby candlelight illuminated his full lips and wide jaw line.

He sensed my stare and eyed me sidelong while tracing the rim of his whiskey glass. When his eyes settled on mine, I looked away. Shit.

His bar stool slid back followed by the click of his boots across the floor. The pistol grew heavy on my thigh. Shit. Shit. Shit.

The boots stopped at my table. Malt whiskey wafted over me. I kept my eyes locked on my empty pint while I unsheathed a blade under my cloak.

He put his palms on the table and leaned into his arms. I tightened my grip on the knife. One swipe would slice off his sprawled fingers. I would use that moment of surprise, aim the knife up and bury it in his throat.

"May I sit?" he asked with a thick Irish accent.

I made no answer.

He leaned in closer. "Please den' be afraid. I am only curious." He paused. Waited.

The dagger's hilt burned in my grip. I didn't respond.

A few heartbeats later, he straightened his stance and opened his coat. Underneath, he donned a black button down cassock, a rosary and a white collar.

"May I sit?" His brogue softened the vowels.

I remained silent and paranoid.

He kept his post and tilted his head. "Are ye still peckish?"

If I ignored him long enough, would he go away?

He motioned to the bartender. "Em...Lloyd? Another boul of your insatiable stew."

Lloyd's shuffle faded into the kitchen.

The hovering presence held out his hand. Scars bubbled across his knuckles, some freshly pink. "I'm Father Roark Molony."

He waited, allowing me to peruse him. I struggled to believe this man was a priest. His course dialect and bulky physique suggested a harder life. Yet, I'd wager his age was close to mine. I studied his eyes, his deep pools of jade. Behind them, I saw a disciplined constitution. And he smiled when he saw the woman behind mine.

I wasn't sure if it was my Catholic upbringing that brought on my moment of weakness, but I surprised and frightened myself when I motioned across the table and said, "Please sit, Father."

He lowered his hand and descended into the chair. The movement revealed a shoulder rig and a scabbard on his belt.

I flexed my fingers on the knife and used my other hand to slide my hood back a few inches. "What gave me away?"

His lips twisted. "Your dainty fingers and small stature."

At least he didn't blame my attempts to walk like a man. "I'm Eveline Delina. Evie."

He widened his eyes and gasped. "Hallowed be thy name."

"I'm sorry?"

"Your name. Eve." He stroked the cross hanging from his neck and stared at me.

I blinked, pretending ignorance to the obvious reference. "It's Evie."

"Right. Ye know the book of Genesis? Genesis 3:20, 'The man named his wife Eve, because she would become the mother of all the living.'"

I dropped my head as Lloyd slid another bowl of stew on the table. When he returned to the bar, I raised my eyes. "Of course I know it, Father. And to this woman, your god said 'I will make your pains in childbearing very severe; with pain you will give birth to children. Your desire will be for your husband, and he will rule over you.' Let us be clear. You will not preach your dogma to me. I served my time in the Catholic Church and I have no use for it."

He bristled. "No offense intended."

Damn my temper and cursed Catholic guilt trip. I forced a steady exhale. "Besides Father, given the current affairs, shouldn't you be looking for someone from the book of Revelations?"

"Perhaps." He smiled. A boyish smile I found comforting. But that strong chin made it sexy. I shoved the thought away.

"Please call me Roark." He swallowed. "Are there others? Women?"

I tilted the bowl to my mouth and shook my head. "I've come a long way"—the stew was lukewarm sliding down my throat—"and I haven't seen any. Human women, that is."

He closed his eyes and steepled his fingers in front of his mouth. "How is it that you're here? When no other women survived?"

I sat back and sheathed the blade. Did a day go by when I wasn't asking myself that question? "Can't find that answer in your bible?"

The corner of his mouth lifted. Was my disrespect amusing him?

Broth sloshed out of my bowl, quivering as it escaped. Was my hand shaking? Or was it the room? I set it down and rubbed the gooseflesh on my arms.

The temperature dropped and the air seemed to swirl and gather by the front door. A mist of smoke seeped from the keyhole and, within it, floated Annie. A grin lit her face and her feet found the floor, framed in tendrils of gray fog. The folds of her eyelet dress licked her legs as she skipped to the bar, curly pigtails bouncing.

I trembled, unable to meet Roark's eyes, though I could feel them on me. He couldn't see her, my delusion.

At the bar, she reached for the circle of sconces. I pressed myself into the chair when her fingers neared the candles. She brushed over one burning wick as she chanted.

The Jabberwock, with eyes of flame

Came whiffling through the tulgey wood

Her grin fell and her head jerked toward the door.

And burbled as it came!

Her fingers melted into the flame. The skin on her arm, then her body, followed the liquidation. Why was she doing that? Was she trying to tell me something? Please stop, Annie. Oh God.

Exposed shreds of muscle pulsated in the candlelight, clinging to her tiny frame. Still, the front door held her attention.

The candles sizzled, vaporizing her transparent figure into the smoke. My stomach rolled under the miasma of burning flesh.

I grew wary of the front door. A sting bit through my guts. I knew that feeling. My muscles tensed, readied for attack.

"Evie? Evie?"

The flames consumed her and the candlelight extinguished with a *pop*.

Roark muttered through the dark, "Wha' in under feck—"

"Shh." I swooped up the carbine and pointed it at the door. His hand found my back.

"I hope you know how to use that pistol," I whispered. "They're coming."

"Why? Wha' are ye—"

The door swung open and smacked the wall. A chilling gust swept through the room and with it the hum of hunger.

One, two! One, two! and through and through
The vorpal blade went snicker-snack!
He left it dead, and with its head
He went galumphing back.

Lewis Carroll, *Jabberwocky*

CHAPTER NINETEEN: THE GOSPEL BLADE

I discovered in Pomme de Terre the best way to kill an aphid was in or near the eyes and doing so required a fast hand or an accurate bullet. While I prided in both most of the time, I wavered when the luminous figures floated into the pub. Numbers in the teens, they stacked together to move through the crowded doorway. The way they hugged the walls and swept the room made it hard to believe they were blind and weaponless. Still, I kept my finger off the trigger, remaining silent, buying time.

Buzzing and vibrations bounced between them. The aphid at the front held up a claw. Another scurried to the back room.

Pans pinged across the kitchen floor. A scream followed then died. The absence of candlelight blanketed the dining room in black.

"Roark, can you see them?"

The glowing bugs paused and pointed their profiles in my direction. I tightened the carbine against my shoulder, wincing at the twinge in my damaged chest.

"There's movement in the shadows." His voice rasped at my ear. "Let's flit to the door."

We'd never make it. "Aim for the eyes. How many rounds do you—"

The priest hissed and steel whistled. A sword? His attacker fell headless at his feet.

Exhale. Squeeze. The *vhoomp* of the spring recoiling in the buffer tube soothed me. With the clanking of the priest's sword behind me, I slaughtered my way across the pub to find Lloyd.

An aphid blocked the kitchen door. It straightened its legs, rising to its full six-foot and many more terrifying inches. A spray of flinging drool drenched my face.

The aphid sprang and hooked a claw around the carbine. Metal clanked the floor. What the fuck? I freed a dagger and buried it between the eyes.

Another aphid filled the doorway. Oh hell. That one was bigger than the last. It bent over the body at my feet and screamed. Its mandibles flexed and trembled. Was it mourning its fallen comrade? A moment of hesitation slipped by. A moment of sympathy.

But I didn't subscribe to sympathy. Not if I wanted to survive.

I drew the pistol. The bullet aimed true. Vile black matter rained from the eye socket and it crumpled upon its friend.

Did I imagine the aphid's show of emotion? I hadn't quite worked through that answer when I located my pack, the Maglite, and pointed the beam on the last mutant flailing under Roark. His fists thudded. *Smack. Smack.*

My lips twitched. Funny just a year earlier I thought I'd never look at a man like that again. Then I'd found Jesse. And there I was, adjusting the Maglite so I could watch Roark's biceps move under his priest uniform. There was substantial muscle on that broad frame, enough to heave steel through dozens of necks without breaking a sweat—

Fuck. He was a priest. As in the celibate kind. If I didn't wipe the hungry look off my face, I'd find myself alone again. I lowered the light. "Lose your sword?"

"This one"—*smack, thud-thud*—"wanted it the hard way."

I crouched before them. The skull crunched under each blow, the jaw snapping open and closed, the tusk missing. He must have sliced it off, removed the risk.

I held up a knife. "Time to end it."

"Right."

I plunged the blade and sat back on my heels. "Not that I'm complaining but what do you have against guns?"

"Who says I do?"

"You didn't use your gun. Seems like it would've been easier than"—I swept the beam across the decapitated bodies—"the alternative."

"Gun ownership was strictly regulated in Ireland. Never held one till the outbreak. I prefer me sword."

"I see." I didn't. "Can you see them in the dark? You know, do they glow?"

He skimmed the carnage and looked back at me. Frown lines marked his forehead. "Glow?"

"This pub has no protection. I checked the perimeter for hours before entering. Where the hell did they come from?"

"Right. I kept this area clean. Ye seemed to have brought them with ye."

"No. I—"

A groan bellowed from the kitchen.

"Oh, shit. Lloyd," Roark breathed as he ran to the bar and lit a candle. I hurried after him, clenching my teeth at the soreness on my chest. The bodies led us to the back room.

Lloyd's mouth hung open, foaming into a gory puddle. Sightless orbs fixated on the ceiling. His torso twisted in alien contortions. I drew the blade. Roark's hand caught my wrist.

I pulled away. "We have to—"

"The Extreme Unction. I need to administer Last Rites."

"Oh."

He gestured toward the front. "Will ye stand watch? I just need a moment."

I nodded and went back to the bar. A few minutes later, Lloyd's cries quieted.

Roark emerged in the doorway and thrust a thumb over a slumped shoulder. "This way."

We stepped around Lloyd's headless body on the way to the back door. I dug my nails into my palms to distract me from the fist of remorse punching my gut.

Sword drawn, he walked the back lot. Thanks to the mysterious sensor that rattled my insides when aphids approached, I knew there wasn't an immediate threat, but I wasn't about to announce it.

He stopped behind a dumpster and rolled out an enduro.

"What is that?" It was more than a dirt bike fitted for street riding. Olive-drab paint, knobby tires, a weapon carrier and luggage rack?

"Ah, now this is a bloody Harley Davidson MT 350E army bike." He smirked and regarded the ground. After a few moments, he met my eyes. "Ye must be knackered. Come with me. You'll be safe. It's dodgy, but—"

"Do you live alone?"

His nod gave me the answer I needed. I didn't think I misjudged him, but I wouldn't want to be outnumbered if I found out I was wrong.

I had to ditch Jesse's bike miles back because the sound attracted aphids. Was riding Roark's bike worth the risk just for the chance at a full night's rest under the protection of a sword toting priest? "Yeah. That would be nice."

He saddled the bike and patted the seat behind him. "Just a few kilometers up the road."

I hugged his waist and clenched my thighs around his. Heat spread through me. Was it from the sharing of body warmth? Or was it a sudden surge in my libido?

He sped out of the lot. The moldering bones of the surrounding buildings chipped away in the absence of life.

Where was Jesse? A void resonated in my chest. A wanting wrenched my gut. He was a piece of me and that piece wasn't where it should be. At that moment, that piece could be anywhere, fighting to stay alive, or already dead.

As the wind whipped past us and battered my body to exhaustion, I clung to the priest and what was left of my composure.

Roark slowed the bike on a narrow street lined with skinny double story pads set a few feet from the road, all connected with single garages. He throttled the motor. We coasted in front of their brick facades and picture windows bordered with frozen flowering baskets. The bike stopped at a white garage door, which looked identical to all the others in the row.

He lifted the unlocked door. Once inside, he locked it behind us.

I paused at an uncovered window. A graveyard of flies and gnats littered the sill. Brittle legs curled against dried up bodies. How different were their humanoid adaptations?

"How long do they live?" I turned to find him staring at me.

"Who?"

"Aphids."

His expression transformed from quizzical to pained, taking me with him. "I den' know."

Did anyone know what we were up against? "Can they starve to death?"

He pushed a ropelike braid behind his ear. "I should bloody well hope so. This way." He pulled a large duffle off the bike's luggage carrier and strode to an opaque corner in front of a short bed Nissan truck.

His broad body folded into a graceful squat beside a lid on the concrete floor. "It's gonna be a wee bit baltic." He slid the lid to the side and eyed my feet. "But your stonking boots should keep ye dry."

A ladder receded into a dark cavity under the garage floor. "What the hell is that?"

"No foostering. We're not safe till we're through the tunnel." He threw our gear in the hole and descended. From the bottom, he shouted, "Pull the lid back on your way down."

An underground tunnel was not what I expected. If Darwin was with me, I'd know if I could trust that man. I eyed the enduro. What I needed was clean clothes to redress my wound, and a good-night's sleep. The priest was my best option.

I drew a knife from each arm sheath and dropped in the hole.

The bore at the bottom stretched six feet in diameter and held about a foot of water. I followed the priest through the tunnel system. For the first ten minutes, I kept a map in my head of the paces between left and right turns, but as we sloshed on I gave up.

"Does the water keep the aphids out?"

He paused at an alcove in the sewer. "Mostly."

Water dripped from the ceiling, echoing from one end of the tunnel to the other.

"Mostly?"

He crouched at the rear of the recess where the shadows concealed a portal secured with a large oval submarine door. "Seems some of the mutants are adapting their skills. Some can crawl through these pipes without touching the water." He shrugged. "Some can't."

"Are you sure?" Evolving skills would explain the aphid battalion at the pub.

"They've been maturing in the last few months." He ran his hands along the seal around the door.

"What is this?"

"It's me dodgy bunker. Bugger is"—he removed something from the seal and opened the door—"it doesn't lock from the outside. A bloody bother. So I rig it a bit."

He held up a small square box wrapped in plastic with dangling wires. "Just a wee explosive to let me know if any gits been faffin' about." Then he bowed. "After ye."

Hand on my back, he guided me through the dark. His hand moved away, a rustle of clothes, and light flooded the room.

The entry opened into a large domed room with exposed beams and pipes.

My inhale filled the silence. "Electricity?"

"Solar. Lashings of panels on the houses we passed above."

"You built this?"

He closed the door and turned a wheel that slid three heavy bars in place. "It was here. Built pre-outbreak by some paranoid fanatics." He chuckled. "Not so paranoid, em? I spotted the panels from the overpass and traced them here. Thought I was a bit of a mentaller, but I eventually found it."

The room's stone walls compassed a bench press, free weights, a stationary bike and other sundry weight machines. At the apex, a heavy bag hung from the ceiling.

He eyed my boots again. "Did ye manage without a posser?"

I held up a foot for a closer inspection. "A what?"

A grin sprouted on his face. "A wet foot, bonny girl. Ye get a wet foot dabbling through the pipes?"

"Oh." I wiggled my toes. "No wet feet."

"Right then. Follow me."

We trudged down a long passageway, boots squeaking on the concrete floor. It emptied into a one room spread.

A metal island overwhelmed the left side. Behind it, a concrete counter lined the wall, littered with propane burners. A worn plaid couch sprawled in the center. Stacks of books and newspapers scattered around it. On the right, sat a single bed. Next to it, a three foot crucifix hung above a prayer bench, surrounded by drippy candle sticks.

He dropped his duffle on the island and pointed to a doorway beyond the bed. "Round back is the bog with running water. But water wen' be hot till morning."

My jaw dropped. "How is it done?"

He leaned a hip against the island and removed several wrapped Bushmills bottles from the duffle. "Tomorrow." He pointed to the bed. "Now ye sleep. I'm taking the couch."

His glare told me arguing would've been fruitless. Besides, I didn't have the energy. My chest felt cold and wet. I still needed to deal with that. "Do you have a needle and thread?"

He headed to a rack where his clothing hung. "I have plenty of clothes. I'm sure somethin' fit ye."

"It's for a...cut. I need to stitch a cut." Unless the infection was lingering.

Eyes wide, he reached my side in two long strides. "Where? I didn't know ye got scratched—"

"No." I waved him off then glimpsed his hand clutching the pommel of his sword. Shit. "It wasn't tonight. I'm not infected." I stretched my jaw wide and stuck out my tongue. Closed it. "We good?"

A beat. A grin. "Sorry. Right." He backed away. "I'll just get the first aid kit. We'll take a gander."

Shit and fuck. "No, it's...uh, my breast. I can manage myself. If you have a sewing kit?"

He dug through the kitchen and procured a dull needle and a black thread. Then he handed me a dram of whiskey. "It's all I got. Ye sure?"

"I've got it. Thanks." I shut the bathroom door and stared longingly at the bathtub. Did he say hot water in the morning? I couldn't believe it.

I sipped the whiskey, removed my sweatshirt. The turquoise stone lay on my bare chest. No bra. Not since my father's house. Under the stone, raw florid skin edged the *C* shaped gash from my collar bone around my tit. I was relieved to see the bacitracin from the pharmacy and iodine from my first aid kit had killed the last of the infection, which meant I'd be sewing after all.

I rinsed away the blood, threaded the needle and splashed the whiskey on my chest.

The task was grueling. Every poke through the skin, every pull on the string, grew more tortuous. When he tapped on the door, I had no idea how much time had toiled by.

"Evie?"

I clenched my teeth. "Hmm?"

"Ye okay?

"Yep. Fine."

"Let me help. I'm a priest. I wen' molest ye."

I flinched at the suggestion. To be honest, I did trust him. But I hid deeper wounds. If he prodded around this one, he'd likely stumble on others I wasn't ready to lick.

I hollered through the door, "Almost finished."

Hell has three gates: lust, anger, and greed.

Bhagavad-Gita

CHAPTER TWENTY: THREE GATES

I shivered awake. For a fleeting moment, I didn't know where I was.

A wooden Jesus hung from a huge cross on the wall. Two worn imprints dented the cushion on the prayer bench below it. A flame stood still on a single candle. Across the room, folded blankets lay on the empty couch. Muffled thuds clapped from the hallway. Roark?

Blood crusted my jeans, which were wadded on the floor. I pulled up the drooping neckline of his borrowed tee and covered my shoulder. If the hem at mid-thigh didn't make me feel vulnerable, the fact that I'd discarded my last pair of panties in Dover did.

A wool robe draped a chair by the bed. I kicked off the blankets, grabbed the robe and stabbed my trembling arms through the sleeves.

Thump. Thump-thump.

I stilled. What the hell was he up to? A hiss echoed every hit. Ah. The heavy bag.

My rumbling stomach led my feet to the kitchen. A can of coffee and a coffee press sat behind first cabinet door I opened. I sucked a breath through my teeth to keep from drooling. Within minutes, I pushed solar heated water through the grounds in the press. The rich roasted beans enveloped me with the sweetness of Saturday mornings with Joel and the A's...I swallowed back the lump in my throat and rifled through the next cabinet. Rolled oats. Brown sugar. Canned pears. The makings of an actual meal.

While I savored the coffee, I flexed my arms, twisted out the kinks in my back, and massaged my sore thighs. My muscles, joints and mind exhibited a liquidity and clarity only a rested night could bring.

Rhythmic thuds marched down the hall. Each jab hit in a pattern. His vigor never faltered. The sweat was probably beading across his broad back. I bet his blond curls were damp with it, clinging to his flushed cheeks. Shit. I rubbed my hands on the robe and headed to the bathroom to brush my teeth.

A note was adhered—with chewing gum?—to the bathroom door.

HELP YOURSELF TO A SHOWER. HOT WATER WILL RUN 10 MINUTES.

Coffee and a shower? I had to be dreaming.

Despite my searing stitches, it was the best shower in memory. I finished in five minutes, hoping to have left him enough heated water. Then I borrowed some cotton pants, fixed breakfast, another canter of coffee and carried a mug down the hall.

I froze in the doorway. His fist slammed into the bag. The brute force punch followed all the way through. And he didn't look tired. Each blow landed as strong as the last. Sweat dripped in rivulets down the cut valleys of his naked back. Black workout shorts hung on his too perfect backside. I wanted to rake my fingernails down his twitching lats and press my lips against his—

"Mornin'." He panted and rested his gloved palms on either side of the heavy bag to steady himself.

His shoulders rose and fell through heavy breaths. I wrestled to control my own breathing. Ugh, what a pervert. I had managed to ignore my libido for months. Why was I losing it so suddenly? He was a priest for fuck's sake.

A damn fine priest of masculine perfection.

"Good Morning." My voice was weak. I cleared my throat and tried again. "I brought you coffee."

He kept his back to me as he grabbed a rag and wiped his face.

"Um...I'll just leave it by the door," I said. "And I made breakfast and hopefully left enough hot water." I bet my face was flushed. I turned to leave.

"Evie?"

"Hmm?"

"Thank ye. I'll be on me way."

I swept from the room with an annoying flutter in my belly.

Showered and fed, Roark sat at the island and watched me peruse his CDs. I held up a Ramones album. "Sheena is a punk rocker."

"She was." He sidled next to me on the floor. His cargos and T-shirt were a nice change from the prior night's cassock and collar. A reminder of my filial guilt and disregard for the Catholic Church.

His jade eyes gleamed over freckled cheeks as he regarded me.

I fought the urge to scoot away. "Thank you for the shower. I almost forgot what one of those felt like."

He beamed.

"Tell me how you keep it going. The electricity and water system."

His smile widened, filling my vision until it was all I saw. "Of course. There's a network of rain collection pipes running through the neighborhood. The water containers are down here, below the freeze line. The solar panels power the electricity and heat the water. But heating the water alone takes a rake of energy."

He raised a brow as if waiting for me to interrupt. "I figured out it takes all of the hundred and fifty square feet of solar panels about seven hours to generate enough power to heat twenty-five gallons. And there are lashings of batteries to store the power."

"A ten minute shower uses twenty-five gallons of water?"

"Right ye are. To conserve, I use the propane cookers to boil water for dinner and tea." He gestured to the scattered burners in the kitchen. The scars on his knuckles rippled with the movement.

"Where'd you learn to hit like that? Last night with the aphids and this morning on the bag?"

"Ah, now I never tell that one." He stared at his hand and stretched his fingers as if recalling a memory.

"I'd love to hear it." I made a dramatic scan of the room and lowered my voice. "I won't tell anyone."

He grinned and shook his head. "Here I sit with the last lass in the world and she wants to hear *me* story?"

His smile was infectious. I knew I was grinning like a fool, but couldn't stop myself.

"Right." He picked at a wool loop in the rug. "Then I'd like to start a' the beginning if ye den' mind."

"Please." I leaned against the bookshelf and met his steady gaze.

He bent a leg and draped an arm over it. "I was raised in Northern Ireland. The streets were uneasy. A sectarian environment. Ye know the conflict between the Catholics and Protestants?"

At my nod, he said, "Like the other boyos I grew up with, I learned how to fight and defend myself. But I wanted out. So I entered the seminary to become a religious priest. There, I committed me life to vows of poverty, obedience and chastity."

He sighed. "I have continually fallen off the road to poverty. Matthew 19:21 says 'If thou wilt be perfect, go sell what thou hast, and give to the poor.' It sounded so easy, that's for sure. But as a priest I lived a community life. A middle-class lifestyle with a car, a housemaid and a piped telly. I had a secure job and a salary. I wasn't free of all worldly goods."

He glanced around the room. "Even now, I den' live in poverty and there's no poor to give to. That brings me to me vow of obedience. Ye said ye spent time in the church? Do ye know this vow?"

I shrugged. "Mind your superiors, right?"

He smiled. "To be a good example of Christlikeness, obeying your superiors was a means to do so. Obedient humility." His smile fell away. "I lived this one well till…"

His voice trailed off as he secured his unraveling dreadlocks behind his ears. "I stumbled upon a wee Irish lad getting reefed by Brit soldiers. They were ridiculing him for his accent. Made him say things…anything…then clatter him in the gub for saying it." He rubbed the scars on one hand. "I lamped every one of those Brits out of it."

"Serves them right."

"Right. Bugger is…I couldn't stop scrapping after that. I lost me head at the first sign of trouble. Then I got a reputation. I got approached by folks involved in underground boxing. They wanted to train me and put me in a ring. At the time, I thought I'd become a better boxer so I could help more lads. I learned from the best and got real good. Won a rake of fights and gave away me earnings. I've been milling ever since. Me superiors never knew."

Creases furrowed his forehead. "I'm sorry. It's not like me to rabbit on like this."

His decency warmed me even if I couldn't sympathize with his vows. "I'm glad you told your story." I nudged him with my elbow, grinning. "And no doubt your pugilism saved the world's last lass."

He chuckled. "I think the world's last lass was holding her own brilliantly." He dropped his head and pinched the bridge of his nose. "That's two of three vows failed, then. All I have left is me chastity."

My breathing hitched.

He lifted his eyes, captured mine. "I've held this vow for donkey's years. It's been the bloody hardest of the three, yet the only one inviolate. I den' take it lightly."

I squirmed under his gaze. I was probably the only person left who could stand in the way of his treasured vow. I had enough things to worry about. Walk away. Don't do this to him. I stood. "Father Molony, thank you for—"

"Who's Annie?" He remained on the floor, staring up at me.

My heart pounded in my chest. Heat tingled my cheeks. "What?"

"Ye screamed her name in your sleep."

I turned away. Exposing my vulnerabilities to a stranger was stupid, stupid, stupid. His clothes swished behind me. His footsteps approached.

"I usually remember my nightmares. I wake or get woken." I faced him. "Why didn't you wake me?"

He held his position a breath away. "Ye couldn't be roused. These nightmares...they happen often?"

I didn't respond.

The lines in his brow deepened. "Wha' have ye been through?"

I shouldn't have come there. I didn't know him and he was too damn perceptive. I reached inside, in my chest, in my gut, and sought the tug that guided me across the Atlantic. Nothing. Just the race of my heart as his eyes dimmed to a dark jade in quiet patience.

I took a deep breath. "The nightmares come and go."

Annie's graceful smile tapestried my mind. And Aaron, tethered to his Booey. As horrific as their visits had been, they were my torches, my guides in the dark. "Annie was my daughter. And I had a son, Aaron. I lost them to the outbreak."

His arms reached to embrace me, but something in my expression stopped him. Did I want his comfort? He must have read my confusion.

He rescinded his arms. "And their da?"

"I lost"—my voice cracked—"I lost my husband a year ago."

He bent his knees so he could look in my eyes. "Ye have come a long way with such a heavy heart. And to survive the aphids—"

"Aphids are nothing to the hell our own race has put me through."

He widened his eyes and swiped a hand over his mouth. "Last night...in the local...that's why ye were hiding your identity. From men? From *me*?"

Could he hear my teeth grinding? "I've only encountered a handful of men who didn't want to rape or kill me as soon as they saw me. Most are friggin' sanctimonious. Their slurs. Their intent. You'd be amazed."

He remained motionless, his sympathetic eyes holding me with him.

"They think I've lost what it was to be a human woman. I wonder if I ever had it to begin with."

Those eyes went slits. "That's a lat of shite, lass. Ye know that full well."

"Doesn't matter." I couldn't change what I was, whatever that was. "I need to go." Maybe I'd feel the tug again if I kept moving.

"Where?"

I stroked the turquoise rock lying against my chest, despising the emptiness underneath it.

"That's okay, ye den' have to tell me. But I'm going with ye. I promise"—his pause snared my eyes with his—"I promise, ye wen' have to fight them alone."

"Okay." I clamped my mouth shut, stared at my boots. Shit. That naive response had tumbled out without thought. And why did it sound so breathy? I didn't trust his words or the tingle they produced in my womb.

I avoided his eyes and fled across the room, under the guise of gathering weapons. "Just don't slow me down."

A few wading steps ahead in the tunnel, Roark stopped and looked over his shoulder. "Wha' are we doing exactly?"

Looking for Jesse. Maybe rousing my tug. "Just need a few things before I move on."

"Right then." He plowed forward, the hem of his coat sloshing in the shallow water. As it turned out, he had to go just to lead me out of the pipes. I lost my way after the first turn.

He approached the ladder and climbed. The pistol in his palm clanked against the rungs. I waited at the bottom until he hollered, "It's safe."

His outstretched hand greeted me at the top. I ignored it and climbed out. He grinned and damn him if I didn't grin back.

"Bike or van?" he asked.

"You have a van?"

A wrinkle formed on his brow and he glanced at the truck.

"Oh. We're not in Kansas anymore."

The wrinkle grew more pronounced.

Bike or truck. The bike had speed. But maybe I'd find more ammo, warmer clothes, or…a Lakota. "Let's take the tr…van."

He drove us out of the neighborhood. Piles of bodies blurred by as we entered the motorway. "Got some petrol in the bed," he said, "but we should look for more."

I nodded, scanning the bodies for forgotten arrows. The various stages of decay glistened under the noon sun. Most just bone and tissue. Some of the fresher bodies were headless.

"Does 'Shall not kill' only apply to humans?" I asked.

He flicked his eyes to me, expression blank. "It's open for interpretation."

"Apparently," I mumbled.

"If you're not gonna tell me where we're going, mind if I make a stop?"

I shrugged. "You're driving."

Ten minutes later, he motored along a skinny street in a small shopping district. He stopped in front of a two story building with moss covered bricks and white shutters. A weathered sign hung next to an arched door.

THREE GATES FUNERAL HOME

"You can't be serious."

"Can't I?" He was out of the truck with his sword drawn before I could respond. I jumped out and followed him up the stairs.

At the door, an uncomfortable compulsion pressed inside me. I raised the carbine just as an aphid scrambled around the corner of the building, mouthparts snapping. My finger stretched for the trigger. Inhale. Exh—

He arced his sword. The aphid's head rolled to the ground and the pressure inside me released. I lowered the barrel and looked him in the eye. "You should know I don't like coddling."

"Right. And ye should know, I den' like your gun attracting more plonkers when I can kill them quietly."

I sighed. "What are we doing here?"

"Follow me."

He strode through the unlocked door and stopped before a stairway just beyond the vestibule. I didn't move from the porch. He clicked on his flashlight and looked back. "Den' trust me?"

"Nope."

"Smart lass."

Was he fucking with me? "Where do the stairs go?"

"Down." He descended into the dark.

I lifted the carbine and rubbed my cheek against the stock. My muscles relaxed, inch by inch. He was good with his sword but he couldn't stop a bullet. Could I shoot him if it came to that? Hell yes. I crept through the entrance and found him waiting a couple stairs down.

In the basement, we passed several closed doors until he stopped at one half way down. As he dialed in a combination on the padlock, I asked, "Isn't this a mortuarium?"

"Too right." He opened the door and waved his beam over the room.

My mouth hung open. Oh my.

Canned food and cereal, medicine and soap, clothing and blankets and *beaucoup* chocolate, cigarettes and other rare goodies stacked on rows of shelves and overflowed to the floor. I had combed grocery stores and homes from Missouri to England and never stumbled on a find like that.

The muscles under the back of his coat rolled as he dug something from a shelf, messed with it and raised it to his mouth.

"What are you doing?"

He turned with a lollypop stick protruding from his adorable smile.

"How did you find this place?"

"I knew a few blokes who knew a few blokes."

"And these blokes are?"

"No longer blokes."

I plucked the stick from his mouth and popped it my own. The first lick wasn't fruity or sugary. It was better. The taste of a man's mouth. I licked it again. His saliva. Another lick. His breath. I missed it. Christ, I missed Joel.

He watched me with parted lips, blinked. "We should hurry."

What was I doing? Flirting with a priest. Wasting time in the bowels of a building with no look out. "I'm an idiot," I muttered around the stick. "What do we need?"

He tossed me a large burlap bag and bent over a crate of whiskey on the floor. "I'm here for the Bushmills. Get what ye need. We'll make one trip out."

"Do you have a grocery list—" I slapped a hand over my stomach, which buzzed like a nest of bees. "Roark?"

His head shot up at my tone.

I spat out the candy, lifted the carbine. "Is there more than one way out?"

"Wha' is it?"

"Aphids. A lot of them."

The floorboards creaked above our heads. He drew his sword and pulled me into the hall by my arm. Then he dragged me the opposite direction we'd come.

Up ahead, he slammed his shoulder into a door and hustled me inside. A high window reflected light off the stainless steel cabinets and counters. A collapsible gurney stood in the middle of the room.

He hurled an oxygen tank at the window. The glass shattered. Then he pushed the gurney under the opening. "Hop up."

I did, and in the next moment found myself hurtling halfway through the window and face down in frozen weeds. Ow, my fucking chest. "You didn't have to shove me."

"Move your arse," he bellowed behind me. I pulled said arse through the window and backed up, carbine in high ready.

He crawled through. "They're right behind us."

"How many?"

"Too many. To the van."

I tailed him down the narrow alleyway between the buildings, staying a few feet behind as vibrations wreaked havoc on my insides. I rounded the corner and smacked into his back. Dozens of aphids poured in and out of the funeral home, shuffled over the front lawn and blocked our path to the truck. Some sniffed the air. Others looked at us. Roark found my hand and tugged me back down the alleyway.

"Now what?" I pulled my hand free to raise the carbine.

He stopped and looked up. An eight-foot brick wall began where the building next to the funeral home ended. He squatted and cupped his hands. "Up ye go."

I dropped the carbine on its sling, gripped his shoulders and lifted my boot. "What about you?"

He grinned. "Aw, ye care."

I narrowed my eyes.

"Right behind ye, lass." He heaved me onto the wall. I straddled it. Aphids plowed into both ends of the alley. Roark jumped. One leg landed on the wall, his other leg kept the momentum, rising up and over. Then he was straddled before me, grinning even more. "Now we leg it."

Aphids hit the wall, climbing as we dropped to the other side. We ran between the buildings and emerged on the next street over. Our feet pounded the sidewalk as we ran past lines of commercial flats crowded on top of each other. The buzzing grew louder. The space between my shoulder blades tingled as the aphids closed the distance. But I didn't dare look back.

He skidded in front of a building veneered with broken windows. "Here."

We jumped through the glassless opening and ran through a lobby. In the back, a marble counter supported a sheet of glass. The glass was unscathed.

"A bank?" I panted.

He nodded as he ushered me through a steel door. "Bulletproof glass."

I scoured the dim room behind the glass. The only door was the one we came through. Metal file cabinets and desks edged the windowless brick walls. A bank safe stood in one corner.

He wrestled with the largest cabinet. I helped him push it to block the door. Next to us, the window rattled.

We turned and backed up. Bodies slammed into the glass by the dozens. Claws struck out, spines scraping with a god-awful screech. Mouths splattered drool, smearing their latest victims' blood on the glass. Moving as one, they crashed into the barrier over and over. The window jiggled and bowed, but didn't fracture. My triple-tempo pulse bludgeoned my ears.

The file cabinet rumbled and began to inch forward as the door jerked. Roark barreled into it. "Evie. Get in the vault."

I spun in a circle. Did I miss it? "Where?"

"The corner. Go."

Surely he didn't mean the standalone safe that wasn't much bigger than a gun safe. I pointed to it. "That?"

His body lurched with the moving barricade. He jumped back to the cabinet, spreading his legs to strengthen his base as he leaned.

"Hurry." His expression was panicked, the whites shining around his pupils.

I ran to it and yanked out the shelves. I was wrong. My gun safe at home was bigger. No chance was I squeezing inside, let alone both of us and our weapons. "We can fight them."

"Like hell," he shouted. "Houl your wheest and get your arse in there."

A crack ripped through the glass. The door crashed from its hinges, sprawling Roark and the file cabinet across the floor. I raised the carbine and popped the bastards as they fell through. Too soon, the carbine went dry. I tugged off the sling. The carbine clattered to the floor. My cloak followed. Then I drew the pistol and backed toward the safe.

Bands of daylight streaked past the bodies writhing against the cracked glass. Blood and drool sprayed from starving mouths. Bugs overfilled the lobby, spilling onto the street and into our room.

Roark scrambled to his feet. His sword and scabbard dropped to the floor. I aimed the pistol at the aphid behind him. It stretched a pincer and clutched Roark's shoulder. I squeezed. The bug let go, blood spouting from its jaw. Roark stumbled forward, wrapped an arm around my waist and lunged us into the safe. His hand clutched the inside handle. I sucked in a breath. He slammed the door shut.

A bang reverberated the safe's walls. We rocked. Then we tipped. The air knocked out of me when the safe hit the floor, his body buffering my fall. We exhaled as one.

He lay under me. "Are ye well?"

"Nice plan, smart guy. At least we die in a coffin."

"It *was* bolted to the wall." His voice was grim.

"Tell me it's not airtight."

His chest rose under me as he dragged in a deep breath. "Ah, now that we'll find out soon enough."

Bang...Bang. Then the scratching began.

Watch and pray so that you will not fall into temptation.
The spirit is willing, but the body is weak.

The Holy Bible, Matthew 26:41

<u>CHAPTER TWENTY-ONE: A NUN'S TITS</u>

"Your smell is intoxicating." Roark sucked in a breath through his nose.

The swell in my throat trapped my speech. With my face smashed against his neck and the screeching outside our tomb, my muscles cramped.

"Gun oil," he went on. "Mixed with embalming fluid and the heady tang of sweat."

My fingers twitched with the impulse to punch him but our cramped quarters kept me in check.

The scratching persisted. The aphids' hunger called to me. And so did Roark's tang. Under the mask of whiskey, an incredible oakiness blended with chocolate and spice. I tried to pry my nose off his neck and my head met the felt lining above us.

I found my voice. "Hiding your fear of those things behind humor?"

"I think I have more to fear in here than what's out there."

My body tensed against the hard ridges of his.

"I can feel their buzzing rippling through ye, lass. And after seeing ye fight last night and out there today, I know ye move like them, ninety to the dozen. Ye could've outrun them if I hadn't slowed us down."

"I'm not—"

"I'm not suggesting ye are. But ye haven't been honest. I think you're the one hiding fear."

The safe's steel casing moaned as aphids piled on. I felt their need like words in my ears. He was right. I *was* hiding my fear. Fear of what I was becoming. Fear of losing my immunity, or never having it to begin with. "I can sense them before I see them. And right now"—for the first time—"I understand them. They're not going to give up until they've fed."

His fingers curled into my hips then relaxed. "It's been ten minutes. Getting enough air?"

I nodded against his neck.

"Then we wait." He rolled his knees out.

I settled between them and eased my grip on his shoulders. God, how I missed the feel of Joel's body under mine. I relaxed into the heat enfolding me. My heartbeat slowed, parroting the steady one below me. "Explain this joke of bank vault we're smashed in."

"It's a bit of a town, lass. Wee families with wee quid."

Something pounded the side of the safe. The door rattled.

"Tell me they can't open that."

"The inside knob slides the pins. But if they can turn the outside wheel, they can open it."

I closed my eyes and focused on the vibrations. Their frustration echoed through me. And their desperation. But nothing intelligible. No way could they figure out the wheel. Right?

"Keep your alans on." He stroked my back. "Why den' ye tell me more about your super powers?"

The corner of my mouth crept up his neck. He was trying to distract me. Maybe both of us. So I told him about the glowing aphids, my fighting speed, my training with Joel. Then I told him about my visions. How I found my father's body, the Lakota and the nymph. And the unexplained urgency to cross the Atlantic. It felt liberating to talk about the spirits of my children. Was it because he was a priest that I was able to talk so freely?

"And this pull, where does it take ye now?"

I shrugged. "It doesn't."

"Ah."

The din of moaning and scraping crept along my spine. I shivered.

His hand skimmed over my ribs. "How about your nightmares? How do I lull ye from the next one?"

"If we get out of this mess, you'd be wise to get the hell away from me."

"Blarney."

I wished I could meet his eyes. I wasn't about to tell him about skin-to-skin contact. "Your vow."

He sighed and the cords between his shoulder and neck contracted against my mouth. My lips tingled with the urge to explore. "I'll tempt you. I know I will. I have…issues."

"Like now? Are ye tempting me now?"

His groin was pressed against my thigh. He didn't feel tempted. Though, the predators clawing inches from our heads offered some distraction. But not enough to distract me from the sudden urge to grind against his leg. There was a sure-fire way to send him running. "I sort of have a sex addiction."

The air in safe thickened.

"That's what I was diagnosed with anyway, a few years back. It wasn't a big deal before. I had Joel."

He laughed then. He *laughed*.

"I'm glad you find it so damn entertaining."

"It's just"—more laughing—"it's bloody brilliant."

"Really. Enlighten me."

"You're the last woman left. And ye fancy sex. And now you're trapped in a vault with a celibate priest. Tell me how ye den' see the humor in it?"

Surely he heard my teeth grinding. "How about I tell you how I used my brilliant position to manipulate a boy a few weeks ago. And how my exploitation got him butchered on our arrival."

His Adam's apple bobbed against my face. "Wha' happened?"

I told him how Ian sneaked me on and off the ship. How the crew members caught up with me in the port. How Jesse followed me. I left out the attempted mastectomy. I didn't want his pity or his coddling. "Where's the laughing now?"

"Ye did wha' ye had to do." A pause. "I ask ye to do one thing, lass. Put some faith in me discipline. Me vow is as useless as a nun's tits if I'm spared from temptation. I can handle it, and you're not gonna get me killed."

Fine. He deserved to hear all of it. "What if I told you my nightmares are eased, prevented even, when I'm wrapped naked with another body?" Joel tested the theory and I proved it—semi-nude—with the Lakota and poor Ian.

"Then I'll say a fit prayer of thanks. The bloody couch is brutal to sleep on."

"You assume we're going back to the bunker."

Muffled gun shots rang out. His arms tightened around me. "Aw, pish."

"Shh. Listen." Multiple machine guns fired alongside rifles and shotguns. I counted the discrepancies in the blasts. The aphid vibrations magnified, but their attention was redirected. When I sensed them retreating from the back room, I whispered, "There's at least ten shooters, maybe more. This may be our only chance."

"Right then. I'm gonna take a gander. If the room's clear—"

"The room's clear."

"Right. If the lobby's clear, run. Den' wait for me—"

"Coddling. Just open the damn door."

He did.

Ruts burrowed through the safe's exterior in twisted shards of steel. We collected our weapons and crawled over the bent door. Gunfire clapped from the street.

"Sounds like only five shooters left," I said. "We need to hurry."

Assuming close combat, I held the pistol in my right hand, knife in my left, and followed him through the empty lobby. The aphids weren't far given the pulsing inside me. We stopped behind a pillar at the front of the bank.

Across the street, fifty—maybe sixty—aphids formed a circle. Every bug in sight pressed into the frenzy. Rifle rounds and masculine shouting boomed from the center.

"I've never seen so many in one place," I whispered at his back. The contentment from the feeding washed over me, sickening and sating at the same time.

A man detached from the swarm. He ran backwards, firing his machine gun, screaming. Aphids scurried after him, unfazed by his bullets. Roark squeezed my hand.

The closest one clamped a pincer on the man's neck. His eyes bulged. Then half a dozen mouths pierced his torso. A wet howl cut through the buzzing.

He pulled me through the entryway. We slipped onto the sidewalk and ran the opposite way. When we veered down a side street, the screaming ceased. A muscle twitched on his clenched jaw, but he kept his pace next to me.

Our truck emerged on the hill ahead. The surrounding lawns and homes were barren. Puffs of steam pumped from my burning lungs. My knees jarred with each smack of my boots on the pavement.

A few blocks later, I swung open the truck door and dropped with a slump on the seat.

He turned over the engine and raced away from the aphid rally. "Where to?"

"Anywhere but here."

"Back to the bunker, then. Until we have a plan."

"Okay." I slouched into the seat and rubbed my chest. I definitely needed a plan.

"So, how do we do this?" Roark asked that night.

I lay in the bed in borrowed sweat pants and a T-shirt. "For it to work, skin to skin is necessary."

His mouth twitched. I sounded like a nut job.

"How much skin?"

"When I was with the Lakota, they kept a bare arm around my waist and a bare chest against my back. But here's the deal. If the contact is lost, the nightmare slips in." Which was why I didn't have a single lapse when I slept nude with Joel.

He stood next to the bed and stared down at me, his expression grave. Yeah, he was having second thoughts.

"It's hard to keep contact all night anyway," I said. "Just forget it."

He put a knee on the mattress. "Scoot."

I gave him half the twin mattress and blew out the candle. When he settled behind me, I tucked the hem of my shirt under my breasts.

His warm fingers brushed my waist and settled into a fist against my belly. A few moments passed.

"Evie?"

"Mm?"

"This tug ye talked about. Do ye think it has something to do with your wonder woman powers?"

I shrugged and my cheeks twitched against the pillow.

"And your immunity. Any guesses?"

"We know the virus targeted low testosterone and I have evidence of the opposite."

"Your libido?"

"That's one symptom. I have others."

He opened his fist and tucked me closer to his naked chest. Warmth flooded my body.

His breath brushed my hair. "Have ye heard of the Shard?"

Joel's letter. A twinge burned away my arousal. "Yeah."

"In the early days, they were campaigning to find surviving women."

"I know."

"But the airwaves have been dead," he said. "I haven't heard mention of them for six months."

I didn't want to tell him I didn't give a shit about saving humanity. As a priest, it would be his mission to correct my opinion. I was too tired for that debate. I feigned a yawn.

"Night, Evie."

"Night."

Three weeks later, I twisted and grunted under Roark. I angled my face away from the sweat doused shirt clinging to his pecs and arched my back. My heartbeat accompanied the pounding drums, bagpipe and tin whistle rattling the gym's speakers. I rocked my hips to leverage a better position under him. He slipped through my guard. Then he mimed a knockout punch to my face.

"Arrgh" ripped from my throat. "Dammit, you suck."

I elbowed him off me. His laughter bounced off the concrete walls.

"You learn Jujitsu in three weeks," I shouted, "and now I can't last five minutes with you."

"Woot-hoo-hoo." He rolled on his back, clutching his stomach.

Next, there'd be tears streaking his face. "Fuck you." He could've at least made me feel like it was an even match. I stormed toward the door, my face burning.

He beat me there, blocking the exit and pinning me with those damn jade eyes. "How 'bout I remind ye I had a stonking teacher?"

I sighed and crossed my arms. "Fine. But I'm still in a snit. Warm up the heavy bag. I'm going to…I'm just going."

He stepped aside and I ran down the hall. I knew where I headed and so did he. He hollered after me, "I love that short fuse of yours, temptress. If ye keep showing me your buttons, I'm going to push 'em."

I slammed the bathroom door and yanked my battery-powered bullet out of the drawer. Then I slid to the floor.

He called me temptress. It became a running joke when he gleaned I was escaping to the bathroom with my bullet every time my libido triggered. He called me temptress because I behaved contrarily. I vacated at the first hint of indecency between us. He, on the other hand, was insufferably flirtatious and enjoyed roiling me then watching me run to the bathroom.

I lay on my back with my feet on the door and clicked the bullet on and off with my thumb.

The teasing, I could endure. But I knew under every tease lay a reciprocated truth. I heard it in his cracked voice when he whispered good morning in my ear. I felt it when he touched my hand as he passed. I saw it when I caught him watching me from across the room. And I dreamed about it when he snuggled at my back every night.

I wet the bullet with my mouth, clicked it on and eased it over the throb inside me. My mind was crowded with fantasies and they all fed an impossible hope. Jesse was gone. Roark was celibate. And a battery-operated apparatus was no replacement for the real thing.

But I closed my eyes and let copper ones fill my vision. Jesse's body pressing mine into the floor, lips parted for ragged breaths. The music of his Texas drawl moaning my name. I found my release with my imaginary lover and emerged from the bathroom, both hurting and feeling better at the same time.

Time toiled by under the freeze line. Snow and bitter temperatures shut us in for weeks. Roark's stores of food and supplies could last months. But I could not.

"I made a list of travel supplies." I took a steadying breath. "I'd like to move on in the next couple days."

He eyed me from the opposite end of the couch, our legs intertwined. "You're off your bloody nut. Ye want to travel now? In January? It's the coldest feckin' month of year. Ye den' even have a plan. Ye den' even know where you're going."

I turned a page in *The Hound of the Baskervilles,* my favorite in Roark's collection. I lifted the frayed hardback until it blocked his face.

He knocked a knee against mine.

While the bunker offered us secrecy from the threats prowling above, we had little privacy from each other. I palmed the stone that lay on my chest. I managed to keep my healing wound concealed from his probing eyes and he stopped asking about it. The scabs and stitches were gone, leaving my chest puckered under a hideous pink scar.

He tapped my knee again.

I sighed and closed the book. "What?"

"Where'd ye get that necklace, temptress?"

The nickname had to go. I dug a toe in his ribs.

"Ackk," he shrieked.

"You scream like a girl, fickle priest."

"One of us should play the part." He caught my foot and kissed it, his smile flashing around white teeth. If only his playfulness could loosen the tension within me.

I traced the veins that webbed the stone. "It was a gift."

"Tell me." He massaged my toes.

I told him about my time with the Lakota. About the Great Mystery, the circle, my healing and my peculiar interactions with Jesse. "Besides Ian, the Lakota are the only men who have shown me civility since the outbreak."

He crooked a brow. "Wha' about your fickle priest?"

"Hmm. Jury's still out on that one."

He locked an arm around my thigh and attempted a hyperextension on my knee. I rolled, twisted out of it and into his lap. He released his grip but kept his arms around my waist. His throat bounced around a swallow, eyes mirroring my hunger. I wanted to close the inches between us. I wanted to find out if he tasted as good as he smelled.

His brogue rumbled from his chest. "Temptress."

"Prude."

"Opinionated heathen."

"Brainwashed god-fearer."

His gaze drifted over my face, returned to my eyes. "Bugger, you're so beautiful."

I swallowed past a tight throat. My self-control was no match for his. I leapt off his lap and ran toward the workout room, the farthest place I could get.

He caught my arm in the hallway. My back hit the wall, held there by his hip.

My thoughts were everywhere and no where they should be. "We need to stop this."

"It doesn't have to be like this." His breath was hot on my temple, his accent thicker than usual. "Trust me, lass. Den' bolt. Close your eyes."

Put some faith in me discipline.

I took a shaky breath and did what he asked. A few heartbeats later, his fingers brushed my cheeks. My pulse raced. My clothes felt tight and itchy. He pressed his forehead to mine and inhaled through his nose. His fingers sank in my hair as he whispered at my mouth, "Can we show each other affection without making it about shagging?"

I opened my eyes. "Impossible." For me, at least.

"We're both lonely. We have no family and friends to hold or care for. But we have each other."

Deep breaths. "What kind of affection?"

He cupped my face. His lips touched my forehead. My heart thundered. He tilted my head back and dropped a kiss on the bridge of my nose. Then the tip. I held my breath. His mouth swept over mine, soft and warm. He lingered on my bottom lip.

I didn't kiss back. My insides flailed in objection.

He released my face and placed his hands on the wall, caging me with his arms. Then he dipped his head to meet my eyes. "So?"

I stuffed my hands in my pockets to keep from yanking him back to my mouth. "I've worn out my welcome. It's time I go. Alone."

"Hmm." He dropped his hands. "There'll be wigs on the green, then. Till my last breath, I'm going to protect ye."

His unblinking glare said he'd tie me up with rosary beads and stuff an alter cloth in my mouth if I challenged him. A challenge I would normally not back down from.

"I won't be responsible for your vow."

"Aw, ye pain in the hole. Ye know full well the vow is futile without ye."

I rolled my head back against the wall. "Like tits on a nun."

"Feckin' apt. Dried up useless tits. Now let's go see wha' we can scrape up for dinner."

"Jaysus' bloody bitch-bag." Roark's roar jerked me awake the next morning. He was in the shower.

I snorted as I rolled out of bed. Bet that mouth had earned him hours of penance.

"Everything okay in there?" I asked through the door.

"Out of water," he hollered back then opened the door and kissed my cheek. "Sorry I woke ye."

I followed him to the clothing rack. What would he do if I tugged the towel hanging on his narrow hips? Oh so tempting…

"Pipe must be crocked," he said. "I have to go up."

"Crocked? Like broke?"

"Aye," he said, distracted.

I fixed breakfast while he dressed. After we ate, he checked the pipes running through the bunker. I gathered my weapons. I could look for more clothes. Replenish the mags for the carbine. Maybe rummage through a library. Look for Jesse.

He caught up with me in the kitchen and snatched the pistol from the island. "Quit your running around like a blue-arsed fly. You're not going."

"Hell if I'm not. Give me back my gun."

He flipped it over. "Where's the safety?"

Duh. Big lever on the side. "In the trigger. Now give it." I held out my hand and curled my fingers back and forth.

He crouched in front of me, flicked the strap on my thigh holster and seated the gun. Then he rose, his green eyes as still and deep as a Scottish loch and fixed on me. He murmured from inches away, "I'll feel better if ye den' go."

"And I'll feel better if you stop thinking of me as a weak little bitch."

"I den'—" A muscle jumped in his cheek. He leaned in and caressed my lips with his Irish lilt. "I think you're the only lass left in the world and not worth risking on a water errand I can do alone."

I resisted the urge to step back. "Too bad. Oh, and while we're out, we're swinging by a library. And shopping. I need clothes."

He scowled.

Oh my, that didn't look right on his gorgeous face. Still, "You can't keep me here."

He gripped my jaw. "I know it, ye obstinate woman." He lightened his grip. Swayed close. Closer. Deliberate and watchful, he kissed the corners of my mouth.

My heart picked up its pace. His lips parted over mine.

I stepped back. Affection without making it about shagging? Did he part his lips when he kissed his mother? Who was he kidding? I didn't run, but I didn't linger. Besides, I had blades to sharpen and ammo to don.

Twenty minutes later, I waited for him by the oval exit in the workout room. I traced the blood stains on the fur sleeve of my cloak. Blood from a chest wound that would've been fatal if Jesse hadn't arrived when he did. Why did he follow me across the Atlantic? Had he followed me to the bunker as well? Could he still be up there?

I blew out a breath. I'd been hidden down there for a month. How stupid to think he waited.

Roark's boots echoed in the passageway. A gasp escaped me when his unsheathed sword glinted in the doorway. Clad in full cassock, rosary and collar, he read the amusement on my face and grinned. Then he raised the sword. "Hello. Me name is Inigo Montoya. Ye killed me father. Prepare to die."

I laughed with pangs in my side at hearing the *Princess Bride* quote inflected with his accent. He sheathed the blade and approached me while he elided, "*El* bonny *lass-ocho,* ye *muy* beautiful *temptresta.* Ye put *fire-ito* in me burrito and make me feel like *elwanker-ito.*"

Between fits of laughter, I said, "I don't know Spanish, but I'm pretty sure you won't find *wanker-ito* in the dictionary."

When he stepped toe-to-toe with me, his repartee came in hot breaths on my neck. "I may have *muchocabeza* and *uno* wee *heart-ito* but *te amo mija.*"

"*Te amo mija?*"

He spun the wheel on the door and led me into the alcove.

"Roark?"

I waited in silence while he installed his *wee* explosive. When he stood and faced me, his expression was fierce. "Ye be dog wide up there."

Dog wide? "Seriously, man. I don't understand half of what comes out of your mouth."

He grabbed my wrist and hauled me down the tunnel. "Keep your backside safe, lass."

The midday sun did nothing for the bitter chill that slapped my face. I squinted watery eyes to shield them from the glare. Add to that the wind speed from the bike. We found out just how fast the Harley could go as we left the neighborhood. Aphids fringed the street as if they lay waiting for our emersion.

"Lanky wasters," Roark shouted as he yawed the bike in and out of mutant strikes. I sighted the pistol on the closest ones as we passed. One…two…three down. Their buzzing surged through me. Along with a rush of energy. A quirk pulled my lips.

The bike slowed to round the corner. The wave inside me lurched into a rhythm. Up ahead, a single aphid stood in the street, rooted to the pavement. It turned its head. Our eyes locked. Then its wide body quivered in tempo with mine.

Drrrrrrrrone penetrated my chest. Not my ears.

Roark zigzagged the bike through lawns as we passed it. I looked over my shoulder. The mutant didn't budge. Not even when the spasm of aphids parted around it.

Drone-drone-drone vibrated through me. Still, it didn't move. Its eyes bored into mine. A knowing rammed my chest. A calling pulled me to it. I had to go back.

Would Roark stop the bike? Not a chance. I released my hold on his waist, tucked my chin and arms, and rolled off.

"Evieeee. Bloody hellllll."

My shoulder hit the pavement. Ow. Fuck.

Tires screeched behind me.

"Evie. I'll feckin' kill ye myself."

I tumbled to my feet and ran toward the fray.

Every conquering temptation represents a new fund of moral energy.
Every trial endured and weathered in the right spirit
makes a soul nobler and stronger than it was before.

William Butler Yeats

CHAPTER TWENTY-TWO: A COWARD HAS NO SCAR

The furor of aphids sprang toward me, but my focus narrowed on the one who stood still. I braced my wrist and deflected an oncoming claw with my forearm. Then I swapped out the pistol for a knife in midstride.

Roark's sword clanged behind me. I moved through the horde, slicing and piercing any in my way. Bodies thudded on the road and I spun free of the fight.

The wind blinded me. Blood and drivel clumped my eyelashes. Yet through the haze, I met the rage burning in Roark's eyes. So what? He didn't have to follow me into battle. He could've left my ass. But there he was, pissed and fighting, instead of dodging and hiding. I'd deal with that complication later.

I turned back to my target, its posture inert. The churning in my chest drew me closer, the knife's hilt warm in my hand. The aphid's pearlescent orbs were as unwavering as its body. An invisible current writhed between us. I raised the knife and let its gaze consume me.

Fffffound you marched through my veins.

"Me?" I asked aloud and felt foolish doing so.

Foooound.

The aphid blurred to the side and disappeared between two houses.

Behind me, the last head thumped to the pavement. Roark panted. I could feel his eyes burning a hole in my back.

"Evie."

I turned around. He leaned on his sword. The death that clung to him matched the glare he aimed at me. I squared my shoulders and walked forward, stepping over the headless bodies encircling him. He didn't move as I brushed back the bloodied hair that matted his forehead.

"I might consider forgiving your daft theatrics"—he waved his hand to the bike sprawled on its side—"if ye tell me wha' you're about."

I just had a conversation with an aphid. He wouldn't understand what was going on with me. I didn't even understand it. "I don't know."

He ground his teeth and sheathed his sword. "We fix the banjaxed pipe then back to the gaff straightaway."

"No." My chin thrust out, as did my chest. "I need books." I nodded to the carnage. "Insect books."

Fury seared his every syllable. "I had a canary when ye leapt off the bike. So you'll tell me wha' ye were doing with that messenger bug."

"What? How do you know it was a messenger?"

"They den' fight. They gawk."

"And you know this how?"

"Lloyd." A heavy sigh. "He heard a rake of stories from the minks passing through."

"If that was a messenger, was it here to deliver a message?" From who? A human? Another aphid?

"They collect information and take it back to their hives."

"Hives? Dammit, we've been together for months. Why am I just hearing about this?"

His whiskered chin tipped to the sky, an exhale pushing through his flared nostrils. Then he dropped his head and leveled his glare at me. "I'm not withholding anything from ye. I told ye they were evolving. The messengers, the hives, I den' know what it means."

"I understand them. I swear I felt it say 'Found you.' *Felt* being the operative word, Roark." After it chanted *Drone* through my veins. The hairs on my neck rose. "Something's not right with me, and to understand what's going on, I need to understand them." If I could get my hands on an entomology tome or maybe layman's texts on natural selection and DNA mutation..."I need a fucking library."

He squinted at his curled fingers. I followed suit with impatience. What, did he need manicure?

When he raised his gaze to mine, my stomach dropped. My theatrics had put shadows in those deep green eyes. Oh, my fickle priest. What had I done?

He watched me, seemed to be debating something. Then he straightened his back, decision made. "I must be a gobshite." His tone was on the hurtful side of contemptuous.

He stalked to the bike. "There's a university a few kilometers north."

Roark found and repaired the break in the pipe without incident. A couple hours later, we stood in the cathedral style foyer of the college library. The mustiness of unused books stagnated the stuffy space. A high window streamed a golden bar of sunlight across the brick floor and illuminated the cloud of dust stirred up by our boots.

A whisper of jade peered from under his lowered lashes as he stepped before me. "We den' know if we've been followed. Root quickly and den' put the heart crossways in me again."

"Hold on to your canaries. I'll steer clear of trouble."

Even bleak in spirit, his beautiful lips turned up. I rose on tiptoes and tilted a closed mouth over his. He met me with a tentative caress of lips. Too soon, he pulled back.

Head down, he nodded to the right. "Science and Nature is that way."

We secured the building then separated in the closed off corner of the library. Three stories of stained glass windows veneered the west wall and soaked up the last hour of sun. I scuffed down the aisles, loading my arms with every primer I found on bugs, evolution and genetics.

Honey-tinged curls flashed between the books one aisle over. I leaned on the shelf that separated us. He pretended to ignore me, keeping his eyes on the text he cradled.

I pushed a few books out of the way. "You must be in the *1000 Ways To Pleasure a Woman* section?"

His lips teased a smile. "Actually, this is *Temptress for Dummies*, but"—he glanced up—"I'm on me way to the *How To Make Her Bugger Off* aisle."

Dusty hardbacks framed his sculptured face. As we stared at each other through the opening, something crept from the green lagoons of his eyes. That something spiraled through me, reaching places I couldn't reach myself. The way he looked at me, I felt attractive, admired, and secure. My body went rigid. I squeezed the books in my arms, thankful for the bookshelf between us.

He nodded toward the end of the aisle and disappeared in that direction. I followed. Snapshots of his heated expression flickered between the books as we advanced.

My mouth went dry. I planted my feet. What would I find at the end of the aisle? A neglected vow? If his control wavered, could I be strong enough for both of us? An irresistible impulse hummed through my body.

Listen to the song.

I lingered in the too quiet stillness, longing to go to him, arousal pumping my pulse.

The scuff of boot treads sent a bird flapping to the rafters. A soft thump up ahead. Another. Then Roark's shout. "Run—"

My body jerked forward, my feet stumbling to catch up. Toward his voice and around the corner. The books plummeted out of my arms.

He was on his knees. A shotgun barrel pressed against his temple. The man behind the gun eyed me up and down. Twice. Deep pockmarks pitted his face. The curved beak that was his nose angled to the side, the misshaped cartilage toughened and old. His boot pinned Roark's sword to the floor and out of reach.

A fist wrapped around my hair. "I don't believe it," a second man whispered, his pierced lips hovering inches from my face. Faded tattoos sleeved his arm, which aimed a sawed-off shotgun at Roark. "Are you real?" Rot wafted from his gaping jaw. His too-large head bobbled on a pencil neck as if it might fall off if he moved too quickly.

The daggers itched on my forearms. I could maim Pencil Neck next to me, but I wouldn't be fast enough to stop Broken Nose from pulling the trigger. I needed one or both of them distracted. So I improvised. "I'm a demon sent by God in his scorn for man's sins to entice thee with"—I cringed—"a voodoo vagina."

Roark's eyebrows climbed up his forehead.

"Release this soldier of Christ and God will show mercy."

Silence blanketed the library.

Broken Nose's saucer eyes didn't blink. "I thought women...I never thought I'd see one again. But here you are. In the flesh." He thumbed his ill-fitted nostrils. "Let's see the voodoo vagina."

Damn. Not the usual god-fearers. Plan B. "Listen fuckers. I'm a hybrid nymph. And I'm hungry enough to dine on your low grade sap."

Pencil Neck yanked back my head and wedged the gun barrel in my mouth, prying it open, gagging me. "No mutated bits in there. Aw God, her throat is perfect." He shut my jaw and turned the gun back to Roark. "She's going to take my cock in that sweet throat"— he thrust his enlarged groin against my hip—"while her soldier of Christ watches. If he behaves, he can have a go at her ass while we take turns filling her cunt. And I can see the weapons under that coat. Those come off first."

I met Roark's eyes. I'd seen that torment before. In my father's basement.

"No, Evie."

I rubbed my wrists. I failed Joel. I wouldn't fail Roark. I removed the weapons and cloak. Roark didn't lower his eyes from mine when I shed my shirt. The frigid air trailed cold fingers along my scar. Would its hideousness be enough of a diversion? I puffed out my chest.

Broken Nose made a choking sound. "Holy fuck."

Wide-eyed, Pencil Neck lowered his barrel to bend down for a closer look. I shot my shin up and out, cracking his jaw. Then I kicked again, knocking the shotgun from his grasp and catching it before it dropped.

Broken Nose fired as Roark dove. Confetti of books showered the far side of the room. I flipped the shotgun and reached for the trigger.

"Den' shoot." Roark fisted the sword, angled like a hatchet over Broken Nose's bowed head.

"Fuck that." I shoved the shotgun against the other man's trembling chest.

"If we kill them, we're no different than they are."

"You have no idea what kind of monster I am." I put pressure on the trigger.

"Look at them. Look close. What do ye see?"

I looked into the eyes of the man who was willing to take turns raping me. A wet sheen rose over his gaze and broke free in one pathetic plop on his sunken cheek.

"Fear," I said, "follows evil, and its punishment."

"It also follows suffering. It weakens a man, makes him desperate. They're scared, lass. Just like ye. And me."

My trigger finger wobbled, strengthened. "If we don't kill them, they'll come after us."

"No more blood, Evie. We'll tie them up, find another way."

Something moved near Roark's boot. Broken Nose's hand twitched over the hem of his bunched up pant leg. Then a flash of metal. Another goddamn gun.

I swung my aim and fired. His broken nose burst in bits of bone and flesh. A pitted flap of skin hung from his chin, quivering on his neck. His body toppled to the floor.

Pencil Neck launched, barreled into me. His hand wrestled mine for the aim of the shot gun. He was stronger, had more leverage. The barrel rose up, up, up until I was staring into the dark hollow tubes.

The sword whistled behind me. The shotgun dropped, followed by Pencil Neck's too-large head.

Adrenaline drained from my shaking limbs as I scooted away from the headless corpse. I dressed and strapped on my weapons, fearful of meeting Roark's eyes.

He was crouched over the bodies, murmuring what I presumed to be Last Rites. When he stood, I approached his back and leaned my forehead against it. His body stilled.

"I'm sorry." For jumping off his bike. For the blood on his sword. For hiding my scar.

He stepped away and scooped up my abandoned books. "We're leaving."

I stepped out of the bathroom. The sweatshirt and cotton pants did little to calm my shivering from the ice cold shower. Roark sat on the edge of the bed, already showered and in his wool robe.

His gaze swiveled to mine. "Come here."

When I sat next to him, he gripped me in a painful hug.

"Roark—"

"We have scads to discuss." He released me. "But right now, I can't get past the scar." His fingers yanked through his wet curls. "Tell me that's not the wee cut ye were stitching the night we met?"

I lowered my eyes.

"Bloody hell. Why?" He knelt before me. "I was right here. I could've helped ye. I should've helped ye."

"Well"—I shrugged—"I was still trying to get over the fact that some bastard wanted to give me a mastectomy. I wasn't really in a trusting mood."

His jaw set. Red spots bloomed on his neck and cheeks. "And now? If it happened now, would ye let me?"

I cupped his face and rubbed my thumbs over his whiskers. "Of course, I would. I trust you."

"Then show me the scar. I want to see it."

I arched my eyebrows and tried to hide my surfacing nerves with humor. "I'll show you mine if you show me yours?"

"Ach, I'm not coddin' ye. I can't be more serious in me request."

"Okay." I threw up my hands. "Fine."

He remained on his knees, eyes on mine.

"Now?"

He nodded.

So many times, I lost myself to fantasies of him gazing upon my body with an amorous ogle and a slackened jaw. But I knew his request wasn't about sex. So I pictured my annual doctor's exam. Latex gloves. Cold stirrups. It was just a health inspection.

I shrugged out of my shirt and lay back on the bed, propped up on my elbows. The chill in the room hardened my nipples, pointing them to the ceiling.

He sucked in a breath, his brogue thick. "Aw love, you're a vixen."

Doctor's office. Acrid disinfectant hospital smell. Stiff exam table.

He stood over me. "Ye meant wha' ye said? Ye trust me fully?"

"Yes." That word was so much bolder than the voice that imparted it.

He removed his robe. His bare chest tapered to the slim waistline of his jeans, which hung low on his hips. My heart hammered.

The muscles in his arms twitched in the candlelight as he crawled over me. Sweat lined my palms.

When he straddled my thighs, my teeth sank into my lip. He moved my turquoise stone to the side and bent his mouth over my scar. His eyes held mine.

"Does he live?" he rasped. "The sodding bastard who did this?"

I shook my head. His gaze lowered to my marred chest. My lungs labored under his examination. His head dipped. I held my breath.

Warm lips stroked my collarbone, lingering on the widest stretch of scar tissue, the gouge where the knife plunged. He followed the welt around my breast. I balled the bedding in my fists. His tongue caressed the raised tissue. Each time I shuddered, a sultry exhale escaped his mouth. His tongue never strayed from the gash. When he arrived at my collarbone a third time, he raised his head.

We exchanged reverent looks. It felt so fucking good to feel a man's adoration again. I felt alive. Joy even.

Our foreheads touched. His lips lowered. Closer. Closer. Then they found mine.

He brushed them sweetly back and forth. His tongue reached out, begging invitation. Oh, sweet God, I wanted to. I wanted to push him on his back and ride him until his voice was hoarse and his balls empty. I couldn't. I shouldn't. He drew my bottom lip into his mouth, sucking, nursing. Our breaths united.

He took over my mouth, his tongue moving in and out, his lips massaging. The richness of oak and whiskey and Roark seeped into my taste buds. His lips flowed against mine, his breath a velvet stroke. My veins thrummed in song, tingling the crown of my head, the soles of my feet and everywhere in between.

His fingers dug into the mattress on either side of us. I echoed his moan with my own. The kiss deepened, impatient and hungry.

When he caught his breath, his eyes slammed into mine. His lips were swollen and wet. His pupils widened, flickered, then his expression fell.

He ducked his head and groaned into my shoulder. "Jaysus, Mary and Joseph." He pushed off me and slumped at my side.

I gritted my teeth against the sudden loss. Every sensitive zone on my body pulsated for attention. The hollow between my shoulder and neck. The dark peaks of my breasts. The dip in my waist. The folds between my legs. The more I thought about him touching me, the hotter I burned. So I marshaled my breathing by counting the knots in the wood beams above. One, two, three, four—

"Evie, I'm so sorry."

I rubbed my thighs together. My chest heaved. Beside me, his breathing wasn't any better. He rolled away to his prayer bench and I restarted my counting. One, two, three…

…twenty-eight, twenty-nine. I took a deep breath. The itch was still there, but my frenzied pulse had ebbed.

His silhouette flickered in the candlelight, bent over his bench. His mouth moved soundlessly, fingers sliding along rosary beads in rheumatic strokes. When he reached the rosary's length, he made the sign of the cross and clutched the dangling crucifix to begin again.

"Stop this. Come back to bed."

His eyes widened under drawn eyebrows.

"It was only a month ago you told me you could handle this."

He set down the beads. "I can."

I raised the blanket.

He dove at the invitation, slipping under it and reaching across to pull me to him. He mantled my body with a heavy thigh and bicep. His voice was soft at my ear, "Evie, I'm—"

"Don't. We'll talk in the morning." I wrapped my hands around the arm across my chest and closed my eyes.

"Right. It'll be a brilliant segue into the lecture I'll be giving on the risks involved with offering up a voodoo vagina."

Heat flushed my face. I bit down on my cheek to trap my groan.

I woke later that night, my skin still exposed from the waist up. Whiskers tickled my back. Fingers trailed over the bumps of my spine. A kiss grazed my shoulder. And another. Then lips peppered my nape. He was hugging my back, a knee tucked between my thighs.

My body surrendered to his touch, boiled to its earlier intensity. "Roark?"

He stiffened. He thought I was still asleep?

After a few breaths, he shifted, rolling me in his fold to face him. His jaw was clenched, lips in a slit, but desire fed the blaze in his heavy-lidded eyes. Would he let me run my hand through his curls and suck the tension from his bottom lip?

We stared at each other, nose to nose. I licked my lips, where his oaky taste lingered. His eyes followed.

The muscles in my stomach clenched, rippled lower, and settled into a throb against the thigh between my legs. I meant to push him away, but instead curled my nails into his back. The buildup inside me quickened to the point of pain. This time, it had to be slaked.

I took a deep breath. The words came on my exhale. "Please. Fuck me."

He lowered his head.

God is faithful;
he will not let you be tempted beyond what you can bear.
But when you are tempted,
he will also provide a way out so that you can stand up under it.

The Holy Bible, 1 Corinthians 10:13

CHAPTER TWENTY-THREE: REBELS OF THE SACRED HEART

Roark buried a hand in my hair, knotting a shock of it at my nape. Another hand around my hip, he pressed his mouth hard against mine.

His tongue slipped past my lips, leaving a trail of fire in its wake. I fell into his kiss, clinging to him as tightly as he clung to me. Soft curls tangled with my fingers as I scored his scalp. He responded with a rumble low in his throat.

When I met him, I was injured, hungry and so damn lonely. In a matter of hours, he'd slipped past my guard, sneaked in with a charming smile, and soothed the ache in my heart. But I wanted more than friendly flirting and sympathetic snuggling. I wanted an embedded joining, a molecular connection, a melding of souls.

My body trapped under his, the lean sinews in his back bunched under my hands. His teeth scraped my neck where he nuzzled and licked. Then his tongue sought mine again, tasting as he nudged his thigh between my legs and drove the muscled strength of it against my groin.

Need swelled inside me, tightening my womb and demanding release.

His pelvis retreated. He released my mouth. His eyes searched mine as he molded fingers to the contour of my waist, sweeping them over the edge of my breast.

"I want this," he panted. "Ye den' know how much I want...but I—"

"No," I whispered between clenched teeth. "We both want this. Please."

He squeezed his eyes shut, nostrils flaring. His hand curled into a fist on my chest and his body constricted, pulled away.

"No." I rolled after him, restrained by twisted bedding.

He scooted to the end of the bed, hunched over. His knuckles blanched as his hands made fists in his lap. "God forgive me."

"*God* forgive you?" I sat up, shouting at his back. "Bullshit. What about *me* forgiving you?"

No response.

"Fuck this." I untangled my legs from the blankets and bolted to the bathroom.

"Evie!"

I slammed the door and sent something crashing to the floor. The candlelight danced as I yanked the drawer open. My bullet lay amongst the toothpaste, soaps and razors.

In the mirror, my yellow-green irises flared under the agitated vein in my forehead. My cheeks flushed in coral hues. My hair parted over my shoulder, curling around one breast and miming his caress. I dropped my eyes.

My naval jerked in response to the pulsing below it. I splayed a hand over the curve of my hip, dipped it under the waistband and between my thighs. My body trembled. I plucked the bullet and dropped to my usual spot on the floor. My eyes closed, flooded with the intensity of copper ones. The illusion of Jesse's body wrapped around and in mine as the bullet assuaged my need.

After I cleaned up, I returned to the floor. At least self-pleasure took the edge off. Bet his vow didn't allow him even that.

We stood at a crossroad. The longer we remained confined to the bunker, the more the thing between us would strain. He swore to protect me, asking only for my faith in his discipline. With my growing connection to the aphids, I needed his faith in my humanity.

From my perspective, humanity as a whole was already lost. The cries of the nymph in the cabin, however, still sent shudders through me. What if there were others like her? What if I could aid the research to cure them?

A shadow flickered under the bathroom door. I reached up for the knob and opened it.

He sat on the other side, legs bent, back to the door jam. He raised his eyes to mine and held out my shirt. "I'm sorry. Ye deserve more."

"Don't be sorry. I didn't mean what I said." I sweetened my words, but they tasted like acid in my mouth. I pulled the shirt on.

Behind his grim expression was an unrivaled tenacity. His eyes were vehement in resolve and I found myself filled with admiration. If only I could be that strong.

I scooched toward him and leaned against the opposite side of the doorway.

When he drooped a hand over his bent knee, I hooked my pinky around his thumb. "What do you pray for?"

He stared at our hands. "Forgiveness, guidance, strength"—the corner of his mouth lifted—"ye."

Something in my chest squeezed. "We should sleep separately."

"No." He interlaced our fingers. "Sleeping with me arms around ye is me favorite part of every day. I won't have it another way."

I blew out a breath. That went both ways. How had I allowed him to nose dive straight into the recesses of my heart? "That's probably best. Where we're headed, we'll need to share body warmth."

His lashes flew up. When he opened his mouth, I said, "We're going to find the Shard." If they still existed.

He closed his mouth and rolled his lips as if sampling my words. "And wha' about your animosity toward mankind?"

Was I that transparent? "Ah well, some starry-eyed bloke has shown me the yellow brick road. Maybe I'll find a heart."

That earned me the patented Roark smile. "And wha' if the Shard's just a cantankerous auld man pressing buttons on a ham radio?"

"We won't know until we pull back the curtain."

He raised his hand and smoothed hair from my cheek. "Then pull your socks up. Iceland will freeze the balls off a brass monkey."

Roark spent the next two days scribbling on his maps of the U.K., marking towns along the way that might have the supplies we'd need. I spent that time cleaning my weapons, honing my strength in the gym and scouring the genetics primer from the library.

The night before we planned to depart, he woke me, kneeling beside me, his features twisted in a queer wonderment. "Evie. Evie."

"Mm?"

"Did ye read any of your entomology texts? Or any of the books on aphids?"

Seriously? He woke me for that? My lids fluttered closed and I waved him away. "Tomorrow."

"I read them." He shook me. "Evie? Do ye know wha' the aphid's biggest predator is?"

"My 5.56 round between the eyes."

His hands hooked under my armpits and slid me to a sitting position. I groaned my annoyance. He curled a knuckle under my chin and lifted my eyes to his. Even in the dim candlelight, his jades were fierce. "Aphids. The wee insects. Do ye know their predator, love?"

I exaggerated another yawn.

His hand brushed my shoulder and extended before me. Two ladybugs gripped his fingers.

"Ladybirds. The bloody aphids' predators are ladybirds." He let the beetles wiggle into my lap. "Do ye know wha' this means?"

I flicked the bugs across the room. "We need an exterminator?"

He squinted at me, his tone impatient. "Wise up and listen. I prayed for a sign."

I lifted a shoulder. "Like the spinning sun of the Medjugorje sunset? Or the bleeding Bolivian statues?"

He sidled closer, palm circling my nape. "I very specifically asked for"—his eyes dipped to my lips then darted back up—"I asked for a sign to acknowledge you're more sacred than me vow."

He sat back on his ankles and pulled the blanket away from me. My body teemed with bustling beetles. Ladybugs perched on my arms and thighs and stirred in the bedding that surrounded me.

I jumped out of the bed and swatted them off. "Oh God, where did they come from?"

"Exactly." He ran his hand over his mouth. Creases spread from the corners of his eyes. "Ye are hallowed."

"You can't be serious." I brushed the last of them away and grimaced. "This isn't the first time they've flocked to me like this." My dad's boat. My Lakota name.

He stood still, hands to his sides, watching the bed. "This is big. Bigger than us."

Good lord. "Maybe they're like mosquitoes, only biting certain people. Maybe I exude an odor that attracts them."

"I'm going to wet the tea."

The blankets seemed to move under the writhing red bodies. A shiver ran through me. "Something stronger than tea."

He held up a bottle of Bushmills and patted a stool by the bar. I sat and he filled our tumblers. "Can ye have children?"

My nerves resurfaced. "That's...what? What the hell does my fertility have to do with our insect problem?"

He passed me a glass. "I've wanted to ask ye since I met ye. I decided to come out with it straight away." He sat next to me. "I know it's not an easy question."

No, it wasn't. But I kept nothing from the man. "I had an IUD implanted three years ago. It's like ninety-nine point nine nine percent effective against pregnancy. And no periods, one less thing to worry about. I should get two more years out it."

He traced the lip of his glass. "So if it was removed. Ye could get pregnant?"

Fear and curiosity collided, wrestled. What sort of divine notions had hatched in that mercurial brain of his? Was he going to offer fatherhood? For a child I couldn't have and didn't want? "Conception maybe. But pregnancy to term? Or a baby that lives after it inhales the virus? Just because I'm immune doesn't mean my child would be." The reminder of my A's final hours wrenched my gut. "Why?"

"The Shard. They'll pursue this option."

Oh. The last human woman begetting children. Yeah, that would be a coup. One that ran a chill through me. Maybe I'd agree to be a guinea pig in their research, but I'd die before I'd bring a daughter into a world rife with rapists.

I swilled the contents of my glass and met his heavy gaze.

"Ye know it's different now."

"You're referring to this sign"—I gestured to the bed—"from your god? Now you're suddenly released from your vow?"

"I den' know. I asked for a sign and the aphids' predator rains down upon us. Perhaps, it's a blessing from God."

Oh, my sentimental Irishman. "It's frigid above the freeze line. Bugs come inside, drawn to the warmth."

"Maybe." Thoughts swirled through his expression. "Regardless, I'm bound to ye."

I leaned away. "That's not necessary."

"I'm not asking. Nor am I asking for the same in return. We no longer live in a world that accommodates traditional sensibilities."

What the hell was he getting at? He was bound to me, but wouldn't sleep with me?

He drained his tumbler. "And I will kill any man who tries to own ye like a thing to possess."

I straightened. "Not if I kill him first. And for my part, I'm not a whore." Between Jesse's disappearance and Roark's celibacy, I faced a future of abstinence.

He jerked my stool between his legs and planted his palms on my hips. "No. Ye are hallowed." He touched his forehead to mine and brushed a thumb over my lips. "Times are different now."

First my fertility. Then my fidelity? I didn't know how to respond, so I didn't.

He stood, the Bushmills bottle tucked under his arm, and walked to the stereo. He held up a CD. "Flogging Molly?"

To my silence, he nodded to the bed. "Or ye could snuggle with your bugs."

I grabbed my empty tumbler and joined him on the couch.

The whiskey flowed for the next couple hours. We avoided further discussion on sex, the Shard, or beetles sent from God. Instead, we shared stories about our families growing up and our experiences during the outbreak. And I told him about my nightmares with the Drone.

"I felt his name when we encountered the messenger bug."

"That's why ye jumped off the bike."

I nodded.

"Ye think this…Drone is real? And he's looking for ye?"

I shrugged. "Colorful delusions have become my norm since the outbreak."

He pulled my legs across his lap and bent over me. His lids hung heavy over cloudy eyes. I nursed my own buzz, but he was hammered. He set his glass on my chest, its amber dram sloshing on my shirt. The glass bottom moved over my scar.

"Tell me how that bloody butcher died."

I unfolded my memories of Dover Port while massaging the frown lines rutting between his brows. Then I told him about the basement in Pomme de Terre. Despite my taut throat, I recited the events in a toneless monologue.

He listened without interrupting, but the muscles jerked in his clamped jaw. His arms around my legs turned to stone. "And ye den' remember wha' happened to Joel?"

I shook my head. "I don't want to."

He studied my face with eyes that penetrated a hole in my defenses. "Ye never cry about this, about anything you've been through." His brows gathered. "Ye think emotions are useless to survival."

Christ, he knew me well. "I've learned the hard way."

He pushed off my legs and staggered to his feet. "Then let's not get weighted down with them."

Relief washed over me. He stumbled to the stereo and punched a button. His voice warbled through the basement as "Rebels of the Sacred Heart" kicked off with the vocals.

He turned to me and winked, his beautiful voice hitting every note. Then he set down his glass and prowled toward me.

"Tipsy much?" I hollered over the feel-good Irish chords.

He swayed over me. "Rubbered. Blootered. Pole-axed"—he swished a finger in the air—"Monkeyed. Rat-arsed. But tipsy? Naw."

I ducked under him and stood. "We should get some sleep. Separately."

"Away on a' that. Sing with me." He followed me around the couch, belting lyrics to the rafters.

Holy fuck, he was adorable. His roughened lilt, the cleft of his stubborn chin, the way his boyish smile turned my hardened heart into butter. In matters of intimacy, he was just a boy.

I powered off the stereo mid-verse and tugged him back to the couch.

He fell against me and gripped the back of my thighs. His hands inched up and cupped my rear. "Give me a snog, love."

"A what? Never mind." I wrestled his hands away. "It's bedtime for bonzo." I turned him, gave him a hard push. He fell on the couch. When I returned with a blanket to tuck him in, he grabbed my arm and yanked me on top of him.

I perched on my elbows above him. "What's this about?"

His eyebrows jumped across his forehead. "Den' ye drive all your men to drink?"

"Silly mick, if you weren't drinking yourself stupid, you'd be chasing pots of gold at the end of rainbows."

His grin fell away under red tingeing in his cheeks. "That's mean."

I smirked. "Oh, aye."

He flipped me over and kicked my knees out with his legs. Then he settled his hips between my thighs. "I surrender." Whiskey puffed against my mouth. "If I were honest, I surrendered the day ye walked into Lloyd's local."

For the first time, he let me feel how aroused he was. I grabbed a fistful of curls and yanked his head back. His body followed. Free of his weight, I powered a knee into his gut. His breath rushed out with an oomph.

I slipped off the couch and stooped over him. "You get drunk to work up the nerve to have sex with me?"

"Liquid courage."

A rush of resentment curled my hands into fists. I ached for this man, who would kill for me and die for me, but wouldn't fuck me sober. "Go to hell."

"Aw Evie, it's not like that. It's..." He ran his hands over his face and slurred, "Ye know I'm...I've not touched a woman until..."

His eyes dropped to my chest. I crossed my arms and cleared my throat.

"Ye know wha' I was thinking about that night ye walked into Lloyd's?"

"Altar boys and dried up convent titties?"

"Jaysus, no." He fidgeted with the hem of his tee. "But shagging was heavy on me mind. Sitting a' that bar, thinking I'd never see a woman again, I felt sick. The decision to break me vow—had I wanted to—was taken from me."

"Should've made it easier."

"Easier? Having the existence of women wiped clean from the planet made me realize I would *never* know the love of one."

Never. Despite his slurred statement, I felt the pain of that one word. "That's fucked up."

"Right." He leaned forward, stared at the floor. "Then a woman walked in. The sexiest, most courageous thing I'd ever seen. I wanted...I never wanted something so badly."

"Oh my God." How had I misjudged him so completely that night? "You're a priest. I thought I was safe with you."

His head shot up. "Ye were. I mean ye are. I wouldn't have—" He pushed back his shoulders. "I've never even bashed the bishop."

My jaw dropped.

"Ye know, rubbed one off—"

"Stop. Shit. I know what it means. Christ, Roark." I crouched before him. "You told me to trust your discipline. Despite all your teasing, I did trust you. And now you're drunk enough to forgo it? Your timing sucks." Blood boiling, I paced in front of the couch. "Sleep it off or take a cold shower. And for the record, I fucking hate your vow."

His expression shuttered, fingers digging into his jean-clad thighs. He stared at me for a long time, carving away my anger. But I glared right back, willing him to understand. Then something changed. The air between us shifted, sizzled, charged.

He rose from the couch, stepped toe-to-toe with me, looking suspicious and gorgeous, smiling down at me.

I put a hand over the low waistline of my sweatpants, as if to hide the frenzy pulsing below. "What are you—"

He silenced me with a kiss. Irish whiskey flavored the tongue dancing with mine. My already rapid pulse picked up its pace.

He pulled away. "Of all the carnal temptations over the years, I've never wavered. Do ye know why it's different with ye?"

"Holing up with the world's last lass for endless weeks might have something to do with it."

"Nah, love. Let me show ye."

He pulled my hand from my belly. Fingertips balancing on mine, he slid them over my palm, up my forearm to the inside of my elbow. Goose bumps trailed. In sync, he guided my fingers over his palm, his arm, my caress mimicking his.

Static skated my skin, lifting the hairs on my arms. My body trembled.

"Do ye feel that?"

I swallowed, nodded, swallowed again.

He nodded too, padding a finger across my lips. I let him raise my hand and mirror the movement on him. His mouth was so pliant, inviting. His eyes hooded in sultry slits. Drunk Roark was delicious. My womb clenched.

He pressed his palm over my heart. I followed suit. His beat under my hand, thumping in chorus with mine, surged tingles through my limbs and blood roaring in my head. My empty chest filled with...what? The sensation was fluttery, but intense. I knew that feeling.

"Evie?"

"Mm?"

"Wha' do ye feel?"

Throbbing under my palm, mere inches beneath muscle and bone. His vitality. The thing I fed so ravenously on. The thing that made me long for a future. "The song."

"It's one hell of a feckin' song. Never felt anything like it." A finger hooked my waistband, yanked my body flush with his. He used my surprise to capture my mouth.

What of soul was left, I wonder, when the kissing had to stop?

Robert Browning

CHAPTER TWENTY-FOUR: THE ROAD TO TRUTH

A hundred objections beginning with "Don't" assembled on my tongue, until they melded, transformed, and escaped as one. "Don't stop."

He didn't. Mouths locked in urgency, we staggered toward the bed, stripped it of bug infested blankets, laughing into that kiss and tumbling on the mattress, not once severing our joined lips.

The bunker filled with the rip and rustle of shed clothes. Finally naked, our hands explored. Mine on his chest, the cut lines of his back, the cleft of his gorgeous ass. His drew in, closing around my breasts, following my ribs, over the swell of my belly.

When fingers found the wet heat between my thighs, elation sloughed away whatever willpower I had left to stop it. His mouth took mine and I met his demands, lick after lick, wanting him more and more.

I centered myself in the flex of the body draping mine. The iron erection thrusting against my thigh, miming sex, was affirmation of his intent.

He raised his body, lips parted and watched his fingers move between my legs. In and out. Round and round. "So soft. Slick." Eyes flicked to mine, accent thick. "Sacred."

"Voodoo," I breathed, widening my thighs.

A husky laugh barreled from his throat. "Aye, ye randy temptress."

I closed my eyes, saw myself standing nude under an apple tree. Vines swayed around me. Except one of those vines was a snake hissing in my ear. Temptation. Fruit. Sin.

My lids fluttered up. Through the alcohol and guilt-ridden fog, I found the question still worrying me. "How drunk are you?"

He shook his head, eyes glittering. "Your deadly body sobers a lad straight away."

Conflicting emotions railroaded me. Leading the pack was apprehension. It was going to happen. When the aftershocks settled, where would we stand?

I grabbed his face, held it between my palms. "This can't come between us. Understand?"

Mouth bowed in a lopsided grin, his hips closed the distance, erection replacing fingers, nudging me. Those fingers slipped into my mouth, letting me taste my arousal, then moved to my hair, knotting and pulling. His gaze, as naked as our bodies, searched mine. "This"—he wiggled his hips—"*will* come between us." Then he thrust.

"Ugn." His head dropped, cheek stroking cheek. "Uhh...unngh."

Inch by aching inch, bliss overwhelmed me. My thighs shook with it. Our tongues collided, tangled, and I was lost. Lost in the thrumming of heartbeats, panting breaths, rolling hips.

"Oh, love. Oh, Evie. This is—"

A shudder went through him. He pulled back, mouth agape to accommodate labored breaths. "I can't..."

"No, you don't. Not now." I bent my legs, clamped his torso between my thighs and dug my heels into the muscled meat of his ass.

He released a shaky laugh, hands pinning my writhing hips. "Just need a minute, love." His brogue was intense.

Oh. A smile twisted my lips.

I held still as we stared at each other, ragged breaths mingling, the intimate connection magnifying the anticipation. Moments later, he sat up and crushed my breasts to him. Arms coiled around me, his mouth covering mine, he began to move.

I rocked in his lap, calves sawing against his back. We found a rhythm and the pleasure built. My body tensed, prepared to unfurl. Our tongues disentangled.

"Come with me," he mouthed.

I tightened my arms around his neck. I was there, teetering, nodding.

My back hit the mattress. Muscles trembled above me. Hips met mine, over and over. The pace became harder, more impassioned.

"Now." His exhale heated my cheek.

Deep inside me, his cock enlarged, stilled, released. Submerged in his groans, his scrunched face, the fists in my hair, and the drugging grind of his pelvis against my clit, my cry joined his and I followed, riding his tremors, fully sated.

When I came back to myself, I pushed against the hard muscle crushing me. It didn't move.

"Roark?"

A snore answered. Still buried inside me, his cock twitched. As I succumbed to orgasm-induced sleep, I basked in our connection, his body in mine, his perceptive ability to read my mind, and the way he wound himself around my heart.

The cave bled around me. I rolled, met the gentle features of a woman's face. Her eyes were closed. I shook her shoulders. Her head wobbled and detached from her body.

My heart pounded. Her body lay gutted. Her womb turned inside out. Bile filled my throat.

Laughter echoed. Black boots approached, kicking the swishing hem of a sable cape. "Shh. Do not fear Allah. You are a necessary instrument in my design."

My eyes snapped open, lungs pumping, my hands searching the bed beside me. Empty. I sat up.

Roark stood from the prayer bench, dressed in full cassock, rosary twisted through his fingers, expression severe. It occurred to me then, he dressed that way when he meant business.

I swallowed past a parched throat. "What's with the fuck-all mood?" I glanced at our supplies, packed and waiting by the hall. "Is it the trip today? Or something else?" Please don't let that be resentment in his eyes.

He perched a hip next to mine and cupped my face. "Was that a nightmare?"

I nodded. "They've been worse."

His hand dropped, fisted. "Bloody hell. I'm sorry. I was…" His eyes flicked to the prayer bench then the floor. "Do ye still want to leave today?"

"Yes. You?"

"Ready when ye are." He smiled, but the mirth was missing from his eyes.

I slid a finger under his white collar and tugged. "What's this about?"

He rose, a pained expression twisting his beautiful face. "I'm a man of God. Least I can do is dress like one." Taking long strides, he swept toward the hall.

Unease boiled to realization. "Oh my fucking God. You regret it? You regret what we did?"

He froze, turned. "Ye should find another blasphemy. Coming from a non-believer, that one sounds hollow."

Fire swept through my bloodstream. I marched toward him, gloriously naked, aware of the remnants of sex crusting my thighs and how my tits bounced with every stomp. I put my face in his and shoved him. The mountain didn't move.

"You self-righteous fucker." I shoved again. "Whose name were you groaning while pumping your saintly dick in me?" I cupped my chest. "'Oh, Evie. Oh, love.' Certainly wasn't your god's. You fucking enjoyed it and that makes you feel like a rat-bastard."

His eyes flared, face crimson.

My heart hit the floor and shattered into a million pieces. My voice came out whispered, broken. "You're safe with your vow. I'm going alone."

A hiss whistled through his teeth. "Ballix. I vowed to protect ye, if it's the last vow I can hold." He stepped back. "I'll be waiting by the door." Then he spun, leaving a tornado of emotional debris in his wake.

In the truck, loaded with food, ammo and petrol, our journey north took us through rippling moors and quaint villages. The drive was tedious, dodging men and aphids. And the brooding priest beside me made it worse.

He wouldn't talk about the barbed-wire wall erected between us. His silence only stabbed the spikes further in my wound.

When I pushed, he jerked the truck over and foraged for additional supplies. These unnecessary stops resulted in risky battles with aphids, so I stopped pressing.

At night, we slept in the truck, two feet apart. Might as well have been sleeping in separate countries.

So, why hadn't I shaken free of him? It was as easy as holding the carbine to his head and swiping the keys.

Memories of his drunken laughter, his innocent smile, and his not so innocent lips formed a knot in my gut, replacing the fury there. In my fucked up mind, I convinced myself he was just a sentinel. Someone to watch my back.

Weak. I was so fucking weak.

Several days and seven hundred kilometers later, we reached the basin of the River Tweed, which bordered England and Scotland.

We didn't know how we were going to cross the Atlantic to Iceland, but he planned to filch a boat and use the ferry route to Northern Ireland. The same route he took two years prior when the outbreak forced him afield.

He sat upon a stone wall that edged a moss covered bridge and watched me bathe in the stream below. "Ye think that bloody Lakota is shadowing ye?"

I glared at him and forced myself a final dunk in the frigid water. Maybe the naked show would make his dick so hard it would crack and fall off.

"Would we know if he was following?" he asked.

"Nope."

I waded out, flushing a nuthatch bird from its pecking spot.

He leaned forward, elbows on knees. Our interactions were so attuned, we could communicate with the exchange of a look or slight gesture. As we shared a glance across the space between us, we knew the other's hurt. We didn't need to vocalize feelings or hash out issues. What we needed was an impossible solution.

The sun dipped below the lea that stretched beyond the bluff we parked on. The night was made darker by the wall of clouds charging in.

An hour later, sleet pounded, drenching our clothes and chasing us into the shelter of a limestone cave.

Settled and dried on our bedroll, he sat beside me, his outstretched hand offering an opened can of chili and a spoon.

"Are ye well?" he asked, five days behind.

I snorted.

"This land reminds me of me boyo home."

It rained a lot in that climate, which kept the aphids away. But who fucking cared? "We need to talk."

He dug a spoon in my can then slipped it between his lips, that talented tongue licking both sides. "I know."

My eyes went back to our dinner. Why the hell was I torturing myself? I wanted him, but I couldn't have him. More painful silence stretched between us.

He set down his spoon. "Right then. I'll go first."

Hands gripped my shoulders, pulled my back to his chest, and legs straddled my sides. His breath teased my nape.

My reaction was to explode in a whirlwind of attacking limbs, but it only came out as a flinch and a sputtering broken heart. Never mind days of pent up anger. It was comforting to be close to him. I reprimanded myself, but didn't pull away. I missed him and that was that.

"I den' regret making love to ye. It was brilliant, amazing. Sacred." He sucked in a breath. "I will never forget it."

My chest constricted. "That sounds...final."

His brow touched my shoulder. "I'm still a priest." A heavy sigh. "A priest in love with a beautiful woman. I broke me vow. Doesn't make it go away. I just have to try harder."

Every muscle in my body tensed. In love? Had I become so greedy as to try to turn him away from his god or prevent him from being the man he wanted to be? But I'd felt his desire, he'd been there with me, every step of the way. "So the ladybugs, the song, the magnetism between us...that means nothing?"

His arms snaked around me, squeezed. "It means everything. Wha' we have"—his hand pressed against my chest—"this bond won't go away. I can't stomach the idea of not holding ye, laughing and fighting with ye, kissing ye—"

I shoved his hand away. "Kissing me?"

"Friends kiss."

Friends. "So I let you kiss me and paw me and pretend your steel hard dick—which is currently stabbing my back—doesn't exist?"

He groaned. "Aye right."

I spun in his arms and raised a brow. "And I can prance around naked, use my bullet in bed beside you as long as fiery, sweaty sex remains off the table?"

A bulge bounced in his throat. "Ye wen' make this easy, em? The answer's the same."

I climbed to my feet, a heaping dose of doubt fortifying my stance. "Problem is, Father Molony, we've moved beyond friendship. The little ditty you brought to light—you know, the shivering dance of electricity you feel under our *friendly* touches?—I can't ignore that. So, while you're clinging to your celibacy, remember one thing. I took no such vow. You being unavailable makes me available to others." The thought made me sick.

His gaze drifted up, eyes insoluble despite the wetness there. "I told ye. I den' expect the same in return."

I wasn't sure if I was more hurt by his rejection or the fact that he accepted me sleeping with another man. The agony of it pivoted my boots, sent me tearing through the pelting rain.

Lightening illuminated a rapeseed field in a golden glow. The protection of the rain ensured no aphids. I took advantage of the respite and ran through the sodden stems, leaves clinging to my jeans. On and on I went. My legs softened and my body shook with chills.

Eventually, exhaustion won and I found myself trudging toward the truck, slumping behind the wheel and fighting sleep as the miserable fucking night forced itself upon me.

Tap-tap.

I shivered awake. Curtained by the night sky, stars speckled through the windshield. The rain had moved out, which meant the aphids would move in.

Hard muscle curled around me. Oh, hell no. How had I not heard him climb into the truck?

I tugged his arm from under my shirt and turned it over to read his watch. I blinked and read it again. Almost sunrise. I tossed his arm.

Though his breaths hiccupped, his rigid jaw—which had been locked for days in resolution—was at ease under the pull of gravity. Whiskers shadowed the perfect sculpture of his face. I reached out. Just one stroke—

Tap-tap. Tap-tap.

A fingernail on glass. I scrambled up Roark's chest and away from the driver's side window. Darkness hovered on the other side. I shook his shoulders. "Wake up."

The smooth pace of his breaths in sleep didn't falter. I shook him again. "Roark. Roark?" His head lolled against the back of the seat. I turned back to the window. Yellow-green eyes glowed over the door.

Come away, O human child:
To the waters and the wild with a fairy, hand in hand,
For the world's more full of weeping than you can understand.

William Butler Yeats

CHAPTER TWENTY-FIVE: FLYPAPER

My pulse kept its frantic beat as the glowing discs dimmed and melted into the dark. I hauled the carbine sling over my head and climbed out. Roark didn't stir.

The black sky fused with the black landscape and seemed to drain the winter chill from the air. My socks warmed against the dry ground. Dry? How could that be?

I called out into the night, "Aaron?"

"Mama?"

I spun back to the truck.

Annie sat on the hood, legs stretched before her. "You came."

"I-I didn't"—I swallowed past a burning lump—"Sweetheart, you came to me."

She looked around. I followed her eyes, scanning the darkness that enveloped the bluff. Beyond the rush of my breaths, there was no twittering of nocturnal critters. No ruffling plumage of ducks hunkering in the wetlands. No wind whispering through the frost-laced grasses. No life.

She shook her head. "You're in our world."

Their world? My thoughts traced back to the day I saw them by the pool. The day I cremated my father. The day I woke to discover Joel's death. In those moments, when the absence of life weighed on me, wasn't it an unbalanced ecosystem? Was I treading outside the world of the living? How was that possible?

I moved to the truck's window, pressed my face against it. Roark's chest moved up and down, his eyes closed.

"You brought him here. I like him," Annie said, her smile forever missing the same two teeth.

Aaron climbed onto the hood and plopped beside her. "I liked the ladybugs bestest." He clasped his hands to his chest. "Will you bring them again, Mommy?"

Annie elbowed him. "Not now. We got her across the big ocean. She doesn't have time for ladybirds."

My legs wobbled. I gripped the side mirror. "What do you mean?" My hand went to my chest, where the tug used to be. "That was you?"

Chin raised, she tapped the toes of her tennis shoes together and hummed.

Aaron huffed, "I help."

The burn in my throat worked its way to my nose and spread behind my eyes. "Why?"

Their heads swiveled toward the windshield, their eyes locked on Roark.

"Him?" I asked.

"Your fixer." Annie grinned.

"Fixer?" I stepped toward them until my legs bumped the front tire. "What does he fix?"

She cocked her head. "He fixed your ouchie." Her finger drew a circle over my heart. "Now you care."

My throat closed, strangled my voice. "Care?"

"You'll save them, Mama."

Them? The nymphs? I couldn't ask. I wanted to protect my A's from the world they left. I wanted to spend that time holding them and telling them I would never stop loving them.

I opened my arms, reaching. The vapor that shaped them waved, slipped through my fingers. They didn't seem to notice.

A choke escaped my lips. I pulled back and tucked my clenched fists under my arms. The blaze in my sinuses swelled. After a lifetime of dry eyes, maybe I would finally cry.

A gasp returned my attention to Aaron. His eyes were wide, staring at the lea beyond the bluff. "He's here."

"Who?"

A tremendous roar whooshed from above. The truck wobbled back and forth on its frame.

The sky opened up and peeled away the night in a flash of light. The wind tunneled toward Annie and Aaron, spun their bodies, and carried them away.

I pounded my hands on the hood. "Nooo."

My screams chased the vortex into the blinding rays of the sun. The saturated ground soaked into my socks. The crisp air penetrated my bones, bringing with it the sudden orchestra of chirping birds, the pushing of water between the banks of River Tweed, and the buzzing of aphids. The truck's door slammed.

"Evie. What's wrong?" Roark's hand brushed my cheek. Then he stilled. "Do ye hear that?"

"Aphids." Their buzzing amplified in volume and complexity. I raised the carbine and followed the vibrations to the edge of the bluff.

The hum became more deafening, like the buzz of a million flies breeding on ol' Hurlin's stallions.

At the edge of the bluff, his hand found mine. Hundreds of aphids corralled below. In the center, two human boys clawed and kicked for their lives.

Could we save them? Distract the bugs somehow?

He tugged my hand. "Too many. We need to get away from this cliff. To the van—"

Scraping footsteps crept over my shoulder. We spun, his sword outstretched, his other hand shoving me behind him.

Aphids encircled us. Carbine, leveled, I stepped around him, picking them off, counting down the rounds. Thirty...twenty-nine...twenty-eight...

Buzzing numbed my ears. Beside me, his sword thrashed side to side to stave them off.

The carbine tapped my shoulder. Nine...eight...

There were too many. I needed ammo from the truck, which had vanished behind the quivering swarm.

Two rounds left. The dozen or so remaining aphids shuffled closer with ravenous purpose. We backed to the edge. Their food had nowhere to go.

The buzzing ceased. Roark wrapped his free arm around my waist and mantled me with his body.

A gap opened in the center of the swarm and the mutants calmed. A dark haired man emerged from the parting.

Roark risked a quick glance at me. I shook my head. Not the Drone. Still, the man's tawny complexion and ominous eyes were familiar.

Flanked by several aphids, he swaggered closer. His xanadu-tinged uniform stretched across his puffed out chest and squared shoulders. He stopped a few feet before us and tumbled a chuckle between puffs from his cigar. "So, you're the menacing little chit who's been shooting up my soldiers."

His hair shined as black as his enlarged pupils and clipped close to his skull. A thick scarlet scar zagged his forehead and begged me to sight it with the carbine. I obliged.

"And you are?" I asked around the carbine.

"The Imago." He rolled the vowels.

I laughed. "The Imago?"

"Yes. A title I've earned as the leader of the aphid army."

"These mutants are your...soldiers?" Roark asked.

"Impressive, yes? And this is just a small battalion. There's more to see."

He swept his eyes to the aphids closest to us. "Bring them." He turned, put his back in my scope. I squeezed the trigger.

A streak of green blotted my sight. I lowered the barrel. Black blood coursed from the aphid at my feet. A bodyguard.

I returned to high ready, sighted the Imago's back. One round left.

Roark's sword clanked on the rocky ground. Beside it, he bowed his head, a speared mouth angled at his neck. His captor's hunger tore through me in waves.

I dropped the barrel, fought my panic. "Imago. Call off your fucking bug."

The Imago's soulless eyes appeared over his shoulder. "Relinquish the gun."

"Den' give it," Roark said from his bent position.

Outnumbered, I shrugged out of the sling and offered it to the aphid at his neck. Spit dripped from the sharp beak of its mandible, its pearly orbs hypnotizing. Snarls wheezed past its jowls.

It released Roark and snatched the gun from my hands.

All at once, the buzzing resumed. Roark lurched to my side, arms suffocating me against his tense body. "Ye wreck me nerves, woman. I'll be dealing with ye in a severe and violent manner after this."

"Such optimism."

The aphids pushed us forward with mere intimidation. When we reached the valley, Roark crushed my face to his chest. The boys' transitional cries fractured the icy air. Their mutation had begun.

The Imago prowled through his brigade, chuffing and tapping his cigar. The biceps embracing me went taut every time the Imago cast a look in my direction. I wanted to fight. Or run. I wanted to do something besides stand before that mad man and await our fate. How did he control the bugs? They crowded us shoulder to shoulder.

I could feel their hunger as if it were my own. But not one made a move to bite.

The Imago staked his post before me and sucked from his cigar. With a gloved hand, he lifted my chin. "My brother is here and he will be pleased."

He squinted at the cliff. *Whoomp-whoomp-whoomp* clapped down the rocky crag, a sound I hadn't heard since the outbreak. Then the helicopter emerged in view.

Our hair and clothes lashed around us as it landed. My heart banged on my ribs. Roark enfolded me like body armor, his mouth at my ear. "We'll get through this. Den' lose your head."

The first man disembarked the chopper. Black curls wound over a sable cape. His onyx eyes narrowed on me. The Imago's brother. My nightmare in flesh. Cold sweat trickled between my breasts.

Roark's lilt was low. "Is he…"

He craned his neck and found his answer in my eyes. My wrist ached under the pressure from his fingertips.

A claw caught his arm. An insectile mouth pressed under his white collar. Still, he hung on to me as the Imago pried me from his arms.

Roark was one stab away from infection. All it would take was the slightest pressure from that speared mouth. I didn't dare fight back.

With the aid of his aphid army, the Imago made quick work of binding and gagging us. I twisted my arms against the knots on my wrists. Remembered pain gurgled up. With it, came bile and tremors.

The Imago's brother approached with the second man from the chopper. The brothers exchanged a clasp of hands and the Imago said, "The human boys were like sugar on flypaper. Our little fly"— his eyes lingered over me—"buzzed right to the cliff, unable to flee our sweet trap."

The man with the onyx eyes towered over me. "Eveline"—my name rolled from his tongue like a French wine—"it is a pleasure to meet you. I am the Drone."

Roark's breathing at my side reminded me that crunching the Drone's nose with my head would hurt Roark. They would use him against me, the only reason they kept him alive.

"This is my partner, Dr. Michio Nealy. He is going to help you relax for our trip."

If Dr. Nealy hadn't been pulling a syringe from his bag, I would've admired the chary almond shaped eyes and smooth complexion of his Asian heritage. But as he dripped solute from the hollow point, I fantasized using it as a skewer to pluck those eyes from his head.

The Drone glanced at Roark. "I fear you won't behave when we separate you from your priest."

I bucked in the Imago's grip as he canted, "Nighty-night. Don't let the bed bugs bite."

Roark's gaze steadied me. I lobbed him a silent demand. *Stay alive. Promise me.* Then I lunged against the arms that held me and pressed my face against his. He exhaled a resolute breath around his gag. He willed me to be strong.

A sting pricked my neck. Warmth tingled through me as the sedative pumped from the needle.

The *V* of Roark's brows, the stretched muscles in his neck and his peeled-back lips exposed the wrath that consumed him. His teeth ground his gag, the whites blurring to black.

I held onto the vengeance in his eyes as the ground rose up and slammed into my face.

Rust grows from iron and destroys it;
so evil grows from the mind of man and destroys him.

Buddha

CHAPTER TWENTY-SIX: L'ISOLA DEL VESCOVO

My ears perked to the low hum of white noise, air whispering through a vent. The vibration and whine of engine fan blades indicated transit. The helicopter? Too quiet. Quiet enough to hear breathing. I wasn't alone.

Eyelids, weighed down with sedation, refused to let in light. I willed them open and blinked through the drug-induced fog.

The Drone slid a haughty smile from across a foldaway table. The doctor perched beside him, his nose in a book.

Clouds whisked by tiny windows lining the narrow cabin. Straps over my neck and arms held me firm against one of four leather seats, two facing two, the table between.

Ivory gauze draped my body toga-style from shoulder to bare feet. The knot in my gut tightened. Whose hands touched my body while dressing me? What else had they done while I was at their mercy?

Gloved fingertips slithered along my arm. I jerked as much as the shackles allowed. The Imago hovered a breath away. The black of his eyes matched the lashes feathering his lids. He ridged his forehead, the scarlet scar defying the folds. My fingers curled into the armrest.

Surrounded by three monsters—still men in form, but monsters all the same—what were my options? Without the carbine, it couldn't be solved with a three pound trigger pull.

I pointed my glare at the man molesting my arm. "Which one are you in the trifecta? First, second or worst?"

The Drone's discomfiting laugh rattled the cabin. "Seems my brother is besotted." His tone lowered. "While his attentions linger on your mouth, he forgets the affliction it may volley."

What a douche bag. I showed none of the symptoms. Whatever. Letting them think I was a nymph would discourage rape. I hoped.

He picked up a spoon and stirred a powder into his tea cup. "Only a few more hours, brother, and we'll confirm our suspicions."

Or until I could free him of that spoon and gut them one by one with it. "Where's the priest?"

The Drone's cruel eyes were at odds with the delicate manner in which he placed the tea cup to his lips. "He's en route to Malta."

"What?" My organs crashed into one another in a frantic pounding. "What's in Malta?"

As if on cue, the pilot announced our approach to the archipelago off the coast of Italy. The Drone turned up his mouth. "Your new home."

"Release the priest. He has nothing—"

My tongue collided with the scratchy cloth of a gag. The Imago tightened the tie at the back of my head.

When the plane landed, I remained tethered to the Imago's side. His eyes stalked me as I gnawed at the fabric that desisted my questions.

He tossed me into the backseat of the SUV, an arm stretched across my thigh. Oh, the things I would do if I had a dull knife. I would start at the elbow in my lap, sawing the serrated edge back and forth. A flap of skin. A strip of muscle. And when only the bone kept it attached, I would snap it over my knee and regift the appendage in his very own sodomy—

"Welcome to Manoel Island," the Drone chirped from the front seat. Darkness swallowed the mainland behind us as we crossed a bridge, the doctor driving, the Drone narrating. "This island, *l'Isola del Vescovo* was once home to seven thousand Maltese. Now only those under my command occupy its shores."

Apparently, his command consisted of Malta's mutated humans. The flicker of aphids meandered in and out of the dusty stone buildings that crumbled along the beach. The tide sloshed against the empty docks. No boats and no humans.

We bumped along the disintegrating road into the quiet bowels of the island. From the depths, another shoreline emerged. The doctor slowed before a monolithic stone wall. I sucked in a breath.

"This," the Drone said, "is Fort Manoel. Once used as a military fortification, it has been standing since the eighteenth century." Red veins webbed his eyes.

Towering walls rose out of the Mediterranean, mocking the whipping brine and the crashing tide. A fortress meant to keep out attackers. Would I find a dungeon within? A bleeding cave? I shuddered.

On the other side of the gate, my captors escorted me up winding stairs and through one of the many stone archways that encircled an expansive brick quadrangle. The full circumference of the island was visible from that height. Desolate streets weaved between crowded buildings. Stores, docks and cars were abandoned. Not a single watercraft in sight. Not even a jet ski.

I shivered despite the sultry island breeze. We were surrounded by water, trapped on an island with aphids.

The fort's main tower eclipsed the stars. We entered the tower's anteroom ornamented with marble pillars and tropical florae.

Fingers pressed in my arm, the doctor dragged me through massive double doors. Then he removed my gag and bindings and shoved me into the heart of a hall, enclosed by a living wall of aphids.

The Drone prowled around me, chilling my bones with his glacial mien, penetrating with even colder eyes.

I steeled my voice with an equally steeled posture. "Where's the priest? I demand to see him."

The Drone's fist blurred. I dodged it, but not fast enough for the second punch. I wheeled back, void of weapons and tripping on the skirts of my gown. Blood filled my mouth. I spat, speckling the tile with crimson. The air sizzled with excited hunger. Huffing snarls and quivering limbs surrounded me, overwhelmed me.

"Foolish woman." He rolled his upper lip, revealing human teeth unlike the incisors from my nightmares. A chill oozed from his syllables. "Can you not feel the vibrations of fifty thirsty mouths drumming for your blood?"

I hissed at the bugs and returned to their leader. "You fucking coward. You don't need the priest. Release him."

His laugh cracked through the room and stole the strength from my spine. "Bring the bait."

The Imago appeared in the hall, directing four men with terse commands and a wave of his cigar. They skidded and stumbled with wide eyes and clenched fists. Bruises and gashes marked their naked bodies. Why weren't they fighting back?

A brown skinned man spat at me in an indistinguishable language. An Asian man warded me off with a wave of trembling hands.

Holy hell. These men feared *me*. "Does anyone speak English?"

They panted and scooted away, heels scrubbing the tiles to speed up their retreat.

My stomach clenched. The mutants stirred. Their vibrations increased and their fragile control tipped. What was leashing them? How long could it hold?

An aphid burst from the blockade. In a blink, the Asian man hit the ground in a torsion of human and aphid limbs. I lunged onto his attacker's back and wrestled an arm under its mandible. I hoped breathing was an aphid necessity and put all my strength into the choke hold.

Agonizing moments passed. Then the bug collapsed. Not dead, not from a choke hold.

I jumped back, ready for the next attack.

The Asian man moaned through distorted features. Blood bubbled from the puncture in his chest.

My nostrils flared at the metallic smell of his blood. The scent roused something within me, increasing my connection with the aphids. They smelled it, too. Hungered for it. The united resistance wouldn't hold.

Another aphid jerked. I leapt from its path, rolled onto my shoulder, looked back.

The brown man coughed a wet, surprised gurgle. His gaze dropped to his chest where the mandible's tusk erupted, skewering his heart to his ribs.

The aphid enclosure decomposed in a mass of spines and twitching green bodies. Another man went down. One remained, defending his ground with kicks and swinging arms.

Helplessness glued my feet to the floor. Our captors, who cared so little for human life, had Roark. What would they do to him? My heart gave a painful thump. Without weapons or allies, I'd been stripped of everything I needed to beat them. Everything except the compulsion to live.

The Drone kept watch from afar. When our eyes collided, he said, "Your speed, your agility…very aphid."

A claw snapped toward me. I twisted, dodging it, and jumped on its back. We spun as I used its body as a shield against the others. It wrestled in my hold, turning to face me. We rolled to the ground and I landed with my legs squeezing its chest. I angled its mouth away and plunged my thumb into its eye. It bucked, but I kept my Jujitsu mount planted. With a hefty thrust, I pressed my hand further into its socket and met a barrier with my thumb. Its body went limp.

A vise clamped my shoulder, the sharp point of a mouth scraped my neck.

Pop.

The Imago lowered a dart gun. The aphid dropped with a thud. Smoke plumed from its pores. Its skin hissed, crackled. Then it burst in a gruesome rain, leaving a charred heap of black innards. The remaining aphids buzzed and backed away.

A hand caught my arm, yanked me to my feet. The doctor's jet eyes narrowed. Not a strand of black hair out of place. He stabbed me with a hypodermic and lifted me to his chest. As the chemical cocktail robbed my vision, his voice stroked my ear. "*Nannakola.*"

Pain pounded my temples. Through slits, the room rotated, dipped clockwise then counter-clockwise. I gritted my teeth and waited for the sedative hangover to pass.

The room stopped rocking. I lay upon a bed bordered by three stone walls. Steel bars domed over my cell and made up the fourth wall, caging me from the rest of the chamber. A heavy-duty combination lock—like the one on my gun safe—fastened to the gate. The gate was open.

Polished golden rock stretched to the sky and surfaced the floor. Wind and sun dove through the arched open rafters. The apex of the main tower.

Outside my cage, the doctor sat in padmasana, a posture I'd seen used in Buddhist mediation. Ass on the floor, back of hands on bent knees, ankles on opposing thighs, eyes closed. Another man paced behind him. The pilot maybe?

Beside me, a tray sat on a table laden with bandages, ointments and papers. All useless. Bar the scissors. They didn't know I was awake. If I moved fast enough—

I lunged for the scissors and heaved them full spin at the pacing man. They slipped between the bars of my cage and plunged his throat.

He pawed at them, his mouth working for air against the blood pooling out. Then he dislodged them, stared at them. He staggered, grabbed the back of a couch. The scissors clattered to the floor. So did he.

The doctor didn't move, but his eyes bored into mine. I fumbled through the items on the tray, gripped a pen with metal casing.

Heart thumping, I concealed it lengthwise along my arm and approached the open gate. He remained motionless, his eyes never leaving mine.

Ten feet. I straightened my arm toward his chest with a snap. The pen slipped from my grasp and sped down the invisible horizontal level.

His body bleared, rolled and collided with mine.

I skidded across the floor in a tangle of gauzy skirts. He stood over me, arms to his side, face blank.

Mother fucker. I shook my hand as if something were amiss. "Where's the priest?"

He stalked to the man heaped on the floor. "Not here yet."

I pushed off the floor, launched to his side. "Touch Roark and I'll turn your putrefied heart into a pincushion for your needle collection."

Silky black hair fell over his brow as he examined the unconscious man.

I slammed a fist toward his head. He snapped out his arm and redirected my hit inches from his face.

My pulse raced. I faked the same punch then sent a full speed kick to his groin. He flicked his wrist, intercepted my leg and used it to throw my balance. My ass hit the ground.

Fuck. I released a heavy breath and shoved the goddamn skirt out of the way.

The doctor looked up from checking the other man's vitals. "Are you done?"

I scrambled to my feet. "Not quite. Where. Is. The. Priest?"

The air shifted a half-breath before he did. His palm hit my chest, knocked me back down. The gesture was slight, as if swatting a pesky gnat. Yet it left me wheezing on my knees.

He sat seiza-style before me and tilted his head. "Are you done?"

I took to my feet again and lobbed an arcing punch to his jaw. He floated up and caught my punch. With a twist of hips, he shot out a foot and swooped me to my butt. Agony jarred my joints.

He hovered inches from my face. "Are you done?"

I angled to the side and found my footing. Feet spread, toes pointed in the same direction, I poised my power hand at my jaw.

His arms lolled at his side, legs relaxed hip-width apart. His reflexes paralleled a martial artist, but didn't demonstrate a specific style. And his eyes—caught between shades of black and more black—divulged nothing. His loose cotton pants and shirt couldn't conceal his strapping physique. His attractiveness made me despise him more.

We stared at each other in a suspended moment. I acknowledged the Lakota for teaching me to appreciate tense silence.

Then he was on me. Arm under my neck, I gasped for air as he dragged me to the cell. The more I clawed, the more pressure he applied. White spots dappled my vision. My arms dropped.

He released me in the cell and locked the gate between us. Then he squatted next to the man. "You have questions. I have questions." He hiked the body over his shoulder and turned to me. "So we'll trade answers. Fair?"

No. My freedom would be fair, but I nodded, heat burning through my face. "Is that man dead?"

"Yes." He opened the door. A staircase descended on the other side. An aphid bared its feral mouth from its guard position. The doctor dodged the snapping jaws and slammed the door.

I didn't feel bad about killing that man. I planned to kill them all.

The doctor returned minutes later. He crossed his arms and leaned against the bars. "Who taught you to fight?"

A swallow lodged in my throat. Would that answer be used against me? I didn't think so. "My husband."

"Your priest is on a ship. About a day out. Guarded by men, not aphids. He will not be released. Do not ask it. But he will not be harmed as long as you cooperate." A pause. "Where is your husband now?"

I raised my chin. "Given his skill set, I assume he's sketching my escape and his revenge as we speak."

"Is that how you want to play this game?"

Fists clenched at my sides. "My husband's dead."

He didn't reward my honesty with a reaction.

I narrowed my eyes. "Are you going to kill me?"

"No. Did you have children?"

A burn penetrated my chest. "Yes."

Questions crowded my mind. I needed to know as much as I could about the army. "What was in the dart that smoked the aphid in the hall?"

"Blood from a nymph."

A slick sweat of unease glistened my skin. Don't freak out. Keep him talking. I mirrored his casual stance. "Uh huh."

"I assume you know a nymph is a partially transformed woman. One who didn't fully mutate."

"Yeah."

"Her blood is poisonous to an aphid. The Imago uses it to control the army. One drop burns the aphid from the inside out and explodes the heart."

Fuck. That explained the bursting body parts. Fear of it alone controlled them? But that was a human emotion.

His eyes probed me, unraveling my composure. "How did you know the Drone?"

Damn his questions. "I didn't."

"Recognition lit up your face when you saw him." His glare hardened. "Lie to me again and I'll take the answers through whatever means necessary."

What, did he carry truth serum in those damn vials? Or would he just beat it out of me? Fuck it. "He visited me in dreams." I leveled my eyes with his empty ones. "Explain the human bloodbath in the hall."

"The Drone is Muslim and has a flair for theatrics. Hence, your ceremonial gown. Which reminds me..." He walked to a closet across the room and removed flowing blue garments. "He'll have you veiled from now on." He tossed a long skirt at me through the bars. "This is a *daaman.*" Next came a blouse. "*Pirahan.*" Something like a headscarf landed on top. "*Hijab.* Put them on."

Was he kidding? "When you eat an aphid dick."

He put his face between two bars. "You might be doing just that in the next demonstration if you're not covered."

Nausea waved through me. "You still haven't explained the last demonstration."

"The humans were a test to determine if you were infected. They were injected with antiandrogens."

I met his hard stare and shook my head.

"Antiandrogens make aphids crazed with hunger. Even a nymph can't resist it." He shrugged. "But you did. So the Drone no longer considers you a threat."

Good. Let him think that. The smell of the men's blood in the hall did stir me. Maybe it was the antiandrogens. "So you let four innocent men die? The absence of a spear in my mouth didn't provide enough evidence?"

He watched me through the bars, his body motionless. "Did the virus kill your children?"

"Yes, you unfeeling asshole." Even as I derided him, I suspected he asked to satisfy a medical curiosity. He probably wondered if my children carried the same immunity as me. Still, I wanted to use my dagger to carve a permanent frown on the blank canvas that was his face. "Explain the mutation differences between nymphs and aphids."

"There are two ways to become an aphid." He uncrossed his arms and ticked them off on his fingers. "One. You're a human bitten by a nymph or an aphid. Two. You're the nymph that does the biting."

"Wait. So a nymph can become an aphid?"

He nodded, eyes glinting. He fell so easily into that line of questioning, as if he'd forgotten I was his prisoner. I hadn't forgotten.

"When the nymph feeds from a human, her blood merges with her victim's and completes her mutation to aphid. She also releases a poisonous compound that mutates her victim into an aphid."

So when a nymph feeds from a human, they both turn aphid. Which meant aphids came from men and women. Did they retain their gender? Could they reproduce? The questions piled up. How many more could I ask before he ended the game? Make them count. "Do aphids and nymphs feed from each other?"

"It's not a common occurrence, but it happens. The result is death for both. Their blood is poisonous to each other, as is the compound they release."

Too bad we couldn't just lock them all up and let them kill each other. Except I didn't want that for the nymph in the cabin. If she never fed from a human, she would never become an aphid. How did she avoid it? Did her reclusive home keep her suspended in transition? But I was there. She could've attacked me. She seemed more interested in protecting her dead children. "Do you think will alone could keep a nymph from attacking a human?"

"Don't know. But we know nymphs are extremely rare. The Drone has sent his messengers across the planet looking for them.

And women." He studied my face. "You're the only woman he's found. Your blood test confirmed your high testosterone level, which has something to do with your immunity."

I gripped the bars next to his face. "My blood test?"

He didn't flinch. "Your aggression is a symptom of high testosterone. As is your muscle strength. I assume you also have a demanding sex-drive?"

"What blood test?"

"I took your blood on the plane when I changed your clothes."

Tension racked my body. "What else have you discovered?"

"I'm still analyzing it."

His monotone voice chaffed my skin. "What do you and the sadistic brothers want with me?"

"To study you."

"What are your qualifications, Dr. Nealy?"

"I hold a medical degree and my expertise is in molecular biology and genetics. The Drone is a Biochemist. We want to learn about your survival and your connection to the aphid."

"So I'm the lab rat? To help you control your mutant army?"

"How did you get the scar?" His gaze dropped to my chest.

My hand flew to my neckline, covered by the gown. My other hand shot through the bars, toward his jaw. His body bowed backwards. My fist punched air.

He stepped back. The door crashed open behind him.

"Why isn't she dressed in proper attire?" the Drone shouted through the chamber.

"She refused." The doctor's unemphatic response.

"She refused? She is not allowed to refuse. You assured me you could handle this, Michio. If you are not able to accomplish even the simplest task—"

"I do not need handling," I said. "And I decide what I wear."

The Drone strolled over to the gate. "Open it."

The doctor dialed in the combination and opened the gate.

A brass knuckle dagger appeared in the Drone's fist. He handed it to the Imago, who stood behind him, and floated into the cell, sable cloak slapping at the bars. The sunlight seemed to twist and slide away to oblige his oily aura. The lock slammed in place.

I braced my feet and met his eyes, though every muscle in my body screamed at me to attack.

He pointed a finger at the *hijab*. "You will cover yourself. Now."

The hellish wings and driveling incisors in my nightmares were my own imagining. I supposed him being human was a small relief. Still, a sinister overcast enshrouded him and aroused the hairs on my arms.

I lifted my chin and shook my head.

My back hit the wall. The Drone's nails curled into my neck as he held my face level with his. I gasped for air and stretched my toes, unable to feel the ground.

Cold lips stroked my face. "Just a flex of my fingers, Eveline, and I will squeeze your last breath from your lungs."

Pain seared my throat. I kicked his legs until he pinned my lower body with his. My lungs labored for air. I opened my mouth. His fist trapped my voice. He bent his head and moved his grasp from my jugular to my nape. I gulped, filled my lungs, and whispered through the burn, "Okay—"

His teeth plunged into my neck.

Science has not yet taught us if madness is
or is not the sublimity of the intelligence.

Edgar Allan Poe

CHAPTER TWENTY-SEVEN: SUBLIMITY

Fire lashed my throat and chased a chill down the length of my spine. The Drone's arms and teeth restrained me against the wall.

The doctor's face filled my vision, eyes dark and unreadable. "Let her go." His voice lowered. "And don't swallow. We don't know the effects of her blood."

The Drone's growl reverberated against my throat. He released my neck, his smile brimmed with blood-tinged teeth, and puckered to spit crimson dollops at my feet.

I slapped a hand to my neck and palmed the hurt there. Had he bitten me out of madness or was he trying to imbibe something from my blood? And how would I keep them from using Roark as leverage? The unknowns lumped up in my gut. I tried to smooth them out with fantasies of the Drone's head tilted at an unnatural angle, his spinal column protruding from the stiff collar of his shirt. His necrotic eyes yellowed and his tongue buoying in a mouth of vomit—

"You will cover yourself. If not, your priest will be covered in kind with blood."

I stiffened. My nightmare was true to form, with his ringlets of black hair, sable cloak, even the purr of his accent.

It brought up the troubling question of how I was able to foresee him in visions. Even more troubling were the words he spoke in those dreams. *Together we will populate the world with Allah's chosen.*

Queasiness mingled with my rising blood pressure and laced my rebuttal with acridity. Or stupidity. "Fine. I'll conceal my body to prevent your dick from saluting your desire. It'll make it hard to knock me up. And by hard, I don't mean firm." I pointed my gaze at the zipper of his black pants.

The room stilled, teetered on a deadly edge as if the air itself were afraid to move. The Imago's cigar paused halfway to his mouth. Beside me, the doctor shifted his weight.

The Drone's pupils saturated his eyes. His chest ballooned with an influx of air and his face turned to stone. "What do you know of my plans?"

No way would I reveal my foresight, whatever it was. So I shrugged. "A blind person couldn't miss your narcissist Hitler wannabe act."

The back of his hand slammed into my mouth. Ow, fuck. Real smart. I kept my arms at my sides, face blank, refused to reveal the pain rattling my teeth.

"You will heed the glorious words in Sura 33:59." The black of his eyes, so dense and endless, gripped me in a gravitational pull. "'Tell your wives, your daughters, and the wives of the believers that they should lengthen upon themselves their outer garments.' You *will* obey."

Not fucking likely. I blinked, broke the influence of his stare. Then I wadded up the oppressive garments and chucked them. Cloth billowed around the bars.

Ready that time, I assumed a battle bearing. Raised chin, shoulders back, planted feet, and a do-your-worst glare.

"Blood runs from multiple wounds and still you challenge me?"

I'd prepared for a punch. Not the purr in his voice and the curious glint in his eyes.

He pivoted toward his brother with unwavering equilibrium, as if his feet didn't touch the floor. "When Father Molony arrives, bring him to the hall. Eveline will receive her first lesson in respect."

The spike of my pulse sent me hurtling after him. I smacked into a brick body. Lifted my chin. Followed the peaks and dips of the doctor's chest. Longed for my daggers. When I reached his black eyes, his head shook once.

Over the doctor's shoulder, the Drone's glare exuded a chill I felt in my bones. "I will not deign to your indignities. Remember this. The more you fight me, the sweeter your submission will be." A pink tongue wormed over his teeth. "I can taste it already."

The door closed, leaving me alone with the doctor. He gathered the swaths of cloth and shoved them to my chest. "Pick your battles, *Nannakola*."

I shouldered away from him and those damned garments. "Why do you call me that?"

He spread them out on the bed. "I'll tell you if you tell me about the scar."

"Free the priest and I'll tell you anything you want."

"Get dressed. The Drone will be waiting."

Crescents bloomed on my palms. My nails dug deeper. I forced images of Roark bloodied in chains to hold myself back from smiting the doctor with every dirty fighting technique I knew. A whirlwind of hate crashed through me and poured from my mouth. "I'll pick my battle, you son of a bitch. And when I do, it'll end with your blood on my hands."

All I got was a twitch in his jaw. Then he turned on his heels and locked the cell behind him, keeping his back to me. I let my blood soaked gown drop to the floor and wished I felt as confident as I sounded.

Across the table, the Drone and the Imago stared at me over plates of chick peas, curry, potatoes and naan. I pushed into the back of the chair, seeking another millimeter of separation from their tainted airspace, and was certain the chair's iron filigree would be stamped into my shoulder blades.

The hall's arched doors yawned toward the blotted blues of the Mediterranean. A view I would've appreciated under other circumstances.

Salt and seaweed clung to the drafts left by the two human men, who served us with wide eyes and pinched lips. They hurried away as quick as they came, pitchers quivering in their fists. The tension was made worse by the huffing breaths and jerking torsos waving from the wall of aphid guards. The Imago's dart gun couldn't be the only thing preventing them from attacking. I was certain there was more to it.

The Drone tore a corner off the thin bread and dipped it in a bowl of soup thick with pulses of every color. Beside me, the doctor watched my finger move beans around my plate.

Sweat gathered under my head-to-toe scarves. The wound on my neck throbbed. Each minute dragged in anticipation of Roark's arrival and the *lesson* that would follow.

I met the Drone's glare with my own. "Why did you bite me?"

He tongued the corner of his mouth. "To taste your submission." The wrinkle lines around his eyes didn't move, but his pupils pulsed.

Fuck, he was sick, but he was hiding something. I sat a little taller. "Where are your wings?"

The Imago lost his grip on his glass, dumping its contents in his lap.

The Drone remained motionless, except for the slow climb of one brow over darkening eyes. "Wings?"

"To match your vampire fangs." Pride swelled at the steadiness of my voice. Not a trace of fear despite the wild thumping in my chest. I tried to muster a smile to match but couldn't get my mouth to work right.

He curled his lip, making a show of normal teeth, and reclined in his chair. "I am bored with these questions. Further utterances from that disrespectful mouth better offer a sapid discussion."

How should I know what topics would interest a psychopath? "How did you find me?"

"Aphid messengers. They discovered you a year ago then tracked you in the U.K."

He communicated with them? Sure, I had a kind of connection with aphids, but I didn't speak their language. "How does it work? Do you hold biweekly staff meetings with coffee, crumpets and human hearts? Then you sit back and listen in on the pitch and tone of their vibrations?"

The Drone's smile was oily, slicking its way across the table, thick and heavy and oxygen stealing. The doctor seemed to feel it too if the labored movement of his chest was anything to go by.

"What are your real names?"

The smile dissipated. "Her bold inquisitiveness and shamelessly lifted eyes rub my patience. Yet, I feel compelled to answer. It is...curious." His fingers traced the flat edge of a paring knife that lay next to his plate. "My name was Dr. Aiman Jabara. And my brother was Siraj Jabara."

Was? "Why the self-dubbed titles?"

"We renounced our birth names," the Imago said, "when we accepted our new lives under Allah's guidance. Our titles are appropriate to our stations."

Did they realize how insane they sounded? More so when I remembered where I'd heard those designations. The entomology text stated a drone served one purpose: fertilizing the queen. And an imago was some kind of sexually developed insect. They chose those titles because they were appropriate? A shiver chilled the sweat on my spine.

The paring knife glinted under the Drone's fingertips. I could slip free of the doctor's invisible chain. Lunge across the table. Use that knife to flay the skin from the Drone's face. With the slightest pressure, the razor edge would curl away his epidermis and relieve him of his vile attractiveness. But the doctor proved he was faster than me. Would I be stupid enough to try it?

"Let me see if I understand, *Drone*. You and Dr. Nealy donate your prestigious qualifications to the study of aphids so your brother can control them with blood darts?"

Agitation sharpened his laughter. "You have it partially correct, yet you neglect the crux of our roles. You see, it was Dr. Nealy and I who created the nymph virus and the Imago who delivered it to your country."

His admission slammed into me, squeezed my lungs. I was dining with the murderers of my A's.

Clanking and shuffling stiffened the hairs on my neck. The doctor glanced over my shoulder at whatever activity was entering the hall. I followed his gaze.

Roark hung from the wall at the far end. Shredded cassock. Blood soaked curls. Head bowed.

My heart thudded, ripped open, and propelled me over the table. Eyes on the paring knife. My chair skidded. The table creaked. A dish of stacked noodles clattered to the floor. My hands came up empty.

The Drone jumped to his feet and wagged the knife.

Steel bands gripped my legs and braced me upright. I raised my arms and dropped from the doctor's hold. My knees hit the stone floor.

He bent, reaching, leaving his femoral nerve in perfect range. I rolled to my feet, raised the hem to my thighs, and put everything I had into a Thai round kick.

The line of power from my leg whooshed past him as he side-stepped in a fluid movement, swinging his and whacking me behind the knees. I stumbled and spun away.

Across the room, Roark bucked in his restraints.

I pumped my arms. My outstretched legs ripped through my skirt and closed the distance.

An arm caught me halfway. I pivoted, twined my fingers around the doctor's nape and pulled down. His body followed. I delivered a knee to his solar plexus. It struck brick as I rammed his gut again and again.

Then I slipped free. It was too easy. In the next second, I knew why. Vibrations plagued my insides. The aphid dam cracked.

I skidded to a stop in front of Roark. Curls clung to the dripping red gash along his hairline. Blood caked his eyes and crusted his gag. Metal shackles circled his wrists and ankles and fastened to hooks in the wall. I yanked the chains. No give. Until I found the key, all I could do was shield him.

My fingers, numb like the rest of me, found the tie on the back of his head. His gag dropped.

He blinked through matted lashes. "You're as beautiful and fierce as ever, love."

His lilt was hoarse, pained, but his slow smile sent my pulse singing through my veins. I traced my thumbs over his lips.

Buzzing pitched over my shoulder. I put my back against him. The aphids stalked closer. Why, when they could blur next to me in a heartbeat?

Roark jerked against my back. "You're gonna have to run. Run, now."

My body trembled with their hunger. Their pangs scrambled my concentration. But something else was there as well. A strange hesitancy. Did they fear me? My field of vision extended to my captors. The Drone had returned to his seat at the table, the paring knife twirling between his fingers.

The Imago prowled beside him. The barrel of the dart gun rested on his shoulder.

I met his arrogant gaze. "Call them off."

"Oh, I think it's too late for that." He reclaimed his chair next to the Drone, who was tapping the blade of his knife against the table.

Roark's body would've been a comforting support against my back if his heart wasn't thumping so wildly. "Evie, bloody listen to me."

I rose on tiptoes. The doctor stood behind the approaching aphids, shoulders rolled back, expression vacant.

A crescent of aphids formed around us. Twenty or more orbs locked on the man at my back. I reached behind me. His cassock gaped at his abdomen, the buttons gone. I slipped my arms through the opening and traced the taut muscle around his waist.

"Bloody hell, Evie." His body pulsated, clanking the chains. "I'm gonna ram Lucifer's horns up your arse if ye den' get it moving."

My growl joined his, but I aimed it at the mutants. The warmth of his skin under my hands felt like a jolt, connecting us, strengthening me. He would live, goddammit, and I let that single thought energize every cell in my body.

The segmented feet froze midstride. A few aphids stepped back. Was I doing that? Holding them?

Their bodies shook with need. Their reverberations jumbled their want with mine.

Without turning, I ran my fingers over the shackles and the hooks within reach. "Who has the key?"

He bucked against me. "Evie, be off with ye."

"A little busy. The key?"

A ragged sigh. "The wanker with the dart gun."

No biggie. I felt intoxicated from the energy pouring from the aphids. Their arms stretched, jaws snapping, torsos heaving, but their feet remained glued to the floor.

The doctor walked a cautious circuit around them, studying them, his brows curled in question marks.

Holy hell, they were following my will. I could control them. To what extent? My head felt lighter even as my arms weighed down.

When the doctor stepped around the aphid wall and within kicking distance of me, I reinforced my backbone and my glare. "You said Roark wouldn't be harmed."

"I said he wouldn't be harmed as long as you cooperate." The doctor raised a pair of manacles. "Hold out your hands."

I looked over my shoulder. A petition burned in Roark's green depths. *Fight back,* it begged.

Without looking away, I spun my heel and punched with my other foot. A twist of my hip sent my leg down a straight line and met the doctor's arm. The manacles clanked across the floor.

He lifted his eyebrows. I kicked again to sweep his leg. He rolled out of my reach, landed on his feet. The movement forced me to readjust. In that moment, he closed the distance. Through a soft flowing motion of his arms, he held me, locked me and released me. I felt like water in his hands, as if he took my energy, changed it into any form he chose then overpowered it. He was toying with me.

I made a winding strike toward his throat. He shifted his entire body out of range, yet I never saw him move. It wasn't a discipline I knew. What was my defense if I didn't know what I was up against? I clenched my jaw, spread my feet—weight distributed for a springing attack—and extended my jab hand just below my brow.

He flanked me. His arm came down. I lunged, but he was faster. His hand chopped my neck like a sword. A stitch burst through my head, dotted my vision. My palms slapped the floor.

Roark's shouts swelled and ebbed. Cold metal squeezed my wrists. Then I was standing, supported by the doctor.

"To which martial art do I owe my humiliation?"

His arm around my waist tensed and he whispered at my ear, "An ancient one. But your attention is misplaced. How will you save your priest? For now Aiman and Siraj must follow through on their *lesson.*"

Aiman and Siraj. The Drone and the Imago. Vilely self-titled. Vainglorious, they were, slithering toward us, smirking and whispering.

The Drone raised a hand, fingers bending and unbending. The air stirred, condensed, and the aphids regained the movement of their legs.

Their hum pinched my gut. The doctor's cold arms pinned mine and the Drone's chin rose in victory.

I could really use Jesse's protection right about then, but I'd found the architects of my fucked up genetics. They knew nothing of the abilities I'd gained with it. My revenge would be intimate.

The human being is flesh and consciousness, body and soul;
his heart is an abyss which can only be filled by that which is godly.

Olivier Messiaen

Chapter Twenty-Eight: The Abyss Gazed Back

Roughened stone scratched the backs of my hands. Metal rings protruded from the rock wall, holding my shackles in place.

The doctor's eyes moved over mine as if he could read me. "You look entirely too smug"—he yanked the slack from the restraints—"for someone in your position."

I tried to shrug. The chains rattled. He didn't know the only thing keeping my shit together was the notion that I wouldn't need my hands to turn the starving army against him.

Roark's oaky musk emanated an arm's length away. The sidelong view of his blood-drenched head, drooping under the burden of gravity, constricted my chest. But there was fight in the set of his jaw.

The doctor stepped out of my vision. The Imago moved in, leaned a shoulder on the wall and rooted a finger through my headscarf. When he found an opening on my nape, he drew imaginary circles over the skin, raising the hairs there.

Black lashes spread over his cheekbones. He inhaled and the lashes snapped up. "Ready for your lesson?"

Roark arched his back in a swell of outrage, eyes blazing, and voice wheezing through clamped teeth. "Den' ye bloody touch her."

An exhale oozed from the Imago's flared nostrils. Then he spun toward Roark with an unleashed fist. The wet smack stole my breath.

Roark stretched a toothy smirk through the red river coursing from his nose. "That's all ye got, ye goat-fucking toerag?"

His fist reared again. Roark grunted under the blow to his abdomen, the corners of his mouth rigid.

My pulse raced, faster than I thought possible, leaving me trembling and panicked. So much so, I didn't notice the new threat until hot breath dampened the wrap around my neck.

"Mmm, your quivering is delectable," the Drone hummed in my ear. His hip chafed mine, his proximity oiling away the layers of air between us, seeping beneath the surface of my skin.

He ground his flaccid dick against me, punctuating each word with a pant. "I want to want you."

Fucking mouth-breather. "I want to gut you."

He clutched his side, face twisted, breaths pushing out in sprays of spit.

"What's your problem? Dick won't work?"

He grabbed a handful of my headscarf, hair with it, and yanked my neck down in a submissive bow. "How would you feel if people thought we were lovers? Do you want that?"

"There are no people. And there will never be anything resembling love between us."

He released my head, sending it careening back. The bite from the wall spiked from my crown to my eyes.

When my vision cleared, he was gliding over to Roark in that slimy way he moved.

"Pity to defile such a beautiful creature." He tore the front of Roark's pants open, baring his groin.

Roark growled. My heartbeat swished in my ears and the tension pouring from the leashed aphids stretched to the snapping point. How was the Drone still holding them when his attention was focused on us? Could I wrestle the control away from him?

The Imago circled Roark, blade in hand, slicing away the remainder of his clothes until he hung nude, biceps twitching against his sagging weight.

His wide jade eyes locked on the Drone, who hovered close enough to share his breath. Too fucking close. Even if I could get the aphids to attack on command, no way Roark would come out unbitten. I wouldn't chance it. My stomach dropped.

The Drone's mouth ticked up and his back straightened. A rattan cane appeared from under his cloak.

An extension of his arm, the cane shot up. I stopped breathing as it whistled down.

Roark's torso jerked under the impact. His cheeks paled, flexed, no doubt bottling a scream. A red welt ballooned above his nipple. Oh, Roark.

My eyes clung to the cane as it rose again. "Not him. No more." I rammed my arms against the wall. "It's my punishment. Not his."

The next blow landed below the first. A roar escaped Roark's thinned lips.

I pulled against the shackles in useless thrashing. "Stop, you sick fuck." My voice broke. "Just stop. I've learned my lesson."

His free hand hovered over Roark's chest, fingers grazing the twin gashes, lingering. Then his touch meandered along pectoral ridges to his unblemished nipple, catching it between finger and thumb. Squeezing. Yanking beyond comfortable extension.

Roark's eyes remained fastened on the Drone's, his body otherwise unresponsive.

A peculiar sort of darkness pooled in the Drone's eyes as his attentions moved south, over the bump and dip of honed abs, brushing golden naval hair, caressing that perfect indention where his hip jutted.

Saliva thickened with an onslaught of nausea. "Stop it." It was a shout, but came out as a croak.

The Drone flicked his wrist, catching the bloody nipple. "Ten more cuts from the cane. Each word you utter adds another cut. Are we clear?"

I swallowed, nodded, then closed my eyes. Time to focus on the aphids. Precision would be paramount.

The whine of the cane whipped the air. And another and another. The brutality and force of each lunge and swing made my jumps more violent than Roark's, robbing my concentration, tearing out my heart.

I opened my eyes. Mutated bodies swayed. Tiny pupils trained on the Drone. I couldn't get ahold of them, they wouldn't move, and worse my bones were softening. Feeling escaped my fingers and toes. The sensation of spinning crept in.

I centered my focus on the barricaded doors. If I stared hard enough, put a mountain of hope behind that stare, maybe Jesse would crash through with arrows flying. If I hadn't left the States…if I'd just stayed with the Lakota—

The cane whacked, wrenching a moan from Roark's throat.

Whack…Whack.

Roark's breathing turned fitful. Grunts became gasps. Tremors rolled over strained muscles, sending aftershocks through the chains. And his freckled skin took on a gray pallor that matched my A's in their final hours.

I jerked against the cuffs, helpless and dying inside, desperately reaching for the aphid link. Once again, the connection disintegrated, and stole the last of my strength.

The hall sang with the whir of the cane's blow. A ladder of horizontal cuts lined his chest, swelling and springing blood.

Finally, the cane vanished under the Drone's cloak and he moved away to whisper something to the Imago.

I stared at Roark's hanging head, silently begging him to look at me. All the bullshit between us had dissolved on the cliff at River Tweed. I wanted…needed him whole, canonic vows and all. I wouldn't survive without him.

A burn swept through my throat, behind my eyes. Oh Roark… "Please don't give up. I need you."

With slow jerks, his neck straightened. His eyes rolled up. He glanced at me, didn't seem to see me. Then his eyes focused on mine, lips parted. "I…"

His molars smacked together. The chains strained. He took a hissing breath and widened those eyes that seem to penetrate my soul. "...love..." His voice cracked.

Activity flurried through the hall, but the room narrowed to just the two of us and that thing only we could feel. I'd missed that feeling, how big and alive it was, and pushed it into my face, my eyes, so he could read it there and understand.

His lips quivered. The corner lifted then fell. He mouthed, "Sorry."

I shook my head, brows crunched together, a sob locked in my throat.

"The vow." His lips moved, but it was the Drone's voice that reached my ears.

"Now we feed our army." His arms spread out and he floated back to us.

Feed? Oh no, no, no.

A tear swelled in Roark's eye, fell over the red rim, skipped down his cheek.

The Drone pressed against me and palmed my stomach. A violent flutter sparked under his hand and vibrated bone-deep. As if an invisible wall fell away, the aphids surged forward. The doctor evaded a snapping jaw with an acrobatic tumble.

The hand on my stomach clenched. His voice cut through my tremors. "Your body betrays you." Fingers pressed against my bucking abdomen. "I can feel the croon rising in you. It is calling to me as well."

Was that why the aphids were on the move? "You're directing them?"

I didn't let his manic chuckle disarm me. Think revenge. Mind over body. I projected my will along that invisible thread, the one that led me to the aphids.

The mutants paused, but their line rippled. Their hunger burned like acid in my stomach. I swallowed back the bile searing my throat.

The doctor rolled out from under a bent aphid and landed on óne knee. His eyes pinned me. There was no malice there. No emotion. Of the three, he seemed the least insane. Maybe that made him the biggest risk.

The Imago squatted against the far wall. His dart gun lay across his bent knees as he sucked his cigar. That arrogant bastard had to go first.

I filled my head with images of aphids gathered over the Imago's shredded chest, feasting at a bloody buffet.

All at once, the aphids pivoted then shuffled toward the Imago. The pitch of their buzzing stung my ears and burrowed deep within me. Their need strained. Soon it would crack. Control over them was an illusion.

The Drone jerked away. His shoulders shook. The aphids swung back, their orbs directed at Roark.

I hung onto my will, externalizing it, making it real. Warmth gushed from my nose and trickled over my lip. Copper and iron filled my mouth. Sweat cooled my skin. I gathered my concentration and continued to push images. The Drone peppered with leaking bullet holes. The Imago hanging from a meat hook, fingers dragging through a red puddle. But the aphids' rush toward Roark didn't waver.

Laughter bubbled from the Drone. Arms raised to the ceiling, his cloak spread out and eclipsed my view.

Halos circled the wall torches and teetered sideways. My lungs labored through short breaths. The muscles in my face strained against the pressure of my wordless command.

Roark bowed his back and fought his binds. The aphids crawled over each other to get to him feet away.

My broadcast became vocal. "Stop. Stop. Stop." The ringing in my ears deafened my screams.

A warm palm covered my brow. The skin around the doctor's piercing eyes creased. His touch jolted through me. I shoved my directive at the aphids, with my gut, with my voice. "Stop."

Claws rose over Roark. Too late. Too fucking late. I gulped past razor blades and cried, "Roark. No, God. Please. Roark."

The aphids fell on him, covered him. His name shredded my throat. The torches flickered into multicolored dots, spun around me and blended to nothingness.

My eyes flew open. The sun hung high above my cell and warmed my cheek. My leaden arms lay along my torso. The mattress pressed against my bare chest. I tried to move. Straps on my back and legs held me down.

The doctor bent over me, swabbing something on my shoulder.

"Roark?" The whisper scratched my throat.

"What are these spots on your back?"

I gritted my teeth. "Where's Roark?"

Cold dabs wet my other shoulder. "I've never seen anything like this. Are they bites? Birthmarks?"

"Tell me where Roark is."

"The pigment is unusual. Black. And smooth." He pressed his finger down. "Does this hurt?"

"Get away from me. You...you created a virus, a worldwide massacre. You watched that sick fuck cane Roark. And you're asking about the pigment of my skin? Where is he?"

Was Roark's beautiful body shredded with bite marks? His face sunken under all-white eyes? I couldn't do it. Couldn't bear it. I had to find him and find the cure.

Leather bit into my back. "Let me up." I bucked as the walls closed in. Suffocating. Choking. "Let me up, goddammit." My shouting dwindled to a pained rasp.

Footsteps scraped the floor and the doctor's dabbing stilled on my back. I angled my head toward the gate.

The Drone stood on the other side. His infernal aura slithered through the bars and corkscrewed its way to my gut. "I couldn't let him mutate and taint my army, Eveline."

There were no half-breed mutants. If a man were bitten, he became an aphid. If Roark didn't mutate, then… "You killed him?"

He closed his eyes. "Shh. Now, now. It will be all right." A deep inhale and his eyes snapped open. "A cadaver in mid-transition will be invaluable in my laboratory."

My existence shattered. I couldn't let them see. Couldn't let them know they killed me too. I held the pieces together, forced the air from my lungs. "Get. The. *Fuck*. Out."

"I'm very sorry, Eveline. I'll give you time to…accept." The fan of his cape followed him out the door.

My bindings loosened and fell away. The doctor stepped out of the cell in wooden movements and sat at the far end of the chamber.

I rolled off the bed and sought the corner. Knees to chest, I blanked my face and waited for the doctor to leave.

But he didn't move. The sun circled the sky and the shadows crawled over me. The night showed me mercy, a reprieve from his watchful eyes. It was then that I surrendered to soundless, tearless sobs. The abyss inhaled, and welcomed me back.

The moon peeked around the ceiling gables and cast blocks of gray on the floor. Morning and night, the tide crashed against the fortress walls. I put my fingers in my ears.

The corner propped up my back, as it had done for a day, maybe two, maybe more.

A brown and yellow spider tapped its striped legs on my knee, looking for a place to bury its fangs. Its pinecone body dragged behind it. I hoped it was poisonous.

The gate to my cell squeaked opened. That fucking sound made me cringe. It latched shut and a hand swung at the spider. The ridged body crunched under the doctor's sandal.

"You haven't eaten in four days." He waited for a response. He could go fuck himself.

He crouched before me. "If you don't eat, I can't take your blood. If I don't take your blood, Aiman...the Drone will retrieve it himself. And you already know how he'll do that." His dark eyes lowered to my neck.

Why did he need my blood? I turned away from him, pressed closer into the corner.

He gripped my waist and threw me over his shoulder. Sandalwood billowed from his sweat dampened shirt. The shadows on the floor chased us out of the cell and into the bathroom.

He gathered up my skirt. The stool hit my bare butt. The pipes squealed followed by the rush of water in the tub.

"Go." He gave the toilet a pointed look.

I'd given up on my demands for privacy after the first day. To be honest, I just didn't care. Caring was for people with hopes and dreams. So I let him haul me to and from the bathroom, bathe me, watch me use the toilet. All under the pretense of medical care. I felt like a lab monkey, certain the comparison wasn't far off.

Maybe I should've been concerned about an inappropriate touch or worse, considering he had a regular viewing of my naked body. But, I never glimpsed anything in his eyes or manner to seed the doubt. Maybe if he crossed that line, my body would find the fight that had abandoned it.

Bladder empty, I let him lift me into the bath. Warm water rose to my chin. Each slow drop from the faucet echoed the dirge of my heartbeat.

He ripped away the garment bunched at my waist. His hands moved with efficiency, lathering soap over my body and through my hair. He slowed his ministrations on my back. "I want to talk about these spots."

Not that bullshit again. "Want spots on *your* back? Get me a cigarette."

He clenched his jaw and finished washing me in silence.

In my cell, I returned to the corner. He sat on the outside in a moonlit square and dug in his pants pocket. A pack of cigarettes dropped on the floor before him.

I was in no mood for mind games.

Sometime later, he reached in his pocket again. My battery-powered bullet appeared next to the cigarettes.

I hid my surprise. "Shove it up your ass."

He placed my MP3 player next to the bullet. "I retrieved your pack from the truck at River Tweed. I have all your personal items."

Paper rustled in his hand. I straightened. He laid the stained letter next to the other items. Scrawled words glared back at me. Words poured from Joel's heart.

My hand shot to my forearm, seeking a dagger, fingers curling at its bareness. "You have no right." I scrambled to the bars, reached for the letter. He inched it back.

"It's yours when you eat." He nodded to the plate of food on the bed.

So began my sentence on Malta. Three times a day, the doctor bribed me to eat, taking away the letter when I wouldn't. Every day, after midmorning prayer, the Drone brought an empty vial. And every day, he watched with hungry eyes as the doctor pricked my vein. When the vial was filled, he snatched it and rushed out without a word.

Between visiting hours, I fantasized about Annie and Aaron's world. I knew it didn't exist. Still, I would close my eyes and look for their smiling faces. I would look for Joel and Roark too. But it was always so dark. I'd stretch out my hands and feel nothing. Then I would call out for them, sinking deeper. I thought I came close sometimes. The tide would fade. The wind would still. The tightening in my chest would uncoil. And just when I thought I found them, the doctor would drag me back, forcing fluids down my throat or dropping me in the bath.

Every night, I curled in the corner and plugged my ears against the sea. I let my skirt bunch at my thighs and watched the spiders dine on my legs. Often, the doctor would show up and chase them away. Always, he arrived at dawn to nurse my bites and give me a bath.

I didn't fight him. My fight died with Roark. I kept my gaze on the abyss. Until one night, I fell into restless sleep, and the abyss gazed back.

Grasshoppers chirped. Ice settled in my mint mojito. Perspiration teared on the glass lip and I caught it with my tongue. Something splashed in the pool, drenching the sun warmed towel beneath me.

I leaned over the coping. Annie cut across the crystal bottom with lithe strokes. Her blurry figure approached. My smile widened as she came up for breath.

Her face broke the surface and stared into mine with all-white eyes. Black gore drooled from her broken teeth. A pincer clamped my throat, cut my scream. Water burned my nose as she dragged me in.

The pool darkened. We spiraled down, farther and farther. A sea of ink, the bottom never came. The water began to spin and roar around me.

I stood in the center as it gravitated away. Gravel dug into the soles of my feet. Annie was gone.

Clank. Clank.

The darkness receded into the purple shade of twilight. The post in my father's vineyard emerged. Chains suspended Joel's body to it. Metal links hung from Joel's waist, clanking on the post like a dinner bell. A glowing figure clung to his body.

The distance between us blurred. My hands closed over the aphid's mandible. I yanked. The hole in Joel's chest puked flesh and bone. The insectile mouth slipped in my hands. I tightened my grip, bowed it at a right angle.

The point snapped. I twisted my wrist and stabbed it through the gaping mouth. A spout of blood choked its shrieks.

I moved to the post in the next row, dragging the aphid behind me, and knocked my father's viticulture tool from the hook. The muscles in my arms quivered as I raised the aphid by its head and pushed.

The hook's rusted tip punched through the forehead. I jerked it free and repeated. The hook bobbed in and out of the head. Ribbons of black leaked from its pulped orbs. My arms gave out. The lifeless body slid to the ground.

Joel moaned from the other post. My heart pummeled as I knelt before him. His tiny pupils stared at me without seeing. My teeth sawed my lips. My numb fingers wrestled the chains.

His body fell in my lap. Vibrations pounded my chest. I held my hand over the chewed hole in his.

"Trust," he gurgled.

I shook my head, voice caught. He twisted and bucked in my arms. My stomach did the same.

"Trust mind, body and soul." His hand slapped my chest as if jerked by a string. A fever of compulsions magnetized me to his fingers.

Your guardians. *He said it, but his mouth never moved. His pupils dilated. For a brief moment, he appeared human. Then his hand dropped.*

End it. *His command drifted through me, rode the wind, brushed through the tree canopy.*

Tendons in his neck went taut. Lips pulled away from gums. Porcelain orbs bulged. He dug at the dirt, fingers spread in hardened kinks.

I gripped his jaw and screamed, "Joel."

His hunger rippled through me. His head flopped around between my hands. Blood and spit flew. I strengthened my hold on his jaw. He told me once that after the mutation, the result wasn't human, wasn't the person it was before. Did he still believe that?

"Joel," I shouted.

White eyes glazed over with single-minded focus. Feed.

The tip of my dagger touched his forehead. My palm cupped the hilt, but I couldn't feel it. I couldn't feel anything. I pushed hard and fast.

I woke, jack-knifing in the bed. A sweet, earthy flavor stroked the air, an ilk of sandalwood. It did little to soothe the splintering pain in my chest as my memories rushed in. I squeezed my fist. The dagger was so heavy when I pulled it from Joel's skull. I left it there, in my father's vineyard, where I set the fire. The withered grapevines sparked and popped as the flames engulfed Joel's body. I had only minutes to retrieve clothes from the house before the blaze devoured it too.

My eyes stung. Warm flesh flexed against my face. Arms wrapped around me.

I blinked heavy lashes, tilting my head up. The shadows didn't conceal the flawless skin and almond shaped eyes of the man who held me.

Oh, fuck no. I shoved the doctor off me and fell with a thud from the bed.

Back on my feet, I swiped my face. My hand came away wet. My failure glistened on his bare chest.

"Don't ever touch me again," I choked, backing away.

He stood with the bed between us, arms relaxed at his side. "I'm your doctor, whether you want that or not." He pushed his hand through his hair. "I'm doing my best to ensure your physical well-being, but it's moot if your mental health fails."

I turned away. My feet moved to the corner, to its numbing depths.

"Your nightmares," he said, "and weeks without talking or making eye contact. You value a tattered letter more than your music player, yet you cover your ears at night. And your changing physiology…"

I tuned out his diagnosis. He chatted on as if he hadn't played a part in imprisoning me and filleting my heart.

He was suddenly behind me, his breath brushing my hair. "Come back from this madness."

I had finally remembered Joel's death. Faced what I'd done. But it wasn't enough to mend the hole Roark left behind. Stages of denial, anger and bargaining had come and gone in the prior weeks. Yet, as I spun around, it sure felt like I was back to stage one. "I'll come back when you bring back Roark."

Creases appeared in his forehead and his eyes darted through the dark as if searching for a response. After a roam over the open rafters, his gaze settled on mine. "Then abandon all your senses but the sixth one."

It is by going down into the abyss that we recover the treasures of life.
Where you stumble, there lies your treasure.

Joseph Campbell

CHAPTER TWENTY-NINE: FILLET OF SOUL

"My sixth sense? Intuition tells me you're a liar and a murderer."

A muscle jogged in the doctor's cheek. "So you say. Yet, you've seen me do neither. Can't say the same for you."

My thoughts skipped to my first night on Malta. Okay, so I had a lethal knack for throwing scissors. My fists clenched and unclenched at my sides, thrumming for a repeat. "Spoken by the man responsible for billions of murders, for Roark's murder, that barb has no teeth."

His hand shot through a column of moonlight and squeezed my throat. "He lives."

I swallowed around his fist, didn't pretend to misunderstand who. "I watched him get eaten."

He stared down at me. "No, you didn't. You commanded the aphids acoustically. Just like Aiman does." His hand dropped, head cocked, vertical lines separating his brows. "They responded to you. But the effort made you sick."

I shook my head and backed up. "They didn't respond. He was covered—"

"When I put my hand on your face, I felt a...you stabilized. You stopped them before the first mouth broke skin. And when you lost consciousness, Aiman held them back."

I cupped my mouth and slid down the wall. "I have no reason to believe you."

He squatted next to me and angled his chin toward the night sky. "Like the moon, the truth doesn't hide for long."

"Get the fuck out of my face."

He dropped his head and looked at me through lowered lids. "Give me a question only the priest can answer."

My muscles contracted against the longing in my chest. I couldn't give into hope. Why would the Drone let him live? And what was Dr. Nealy's motivation? He'd taken care of me, kept me alive. Such was a scientist's relationship with his rats. Until the tests began. I couldn't trust him, but I could call his bluff.

"The priest received a sign. What was it?" The memory of that night latched onto my heart. I'd never forget Roark's wonderment as he knelt over me, the depths of his eyes tracking the ladybugs on my body.

The doctor set an apple on the floor at my hip. "I do this at my own peril. Aiman and Siraj wouldn't agree to my methods."

At my shaky nod, he left.

Would the Drone and the Imago kill the doctor before I had the chance? The idea shoved in an ache deep inside me, which should've twinged my conscience. But losing my moral principles was nothing compared to what the past year had taken from me.

I crawled into the bed and sorted through my new memories of Joel. His final words ate at me. Why couldn't he have just told me he loved me? Even amidst transformation, he counseled.

Trust mind, body and soul. Your guardians.

I eventually trusted my soul. It didn't guard me. Instead, it weakened me and took my mind with it. My body would have followed, had the doctor not intervened. Was there another meaning? It wasn't like Joel to speak in riddles. But in the throes of death, maybe he saw things or understood things I couldn't.

Vulnerability settled around my heart. To chase it away, I practiced Roark's boxing exercises, aiming each jab at the slivers of moonlight spearing the room. When the door groaned opened, I was stretched, energized and ready to pound the doctor's lying mouth.

The Imago swaggered toward the gate. His gaze prowled over my body.

I squared my shoulders, fighting the compulsion to back into the corner. Fabric stretched over my chest, inviting his ogle while I catalogued his weapons.

The dart gun slung across his back. A gold Desert Eagle .50 cal seated in his thigh holster. His belt flaunted a Jambiya dagger in a *J* shaped sheath.

"Looking for Dr. Nealy?" The Imago never came alone.

He unsheathed the knife and dialed the combination on the lock. Then he locked himself—and his weapons—in with me. Stupid douche. Even the Drone wasn't arrogant enough to put weapons in my reach.

"I passed him on the stairs and decided to pay you a visit." His eyes continued their greedy perusal.

My pulse was an erratic thrum in my ears. "And so you have. Now you can go."

He scratched his chin with the blade. "I'm a man of opportunity. It's not often Michio leaves you alone. Undress. Or shall I do it for you?" He teased the blade down my sternum. His other hand palmed the butt of the pistol.

I suppressed the telltale bob of my throat. "What's the Qur'an say about that? Big brother likes me covered."

"Quickly." He stomped his boot.

I clutched the hem of my top, prepared to brook any action that would get me closer to one of his weapons.

Heat burned in his eyes when I pulled it over my head, taking the headscarf with it. His lashes dropped with the garments' descent to the floor. Then he was on me, mouth assaulting mine, stabbing with a tongue as stiff and foul as his cigar. I let him back me into the wall and waited for the moment he was caroused on lust.

It didn't take long. He sheathed the dagger. His trembling hand groped my bared breast. His other fumbled with the buckle on his pants.

I tried to endure the next few moments, but my stomach rolled, preparing to blow chunks over the slimy invader in my mouth. I yanked my face back. "Do you like your tongue?"

He grinned, waggling the offensive organ bubbled in spit.

"Put it in my mouth again and you won't get it back."

"I'll take my chances." And he did.

I transferred my attention away from it to the belt under my exploring fingers. I ached to castrate him. He was moments from handing it to me. My thumb bumped the dagger's hilt.

The final button yielded. His trousers sagged to the floor. I held onto the dagger and sank my teeth into the foul flesh between them. Hard.

His eyes bulged. "Ewwaaah."

I spat. Blood sprayed from his mouth and mine.

The Imago threw back his head and screamed. His tongue hung by a strip.

I angled the blade over his softening dick.

A hand circled my wrist. I snapped my gaze up and met the doctor's. Where the hell did he come from?

I tightened my fingers around the hilt. A depression of his thumb forced my hand open. The blade clanked to the floor.

"Ew do?" The Imago cried.

Hands tucked in elbows, the doctor leaned against the wall. "Saved your life."

I looked into the Imago's tear streaked eyes. "Saved his dick, actually. I'm afraid it's too late to save his larger organ."

He pawed at his mouth and ripped the flopping flesh all the way off. "Aaaah. Ew itch."

The doctor remained unmoved. "Get out, Siraj, before you have to explain to your brother what you were doing in here."

A shadow passed over his screwed up expression. He gathered his pants and weapons and shouldered past the doctor. When the chamber door slammed behind him, I found myself locked behind bars with another monster. Unfortunately, the doctor wasn't stupid enough to bring in weapons.

I rinsed my mouth with a pitcher, dressed and sat on the bed. "Let's get this over with."

He held his post on the wall. "Proud of yourself?"

I shrugged. "I've had cleaner cuts with a blade. Didn't get the timing right."

He read my eyes, saw the truth there. "That right?" He pushed a hand through his hair. "I don't hold you responsible for what happened."

"Gee, thanks."

"I talked to your priest."

So his lies continued.

"His cooperation wasn't forthcoming. He decided if you thought him dead, we would lose our leverage."

My jab hand curled in my lap.

"But I made sure he understood that his death had broken you."

I rubbed the vein at my elbow, one of the many bruised blood taps I'd offered without fight. His death *did* break me.

He pushed away from the wall and knelt before me. "In Malta, the children used to sing *Nannakola, mur l-iskola, aqbad siggu u ibda oghla.*" His expression softened. "Ladybird, go to school, get a chair and start jumping."

I gasped and covered it with my hand. "What did you say?"

He pulled my hand from my mouth. "His sign. The ladybirds. The *Nannakola.*" He squeezed my hand. Lifted my chin with the other. "You are hallowed."

I stopped breathing.

"That's what he called you."

Oh, my sentimental Irishman. "Infection?"

"He's human. No bites."

My chest expanded. Then it heaved with the thunder of my breaths. He lived. Oh God, he *lived*.

The lines around the doctor's eyes faded. Tenderness touched his features. Too tender. Was that his game? To break me then rebuild me? I jerked my hand away and jumped from the bed. "Where is he?"

"Two floors down."

"In a cell like this?"

"The same. But no visitors." He tipped his head to the rafters. "And the view's not as good."

No visitors? "Are you starving him?" I couldn't keep my voice from hitching.

"The human staff delivers his meals."

"Why did you let me think he was dead all this time?"

He stood, eyes fastened on mine. "He's alive because if his death didn't break you, his torture would."

My jaw clenched to the verge of pain. "Free him and my cooperation will be without bounds."

"I cannot."

My shoulders sagged. "Let me see him. Move him here. He can stay in my cell."

"Aiman and Siraj cannot know their plan has been compromised."

Or they'd move to Plan B. Roark's torture. "So I pretend to be broken. Why is that important?"

His eyes narrowed. "You've exceeded your questions. My turn. What are the black spots on your back?"

No idea. "Never seen them before."

Lines rutted his forehead. Then he nodded at my chest, where the blouse had fallen away from my scar. "How'd you get that?"

Of all the questions. I gathered the material at my collar, covering the atrocity. "A prig of a man deemed me the devil and attempted a mastectomy."

His face smoothed into a blank canvas. "Does he live?"

Same question Roark asked. I shook my head.

"It was deep. Through the muscle. It hit bone?"

He knew the extent of the damage, had scrutinized it under the slide of soap. I lifted a shoulder.

"The stitching was a sorry attempt. Who did it?"

I shrugged again. "Who cares?" Then his drawn eyebrows compelled me to say, "I did."

He cleared his throat. "I see."

We stared at one another in a suspended moment. Whatever his plan was, he had returned my will to fight. I would escape that damn island with Roark in tow. The key was in my physiology, in the vials the Drone collected every day. What did the doctor know about my blood?

Time to pull my head out of my ass and find out. I crooked my lips.

His brow furrowed and he spun on his heel.

Maybe the doctor wasn't as unaffected by me as I originally assumed. I didn't know his intentions, but I could leverage his give-and-take to find out. I let my smile fill my face as I admired his retreating backside for the first time.

The wind roared with the passing of night, pitching the tide and stuffing the sky with clouds. I lay on my back, unable to escape the taunt of having Roark so close, yet unable to reach him.

Something skittered along the stone balk above, followed by the beat of wings.

"You awake?" I knew he was. The doctor's nights on the couch were as restless as mine.

"What is it?"

"Did you hear that noise on the rafters?" I rolled toward him and pillowed my head with my arm.

"Probably a bat."

I strained to hear its return. Eventually gave up. "Why did you tell me about Roark?"

Silence weighted the air. Then his outline moved through the chamber and settled outside the gate.

A shallow dish tilted between the bars and sailed across the floor. Of course. Always a trade.

Rice clung to the sides. I scooped with my fingers and chewed.

"I told you," he said. "It's my job to keep you healthy. That includes your mental health."

It didn't make sense. They wanted me broken. Was there internal conflict on Team Evil? "Why did you do it? The virus?"

He shook his head, his face slack.

Fine. He could keep that secret. "Why does the Drone need my blood?"

He nodded to the bowl. I plucked another sticky clump and smeared it on my tongue.

"He wants your immunity."

Whoa. What? I swallowed the muck. "So you dumb asses created a virus without a vaccine. One that could come back to bite you." I pressed my tongue in my cheek. "And you think consuming my blood will be inoculative?"

"He hopes it will be a cure."

"He wouldn't need a cure if he kept better company." I flicked at hand at the chamber door where his guards hummed on the other side. "Besides, you intentionally spread the virus. Why would he want a cure?"

His expression remained empty. I rubbed my neck where the Drone bit me. He didn't have fangs and wings, though everything else I dreamt was real. And how could he communicate with the aphids? Something didn't fit. "You still have those cigarettes?"

A cup and spoon appeared between the bars. I scooted closer and accepted the trade. Clams and garlic wafted from the chunky brown broth. I slurped down a fishy bite and made a face.

"Sole stew." He rose as graceful as a curl of smoke and drifted through the room. A moment later, he returned with the cigarettes and…a fire extinguisher?

"You won't need that." Setting fire to my clothes would be one way out, but he'd given me a reason to live.

He lit a cigarette and passed it to me. I coughed through the stale burn. "So what is he? The Drone?"

"His genetic code includes a hybrid of aphid and spider now. It continues to alter and he's desperate to remain human."

So he was mutating. "Did you say spider?"

"He's been injecting himself with a serum derived from genomic macromolecules of various spider species." He dropped his eyes to the bites on my legs. "It was unproven, so there have been some side-effects. But it stinted his aphid transformation."

His frankness thrilled me. Even in the dark, his eyes danced. I'd found his spark. "And a macromolecule is…"

"DNA, RNA, proteins."

I rested my chin on my knee and pinched the bridge of my nose. "So aphid and eight-leggers. No wings."

"There is wing dimorphism in aphids."

My heart sputtered.

"Some aphids—the insect species—can produce winged offspring to relocate from overcrowded or degraded food sources. It's a fascinating example of evolution. But we haven't seen wings in the aphid humanoid species. And the Drone hasn't allowed me a full examination of him."

The perfect segue. "You stole that exam of my body, blood and all. What's the verdict?"

Arm dangling over a knee, he picked at the chipped floor tile between his feet. The wait was torturous.

He licked his lips, met my eyes. "There's neither aphid nor nymph genome stored on your DNA."

Didn't expect that. "What then?"

"I'm still analyzing your blood." His eyes darted away. "The absence of aphid in your DNA chemistry questions your ability to link with them. Aiman explained it as a vibration in his abdomen that presses out through his chest." His gaze returned. "Is that accurate?"

I nodded.

"Insects communicate using visual, chemical, tactile and acoustic means. And aphids have mechanoreceptors—those tiny tactile hairs on their arms and legs—to feel the vibrations you're producing."

I held up an arm. "I don't, yet I still feel them."

"It's acoustic. There's a tympanic membrane, a kind of eardrum, in the insect abdomen to detect sound. That would explain how you *feel* it there." He nodded to my stomach.

"You think I have this membrane? That I'm mutating like the Drone?" Sole stew threatened a comeback.

"Your evolution is the result of adaptation. But it's more complex than that. A physical morphing occurs over generations. Yours is...miraculous."

My stomach settled and a smile crept up. Roark would think so.

"If we evaluate the life cycle of parasites and viruses, which are very efficient at mutating and adapting into different forms, we may find the answer. You're not mutating like Aiman. Your abilities are an environmental response." A sparkle lit his eye. "Aiman was bit."

Wow, he was in rare form and he pulled me right along with him. "Let me guess. His own guards?"

"His lover."

I let out a bitter laugh. A creation that became dangerous to its creator. "How'd he avoid the immediate changes of the mutation?"

"He was already inoculating himself."

With his unproven spider serum. "What about you?"

"I won't touch his experiments."

"I meant did you have a lover? Wife? Children?" Why the hell did I care?

"No."

"No, I suppose you wouldn't considering you created a virus intended to kill them." Hit with the reality of the conversation, I stubbed out the cigarette. "Why are you always in here? Sleeping in here? With your attack dogs at the door, there's no way I'm escaping." Unless I could use my connection to them.

The skin around his eyes creased, no trace of their earlier animation.

I'd annihilated the mood, but one question remained. "How'd you get mixed up with the Jabara brothers?"

"We grew up together in Okinawa. Our fathers were stationed there. U.S. Air Force."

A Japanese heritage fit his silken gold skin, almond shaped eyes, thick black hair. "Your mother was Japanese."

He nodded and eyed my cup. Back to captor and captive.

I gagged down the soup.

"Aiman and I reunited in med school and collaborated on a project. We were pursuing a hypothesis involving the relationship between entomological and viral saltation. I believe that project initiated the design of the nymph virus. But we had a fundamental disagreement that roadblocked our work."

He might as well have been speaking another language in regards to his project. But I could guess the roadblock. "Religion."

"Yes. So I broke off from the project and the friendship dissolved."

"Sounds like you're saying you didn't knowingly aid in mass murder. Yet here you are."

He lifted his head and met my eyes. "I take full responsibility for what happened."

Something lurched in my gut, something corroded and unused. I wanted to forgive him and didn't know why.

We fell silent after that. A short time later, he stood and left the room. I lay on my side on the bed and arranged the robe over me. I pretended it was Roark's wool robe and Roark's bed. I could feel his easy smile whisper against my back, his protective arms grabbing hold of my waist. Every breath was a breath for him and charged me anew. Imagined fingers trailed my body. My skin bumped up. I visualized his generous lips parting over mine. His curls would be soft in my hands.

The threads of the mattress tingled on my fingertips. Warmth stirred through me and pulsed between my thighs, a sensation I'd suppressed for weeks. I sank into the bed and let it take me.

The knob on the chamber door jiggled. A heavy weight crashed against it. The throb inside me was replaced by a different kind of hunger. Scratches climbed the door.

Was it the chemical factor he had mentioned? I'd read how insects used pheromones to attract mates. Had the aphid guards sensed my arousal? Maybe I could use the link to control them. A ticket to Roark. To freedom.

I focused on the streaming vibration. If I could just get a steady hold—

Pain stabbed the space behind my eyes. Stars bleached out the blush of daybreak. I ground my teeth and tensed my muscles to anchor their hunger.

Eveline. The Arabic rumble tossed my gut. The bond between us snapped together. The Drone's anger and surprise became my own, like a violation of my soul. His essence permeated through the floors and laded my inhales. He was coming. What the hell had I done?

"The way into my parlor is up a winding stair,
And I have many curious things to show you when you are there."
"Oh no, no," said the Fly, "to ask me is in vain;
For who goes up your winding stair can ne'er come down again."

Mary Howitt

Chapter Thirty: Winding Stair

Snapshots of congealing blood crowded my awareness, holding my body like a limp thing in my bed. The images were so tangible my taste buds were imbued with pennies. The sources of these sensations, the creatures that once made up the men and women of Maltese society, prowled the compound. Their screeches drifted through the walls of my prison, pushing their hunger, making it my own.

A venomous presence pulsed at the heart of the entangled transmissions. It was him, seeking me internally as his human body closed the distance. I probed the connection, learning it, tracing invisible fingers along the thread and reached.

What I found was an icy void, where his soul should've been. I recoiled, but the chasm bulged, swallowing my strength and screwing with my breathing. I couldn't fight the pull to give him anything he wanted.

Holy Mother, that was how he controlled them, and what it felt like when he did. I had to unplug.

I knelt on the bed and put my palms on the wall. I let out one more trembling breath then slammed my forehead into the stone facade. Pain exploded through my face. I fell back and let the throbbing give way to unconsciousness.

When I came to, my senses were my own. Quiet held outside the door. Thank you, skull-crushing wall. I groaned and opened my eyes.

The sun hovered. So did a man-shaped thing called the Drone. His glossy curls curtained my face. He leaned lower and cupped my jaw, his gentle touch at odds with the sinister vibe dripping from him. "My dear Eveline. It is time."

I couldn't hide the strain in my face as I recoiled beneath my skin and scanned the room. Where was Dr. Nealy?

The mattress sprang up. He strode to the chamber door. "Wear the *chador*. Come."

We were leaving the chamber? My heart leapt as I grabbed the robe and slipped it over my chemise. My longing to get down those stairs outweighed my need to empty my bladder and scrub the grit from my teeth. Still, I questioned the wisdom in going anywhere with him. "Where are we going?"

His head dipped, lower, closer, bringing cold lips to my cheekbone, to the corner of my mouth.

My jaw tightened until I thought my teeth would break. Would he violate me while yanking my mind through our connection and stealing my will? If I fought him hand-to-hand, could I neutralize him?

Whiskers pricked my chin. His lips hovered, separated. Where the fuck was the doctor?

The Drone's right hook cracked my head to the side. I staggered back, bent over and clutched my knees. Big breath. Another. What was that for? I jiggled my jaw and looked up.

His bent position mirrored mine, face constricted and one hand cupping his side. The other popped the lid of a small plastic bottle. White pills tumbled to his tongue and he returned the bottle to a pocket in his cloak.

I punched out my fist. He deflected it with a blur of his own and swept my feet from under me. The crunch with the floor shot pain up my spine.

The kinks gone from his face, he crouched beside me. "Audacity is a plague, Eveline. And your gender is especially susceptible. Your fearlessness in my presence, your attempt to usurp my guards"—a wave of vibration bounced between us—"demonstrate your total disregard for Allah's punishment. It is time you learn humility. Eyes down."

I rose and slid one foot out, centering my stance. I wanted to bend back his dick and drive it up his ass. Would the consequences be worth the reward? I lowered my head.

He bound my wrists behind my back. Then, as if he hadn't just plowed his fist into my face, his arm coiled around mine. "Walk with me."

Said the madman to the fly. I clenched my muscles to suppress my trembling.

He guided us to the stairs. Splinters of wood scattered the floor, gnawed from the chamber door's exterior.

Elbow to elbow, we squeezed into the narrow stairway. Two guards trailed our winding descent. My stomach flopped between their thirst leaking at my back and the anticipation of nearing Roark's cell.

On the final bend, I censored my movements. Loose limbs, steady breathing, and eyes down. Pretend Roark was dead. Pretend to be broken. I forced a pitch of uncertainty in my voice. "Permission to speak?" There, that sounded scared. Maybe I was.

His boots squeaked to a stop, pivoted toward me. His rib cage contracted. Even breaths whispered over my head.

Eyes down, eyes down. Oh, why did I open my mouth?

"Speak."

Shit. I'd lost my train of thought. When he released me to clutch his side, I went with it. "What are the pills for?"

The atmosphere surged with the animosity radiating off him. His hand curled on his abdomen then slid into his pocket, no doubt caressing the pill bottle. "Kidney."

Kidney?

Then we were moving again, double speed. The stairs emptied into a small atrium with two doorways. One opened to a corridor. The other had to be Roark's cell.

He stalled at Roark's door, fingers playing over my arm. My throat closed, but I didn't dare look at the barrier separating me from Roark.

When he tugged me toward the corridor, relief warred with the lump in my throat. Swallowing hard, I forced my feet to keep up.

We passed the hall's double doors. The tower's anteroom. The quadrangle. More doors. Then another stairwell, which took us below ground.

Mold tinged the damp air. A mist chilled the stairs and bit my bare feet. Kerosene fumed from torches marking each curve.

The last step butted a mahogany door. A flutter invaded my stomach, the Drone's cue to his guards. Their feet shuffled behind me as they retreated up the stairs.

As the door opened, he a made a rolling sweep of his arm. "My lab."

Did I expect dripping walls clad with chains and whips, a bedlam of unidentifiable body parts, beakers overflowing with sultry gases, and a skull fringed throne overlooking the savage activities? Yes, I did.

My imagination was amended with fluorescent bulbs swagging from the ceiling, biohazard bins and equipment beeping and blinking on immaculate workbenches.

A microscope slide skidded across the first desk as he passed. "Your survival is…perplexing, yet your blood is ordinary. Now it is time to further our research."

I kept my head down, pretended disinterest.

"In the name of Allah, behold Sura 2:223. 'Your women are the bearers of your seed. Thus, you may enjoy this privilege however you like, so long as you maintain righteousness.'" His tone hardened. "Like a field to cultivate, you will harvest children."

My head shot up. "Oh, and you'll be the sperm donor? Too bad you can't get it up."

He backhanded me. I stumbled, my tied hands hindering my balance. My tongue sloshed in a mouth of blood. I leaned over, let it rope to the concrete. The ache to start swinging was as compulsory as it was pointless.

Dirty fingers invaded my mouth, jamming into the open gash inside my cheek. Fuck, that hurt.

He yanked out his hand, smacked my face. "You'll remember your place."

"There's a hiccup in your plan." I spat more blood and braced for another punch. "I'm not fertile."

His fist slid across my jaw. I spun into a desk. Pain shot through my teeth. In the years I spent learning how to throw knives and tactically clear rooms, maybe I should have invested some time on stratagem and diversion. How the fuck would I talk myself out of there?

"Lying to me will not help your petition. Dr. Nealy confirmed your ovulation and fertility from your vaginal exam."

My whole body tensed. The doctor could've examined me any number of times he sedated me. And he would've discovered my IUD. I knew he hadn't removed it. The string that extended from my cervix was still there. I checked for it regularly to make sure the thing hadn't moved. Either the Drone was lying to me or the doctor was lying to the Drone.

The muffled squall of a baby diffused the room. I turned toward the maw looming at the end of the lab. Another winding stairway. Another basement. Whimpers crept from within.

Sweat formed on my nape. I twisted my hands in the binds at my back.

He gathered his long ringlets of hair into a surgeon cap and slipped on latex gloves, both at odds with the sable cape draping his shoulders. Then he clutched my bicep and hauled me into the black hole. His accent rolled in the dark. "It is time."

CHAPTER THIRTY-ONE: FEAR WHAT IS NOT UNDERSTOOD

I thought I understood fear.

I thought I understood fear when my hands were bound in my father's basement. When my legs were forced open by the man I considered a father.

I thought I understood fear when my dagger tore through my chest. When my breast flopped away from my muscle.

I thought I understood fear when my protector, my lover was chained to a wall and fed to an army of aphids. When only a foot separated us and there wasn't a goddamn thing I could do about it.

But I never had to wait for fear. It always sneaked up and took me by surprise.

It wasn't until the Drone pushed me through the door at the bottom of those stairs that I truly understood. This time, I would see it coming. I would have time to think about it, to dread it. This time, fear was waiting.

All hope abandon, ye who enter here!

Dante Alighieri

CHAPTER THIRTY-TWO: BROKEN WINGS

A cloud of rot chased me back. I stumbled, falling against the Drone's chest. Shock stole my breath and cremated my ability to process the swaying body, metal mask, dog crate, and spanking bench.

The shove at my back sent me hurtling. My toe caught. Graveled dirt smashed into my knees then my chin without my hands to stop the forward motion.

Two iron hooks hung from the ceiling, suspending a girl with all-white eyes. I would've gauged her youth as prepubescent if it weren't for the full-term bulge of her belly. Tiny hands curled around the prongs, which pierced through her palms and held her weight.

Blood stained the butterfly embroidery on her tattered skirt. A molded restraint mask with a barred mouth hole concealed her face but not the terror in her glassy eyes. Green-gray toes stretched toward the ground, toward the reprieve she wouldn't reach.

Bile spurted from my mouth and seeped into the earth. "Free the nymph. What's the point in hanging her like that?"

A boot heel dug into my hair, pinning my cheek to the dirt floor. "To break her."

Cane cuts on her undeveloped breasts expanded with her inhales. Her eyes fluttered closed. Silent. Broken.

Sconces blackened the sweating walls with smoke and cast dim light on the padded sawhorse and the naked body strapped to it. Tawny skin, ass pointing in the air, scar zigzagging his brow, depravity in his eyes. Why was the Imago restrained?

Latex fingers pinched my arm then I was flying toward the dog crate. The steel-toed punch in my back propelled me across the threshold. I curled at the rear of the cage to avoid the next kick. The gate shut and the padlock snicked, giving me a moment's freedom from his jumpy boots.

"What do you want?"

The Drone poked a stray curl into his cap. "Allah's chosen."

"What does that mean?" But I already knew.

"A master race. Human adherents of Islam." His eyes sparkled with delusional dreams.

I fought the scream out of my voice. "When you created the virus to wipe out the heretics"—starting with American women—"were nymphs part of that design?" I couldn't bring myself to look at the horror hanging from the ceiling.

He circled the spanking bench and rested a gloved palm in the spread of his brother's butt cheeks. "Yes. I chose the aphid genome for its adaptive reproductive abilities." He fingered the trembling cleft. "Did you know an aphid can create eggs or live nymphs depending on its environment?"

I lifted a stiff shoulder as his probing finger pulled a gurgled choke from the Imago.

Homosexuality didn't faze me, but incest and rape? The tongue-less protest wrung my stomach and roused a memory from the hall. Roark's abused nipples. The Drone's lingering touches. What if the doctor lied about no visitors in his cell? Bile resurfaced. I would do more than slice out his tongue.

A middle finger crammed past the ring of muscle that protected the Imago's bowels. "I created an evolutionary breed of female hosts. Seeding them with my family blood will ensure a pristine race."

The whacko had exterminated the human species to repopulate it himself. Yet, he rutted on men. And given the bruising around the Imago's rectum, he rutted often. Boy, was that a kink in his plan.

The nymph's moan saturated the room. Movement bubbled her bloated belly, a gruesome reminder that his plan was already in place.

Seeding them with my family blood.

The Imago didn't share his brother's sexual preference. I'd bet my carbine that nymph impregnation was in his job description. "How does one man repopulate the world?"

His mouth parted as he pumped his finger. Butt muscles quivered in the Imago's effort to press them together.

He withdrew his hand. "I isolated specific aphid species. Those that have telescoping generations." He stripped the gloves, donned a new pair and caught the blank look on my face. "It is the ability to carry a daughter within the womb, one who is also pregnant with a daughter. Additionally, the humanoid nymph has a four week gestation and swift healing. Now you see how I can manufacture Allah's chosen race."

The turbulence in my gut was merciless. "Sounds like a race of inbred retards rife with genetic disorders."

A charged current arced between us. "Weak recessive traits will be weeded out."

"Take out the weak and there'll be nothing left."

His boot crashed into the cage, denting the bars. "You will not disrespect my family."

"I'll make sure all future disrespect is for you alone." I was begging him to unleash. Brimming with my own need to lose it, I wanted those soulless eyes within clawing distance.

He grabbed the padlock and fumbled with the dial.

"What happens when all the mammals on this planet have been consumed and the blood runs out? What will your divine race sink its teeth into then?"

His hands stilled. "Allah's chosen race will not drink the blood of mortals. I am perfecting the genetics."

"Perfecting what genetics? You mean trial and error?"

All at once, he stormed to the back wall and stooped over a dark mound, hands digging through shapeless blobs. Fleshy smacks and revived decay filled the air. A baby's cry escaped the pile and tip-toed up my spine.

He flung something at the cage. It clipped the bars and flopped to the floor.

"Look closely, Eveline. Look at the abomination."

Heart pounding, I leaned forward. A tiny genderless body curled on its side. A bony leg angled backwards, jerking. Small wet noises crept from a fanged mouth. The human chest deflated. The spasms ceased.

I buckled over and buried my mouth in my shoulder. A succession of gagging pushed through. "This child's not any less human than you."

He charged the cage and kicked the baby across the room. Bones cracked when it hit the wall. My heart cracked with it.

"You are the key to fix this."

His DNA was altered with aphid and spider genomes. Didn't that make him the very thing he considered unworthy of survival? If the doctor were there, would he have defended that shit?

A pinch yanked my gut, like a hook on a line. I followed it to the torment strung to the ceiling. She didn't move, but her soul flickered and clung to me. I embraced the connection. The beat of her heart fell in sync with mine. Then it slowed. The thread between us snapped. Energy scattered through the room and dissipated.

The Drone followed my gaze. In a blur, he was at her side, hand on the pulse at her throat. "Eveline," he called without turning around. "Bone in or bone out?"

"What?"

"Bone out then." He jumped, cleaving to her body. The hooks ripped through her palms. He landed, gripped her neck and cracked it over his knee. The protruding spinal column gleamed in the artificial light as he swung the corpse toward the wall, where it joined the decomposing mound.

More bile pushed past my teeth, splattering my lap. My hands wrenched in the binds as I screamed, "The baby. Her baby." Oh Christ, why didn't he save it?

He stared at the ceiling, exhaled, then shot me a piercing look. "She was only two-weeks into gestation."

Impossible. "Why did she die?"

"Few survive the gestation period. She was especially weak. "

"She was a child." The burn in my throat roughened my voice as I asked the question my survival hinged on. "Why do you want them broken?"

A wave rippled through his cloak. "A broken winged bird cannot fly."

Neither could a heartbroken woman. Roark was the bandage that bound my wounds and held me together. My scars ripped open when I thought he was dead. Was there a limit to what I could endure to save him? And if I failed, would I have anything left to save myself?

The empty hooks rotated lazily, waiting.

He leaned closer to the bars. "I will break you."

I'd make damn sure he wouldn't. But when he unbuckled his brother's straps, my gut ignited.

The naked man stood on wobbly legs and swiped sputum from his chin. Muscles bucked in his chest and his red-veined eyes narrowed on the Drone.

"Lower your eyes!" The Drone's shout was a thunderclap, sending my chin into my chest though I knew it wasn't directed at me. "Very good. Now we had an agreement. You have earned your reward."

I could guess what that meant. I readied my muscles. Get him on his back. Put him in a choke hold. Then what? Use him as a hostage to get past the Drone? Piece of cake.

The Imago sauntered toward my cage, erection guiding his way. He dismantled the lock and gripped my ankles with sweaty hands. Gravel scraped my back as he dragged me out. I twisted a leg free, hooked it around his.

He stumbled but stayed on his feet. His foot shot toward my face. I rolled to my stomach, panting. He panted, too, crawling atop me, crushing the air from my lungs.

The Drone's boots paced by. "Dear brother, shall I retrieve her incentive?"

Roark. My cheek touched the floor, exhales steaming on the crumbling stone. "That won't be necessary."

Hard-on jabbed in my back, I lay on my stomach and absorbed the enormity of my nightmare. First, he would rape me. Probably in the next few moments. Probably on the sawhorse. Then he would repeat the violation day after day until my womb rounded with…what? A child? A monster? Between coitus, they'd hang me from the hooks. If I fought them and lost, they'd bring in Roark. If I cooperated—my stomach lurched—I'd have nine months to plan my escape. They wouldn't kill me until I delivered. Or worse, they would never kill me.

The ice cold hand of fear took hold of me. It closed my eyes so I couldn't see and clung to my skin in cold beads of sweat. I tasted it on my tongue as my back teeth carved more gashes in my cheeks.

He flipped me over, gripped my jaw and widened his own. A purple stump bobbed around the shouts gargling in his gullet. His other hand held his dagger at my throat, slid it down my sternum. As it cut through the robe and chemise, it caught the leather string around my neck. My turquoise rock spun through the air and landed on the heap of bodies.

My muscles screamed to retaliate. Inhale. Exhale. I would survive whatever they dished out, with Roark and my soul intact. "Do your worst."

The hilt jarred my teeth, whipping my head back. Pain shot through my neck. He used that moment to force my legs apart and kneel between them.

I writhed and bucked, tried to roll from under him. His hand captured my throat and squeezed. My lungs labored and the room dimmed.

"Siraj." The familiar voice pushed through the wave of pain.

The doctor's black eyes came into focus above us. "My recommendation stands, stronger now than ever, that we run more tests before our human host conceives."

Human host? I wanted to stab him. And hug him.

The Imago released me and threw up his hands, eyes flashing. "Ro ew ell."

"I agreed to help you under my terms, Aiman. I expected your trust in this partnership. I will not wager our only human host for your brother's lasciviousness. If you value my expertise and this partnership, you will heed my counsel."

Lines formed below the ridge of the Drone's cap. "Imago, leave us."

Spit landed on my face through the Imago's incoherent utterance.

"Now." The Drone's voice sent a shiver through my bones.

He rolled to his feet and stomped out.

The Drone hauled me up. "I've told you before," he said to the doctor, "you will refer to me as the Drone. And our host is evolving." He spun me, pointing my back to the doctor. "You see?" His finger dug into my shoulder blade. "We cannot wait. You have one week to validate your tests. In that time, we will not compromise her." He shoved me toward the doctor and bent over to clutch his side. "One week."

A shirt fell over my shoulders. The doctor tugged me up the stairs, the lab, more stairs. I tripped and spat blood on the landing. He caught my waist and didn't slow.

I kept his pace. "They were pretty intent on breaking me and impregnating me. How did you deter them so easily? And why?"

A tremor moved through his arm where it wrapped around my shoulders. "They celebrate and fear your survival in equal measures. My warning gave the fear more bite." He gave me a sidelong glance. "The why is more complicated."

Moonlight showered the quadrangle. The proximity of the fortress' exit arrested my feet. The tide howled. The scent of sea plants and stranded shellfish invaded my nose.

He looked out toward the stone archway, conflict waging in his face.

The Imago stood at the center of the open area formed by three main wings of the fortress, blocking the exit, surrounded by aphids. He raised his dart gun, shooting them at random.

Glowing green skin hissed. A series of exploding bodies popped. Insides became outsides. Cooked organs and flesh simmered where they once stood. The remaining aphids skittered back.

"Let's go." The doctor gripped my hips and heaved me over his shoulder. I kneed his chest. He tightened his hold and proceeded down the corridor, back to my cell.

We ascended the stairs. The wound on my heart flared as Roark's door disappeared from sight. The last few hours burrowed further inside me with each step. By the time we reached the chamber, images of the raped nymph and the baby's twitching leg had burned into my eyes.

He locked the gate and removed my shackles. If he noticed his comrades' brutality in my swelling face, he didn't show it. He stood a punch away, watching me, expressionless. A barricade to my freedom.

I shot a straight right jab and startled when the punch connected.

He bounced backwards. Blood gushed from his nose. His eyes crept up to meet mine.

I shook out my hand. "I. Hate. You."

He winced. "Anger and hate are signs of weakness. You've witnessed that first hand today."

I charged. He lifted his forearm to block his face. I hooked my arm under his, twisted and used the bottom of my foot to sweep the back of his leg. His shoulder collided with the floor.

Surprised by the easy take down, I jumped up and away. He rolled to his hands and knees and stared up at me.

"Why aren't you fighting back?"

He dropped his head. Blood gathered on the tip of his nose and dripped to the floor.

I slammed a knee to his side and knocked him over. "I don't care if you are giving this freely so long as you're feeling pain."

He lay on his side, offering an easy kick to his gut. "*Nannakola*, this is not as painful as the hate in your eyes every time you look at me."

I froze in mid-kick and dropped my foot. His expression transformed, swamped with warmth, compassion, attractiveness even. It wrapped around me like a hug. Did he lie to the Drone about my IUD? At the very least, he stopped the Imago from raping me.

There was the corroded wobble in my gut again. "What do you want?"

"To give you something. It's in my pocket."

At my nod, he pulled himself to his feet and dug in his pants. He reached for my palm and uncoiled a leather strap over it.

Black and tan hairs matted the ties. My throat burned as I turned it over. *Darwin* was seared in the tanned skin.

Eros will have naked bodies; Friendship naked personalities.

C.S. Lewis

CHAPTER THIRTY-THREE: EROS' NEEDLE

"Where's Jesse?"

"The savage? No doubt he's sharpening the axe he threatened to use in the removal of my manhood." The doctor crossed and uncrossed his arms. "He intends to rescue you."

"And you intend to stop him."

"No."

I chewed on my lip and tried to suppress the hope offered by the collar in my hand. I thought I lost Jesse in Dover.

"He sent a message. *Wanunhecun* for the third time."

Three mistakes. He said *wanunhecun* after he misjudged my ability to handle weapons. I scratched the scar on my chest. I knew he would take responsibility for my attack in Dover. The third? My kidnapping? "He was at River Tweed?"

"He arrived as we boarded the chopper. He almost freed your priest but the army pushed him back."

"And what? Now he's here? On Malta? How'd you get this?" I held up the collar.

"Last night. When I left here, I crossed the quad to my quarters." His jaw clenched. "An arrow missed my head by millimeters."

A smile tipped the corners of my mouth. "He doesn't miss. He wanted your attention."

"Mm."

Jesse tried to free Roark and didn't kill the doctor. Apparently, he wasn't threatened by either man. Giddiness rushed through me. "What did he say?"

He shifted his weight from one foot to the next.

I laughed. "He threatened you. Tell me."

A sigh. "He said if you get so much as a scratch while on my watch, he will scalp me slowly as he asphyxiates me with my own intestine."

I touched my swollen jaw. "You've got more problems than I do."

His face fell. Something flooded his eyes as they drifted over my injuries. Then it was gone. "He demanded the combinations to yours and the priest's cell. He has a chartered boat. And bodyguards. He's thorough."

How would he get through undetected by the Drone's network of aphid communication? Through them, the Drone had eyes and ears everywhere.

"I gave him the combinations."

My pulse jumped. "So he's coming?"

"He came this morning."

That morning. My eyes shot to the door and the shreds of splintered wood on the floor. "Fuck. The Drone retrieved me around dawn. That was my fault." My hand went to my stomach. "I called him somehow."

His face remained empty.

"But Roark...he's—"

"Free."

"Free? Jesse got past the guards?"

A watchful nod. "Right under Aiman's nose. You had him thoroughly distracted."

Air whooshed from my lungs and with it a heavy weight. I sat on the bed and rubbed my temples, the leather strap wound around my fingers. It caressed my cheek and brought a flood of remembered scents. Dog breath. Mountain yews. Hickory coffee. The same memories stirred by my turquoise rock.

"That Iraqi bastard took my necklace."

He regarded me as closely as I him. "I'll get it back."

I couldn't see past the damn facade that always blanked his face. How could I trust him? Could he have overpowered Jesse? Captured him and collected the collar? No, I had Jesse's message.

"I wasn't the only one distracting the Drone. Did you know they have an incest thing going on?"

A stray lock fell over his brow. "It's not consensual."

"No, figured that much out." My fingers itched to brush his hair back, to see if it was as silky as it looked. And why was that? Jesse remained an unreachable fascination. Roark filled in the void in my heart and kept his off limits. I didn't need the doctor to make things more confusing. Focus, Evie. "Why did Jesse give you the collar if he planned to rescue me himself?"

"Backup plan. In case he didn't make it. He wanted you to know you could trust me. Like I said, he's thought of everything."

"Why would he trust you?"

"He is"—he cleared his throat—"perceptive."

I narrowed my eyes.

He glanced at the chamber door and lowered his voice. "He knew my allegiance lies elsewhere."

"And where would that be?"

"I'm a member of a scientific community looking for the cure."

My jaw dropped. "The Shard."

His shiny black head inclined. "My history with Aiman coupled with certain"—he rubbed his nape—"skills made me an easy guise to infiltrate his activities and ascertain the cure. I established our partnership but ran into two roadblocks. One, he hadn't perfected the cure. And two..." He fastened those penetrating eyes on mine.

"Me?"

He swiped blood from his nose. "When I discovered he didn't have a cure yet, I began plotting my exit. Then, he found you." He blinked at me under drawn brows. "I couldn't stop your abduction without unveiling my disguise and surrendering his captured nymphs. As it turns out, all of the nymphs perished anyway."

I leaned against the wall and wrapped an arm over my twisting gut. "You deceived me."

He sat beside me, leaning elbows on knees. "Would you have believed the truth?"

"I'm not sure what to believe." Believing him meant he wasn't who I thought he was. It meant I'd been a hateful bitch while he risked his guise to protect me.

A bright airy sensation filled my chest. Maybe it was weeks of loneliness slamming into me, but I lifted my hand, held it palm up in his lap.

Quiet floated between us as he stared at it. The wait wilted into sad patience then rejection. The pain of it curled my fingernails into my palm. I pulled my hand away.

He caught it and the moment our fingertips brushed, a jolt of emotion flooded me. Our eyes collided.

His fingers snaked around mine, his other arm supported my back, brought me into his chest. "They'll come back for you." His hug tightened. "Your priest was loath to leave. That arrow-wielding savage hauled him out with his axe at his throat."

Sandalwood smothered my senses. Not cologne. All natural. All him. I nestled my nose further in his neck. "It's a tomahawk."

"It's barbaric."

"Who else knows the combinations? His escape will be pinned on you."

"The cook who delivered his food. He won't be talking."

I raised my head. "How can you be sure?"

"A fierce woman showed me an efficient way to silence people."

I shoved him away. "You took an innocent man's tongue?"

He folded his hands on his hand and looked at me through thick fans of lashes. "Evie, that man beat your priest at every opportunity and fed him only the spoils from the kitchen."

Oh, Roark. I released a shaky exhale. "So that's where you've been all day."

For the first time, his gaze scrutinized my face. "May I treat your injuries?"

I wiggled my jaw. Pain shot through my head but nothing was broken. "Tell me about the botched plan first."

"There are no boats on Malta. The Drone sank them all. The only way on or off the archipelago is by plane. But your savage—"

"Jesse."

"—came by boat. The boat he planned to leave on once he freed you and your priest."

"And you'd let me go? Just like that?" I knew he would. I wanted to hear it.

"I would see you safe. Above all agendas."

I opened my eyes, realizing I'd closed them. "What's the backup plan?"

"I give you the collar and wait. But when I found you downstairs held down by that…" His lips formed a hard line. Then he stood and paced. "I would've hauled you off the island myself if Siraj hadn't been in the courtyard when we passed. It would've been a vain attempt. I had no strategy. I was so…" He cast me dark look then resumed pacing. "This island is guarded by hundreds of aphids, each one linked to Aiman. He sees what they see. We wouldn't have made it beyond the fortress walls."

"That's why you haven't tried to escape with me?"

He knelt before me. "Think about it. Fill your mind with compassion and you'll find the truth."

I licked my lips. I believed him all the way down to the marrow of my psyche. "Can we start over?" I offered my hand.

Fingers slid across my palm. "Call me Michio."

"Michio, I'm Evie."

He tightened his grip. "Aiman cannot know my identity. If he gets a hold of your blood, the consequences—"

"Time out." I pulled my hand back. "You've been giving him my blood for weeks."

He shook his head, sat back on his heels. "A sleight of hand. I always swapped your vial with a substitute. Aiman has been relentlessly studying my blood."

"He's got to know." I patted the bruised vein in my elbow. "Don't men have an extra chromosome?"

"I suggested you are hermaphrodite or intersex with atypical sex chromosomes."

"What?"

"Of course, it isn't true. Besides, looking to chromosomes for gender specification is antiquated. I won't go into that."

He rose from his knees and returned to the edge of the bed. "Your blood confirmed what I suspected." He picked at a fray in the blanket.

"Want to tell me what's making your face twist like that?"

"You're faster than them. You can control them acoustically. You could see them outside with Siraj tonight when I couldn't. Is that right?"

I nodded.

"Then there are the spiders. Your predator. They're drawn to you. The Drone is especially aggressive toward you. He's never bit anyone else. It's his spider genetics, his instinct to do so with you. And there's something else." He stood and gestured for me to follow him out of the cell. We stopped before the mirror above the bathroom sink.

A towel appeared in front of me as he removed my borrowed shirt. Then he offered a small mirror from the drawer and turned my back toward the sink. I lifted it as he brushed my hair over my shoulder to bare my back. A nickel-sized black spot tattooed my shoulder.

"This is what you've been pestering me about. I really have no idea..." I backed up until my butt hit the sink. The roundness of the dot was unnaturally perfect. I reached across my chest and touched it. "…what this is." No pain or sensation. A shiver crept over my spine as I caught his awed expression.

"I do." He tilted my hand. The reflection caught four more black dots, each comparable in size and shape to the first one. Three on one shoulder blade. Two on the other. Like blotches of ink under the skin.

He traced the spots, connected one to the other with an invisible line. "You didn't have them when I examined you on the jet to Malta. They appeared after you passed out in the hall. Was that the first time you tried controlling aphids?"

The mirror shook in my hand. My throat was dry. "Yes."

"Each time you signal them, a new one appears. And your eyes…"

"My eyes?"

"I know when you're communicating because your eyes turn black. Your irises. Your sclera. All pitch black."

My breathing shallowed. "That sounds…bad."

He shook his head. "It's good, Evie. You share the genetic properties of the coccinellidae, the ladybird. You exhibit their strengths and their weaknesses. Yet, you're still human." His pupils dilated. "An enhanced human, adapted to kill aphids."

Tremors infiltrated my body. I handed him the mirror. "I need to go to the bathroom."

He turned his back and filled the tub. Still didn't trust me?

"I can bathe myself."

"Your wounds need cleaning and stitches. I'm still your doctor."

A crimson slash puckered my arm. Where did that come from? I extended my jaw and thousands of needles invaded my head. The ooze from the gash inside my cheek left a rancid taste in my mouth.

He'd bathed me dozens of times, but this time felt different. I flushed the toilet and curiosity sent me climbing into the tub.

He bent over the edge and submersed a sponge. "We have one week. We're not waiting for your guardians."

My guardians?

He cleansed my injured arm and laid it on the ledge. "Let this dry."

As he focused on the cuts on my face, I realized this bath was different for him too. Beneath his clinical movements was a stirring of something intrinsic to a man in the presence of a naked woman. The bead of sweat on his brow. The shift of his eyes. The tremor in his fingers. I found a strange comfort knowing he was as affected by me as I was by him. It felt human.

He made gentle dabs around my mouth. "You can control the army. We just need to hone your command. You have to block Aiman's link to his guards. And blind him. Then we have a chance."

We? My belly fluttered. "Command them how? I get deafening headaches. Nose bleeds. I pass out after mere minutes."

"Yang." His voice was soft.

"Yang."

He lifted his bag onto the toilet and dug through it until a sealed package of needles and thread appeared in his hand. "I can't explain the pigment changes in your skin and eyes without more testing. I've tried to attribute it to bruising, acute shock, blood loss, the spider bites. There's no medical explanation." He prodded the gash on my arm. "I'm stitching this first. Ready?"

At my nod, the needle poked my skin. The tugging was uncomfortable but nothing compared to the pain when I stitched myself in Roark's bathroom.

He clipped the thread, reading my face. "You trust me, don't you?"

"If I didn't, I wouldn't be having this conversation with you while you ogle my tits."

"I'm not—" His gaze flicked to my chest where my nipples poked above the suds. A blush swept over his golden skin and he steadied the needle next to my smile. "We know the"—he cleared his rough voice—"relax your mouth, Evie."

My smile widened. Had he always been that easy to unsettle? After a few attempts, I loosened the muscles in my cheeks.

"We know the ladybird is the aphid's predator. Seeing its physical traits morphing on you...maybe it is mimicry. A form of adaptation assisting you in survival. Or maybe it is teleologic evolution." He glanced at my face. "A derivative of Aristotle's four causes where adaptation occurs for a purpose, an end goal." He pierced another hole. "What we do know is your adaptations are not chance and are undeniable functions of your defenses."

I chewed on his speculation. "So those are your theories on how I'm...evolving. Why do I go into shock?"

"Flip around so I can do that eye."

He stared at his lap as I turned. "Are you familiar with Yin and Yang and its relationship to the body?"

"No clue."

"Yang represents the masculine virtues of nature. The bright burst of a solar flare. The tough shell of a penguin egg. Clay, hardened and fired by the sun. This is balanced with Yin, its feminine polarity. A velvet petal opening under a midnight sky. The roll of a worm pushing soil. A gurgle in an ice water spring." A pause. "Do you feel cold or slowed down when the vibrations hit you?"

I thought about it. "Yeah, but only once did I let the symptoms go too far. That's when I passed out."

His forearms rested on the ledge, drawing his face close to mine. "And that's when I touched your head in the hall. You were summoning the aphids away from your priest. When I touched you, they stopped."

"Okay." I tumbled into his jet eyes, trusting him.

"It was Yang." He stabbed wet fingers in his hair, making the ends stand in chaotic sexy spikes. "Yin and Yang are always vying for balance. The Yang of day turns toward the Yin of night. Without harmony between the two, the body and mind aren't healthy."

"Not sure I'm following."

"Man or woman, all bodies contain Yin and Yang. Yet you're only able to tap into the dark, feminine Yin as your fuel, which is why you needed my touch—Yang—to complete the symmetry. Yang is outward Chi flow. Once depleted, your Yin surges to compensate." He muttered to himself, "Which is why your body goes into shock as you continue to draw from your energy."

He turned my chin to suture the final gash. His eyelashes lowered and the stone set of his face crumbled away. "I won't let them hurt you again."

My heart drummed a furious tempo. "I think you just exposed a feeling, Dr. Nealy."

His iron bound expression returned. "I'm serious. We need to leave." His tone matched his glare. "I thought I had more time to get you out safely, but after Aiman took you down there…he's impatient. Time's up."

I reached for the sponge and gestured him closer. When he dipped his head, I rinsed the blood from his nose, his chiseled cheekbones, his full lips. He was so stunning, my heart ached. "I don't hold it against you for not being there today."

His eyes leapt to mine. A flux of emotions bounced between us.

"Seeing how you were busy helping the savage free Roark."

He looked away, but his shoulders moved closer.

"And you still found the time to rescue me." I lowered the sponge. "Do you forgive me for taking my anger out on you?"

The downcast tilt of his eyes lifted. "There's nothing to forgive." His chest was bent over the tub, arching closer, closer, as if his body was starving for touch. His eyes fluttered closed.

I found myself wishing he would fall in and be forced to remove the shirt that hid his sculpted body. My heart hammered in my ears as I closed the gap.

"Ow." He jerked back.

"What? What happened?"

He held up the needle and rotated his forearm where he'd pricked himself.

I laughed despite the bite of the stitches around my mouth. "Back to this Yang thing. You know I have those nightmares. When I sleep next to a man, I don't have them. Could Yang have something to do with it?"

"Skin-to-skin contact? Yes, of course." His voice jumped. "You're absorbing Yang, strengthening your subconscious against threats."

"It sounds"—I scratched my head—"kind of fantastical."

He released the plug from the drain. "It's the most fundamental concept in Asian medicine, and very important that you understand. Think of Yin as the body and Yang as the spirit. If the spirit returns to the air, the body is restored to the earth. Without the spirit, you'll die." He cupped his hand with water and let it trickle over my leg as I stood. "It could be our way out. We have to test it." He wrapped a towel around me and dropped his voice. "But only while I fuel your Yang."

"How will we do that exactly?"

The Valley Spirit never dies
It is called the Mysterious Female
The entrance to the Mysterious Female
Is called the root of Heaven and Earth
Endless flow
Of inexhaustible energy

Tao Te Ching

CHAPTER THIRTY-FOUR: INEXHAUSTIBLE ENERGY

Dark and drippy clouds floated above the rafters and spat a mist into the ceiling-less chamber. I wiped my brow. "The Drone's going to feel me doing this."

Michio raised the hem of my shift to my nape and drew my back to his bare chest. "Try to relax."

"Trying. I should be exhausted since I didn't sleep last night."

"You know how to prevent those nightmares." His gentle tone stroked private places inside me.

"We'll talk about it later." When his lap wasn't cupping my nude backside.

"I'm going put my arms around you now."

I pulled my lips between my teeth and nodded. Two tentative hands eased under my gown. Forearms on my abdomen shifted us deeper into the couch. Drops of rain trickled off the waterproof cushions.

"Just take your time." His voice brushed that sensitive spot below my ear. "When you're ready, call the guard into the room."

The couch faced the chamber door, which was closed but not latched. I sucked in a needed breath and focused on the ever present hum on the other side. My command poured forth like words from my mouth. *Come.*

A pulse, unlike my heartbeat, rattled in my chest. The door held still.

I dug deeper. Yin or Yang, whatever it was, I amassed my fuel. I imagined it in a tangible form, like a vapor writhing around me. It crept up my spine and stretched over my ribs. But it was weak, as if a heavy exhale would wisp it away.

I reached under my gown and ran my arms along his until our limbs intertwined. Then I tried again. *Come.*

A bright light accompanied a warm wash of my senses. My skin heated where it made contact with his as I siphoned his vitality and replenished mine. The energy propelled from my backbone and out through my chest, taking my breath with it.

The door crashed open and the aphid guard filled the frame. Glassy eyes pointed at me.

I coiled my mind around the connection, solidifying it. *Closer.*

A flow ignited between us and the tiny setae on its green arms bristled, catching my transmission. Jaw-snot sprayed the floor. Segmented feet scuffled. One step. Two.

Its body jerked. Rain drops sizzled on its skin.

Oh shit. "The rain. Water will kill it."

The tenuous thread gathered size and strength, straining to pull away.

"Just sprinkling." His whisper was distracted and rapt with awe. "Keep your focus."

"It's fighting me. Still think I can do this without getting eaten?"

"You're doing it. The mind is everything. Center your thoughts, let it empower you."

I closed my eyes. Control the aphid. Take over the army. Find Roark and Jesse. Kill the psycho brothers. Get the hell off Malta. Oh, and discover the cure. My eyes popped open. "Right."

"You cold? Dizzy?"

His body against mine warmed me inside and out, enough that the memory of it would keep me warm as I slept alone that night. "I'm good."

He skipped his hands along my torso as if trying to catch the weightless sensations bouncing between me and the salivating creature. "Bring it closer."

Inhale. Breathe out. *Closer* leapt from my chest.

The aphid slid two more steps, its bowed body quivering.

"Look at that. Incredible." His admiration penetrated the static charged room. "Do you sense Aiman?"

A network of electric-like trails crisscrossed my mind's eye. The strands thrummed with single-focus, consistent with aphid hunger. "The only crazy I'm sensing is coming from this couch."

His chuckle danced against my back where our skin touched. I wanted to turn and see what his beautiful face looked like wearing a smile, but a clawed foot dragged over the tiles. Then the other foot. More dragging. Getting too close. My order burst from my tailbone and escaped with the air from my lungs. *Stop.*

It halted an arm's span away and cocked its head. Tiny pupils arrowed on me. Tubular parts slid over one another in its throat, connected by strings of black snot.

"I'm doing that," I whispered. "I'm controlling it."

When the arms around me squeezed, I realized he was putting his life in my hands. If I didn't trust him, if I wished him harm, I could use the aphid to attack him.

The skin between its exoskeletal scales twitched with restrained hunger. I probed the thread that linked us. "It's afraid of me. And the rain's pissing it off. But there's also...curiosity."

"You feel all that?"

"Don't ask me how—"

My stomach bucked and forced a yelp from my throat.

He tightened his embrace. "What was that?"

"The hunger. The Drone's starving them." A chill crept over me, followed by an onslaught of dizziness.

"Evie?"

I burrowed into his chest and braced for another shiver. "It's really hungry. Trying to break my hold." My teeth clicked together. "I'm cold."

"Hang on." He half stood and pushed down his pants without releasing his hold around my waist. Then he sat us back on the couch, legs bare under mine. Only the thin material of his boxers lay between us.

Warmth replaced the chill. Tension left my body and the wooziness passed. I swallowed. *Leave.*

The trudge of retreating feet scraped through the room.

"Well," I said, "the Yang thing works."

He nestled his face into my neck. The intimacy of his lips sent a different kind of warmth through me. I held my breath, confused by his affection at the same time savoring the tingle pulling through my womb.

The aphid froze at the door, crouched, pincers raised. Its torso heaved as sucking parts punched from its gullet.

Leave bloomed in my chest and sprang free.

It straightened, a tremor rippling its limbs. Then it scurried out.

I pivoted in his lap. "That last move you did...you can't do that."

His inky irises peeked from under half lids, regarding me, not as my doctor but as something else. His hands, a heavy heat on my thighs, crackled electricity over my skin.

"Dammit, Michio." My feet hit the floor and my shift fell in place.

The aphid hunkered just outside the chamber. I jogged across the room and slammed the door shut.

He hauled on his pants. "What happened?"

"Arousal. That's what happened. Shit. That's how I called the Drone last night." I held my hand over my stomach and searched for his poisonous chasm amidst the psychic threads. "I don't feel him."

He eyes roamed my face and his brows snapped up. "Pheromones. Chemical communication. That's what you're broadcasting."

"Yeah."

"That could be bad."

"You think?"

"Let's try it again. This time, beckon two guards from downstairs."

That night, I lay in bed and watched the subtle movement of Michio's chest on the couch. He wouldn't leave the chamber despite my demands that he search for Jesse and Roark. And I couldn't sleep mulling over the risks they were taking on an island of aphids.

Roark's flirtatious smile appeared every time I closed my eyes. His drawl purred through me and curled my toes.

Then I saw Jesse's copper eyes, rough-hewn jawline, pillowy lips. When our paths collided in the foothills of West Virginia, those exquisite features would twist up as if I disgusted him. Yet, he left his brethren to follow me across an ocean, a continent.

Even more conflicting than my relationships with a celibate priest and a half-mad Lakota was the man sleeping feet away. I wanted to know him better, and I would. Until then, I didn't know if, behind his tenting fingers and penetrating eyes, he was analyzing my evolving genetics or memorizing my features the way I memorized his.

I felt gluttonous taking inventory of the men in my life, yet I couldn't ignore the fullness they gave me. Their protection, their devotion settled deep inside me, taking up space in the lonely places of my heart, making me feel a lot less lonely.

And a lot more needy. My fingers meandered over my hip, stretched toward the heat between my legs. I imagined they were

Michio's fingers rubbing the bud of nerves there. In thirty seconds, the ache would be soothed.

Bannnng. Bang. The door shook. I bolted upright.

Michio's bulky silhouette appeared at the gate. "Evie?"

"Shit." I clenched my thighs and dropped my forehead to my knees.

The gate snicked and the mattress dipped. "What are you thinking about?"

Not going there. I stared at the wall beside his head.

His nostrils flared and his eyes captured mine. "You're aroused."

The heat in my cheeks extinguished any chance of escaping with my dignity. "I'm not."

"Turn it off."

I shifted my hips, unintentionally rubbing against his. "You give really shitty advice."

He reached for me and hesitated. A sigh floated between us. "Bet that mouth gets you in a lot of trouble."

My face burned hotter. "Bet you'd like to find out."

The brush of his thumb on my jaw belied the professional detachment in his voice. "Your testosterone levels aggravate your aggression. And your arousal."

The pulse between my legs agreed.

He lowered his voice. "I can numb it."

I pretended to misunderstand. "I don't want to be sedated. Thought we were past that."

The clement breeze fanned his sandalwood scent around me. My breaths quickened and I knew he noticed.

A hunk of black hair fell over his bowed head. "Let me ease you, *Nannakola.*"

I flinched, even as my heart stretched in my chest, reaching for him. "How would that work? Arousal's the problem. You're making it worse."

"If you can't shut it off, you need an outlet. Direct it to me."

I'd learned that morning I could isolate my transmissions to a specific aphid. Since I didn't know how to turn off the pheromones, it meant I could funnel the waves to him and deflect the aphids from feeling it.

I strangled my enthusiastic heart with the knowledge that his offer was a medical diagnosis, not some romantic attempt to make out with me. "What's behind door number two?"

He reached in his pocket, bent across my lap, and set a syringe on the side table.

Ugh. That would work if the wall-imparted lump on my forehead was anything to go by.

A growl rumbled through the door followed by the cracking of wood.

I chewed my thumb nail. Shirtless, his well-cut shoulders blocked out everything in the room. It'd been so much easier to ignore my attraction to him when he was my enemy. "What did you have in mind?"

"Come here." He patted his knees.

When I leaned toward him, he curved a hand around the small of my back and guided me into his lap. His other hand traced my collarbone, bared above the wide neckline of my chemise. He followed the contour of my neck and tipped up my chin. I forgot to breathe.

His thumb padded my bottom lip. "Breathe, Evie."

My lungs emptied in a whoosh and his mouth fastened to mine. Our lips moved together in silent exploration, a tongue touch. Tenderness without expectation. I liked it. Too much.

He flexed everywhere I put my hands. Skin stretched over the cords of his shoulders. The wide column of his neck contracted as his tongue chased mine, seductively, expertly. Every taste he gave and took fed the blaze within me. Our breaths became one. My body sang.

But beneath the feel of his lips and the tingle of his fingertips on my jaw, I sensed constraint. The edges of his mouth hardened. His hips made a slight roll. Still, he kept it soft and steady, holding himself away from me. Just like Roark.

A twinge stabbed my heart. I broke the kiss and tucked my fingers in my elbows.

Silence waited beyond the door. He wore his usual stone mask. "It worked."

I touched my lips. His eyes followed my fingers, his voice passive. "You're thinking about the priest."

A swallow bounced my throat. "He's celibate. We don't have that kind of relationship." The twinge in my heart sharpened.

He remained quiet, the moonlit sky graying his flawless complexion. I fell into the hypnotic trance of his eyes as they watched me with too much knowing. My libido was calm but his beauty prompted me. "Stay."

His body hardened. Then, with each breath, the woodenness rolled away. He leaned in. "What do you need?"

I lifted a shoulder and let my eyes fall to his naked torso. "Skin."

He stretched out on his side in the space I gave him, looped an arm over me and tugged my chest to his.

My nose settled in the hollow of his throat. He smelled so clean, I wondered if I pressed closer I could absorb some of his humanity. Could I inhale it from his lips to mine? "I never thanked you."

"For what?"

For the forced meals. The baths. Fending off spiders and infection. "For keeping me alive when I didn't want it."

His chin settled on my head. "Hunger of heart is the greatest sickness. I don't know how to heal that." Pain tinged his voice. "I failed to guard your heart and your mind."

He felt right in my arms. "You guard my body. Even from myself."

"Until the day I die."

His words moved something inside me. I strengthened my hug around him and buried my smile in his chest. "Till you die?"

"Not a day sooner."

My smile grew so big, it exploded across my face. My cheeks strained to hold it, hurting even, but I didn't want to let it go.

The tightness of the robe was suffocating. So was the air of impatience wafting off the Drone as he circled me. In his daily visits, he hadn't once mentioned Roark's escape nor had he found Michio alone to confront him. "I want progress."

"And you'll have it," Michio said with a bored tone.

"It's been four days. My doubt in your success is surpassed only by my frustration with the two months you've wasted with her."

Which meant it was April. Two years since the outbreak. Annie would've moved on from ribbons and dolls to earrings and boy bands. Aaron would've climbed the ranks in Karate, perhaps knotting a brown belt with a glowing smile dimpling his cheeks. My chest squeezed.

The Drone bent his head, his mouth a scant inch from mine. "Three more days," he breathed in my face. He smiled and the flash a sizable white tooth stole the air from my lungs. Behind him, the muscles in Michio's throat strained and his eyes smoldered.

All at once, the Drone's face contorted, his hand pawing at the lid of his pill bottle. Then he blustered out in a rustle of papers, shocking my lungs back into action.

I rubbed my neck where his bite had healed. "I think he has fangs."

Michio remained rooted beside my bed, his body taut. "We need to leave. Now."

"I bet he wears that theatrical cape because he's hiding wings."

He didn't move. His arms hung at his sides but his chin seemed to lower. His body grew stiffer.

"What's wrong with you?"

He shook himself. "I used to be better at hiding it." Two long strides and he towered over me, hand around my nape. "I have never wanted him near you. He's getting too close. We need to leave."

"We're not ready."

"Did you hear him? Three days."

"I heard. Three days and it's back to the dungeon." I squared my shoulders. "Believe me. I know what the brothers have planned for me there."

"The way Aiman pops his pills around you, I'm not so sure—"

"His pills? For his kidney?"

He stared at me for a beat that trickled into five. "There's nothing wrong with his kidney. He's feigning symptoms in attempt to draw his attention from the real problem."

"His metamorphosis?"

"His repulsion of women. Of you."

I burst into laughter, choking my words. "Why would he do that?"

"The lie is more comforting than the truth."

"The truth that he's a fucking psycho?" My laughter reached hysterics.

He talked over me. "We don't know how far his repulsion will take him. We're leaving now."

I sobered. "We're not ready."

We'd practiced my communication with the aphids every day. As long as I kept physical contact with him and quashed my arousal, they followed my command. My communication even reached to the ground floor but I could only juggle three under my control at one time.

His grip on my neck tightened. "We are."

"We're not." The Jabara brothers prayed five times a day. During their prayer time, Michio walked the quadrangle to draw out Jesse. "We agreed to give Jesse one more day to contact us." Then we'd leave the fortress, with or without his help. If I could control every aphid we encountered, we'd escape under the Drone's radar. But outside the fortress, we'd have to find Jesse and his boat.

My hand went to my forearm. "I don't even have my weapons anymore."

"You don't need them." At my glare, he grabbed my hand and led me to his laptop and scattered notebooks on the couch. "I want to show you something."

He tapped the screen. "This is premature, until I can prove it…"

Always a disclaimer. "Spit it out."

"It's just…look at this."

A 3-D image of DNA rotated in a kaleidoscope of colors.

"That mine?"

His head inclined. "Your make-up is dynamic. It resists everything I throw at it. According to my tests, your blood's not only poisonous to the aphids but exponentially more potent."

My pulse fired in my throat. "You said I was human."

He scrubbed his hand through his hair. "You are. But as a human with these traits, you can likely withstand an aphid bite. And if that's the case…Evie, you carry the cure."

I stepped back. "The cure to reverse the aphid mutation?"

He stared at the screen. "No. That morphogenesis is final. But through our research in Iceland, we discovered in nymphs a genetic code that isn't transformed when they evolve. It's dormant. You might carry the key that can reactivate it."

"So let's test the poison theory. Call in an aphid. Inject it with my blood."

"How would we keep Aiman from feeling its exploding heart?"

"Good point." I narrowed my eyes. "You've been keeping this from me."

"I had to be sure."

Of course, he did. I paced, pausing to gather the skirts of my gown in one hand. "Now what?"

The scuff of sandals sounded his approach and his hand caught my waist. Warm lips moved along my hairline, trailed down my cheek and hovered over mine. "You have become the path. Now you travel it."

My hands crept up the carved brawn of his chest. "You may not want to follow then. I'm pretty sure it's the path to hell."

His fingers ambled around my back. "Can we leave now?"

I crushed my hips against his. "One more day. Find Jesse—"

A scratch screeched along the door. Then the banging began.

"Dammit." I blew out a breath and skated away from him.

He stalked me in a graceful move of muscle. "We'll give your savage one more day, but you should know I will not share you."

My eyes widened, probably bugging out of my head. "I'm not yours to share—"

"You have a fierce exterior, but hidden beneath glows something precious. It offers promise to dreams this world hasn't had in two years, dreams I haven't had in a lifetime."

My lungs filled and emptied as I lost my self-preservation in the burn of his gaze.

Hands at his sides, he stood before me, around me, consuming me. His voice was thick. "I love when you look at me like that. Even when you don't speak, your stunning eyes hold nothing back. Your expressions are so heavy I can feel your emotions in the marrow of my bones."

Aphid vibrations swarmed my gut, but my hand clutched my chest. "Michio."

"I love that you were a mother and that you carry that experience with you always."

His words landed a direct hit on my heart and my rib cage bucked under the impact. "Michio—"

"I love spending time with you." He traced the stitches around my mouth. "I crave our talks, your baths, your tantrums, our fights—"

"Fight me now."

His brows drew into a *V*.

To keep my pheromones directed at him only, I needed Yang to fuel the effort. Wrestling would put me right up against him. My hands found his chest. "If I get scratched, I'll tell the savage to make your scalping quick."

His pecs bounced under my curling fists, expression unreadable. "No holds barred?"

I shrugged.

He shifted his weight, pushed closer. "Tap out rules. *My* tap out rules."

Sandalwood drifted from his thin shirt, beckoning me. My face dropped to his chest. "Hmm?"

"If you tap, you allow me to ease you." The way he softened *ease* made me gulp. "I'll start chaste. As the taps accumulate, so will the intensity."

"Ease me how?"

"You know how," he mouthed.

My nipples hardened. How far would it go? Kissing? Sex? "And when you tap?"

"*If* I tap, I'll reveal a secret about my discipline."

The bastard. I wanted answers regarding his fighting techniques. "What about the Drone?"

He nuzzled my neck. "Won't be back till tomorrow."

A swelter funneled between my thighs. I fought it. The buzzing beyond the door magnified.

I stepped back and stripped my oppressive garment. When only my chemise remained, I kicked at the skirt around my ankle. Then I ripped the material away to mid-thigh. It felt a little vulnerable without underwear, but I shook off the feeling and faced him.

He raised a brow.

"Really, Michio. It's not like you haven't seen it all already. Besides, how would I pummel your ass when I'm wrapped like a goddamn mummy?" I kicked away the shreds of clothes on the floor.

"You agree to the terms?"

I nodded and centered my stance.

You suppose you are the trouble
But you are the cure
You suppose that you are the lock on the door
But you are the key that opens it
It's too bad that you want to be someone else
You don't see your own face, your own beauty
Yet, no face is more beautiful than yours.

Rumi

CHAPTER THIRTY-FIVE: TAP OUT

Michio's slouched posture seduced me into action. I aimed for his throat. My fist hit air.

From out of nowhere, his forearm crossed my neck and pitched me backwards. My eyes closed for the impact, but my downward motion ceased mid-fall.

I cracked an eye. Almond shaped ones stared back and my body hung in the cradle of his arms.

He leaned in, his breathtaking face filling my horizon, and kissed me with lips as strong as the rest of him. Just as quick, he set me on my feet.

I rose to my full height. "I didn't even tap."

He towered over me. "You would have. When you hit the floor."

"If you were an aphid, I'd already have you squashed under my boot."

"Your aphid speed only works against them."

It wasn't a question. He knew this. "I don't need it."

"Sure you don't."

My arms came up, spreading like a flower. I closed the flower with downward hands, knocking his out and away.

Past his guard, I struck with my elbow. Our arms smacked. His hand trapped mine. His other pulled down on my neck. Between his weight and his strength, he had me on the floor in a heartbeat, pushing an oomph past my lips.

Sweat dampened my skin. My fist hovered next to his groin, seized between his thighs. He squeezed my neck and applied pressure to the lock on my arm, coaxing my free hand to smack the tile.

The burn from the hyperextension dimmed in my arm when his mouth fell over mine. My lip caught between his teeth and he bit down. I held still, absorbing the pain, the taste, the feel of him, wanting more, and communicating it with my eyes.

He read me and angled his mouth, taking over. I gripped the hard ridges of his ass and held on.

My name escaped the corner of his lips and his tongue thrust harder. Buttons plinked the tile as his shirt ripped from our tangle of body heat, my palms skimming through a coat of perspiration.

Time passed without us. Eventually, I murmured into the kiss, "Feels like we're keeping this contained." The aphids were a silent presence in my head.

His eyes darted to the chamber door and he continued kissing through his response. "Uh huh."

Wedged in the *V* of his squat, I swiped my swollen lips and narrowed my eyes. "Is defense all you got?"

Was that a smile? I couldn't be sure because I was spinning and my back hit his chest. The inside of his elbow connected with my jugular, pinching it.

I pulled my feet beneath me and dug my chin under the lock. His arm tightened and cut off my airless grunt. My hands slipped over the velvet skin of his arm. The pressure in my head mushroomed and my vision dotted. My stroking fingers became an urgent tap.

His arm lock melted into a meandering hand and hovered over my breast. Powerful thighs locked me in place. Lips flitted to my nape. Each lick swept chills down my spine.

When he tweaked my nipple between two knuckles, I sucked in a breath and arched into his hand. My knees weakened under my half-crouch.

The room spun again and his mouth latched onto my breast. Hot puffs wet the fabric of my shredded chemise. The graze of his teeth channeled shivers bone-deep. My hands sailed through his thick cropped hair.

Then I was back on my feet, wobbling. His eyes flicked to the door and settled on my face, consuming me with their alluring depths.

He traced my jaw with a thumb. "I've trained with master fighters most of my life. Yet, here you are humbling me."

My brows knitted together. "If you're humbly kicking my ass, what's that make me?"

"Fearless." His palm cupped my nape. "You possess a passion, a beauty, unequaled." Each word was heavy, carried with emotion.

"It's called stubbornness. And you're blind."

He swayed closer. "You are diligent, the way of the wise. And my eyes don't deceive me. Neither does my heart."

The certainty in his tone flooded my chest and sent my thoughts hurdling into the future. Once I put a few thousand miles between myself and Malta, would I seek the Shard? Or prowl the planet slaying aphids? I didn't dream of doing those things without Roark and Jesse at my side. As my fingers swept around Michio's waist, I knew my future included him as well.

But first, I had to deal with the Drone. Given the chance, I would take a potato peeler to his body, dehydrate the peelings under the hot Malta sun, and fold the paper skin into ornamental bugs.

"What are you smiling about?"

"Epidermal origami."

Michio's grin floated to mine.

But the game was still on. I pulled in his hips and drove my shoulder into his gut. My foot slid back, shifting weight to take him down. He made an elegant adjustment of his pelvis and rolled. His fist clipped my chin, the angle perfect. My balance wavered.

He yanked me against him, lips at my ear. "You also fight dirty."

"I do a lot of things dirty." I raised my knee to his groin. A pang ricocheted through my leg as he caught it, paralyzed it and bent it backwards.

I tapped in surrender, agog over the true surrender that would follow.

The couch caught my fall and he pitted me into the cushions. Sea and sandalwood soaked into my taste buds as his lips fed on mine. Then they left my mouth to chase curves around my jaw, down my neck, over one breast, the dip of my waist, and tarried on the ripped hem at my thigh.

His body trembled around me. Mine responded in kind. We sighed together and for a dimwitted moment, I thought he was done.

A clever hand vanished between my legs, searching, stroking, and spiking my pulse. I fought for air. Each curl of his fingers cranked my knees farther open. Hand-to-hand combat wasn't the only skill benefiting from his knowledge of anatomy. His touch reduced my body to a panting needy blob.

My pleasure climbed, teetered on the edge. I reached for it. Just another second—

He leaned back and straightened my tattered chemise. Then he heaved me to my feet with fingers wet from my arousal.

My face fevered. I ground my molars and met his eyes. "You're teasing me."

He stepped closer, lips rolled between his teeth, eyes glittering.

"Bastar...arrgh." My shoulder popped. I blinked. Both my arms were disabled behind my back, extended at the elbows. Hands numb and growing cold, I gave him wide eyes. "Tap."

He lifted me. The gate clicked. Trousers and boxers dropped in our wake. The mattress creaked. He pinned my hands above my head and covered my body with his.

Locked at the lips, neither of us moved. Anticipation puffed and mingled in steam from our noses. I burned under his weight, crushed by packs of muscle from his chest to his thighs. My legs squeezed around him. My pleasure hung on the precipice, waiting.

He lined up and drove his hips, his mouth catching my yelp, the feel of him hurtling me toward heaven. Hump after hump, my bliss built. By the fourth thrust, he discarded what was left of my shift. Two more and my defeat erupted in hoarse cries.

When my full-body tingle tapered, I peeled my cheek from his pounding chest and spied something on his face I'd never seen there.

"What is it?" He tucked a stray lock behind my ear.

"Your smile. Perhaps I shouldn't inflate your head, but you're fucking gorgeous."

He widened it. "Ego's still at a safe level."

"For now."

His nose traced mine. "Are you sated?"

"Ditto on the for now," I roamed a toe along his leg.

He chuckled and browsed my lips, his bowing up in a beautiful curve. Then he slid off the bed and glided to the gate.

The shock of his sudden exit left me stammering, "W-wait. *You* aren't sated."

"The terms were *I* ease *you*." His neutral voice reeked with an undercurrent that said he was anything but neutral. I didn't remember his terms barring reciprocation? What was he trying to prove? Stupid men and their egos.

He breezed to the bathroom and dammit if the muscles in his sculpted bare ass didn't ripple through his strides. Then my panorama faded behind the door and snapped me out of my stupor.

I nibbled my lip for one breath, two…five, leapt from the bed and dialed in the combination. Maybe he forgot he gave that to me.

The door muffled the spray of water from the shower head. I slipped inside.

"Evie." His groan floated from behind the curtain. "If you come in here, my restraint will not be repeated."

Good. I pulled back the drape and held my breath. Palm flat to the wall, head dropped on his arm, his other hand wrapped around his erection. Water sluiced off the ridges of his lats.

I ducked under his arm and shimmied around him. A hum rumbled from his chest. He gripped the back of my thighs and planted my butt against the rock wall.

In the next breath, he filled me. The clench of his hands pinched my skin. The pain sweetened the sensation. I gave him a rough shove with my hips and smiled up at him.

Lines appeared between his brows and his mouth opened. I silenced him with a kiss that was as hungry as my body. All around me, his limbs hardened. Then his restraint snapped. Fingers readjusted on my thighs, digging further into flesh, and his pelvis pounded with a force that ensured I'd limp away.

I clutched the shower curtain to brace for the impacts. The hooks squealed along the pole. Fabric tore. His hips surged on.

A heady rush enveloped me. Climatic spasms racked my body and still, it screamed for more.

Then something flashed in his wide eyes and he caught my face between his palms. "I'm hurting you."

"Hell, yes. Shut up and keep moving."

He squinted and stilled his thrusts. Steam thickened the air. His body shook.

"Come on, gorgeous. I can take it." I compressed my quadriceps around his waist for emphasis.

A moan vibrated low in his throat, but his hips didn't move.

I dropped my legs and slid to my knees. My fingers made slow circles up the bunching tendons in his thighs. His erection jerked and I lowered my head. Then I savored him with a gluttonous mouth.

He clenched all over as I pulled grunts and groans I never imagined hearing from him. Hands threaded through my hair, ripping at the roots. "Baby, you're killing me."

Water sprayed my upturned face. I held his dark gaze and swirled my tongue over the glans. "You'll live."

Then I took him deep and absorbed his responses. His head falling back, his labored breaths, the twitch of his cock against my tongue, his bucking hips. Then it all ground to a halt as the master of emotion lost the rein on his release in a raw and beautiful contortion of features.

The warm splash of salt and man washed down my throat. I licked him and my lips.

His laughter wrapped around my heart. "Christ, Evie. That was…" He leaned down and took my mouth, untamed and filled with fire. "I need a few minutes."

He yanked the faucet to fill the tub. His fingers wrapped around mine, pulling us to sit, me straddling him. I gave him his recovery time then melted onto him, taking him in, rocking my hips.

The way he watched me, his smoldering eyes roaming my nudity, rivaled the heat in his voice. "Just when I thought you couldn't get more beautiful," he whispered, "seeing you wild and happy like this knocks the wind out of me."

His words, his timbre, the flame in his eyes sent another release through my body. When strength returned to my limbs and the water level submerged where we were joined, I turned off the tap.

We soaked the bumps on our well-loved bodies. My chin rested on his chest and he traced my back. His finger paused. "You're bleeding."

"Red sweat," I mumbled in a lazy voice.

"I'm supposed to take care of you. Not injure you."

I flicked water in his face. "You did take care of me. And now you've set the bar. Better get some more sewing needles."

His arms snaked around me, pulling me up until our eyes were level. "Do you know how many times I wanted to crawl in behind you in this tub and hold you like this? To offer some kind of reassurance that you weren't alone?" His biceps flexed around me and rippled the water. "I was so worried in those early days, when you disappeared inside yourself. Took everything I had to keep secrets from you." His voice softened. "You nearly dragged me into that pit with you."

I put my smile against his lips. "Instead, *you* dragged *me* back." I drew up and planted my hands on either side of his head. "I like being with you, too." More than liked it. I held the eyes of the man I trusted with my life, watched them soften. "If we ever get off this rock, I want to go with you. To Shard. To wherever. Got a problem with that?"

His smile lit up his face. "Only way I can protect you, *Nannakola*."

Till the day he died. I smiled back, knew my eyes were brimming with it. "Even if I have a priest and a savage in tow?" They'd come with me. I'd make damn sure of it.

He gave me his answer in a kiss then whispered into it. "Sun down tomorrow. We're breaking out."

My robe dusted a path in my cell. Michio hadn't returned from his final walk in the quadrangle. He was supposed to check for Jesse and come right back. Then we'd escape.

The sun dipped past the rafters hours earlier. Two prayer times came and went.

Perhaps he found Jesse. Or maybe the gig was up. The Drone approached him in the kitchen that morning, said he found the tongue-less chef, that Roark had overpowered him, taken his tongue and fled. He also assumed it was Roark who severed the Imago's tongue during an unscheduled visit to his chamber.

My stomach cramped and my head thrummed under a sheen of sweat. What if the Drone had since figured it out? I stopped at the gate and pulled off my headscarf. Fuck that.

It took three attempts to get the combination on the lock to click. I sprinted to the chamber door. Michio could come and go because the Drone allowed it. The guards were his eyes and ears. As soon as I opened the door, he'd know. I'd have to be quick. Didn't Michio say the kitchen was next to the hall? If I could get there, I'd find a knife.

I reached inside and gathered my guts. I didn't have Michio's Yang to power my whatever, but I could do it. I opened the door.

The guard crouched. Spit flew from its snapping jowls.

For a fearful moment, I locked up. Forced a breath. Then pushed my command. *Stay.*

Black veins pulsed under its glowing skin. Its pincers clicked. I sidled around it. *Stay* beat with every breath I took.

The dizziness crowded in. I tripped down the stairs and bounced off the first bend in the wall. Nausea chased me. But the guard didn't.

Despite the fog in my head, the stairway was clear. I stumbled off the bottom step and released my hold on the chamber guard. The strain inside me receded.

Slithering feet crawled through the adjoined corridor, followed by hissing and the waft of blood. I waited.

Heart-pounding moments later, the unlit tunnel drifted to silence. I forced my feet to move.

Sconces illuminated the end and framed the double doors to the hall. I slipped out of the corridor and remained in the shadows. A large swinging door loomed ahead. The kitchen.

Big breath. Then I ran.

A buzz spiked through me. A clammy arm slammed into my throat. My face skidded along the rock wall.

I pawed at my neck, gripped the pincer that held me. *Back, back, back* I shoved from my spine.

A mandible yawned next to my face. The spear telescoped out. A drip glistened on the point.

Your blood's not only poisonous to the aphids but exponentially more potent.

No time like the present to put Michio's hunch to the test. I caught the spear and squeezed the razor edge. Pain streaked up my arm. Wet warmth poured over my fingers. I let go.

The tube receded, stained with my blood. Pressure eased from my neck and the claw dropped. Fumes of burnt hair assaulted my nose. Then the violent release of flesh and blood sprayed the floor, the walls, my face.

I plodded through the sludge and banged the kitchen door open with my shoulder.

Two pairs of wide human eyes looked up from bubbling pots and locked on my bleeding hand.

"English? Do you speak English?"

A pan dropped, scattering fish heads across the floor. A man with wild hair and lanky limbs crumpled like a marionette and canopied his head under trembling arms.

The second man's neck sank into his shoulders, a surprising feat given the rotund folds engulfing it.

"Knives? Pokers?" I made a jabbing motion.

Their eyes bugged and their mouths sucked air. Useless.

I jogged through the room. Copper pans and ceramic plates cluttered the stainless counters. Nothing sharp or dangerous.

My foot slipped on fishy parts. "How'd you cut the damn heads off?" I gestured to the eyeless faces on the floor.

The fat man stabbed a shaky finger at the rack above the next counter. Torchlight flickered on a half dozen steel blades dangling from the ceiling. Jackpot.

I leapt onto the counter and rolled the knives into a nearby towel. "The doctor? Have you seen him?"

The marionette on the floor curled farther into a ball. The fat one blinked. It was possible one of these asses was missing a tongue.

I yanked up my sleeve and pointed at my stitches. "Doctor?"

Layers of chin rolls shook side to side. His belly jiggled with his backward shuffle into the counter.

Jesus, fuck. Knife in hand, I tied the rolled spares at my waist with the sash on my robe. Then I touched the door and put out feelers. Hunger pushed back. Enough for a single aphid. Close. The other side of the door?

Fffffound rattled through me.

I leaned into my back foot and kicked out with the other. The door crashed into a blur of swinging green limbs. The aphid's back smacked the floor. Double-jointed legs buckled under it. I jumped on its chest and raised the knife.

"Found what?"

An accented purr rolled down my backbone. *Your doctor.*

I buried the blade in the creamy white orb.

Once more into the breach, dear friends, once more

Henry V Act 3, Scene 1
William Shakespeare

Chapter Thirty-Six: The Breach

I planted my feet shoulder width apart on the kitchen floor and packed my voice with authority. "Take off your clothes."

Creases deepened around the fat chef's puffy eyes.

God knew what was happening to Michio at that moment. Every second counted. But I wouldn't go after him without a plan. "Understand anything I'm saying?"

His jowls trembled. Sausage fingers clutched the counter behind him.

"Fine. Watch." I untied the knives and removed my robe. "Now you." I pointed a blade at him. "Quickly."

He fingered the collar of his shirt. I gave him a long nod.

The marionette man scrambled under the counter. I grabbed his bony ankle and pulled him back. Unidentifiable words spewed from his chattering jaws as his hand shook through the sign of the cross.

I ripped open his shirt. Spit sprayed my face and dribble clung to his unshaven chin.

My blade bit his neck. "Clothes off. Now."

He touched the nick and screamed at the smear of blood on his hand. I returned the knife to his neck. He jerked back and stripped off his clothes.

The fat chef's pants smacked the floor. A white swath of material peeked from beneath the bulge of his hanging gut. He slipped his thumbs under the remaining waistband.

"No, no," I shouted. "That's enough."

I yanked off my chemise and ripped it into strips to tie across my chest and waist. Red tinged the fat one's cheeks but he didn't utter a word.

Then we shuffled as one to the door. I should've felt guilty ushering them at knife point wearing only their underwear, but Michio was my priority and I needed their Yang. With the quivering man hooked to my side and my chest and the knife pressed to the back of the fat chef, I sucked in my fuel and filled my nose with fish and sweat.

Aphids lined the walls and pushed through open doors. Barbs on their forearms stood at attention. We hobbled through the corridor, past the anteroom and the quadrangle. Energy pooled in my belly and traveled up my spine. *Stay.*

The aphids growled. Claws raised and reached, but their segmented feet remained rooted to the floor.

At the end of the hall, I stopped before a lone, driveling bug and extended an image of the Drone onto the unseen bond.

The aphid pivoted and led us to the stairway. The stairway to the lab.

Leave, I commanded.

It lowered its green hunched body and hissed. I drew back the knife, exhaled and let it fly.

It clinked off the rock wall.

Mother fuck. Another knife. Another breath. Release.

It landed with a thud. The hilt protruded from one eye. The other eye rolled to the ceiling and the aphid collapsed.

I plucked the blade from the skull and pushed our huddle forward. Marionette man shook harder with each stair to the Drone's lab. At the last step, he twisted out of my grip. I lunged for his legs. My fingers slipped down his clammy calf.

His screams followed him up the stairs and faded into the dark depths. Fuck. There went my contingency plan. I touched the knife to one of the big guy's neck rolls. "Don't even think about it."

His mouth dropped and his head whipped in sharp shakes. I opened the door to the lab.

Our bare feet whispered along the flagstone, my knife angled at the potbelly. Traces of rubbing alcohol whiffed by. Machines beeped. One more staircase to go.

I unraveled the knife roll bound to my forearm, the steel jangling in my trembling hands. Then we stepped into the black hole and descended into the bowels.

I nudged the door. Its creak cut through the dark. The chef's hand flew to his face against the onslaught of death and decay.

The dull glow of a sconce guttered next to Michio. His body, shackled to the wall, was a punch in the gut. I knew he wasn't invincible, but seeing it was difficult to swallow. How had the Drone managed to restrain him? I imagined the army surrounding him, preventing escape. My heart knocked against my ribs.

Eyes closed, his head hung on his chest. No visible wounds. Maybe I wasn't too late.

"Will you cooperate or join the doctor?" The Drone floated from the shadows, eyes seizing mine. His stiff slacks, collared shirt and long shiny curls, all black, melded with his sable cloak.

I shoved the chef in front of me, knife at his back. "What did you do to Dr. Nealy?"

"He is sleeping." He slapped a painful hum at my chest, inflaming the ever-present network of aphid links battering me. "His supreme lack of fear for Allah's judgement is arrogant. And unforgivable." Venom laced his inflection.

My gut tightened. A buzzing hunger swirled around me. I kept my body angled behind the chef. "Release him. It's me you want."

"Release him?" He clicked his tongue. "Do not insult me, Eveline."

The Imago stepped around the door. His smirk hovered over his .50 cal Desert Eagle, the gold barrel trained at my head. Two aphids crouched behind him, rib cages contracting, bodies swaying with unraveling tension.

I tested the knife's weight, let it drop from my palm to my fingers. Could I chuck it and release a spare before the chef ran? Before the gun fired?

Deep breath. I spun the knife.

A boom shattered the room. Gun powder and dust clouded the air. My human shield slumped to the floor.

I enjoyed a moment of victory when the Imago gripped the hilt jutting from a spurting hole in his shoulder. He dislodged it, sent it clanking across the room. His pistol remained pointed at my head. I raised another knife.

"I can sense your telekinetic presence now." The Drone cocked his head and flicked his eyes to the dead cook. "But it was invisible just a moment ago. Somehow, you are slipping behind shields and taking command of my troops." A terrifying smile warped his features. "But you have a weakness. Something is keeping you from turning these guards against me now."

Damn Yang. The aphids' strings waited in my gut, thrumming to be plucked. But if I took hold of them, I'd pass out and reveal my weakness. Then I'd be hanging next to Michio. Or worse.

His long fingers vanished beneath his cloak and reappeared with a syringe. He uncapped the tip and touched it to Michio's bent neck. "Drop the knives and stand here." He nodded at the empty wall beside Michio.

My body hardened, primed for a fight. "What's in the injection?"

"I have an exuberant supply of submicroscopic agents and genetically designed toxins. What should he be, do you think?" He dragged a pointed fingernail along Michio's bicep. "He has the form and stealth of a mantis, but I bet he fucks like a scorpion's dance. Did he give you a cheliceral kiss, little fly?"

I let the knives clatter at my feet and leveled a glare at the bane of mankind.

The Imago pressed his pistol into my back and nudged me forward. If I could touch him—any of them—and maintain contact, I'd own the guards. The opportunity would come. It had to.

At the wall, the Imago clicked the buckles in place. Minimal contact with his skin offered only feeble attempts at imbibing his energy.

He stood back and admired his work. My hands and legs, locked in restraints, stretched in an *X*. My options sucked.

I looked into the eyes of the monster fingering the plunger of his weapon. "I did what you asked. Lower the syringe. I promise I won't be any trouble."

"Women and their promises." He pressed the plunger with the needle buried in Michio's neck.

Panic burned through my chest, stole my air. A horrible sound burst from my throat.

"Charming, Eveline. Please don't wet all over my floor."

"You sick bastard. What did you inject him with?"

Michio's chin lifted. His eyelids fluttered and his jaw worked against his gag. Then his eyes met mine and widened.

"Michio." The Drone traced his lips, spread around the gag. "Assure Eveline that the dose I just gave you was a stimulant to wake you. Do you feel human?"

Michio's head dipped, raised, dipped again. The fire inside me dimmed. Only a little.

"Very good. Now, the reason you are here. I made a fascinating discovery when I compared your blood to the samples you've been providing." His cape whistled as he swung a fist into Michio's gut. "Our friendship, all the years we worked together, you were family." His voice broke. "You kept her blood from me, knowing how much I needed it." He bent, clutched his abdomen. The air around him seemed to rotate, thicken. He straightened and smacked his lips. "Your betrayal tastes so bitter, it will linger long after I dine on your girlfriend."

Michio's expression gathered into a silent and deadly storm behind his gag.

"Ewl em." The Imago shoved his gun against Michio's brow.

"Don't be rude, Siraj. I much prefer him alive." The Drone turned to me and caressed my face.

I pulled on his energy, one vile spark at a time. One stroke. Two. Then he yanked my head to the side and lowered his mouth to my exposed throat.

"Wait." My lean into his grip belied my command. "You can't ingest my blood. Your body wouldn't absorb it."

"You have no idea what my body can do." Beneath the aroma of chemical cleansers, seeped something sinister and stale.

"You smell like your brother."

Teeth grazed my skin. "My brother smells divine."

I consumed his Yang through the tips of his meandering fingers and reached for my telepathic connection with the guards. The threads wavered. I grabbed hold with mental fists.

The Drone's eyes slammed shut and his body hardened against mine. Silence. So heavy there was only the roar of my heart in my ears. Something was happening. The movement under his eyelids and the tremble in his shoulders told me he was communicating with his army.

His head snapped up. "We have a breach."

Oh shit. Me?

The Imago stiffened behind him, turned toward the door.

Ba-boom.

An explosion vibrated the foundation, loosening rock and silt from the walls, and jarring my bones.

"We must hurry." The Drone was already at the door, waving to his brother to follow.

The Imago hesitated, narrowed hard eyes on me.

The Drone followed his gaze. "You're right. Stay with her. But I will not leave the guards." He flashed me a horrific smile, one that would stick with me for a long time. "Do not release her." He vanished through the door, the guards on his heels.

The Imago lapped the room, swinging his pistol and winding my body into a torsion of anxiety. Michio remained motionless, but his eyes darkened with every pass.

My throat tightened in a hot tangle of uncertainty over the explosion and fear for Roark and Jesse. My muscles thrummed to go after the Drone, but first, I had to take down the asshole guarding us. To do that, I'd have to bait him. "Your intimidation is only effective with me unarmed and restrained. Unlock my restraints and fight me like the little man bitch that you are." I returned his scowl with a grin. "Unless, of course, your spear is too small."

His pistol moved in a streak of gold. The butt whacked my face and sent my head careening into the wall. He crouched before me and unsheathed the Jambiya dagger. It whirled around his fingers and halted on my inner thigh. He leaned closer in a fume of stale cigar. "Awl ahh ew."

A biting pain ignited under the dagger. "What? Didn't quite catch that."

He lanced the edge downward along my inner thigh. Then his mouth fell upon the wound. The suckling pitched fire through my leg, a melting of flesh from the inside out.

Through the haze of pain, I sought the closest aphid in the psychic cosmos. There, a jolt. I followed the source. The corridor. Near the stairway to the lab. The link iced the heat racing through my veins. *Come.*

Hands traveled up my thighs. An influx of power spread through my limbs, calming me. *Come.*

A green shape filled the doorway. Translucent skin rippled over quivering forearms. Its spear extended in response to the blood dripping down my leg.

Attack, I pushed and layered it with images of the Imago.

The Imago jerked his mouth from my thigh, face bloodied, and reached for the dart gun slung on his back.

I dipped into my power. *Attack.* My heart rate crashed as I drove the command over and over.

Blurred snapshots of insectile arms wheeled around me. The dart gun clattered across the room. A warm gush poured from my nose. My chin fell upon my chest and I clamped my mouth shut to hold back bile.

The Imago dropped at my feet, held down by the crouching aphid. He babbled incoherent sounds, staring at my eyes, and I wondered what he saw there, if they were filled with solid black.

"I'll call it off if you release me."

Eyes round and glassy, he nodded.

I sucked in air and sent a prayer to hell for enough juice. *Back.*

The bulbous body rose to its full height, but did not back away.

The Imago jumped to his feet and freed the key ring from his belt. His clammy hands gripped mine as the locks sprang open.

Beside me, Michio grunted, eyes on the mouthparts arching from the depths of the aphid's gullet.

Stay. A weak command, wrapped in numbness. The link was disintegrating. "Hurry. I'm losing it."

He dropped to his knees and released my feet. My languid body crumpled into his arms. A metal click told me he'd returned the keys to his belt, then he spun, clutching my back to his chest, hiding his trembling frame behind the cover of mine.

Idiot. I slumped against him and collected spurts of energy from multiple points of contact. His vitality energized my weakened limbs, the very weapons I would use against him. A deep breath. *Attack.*

I ducked. The first claw swiped the crown of my head and knocked the Imago to the ground. The second landed in my chest. I stumbled back, tripped over the Imago's legs and fell upon him.

Hold. I sent images of his arms, locked down by claws. If I killed the Imago, I'd lose my Yang source and the aphid would turn on me, a risk I hadn't considered when I called it down there. If I killed the aphid, I'd lose my weapon against the Imago. To buy time, I chanted, *Hold,* aloud or in my head, I wasn't sure.

Pincers hooked around the Imago's arms, pinning him to the floor just as I envisioned. But my effort to maintain the choreography caused an exodus of energy.

I slid my hands over the Imago's belt, his chest, his arms. Finally, I bumped his dagger, clutched it. Dizziness and gelidity crept through me. Consciousness began to slip. I cut away his shirt and rolled onto his bare chest.

Warmth and light infused my senses. I fought the revulsion from the slime of his skin and soaked up his Yang. Then I strengthened my hold on the guard.

Its wavering pincers stilled, clamped harder on the Imago's arms. Its head bobbed inches from mine. Frown lines, eyelashes, even a pierced ear reminded me this creature was once human.

I gathered my strength and scooted down his legs, cutting away his pants as I moved. His flaccid cock flopped on his hip. I gripped it and raised the knife.

The zagged scar on his forehead reddened. He writhed under the guard's hold. Tears slicked his lashes.

The fucker was responsible for billions of deaths. He stole Annie and Aaron from me. Corpses rotted feet away, a reminder that his delivery of the virus was only the beginning of his bloodshed.

I brought down the edge. An arch of crimson spurted from his groin and striped his chest. His pathetic shrills stung my ears as he convulsed under me. I wanted to stuff his dick in his mouth, but my vision swam with black dots and my body shook. I tossed the severed flesh.

With numb fingers, I unhooked the key ring from his belt and pushed to my feet. My legs gave out.

Should I kill them first? What if the key didn't work? Would I need to use the Imago as a hostage?

I scraped the Jambiya, the keys and my knees over the dirt floor and crawled to Michio.

The aphid yanked on the link, testing its snapping point.

Hold goddammit. With each dragged limb, my vision dissipated in strobe-flashes. Minutes felt like hours. The beat in my ears pounded out the Imago's tongueless cries. Just had to hold the aphid, move toward the wall. Deep breaths.

The knife clinked the wall. I swiped my eyes with the back of my hand, tried to clear the visual snow. A shadow on my left. I dropped the knife and reached for it. Warmth. Muscle. Michio.

My hands climbed his legs, found the button at his waist. His pants dropped. I hugged every inch of flesh in my reach. Nausea retreated. The golden perfection of his skin came into focus and my body heated.

I crawled up his torso, keeping contact with as much of him as possible. His hips rocked in urging taps. His voice hummed behind his gag.

The keys fumbled in my fingers. At last, the lock snicked. Oh, thank Christ. The shackles fell open and strong arms caught me. I tugged at his gag until it fell away.

A roar burst from his mouth. "I'm going to kill him." His anger rolled off him in shuddering waves. He pulled away and angled his body toward the Imago.

"No. Don't let go of me." I clung to his neck.

"Then let the beast go, Evie. Let it have him."

With his strength, it was easy to clip my leash on the aphid. I simply willed it. The Imago's final shriek gave way to greedy slurps and sucking.

Michio shrugged out of his shirt and pulled up his pants, his movements clumsy with the aftereffect of sedation. We slid to the floor and his gaze drifted over my shoulder. A smile stole over his face.

The swoosh of steel erupted behind me. A wet smack followed. Then another. I turned in his arms.

Roark stood over the headless aphid, gore clinging to his sword and cassock. He tapped the Imago's head with his boot. It rolled from the body.

Jade eyes rose, searched mine. He sheathed the sword, crossed the distance between us in three huge leaps, and pulled me into his embrace.

"Love," he drawled. Ah, the lilt of that one word. A silken caress.

Giant hands framed my face. I reached for his, mimicking him. Whiskers scratched my palms. Our eyes locked. His exhale was my inhale. So much was said in that shared look. I knew his regrets, his fears, his heart and he knew mine.

Then he took my mouth, a dusting of lips in tender greeting. All too quick, his reluctant release tugged at my bottom lip, a pledge for another time.

Michio staggered to his feet. Something dangerous clouded his eyes, and it was aimed at Roark. "We need to go, *Father* Molony." Then he wrapped a possessive hand around mine and pulled.

I pulled back, spearing him with a look that unclenched his fingers, and turned to Roark.

Dark membranes caked his face, his curls, his calloused hands. He'd sliced his way there. Getting out would be much of the same. My chest clenched. "Lose your clothes."

His freckled forehead scrunched into his hairline.

My lips twitched. "You can keep the pants." I tackled the buttons at his chest. "Don't have time to explain. Just trust me, okay?"

His hands brushed mine aside. A moment later, his cassock and shirt hit the floor.

"You siphoned him to get past the guards upstairs?" Michio gestured to the dead cook.

"Yeah. And you were right about something else." I raised my chewed up palm. "Toxic blood."

The rip of fabric responded. Michio held up long pieces of his abandoned shirt and tied one over my hand.

Deep grooves bracketed Roark's eyes, which were locked on my bandage. "Wha' toxic blood?"

Michio secured another strip around the gash on my thigh, a smile in his voice. "Hers. It's poisonous to the aphids. We can discuss the mechanics later." His eyes turned to me. "Head up with the priest. I'm two minutes behind you."

I ran toward the exit. "Where's Jesse?"

Roark's drawl followed me into the stairwell. "Distracting the Drone."

The feeling I'd been ignoring, the one tapping at the edges of my mind, materialized like a knife in the chest. Jesse was the breach, the explosion.

I raced out of the bowels of one hell to rise into another.

Though my soul may set in darkness,
it will rise in perfect light.
I have loved the stars too fondly
to be fearful of the night.

Sarah Williams

CHAPTER THIRTY-SEVEN: RISE IN PERFECT LIGHT

Humidity thickened as we rose from the basement. Roark in the lead, we took the stairs two at a time. The steps behind slipped into nothingness.

"Michio," I shouted into the black cavity.

"Two minutes behind, remember?" Roark's naked lats contracted through his jog. "Tell me"—he panted—"why I'm not wearing me duds."

"You know how skin-to-skin blocks my nightmares?"

We stumbled on. A passing torchlight illuminated his nodding head.

"Same thing helps me communicate with the bugs. I can control them. There's a masculine energy—Michio calls it Yang—that I can somehow borrow for strength, through skin."

"Sounds like ye got lamped in your noggin, love."

I touched the swelling egg on my head. Yeah, lamped by an obnoxious gold pistol.

A few silent strides later, he said, "Last time I saw ye, I was scran for the aphids. Ye saved me life."

"I don't know how, but it works." I gave him an abbreviated explanation of Yin and Yang and the body. My voice whispered along the flagstone walls until we paused at the final step. Footfalls padded from the depths below. Michio's jet eyes emerged from the dark.

"What took you so long?" I asked.

Three knives were pressed against my chest. Then the turquoise rock swung above me, dimmed gray by the dark.

A fist of emotions grabbed hold of my esophagus and squeezed. He delayed, risked his life, to collect my knives and my necklace. "Michio." A choke.

He tied it around my neck, staring into my eyes. I tried fill my expression with all the things I wanted to say, feelings I couldn't form into words.

Too soon, he looked away, blank mask in place. "Can you feel how many?"

I touched his face, angled his cheek against mine, and imbibed his Yang. My stomach stirred and the trill coiled up my spine. Fingers of energy stretched from my chest, seeking. Vibes bounced back along a dozen invisible threads. "Twelve, at least."

The muscle in his jaw twitched.

I leaned back. "I held at least that many to get here."

Lines crimped his brow and vanished just as fast. His chest flexed under the strap of his bag as he reached behind his back and pulled out a long narrow staff. Where the hell did that come from?

"I'll lead." He glared at Roark. "Constant contact with her will be more effective than your sword."

"Hmm. A weapon upgrade. I'm trading up for one with curves."

"Stop it." I tried for a scolding tone but my smile ruined it.

A gruff noise scraped from Michio's throat and his eyes hardened, locked on Roark. "Where was the explosion?"

"Southwest corner." Roark pushed away from the wall.

Black eyes narrowed. "The drive entrance? Our only access to the street?"

Roark grinned. "Wen' be needing a car."

Understanding softened Michio's features.

Confusion twisted mine. "The explosion was you?" I asked Roark.

"Jesse."

It sounded both odd and strangely comforting to hear Jesse's name whispered in Roark's lyrical accent. "And we're meeting him where?"

"The dock," Michio answered. "Ready?"

I solidified my link with the aphids. "Red-eyed and hair-lipped."

Two gorgeous faces, frozen in puzzlement, stared at me. I sighed and shooed them with the knives.

Blackness draped the corridor. Our pace plodded until our eyes adjusted. Illuminated silhouettes wavered at the end of the hall.

"Eight behind us," I whispered. "They don't see us."

Shadowed heaps came into focus as we stole through the passage. Bodies stacked waist high, sans heads.

"Well done, Father." Michio nodded, sidling around a headless slump.

The husk of a sconce dangled on the wall next to my face. "Something ate the torches."

"Sorry, love. Me night vision is better than the sodding snarlies'." Roark lifted a shoulder. "So I killed the lights."

The coppery scent of blood smothered the narrow space. Thick plip-plops resonated between the suction of our bare feet as we mucked through.

I jumped over a stretch of disembodied parts with the help of Roark's hands on my hips. He set me down, but his arms wrapped around me, fingers tracing my ribs. "Ye lost a rake of kilos."

Michio cut his eyes at me. His expression said nothing. It didn't have to. After weeks of forced meals, I knew what he was thinking. "I'm fine."

"Ach. You're a pull through for a rifle, love. Feels like I'm hugging a throwing star."

Hard to sound threatening while leaning into his attentive fingers, but I gave my best growl. "This is not the time—"

He pinched my ass. "Den' get narky." His head lowered. Lips brushed my earlobe. "You're still sexy as hell."

"Nix the flirting—" My insides jumped.

A green flicker sprang from the bend up ahead. Three more followed. I shaped my command, sent it winding up and out. *Stop.*

A slow hiss replaced the scraping of feet. The glowing forms stilled.

"There's four ahead, blocking the door. Roark, I'm going to move to Michio. Then I'll hold them while you gut them? 'kay?"

He pressed his lips to my brow and turned us, guiding my back to Michio's chest.

I clutched the arms snaking around my waist and followed the wall. Bones cracked underfoot. Mold and death weighted the air. And *Stay* was a staccato beating on my ribs.

We approached the waiting chomps of jowls. Strings of ichor-like dribble doused the walls. Ribs expanded and vibrated under their diaphanous skin.

I hissed back and reinforced the invisible wall of resistance.

The sword whooshed. A wet thud followed by another. Two left.

All-white eyes held mine, silent and steady, despite the distortion in its androgynous face. Then the eyes went flat and the head rolled off the shoulders.

"Bloody hell, that was easy." Roark grabbed my hand, pulled us forward. "Could've used ye on me way in."

I stepped around the fourth body, one I hadn't even seen him kill.

A few paces ahead, we stumbled into the quadrangle. My stomach churned. Dozens of silent cravings stitched through me.

"Oh no." I ground my teeth as the demands multiplied, fragmented my own. "We're not alone."

The rosy slivered moon offered no light. Not that I needed it. A fluorescent ring of squirming mouths and striking claws erected around us.

Weapons shot up. Roark's sword. Michio's staff.

"Where's my carbine?" Trapped and outnumbered, I shook with the effort to hold the aphids with will alone.

"With your Lakota," Roark said, eyes probing the dark.

"Where's my Lakota?"

He spun in a circle, lips pinched. "Plan A, we meet him a' the boat."

"And Plan B?"

"We meet his team a' the boat."

If we made it to the boat. My throat dried up, strangled by streamers of predatory need.

"How many?" Michio's neutral voice.

I blew my hair out of my face. "Dozens and growing. I can hold some of them but we're fighting our way to the exit."

"And Aiman?" Michio asked.

The warmth of the bricks soaked into the soles of my feet. A tepid gust swept in with the thunder of the tide. My stomach growled with hunger that wasn't mine. I reached beyond that basic need and followed the darkest thread. Flickering and angry, it led me up, up, up...there. "The tower. My chamber." Then, with a snap, the connection blinked out. Dammit, he knew how to shut me out the way I shut out him.

Michio tilted his head and studied me sidelong. "How many can you hold?"

I pulled his back to my chest without losing contact with Roark. "I'm holding the ones in front. The rest are mindless with hunger. I can feel them pushing through the horde, getting closer."

We sidled toward the exit, the circle of aphids shifting with us. Then the inner ring shrank, halting us.

"We'll fight them off with our backs to you, Evie." Michio glanced over his shoulder at Roark, who gave a swift nod and glued his back to mine.

Behind me, a glowing figure darted from the front line. Roark broke away from my embrace in a flash of steel. A head rolled. Then another.

The vigor powering my command dimmed and my vision went with it. My limbs turned to cement and I sagged against Michio. His arm looped back to catch me. The band around us wavered.

Roark returned to my back in a rise and fall of muscle. We gained a few more steps. Points of skin contact came and went. A fleeting grip. A brush of fingers. I pulled energy when and where I could, gathered it into myself, and released it with everything I had. *Leave.*

The aphids faltered, allowing a reprieve to run. The swoosh of the sword led the way. Michio's stick snapped through the air unheard and with a long reach, fending off those closest on our heels.

Blinking sweat from my eyes, I held the knives at my sides and clamped down on the network of threads heating under the passage of my commands. Their numbers grew. Too many were gaining too close.

Our feet slapped across the quadrangle. A swarm rose up from the side. I released a blade and missed. "Michio, watch out." My teeth sawed my lip and I tasted blood.

A chain whipped out from the end of his cane and disabled a row of double-jointed legs.

"Behind you." His tone was calm, at odds with the fierce movement of his arms.

I spun, swapping the knives in my hands, double-fisting, and collided them into both sides of the bulbous head crashing into me. My back hit the bricks and my heartbeat screamed.

Eerie shrieks ripped through the night. The pit of bugs squeezed in.

Arms gripped me, lifted me over a bare shoulder. My energy spilled out, tendrils elongating, skirting the tubular suckers, the snapping pincers, and the hunched torsos. The web spread, ensnared everything in its path. My muscles trembled under the exertion.

Aphids invaded from all directions, flooding my horizon with green. I sucked in a jagged breath. "How far to the exit?"

"Ten paces." Michio's voice vibrated beneath me.

I pictured the arched stairway, the freedom beyond. Then I poured out my essence. My body fought it. My mouth watered, imbued with acid. *Move.*

The crowd of creatures divided, opened a path. The bricks ran together under my hanging feet. An inner agitation tore along my spine. The pain rippled up, bowed my back. The stone archway passed overhead and blocked out the floating crescent in the sky.

"Evie? Evie?" The voice faded. The arch tilted.

Brine teased my nose. I opened my eyes. "Did I pass out?"

"Where to?" Michio shouted.

My waist bounced on his shoulder, arms lolling down his back. Sea breeze whipped my hair as he glided through the dark.

"The boreen. There," Roark said, winded.

Sand sprayed under Michio's feet as he reeled in a circle. A narrow path flickered by. Water slapped at a huge boat docked at the end.

Michio grunted and jerked to the side. His body flowed through the swing of his free arm. A meaty smack followed. When he whirled again, I craned my neck. A sea of green stretched to the horizon. Driveling mouths struck at our heels.

A long-necked bird winged into the night and rose above the aphids. Its white plumage glistened as if absorbing their glow. Convenient that it was there. I couldn't command it, having no connection with it. But I could command the aphids to follow it.

The wings snapped, soaring, taking it away. I focused on it, fed my energy into the image of it. *Follow.*

Waves of light rippled through the predators. Their virescent bodies turned as one, climbing over each other, chasing the feathered star.

Follow, I pushed. Spasms seized my muscles. So many frenzied threads. Too many to command. My tongue flopped between stabbing teeth. My stomach heaved.

Michio's arm clenched around me and the ground blurred under his feet. An engine rumbled.

"Did it work?" I slurred. "Are they following it?"

"Get her on the boat," an unfamiliar voice shouted. "We're pushing off."

"J-J...see." What was wrong with my speech? Roark voiced what I couldn't. "The Lakota."

Multiple footsteps pounded the ramp.

"Didn't make it." Michio's lips brushed my cheek. "You were amazing back there, Evie. Just hang on."

No. No. No. My screams didn't escape the convulsions in my throat.

"My bag." He shifted me in his arms. "Out of my way, Roark. She's seizing."

Our bodies lurched against the sudden motion beneath us. Sandalwood mingled with a mist of salt and algae. Michio's chest bolstered the battering contractions.

The jade of Roark's worried eyes blinked in and out of my vision. His trembling hands cupped my face. "Bloody hell. Do something."

The wind stilled. The tide hushed. Amidst the darkness, the perfect light carried my body and my soul.

Reason is our soul's left hand, faith her right.

John Donne

CHAPTER THIRTY-EIGHT: REASON

I woke to a sharp prick on my lip, the slide of thread tugging at the hurt.

"Aiman's fist," Michio whispered.

"And the one above her eye?" Roark's brogue was tight, his arm a heavy drape on my waist.

"The same."

The arm around me hardened. "I want to beat the bag outta him."

Silence. Then Michio shifted, followed by the creak of leather and slide of zippers. "That's the last of her old stitches." His hushed voice followed his retreating footsteps.

Roark's fingers perused my body. The lump on my head. The cuts and bumps on my face. The wound on my palm. "They put her through hell."

A tired sigh. "She held her own."

There was too much regret in their voices. Time to move on. I dragged my eyes open. Jade ones stared back. His were alert and so very green. I smiled into them. "I've been awake for a while."

Honey-tinged strands curled around the sharp angles of his freckled cheeks. "I know it. Ye have this adorable habit of wigglin' your Indian joes when ye wake."

"My what?"

His chuckle brought me home. "Your toes, lass. Ye wiggle your clever toes."

Said toes explored the legs intertwined with mine. Ah God, I missed him. I missed this, my hand reaching, strolling along his jaw. My arm wobbled, dropped to the bed. "Where's Jesse?"

"How do you feel?" Michio leaned against a rich veneered cabinet, which hovered over bench seats and more cabinets. Candlelight danced across his severe expression. "Any pain?"

I rubbed my eyes with a finger and thumb and rolled to my back. "I feel numb at the moment."

The double bed I shared with Roark engulfed half of the windowless room. Two oval doors crowded one wall. Clothes swayed from hooks in the ceiling.

Roark pillowed his face on his bicep and regarded me from under hooded eyes. "We're in the stateroom aft of the yacht, love."

There was that beautiful smile. The smile I thought I'd never see again. I touched the turned up corners. "Missed you."

He tilted his head and pressed a kiss into my captured palm. "Missed ye more."

Michio shifted his weight and crossed his arms. "It's important you tell me if anything hurts. You had a seizure."

"I'll feel better if you tell me where Jesse is."

Another shift of hips. "He went after Aiman."

When I opened my mouth, Roark pressed a finger over it. "He's got a pilot with him. He'll meet us in Italy."

If he survived the Drone and his aphid infested island. "That's his Plan B?"

His knuckle tapped my chin. "He'll catch up."

Michio shoved medical instruments in his bag with impatient and uncharacteristic jerks. "Your vitals are normal, but your body underwent a lot of shock last night."

"I feel fine."

That turned his head to look at me over his shoulder. "You did good, Evie."

Roark's hand squeezed mine. "Ye redirected hundreds of aphids before ye couped. If ye hadn't held them a' the end—"

"Don't." I sat up. "Not till we know Jesse's safe."

The bedding gathered around my waist, the remains of my chemise gone. The puckered pink *C* on my chest gleamed against my pale complexion. I shoved the sheets out of my lap. Neat stitches crossed the cut that started at the apex of my inner thigh and stretched as long as the length of my hand.

"You're a much better tailor than I am," I said to Michio.

He straightened, watching me. "It'll scar."

I shrugged. "No worries. I'm collecting scars like Roark collects sins. All in the name of greater good."

Roark sprinkled kisses on my back. "Scars, sins and"—his lips hovered—"spots."

Michio's frown deepened, his agitation impossible to ignore.

Maybe I should've squashed Roark's open affection. But I had no shame when it came to either of them. I put a hand on Roark's arm. "I need to tell you something." I let him read my face while those gorgeous pools of jade melted things inside me. I cleared my throat and steeled my spine. "I slept with Michio."

A smile split his face, but it wasn't his easy smile. It seemed forced, tight in the corners, and didn't sparkle his eyes. "I did too. He hogged the feckin' covers all night."

That surprised me. They both slept in that tiny bed with me? "You know what I mean."

His mouth slacked and his arm left my waist. "I know."

"I told him." Michio's careful tone.

"Oh." I plucked at the sheets. "Now what?" Would they make me choose? Would it be a slow buildup of insecurity, jealously, rivalry?

Roark blew out a breath and slid from the bed, donned only in a pair of cutoff sweats. "Doc and I agree on this: we love ye, we'll protect ye, but we will not possess ye. And seeing how you're hauling yourself into danger all the time, I'll be resting easier knowing you're wearing a doctor a' your side." He glanced at the other man. "But we'll have to do something about the swot's bealin' lack of humor."

I was still stuck on *we love ye*. Thinking it was one thing. But hearing it…it was balm to my damaged soul. I just hoped there was enough left to love.

Michio turned to open a cabinet, distracting me with the way his cotton pants hugged the swell of his backside. "All your personal things are here."

Darwin's collar, my music player, Joel's letter. It didn't pass my notice that my bullet wasn't among the collection.

"And here." He crossed the room and unlatched a tall cabinet. Soft light splashed over my carbine, pistol and arm sheaths hanging from the racks. "These are your Lakota's doing."

A ridiculous rush of relief swelled inside me. "I love that man."

Roark and Michio froze. Shit. "I didn't mean…slight figure of speech." I stared at the space between their rigid bodies, waiting for someone to say something.

The air in the small room thickened and swirled, stirring up the tension I'd been trying to ignore. I cleared my throat. "All right. Let's hash it out."

Roark turned to leave. Heat surged in my cheeks. "Oh no, you don't." I squared my shoulders. "Toss me that shirt."

He yanked a man's tee off the hanger, wadded it, and sent it flying at my bare chest.

I grabbed the closest thing in reach, a pillow, and hurled it at his head. Direct hit.

His hands went to his hips. "Real mature."

"You're one to talk."

"Enough." Michio didn't move, his face stoic as always. "What's on your mind, Evie?"

"Same thing on yours. What to do about jealous, possessive—"

"Guardians." He dropped his voice. "There's a lot more to worry about out there"—he jabbed a finger at the door—"than the soap opera about to play out in this room."

"Bullshit." I dragged on the shirt. "Because if we don't square our shit away here"—I pointed a circling finger at the mattress—"then we won't be united to fight the shit out there." I looked at Roark. "And you. You flirted your way into my pants and my heart. The moment you gained access, you didn't want it anymore. That forfeits your rights to jealousy."

Michio's fist clenched. Mid-swing, I jumped, tackling him to the floor.

Red splotched Michio's golden complexion. "Get back in bed, Evie."

Roark jerked me to my feet and took my place, legs straddling Michio's, arms outstretched. "Go ahead. Lamp me, ye sod."

Oh, for fuck's sake. "You gonna pound your chest, too? Get off him, you big ape." I grabbed a wayward curl and yanked. Hard.

"Ow." Roark twisted a finger into my fist and released his hair. Then he stumbled to his feet. "Feck aff. I'm outta here."

I beat him to the door, met his angry eyes. "Me or the vow. Decide now."

His teeth ground so loud, he could've spit enamel. "The vow. It's always been the vow." He moved around me and slammed the door.

I leaned against it. "Well, that sucked. Out walked my heart all over again."

Michio remained on the floor, arm dangling over a bent knee. His features were soft, sympathetic.

Picking fights wasn't his style, which meant, "You didn't know I slept with him."

He lowered his head, pushed a hand through his tousled hair. "No. But it explains a lot."

"Rest assured it'll never happen again."

"I'd peg you as a lot of things, Evie, but naive isn't one of them."

I threw my hands in the air and paced. "Are you serious? You had a front row seat to that." I jerked my thumb at the door. "He made his decision."

"Maybe so. But you"—he gritted his teeth—"have not."

I sucked in a sharp breath. I endured two months without Roark. Two agonizing, lonely months without his affection and companionship. I'd fight to the death to avoid suffering that again.

He stood and moved to the door. "But you're right. He's not going anywhere and, regardless whether we get along or not, we're on the same side. And Evie"—he paused at the threshold, gripped the doorframe, eyes on me—"I'm not going anywhere either. Not the sharpest blade, not the fastest arrow, not even the fate of man could take my love from you."

His words solidified as his retreating back faded in the darkness of the galley beyond.

My feet were moving before my brain was. I ran through the door, slid around him and jumped, wrapping him in a hug with arms and legs.

He stumbled back, hands on my ass, and spun. When my back hit the wall, I looked up at him and fell into the bottomless black of his eyes. He gave me a smile so rare and beautiful I touched it, tried to hold it in my hand.

"I love you, too," he whispered through my fingers.

Then his mouth claimed mine. It was a New World exploration full of ventures and dreams, and I was right there with him, meeting the thrust of his tongue with the whole of my heart.

Our hips moved in sync with our lips, and my hands slid through the thick locks of his hair, glided down his ribs, and found the flex in his backside. I wanted more. I wanted—

"Dr. Nealy," Tallis shouted from the top of the stairs.

He pressed his face into my neck and groaned.

"Ignore him." I turned my head, seeking his lips.

His long fingers framed my face. "They're waiting." He sighed. "Get dressed. Drink the water I left by the bed. I'll meet you up top."

When he slipped away, I returned to the room in search of my weapons, my clothes, and my game face.

The yacht was longer than a school bus and twice as wide. I leaned into the *V* railing at the bow and waited for the men to gather. Sandy ridges rose from the crystalline waters along the eastern horizon. Boxy white-washed buildings scattered the closest island and overlooked sailboats toppled in the ghost port.

A hand settled next to mine on the railing. "The Egadi Islands." Michio's voice was as guarded as the day I met him. "We're heading into the Tyrrhenian Sea." He pointed at the frosted waves sloshing to the left of the morning sun."Ready to meet the crew?"

I searched his blank face and found what I was looking for. His mask. Worn to disguise his weaknesses from those he didn't trust. But, slow as I was, I finally recognized what was beneath that mask. A whisper of love to match his words in the galley. It made me want to sing to the vast openness of the sea and sky. Instead, I rearranged my face into one that might mirror the seriousness in his and nodded.

He led me across the teak-laid deck. Roark and two others talked over maps in the cockpit, encircled by deep couches. The man nearest Roark stood a few inches over him. Streaks of gold weaved through his headful of bushy brown hair.

I stopped before him and raised my chin to hold his steel blue stare. His swarthy face froze as he looked at me agape.

"What?" I asked.

"I'm sorry. It's just...Beckett said you were breathtaking, but that was an understatement." An Australian accent. "I'm still trying to catch my breath."

Jesse Beckett and I were going to have words. "What else did Beckett say?"

The other man replied, "If we touch you without your consent, our balls will hang like baubles from his Humvee's rearview mirror"—he eyed my outstretched hand and looked away—"ma'am."

The Australian gripped my palm. "Tallis Reynolds. Nice to meet you, Ms. Delina."

"Call me Evie."

He turned to the other man. "My mate here is Cliff Dilman."

Cliff tipped up his baseball cap and gave me a demure smile made for charming small town girls. "Nice to meet you, ma'am."

"Same. Did you say Jesse has a Humvee?"

"Yes, ma'am. It's yours. Said he brought it over on the very ship you were hiding on."

"No shit." Sneaky bastard.

"He's got your MT 350E army bike, too," Tallis said.

"Son of a bitch," Roark huffed. "Where?"

"He left it in Genoa," Tallis replied, "where we'll be docking."

"So you both work for Jesse?" I asked.

Tallis rocked on his heels. "On and off the past seven years."

I refrained from rubbing my palms together, anxious to dig. "Doing what?"

"Bodyguard, muscle, hired gun, whatever you want to call it."

Michio folded his arms over his chest. "What does Beckett do exactly?"

Cliff shrugged. Tallis said, "Some kind of underground international humanitarian, perhaps? That's my guess given the secret nature of his activities and the types of services he requires."

"Humanitarian," Roark prompted Tallis, avoiding my stare.

"His methods may be questionable, but he seems to always be on the right side."

Whatever his job was, he wasn't doing it anymore considering he spent the prior eighteen months at my heels. "What types of services are we talking about?"

Tallis grinned. "Let's see, a week before the outbreak, I helped him shovel through innards on a blown up Afghani sidewalk looking for"—he rubbed his nape—"this and that. That same night—"

"I escorted him to Tibet," Cliff said, "to have tea with the Dalai Lama."

Michio's brows shot to his hairline. "Bull."

Cliff shared a smile with Tallis and lifted a shoulder. "The man has more connections than anyone I know."

"Had," Tallis said. "Most of them suck blood now."

"Who does he work for?" Roark asked.

"No one knows." Tallis plopped onto the couch. "Beckett carries himself like a military attaché, yet he lives like a spy. Every assignment is flawlessly planned, heavily clouded, and approached with zero emotion." He darted his eyes at me. "Until this one."

"What's that mean?" I asked.

"When he sought me out a month ago, he wasn't his usual cryptic self. He was fidgety, short-tempered, running around like some obsessed person. He kept going on about this beautiful kidnapped woman." He paused, held my eyes. "He'd even traded in his rifle for arrows and a tomahawk. His behavior made me nervous and the shit about saving a woman when I knew none had survived...I turned down the assignment." He exhaled. "In the end, he was very persuasive. And I get it now. In the matters of humanity, this billet makes all the others negligible."

"It's not just that," Cliff said. "He's made this one personal."

Personal. I decided to analyze that later. "So what was your assignment from Beckett?"

"Get a yacht, pick you up from Manoel Island and meet him in Genoa—if he wasn't with you in Malta."

"And above all," Cliff said, "guard you with our lives."

Michio watched them with the same scrutiny he watched me. "What happens in Genoa?"

Tallis leaned into his knees. "Doesn't work that way, mate. Beckett never shows all his cards."

Lines formed on Roark's brow. "When the wanker dragged me from the fortress, he had a pilot with him. A French bloke." He looked at me for the first time. "He said he'd fly ye to Iceland."

To see the Shard. Michio knew them, trusted them. Still, my stomach churned. Did I want to know if I carried the cure? And if we did find it, what would keep us from repeating our failures, pandering our human-centric gods and destroying ourselves all over again?

If the Drone hadn't killed the last of the nymphs, what would they endure to test the cure? Even if we found and cured twenty nymphs, I knew all too well the hardships each would suffer as rare human women.

Bile simmered in my throat. I braced my hands on my knees. Roark took a step toward me then seemed to think better of it.

"And if Jesse failed to kill the Drone?" I asked to no one particular.

Cliff's voice whipped with the ocean breeze. "Beckett never fails."

I wasn't convinced.

Several hours after retiring to bed, I lay curled around Michio's back, seeking comfort in his steady breaths.

Sleep hadn't taken me and I knew why. I was waiting, hoping.

Wooden boards creaked. The room lolled with the rock of the tide. My eyelids drooped. Just as I was about to give in, the reason for my wait slipped into bed behind me.

I shut my eyes as his hands sought a place to settle, a place against my bare skin but far enough away from Michio's. The back of my thigh. The dip of my waist.

I fell asleep loathing my guilt of wanting more from Roark, but content with having him there. It would have to be enough.

We left the steep mountains of Corsica and sailed around Capraia. I stood opposite Michio on the yacht's port quarter and narrowed my eyes at him. The combination of the open sea and the perspiration beading on his hulking frame made me dizzy and restless.

Two days on the boat, rife with sexual tension. All three of us felt it. I didn't have a clue how to approach it. So, I did what I always did and escaped to the bathroom. The loss of my bullet only fueled my frustration.

"Evie. It's important that you press your free hand into your opponent's throat when you're locking the arm. Try again."

I'd asked Michio to teach me the arm bar he used against my flower technique. The one that put my hand so temptingly close to his groin and my submission to the head. After forty-five minutes, however, I regretted the request. I couldn't drag my thoughts away from the ache between my legs or the brooding priest polishing his sword a few feet away.

His honey curls glinted red in the sun and lifted in the breeze. Each time I stole a glance, the corner of his mouth pinched, but his eyes remained on his sword. Damn, damn, damn the stubborn bastard.

I lunged. My forearm slid over Michio's chest. I swept my leg behind his. The mountain didn't move. The momentum sent me hurtling past and head first over the side.

His arm stopped my legs from following and hauled me to his chest. I slumped in his embrace and squeezed my thighs together. Time for that bathroom break.

"Evie." Michio's rasp tickled my ear. "Go talk to him."

I cocked my hip and tilted my head. "You go talk to him."

His lips twitched. "I'm the problem, Evie. And as long as I'm in his face, this standoff isn't going anywhere. And you need to work it out while on the boat, safe from danger. Rekindle whatever you had, do whatever you do with a celibate priest, down in the stateroom where I don't have to watch."

I leaned back, brows arched.

He brushed his lips over my gaping mouth. His heady, exotic taste overrode the salty air. "That's a heavy emphasis on celibate, Evie. Bold, italicized, and underlined."

"Michio—"

"Go before I pound my chest."

I would've kissed him again if I wasn't already moving. I skidded past Roark and met his eyes. Then I ran to the stateroom.

The door crashed behind me. Roark leaned against it and dragged in a breath that shuddered the naked muscles in his chest, his neck drawn in an iron sinew.

He uncurled his massive body, jade eyes blazing through fallen curls, and stalked toward me. "I'm sorry"—his palms captured my face—"for this."

His tongue pushed into my mouth. I caught it between my lips and sucked.

Fingers stabbed through my hair, tilting my head the angle he wanted. My feet arched on tiptoes as I stretched to meet him.

"I missed ye so much," he said at my lips, "I can't stop this."

Oh no. *Stop* was on my tongue, but his swept it away. Oak and chocolate filled my mouth. Desire pooled between my thighs. Didn't I learn last time?

I shoved his chest. "Talk, Roark. That's why we're here."

Strong fingers yanked my waist toward the bed. He fell with me, pinned me with his hips.

"We'll talk like this." His brogue was deep and very male.

I groaned. "No way."

His thumb bit into my bottom lip, parted it. His mouth opened over mine, hovered. "Talk."

"What is this?" I rocked against his erection.

A rumble vibrated low in his throat. "Ye know what that is."

"No. You doing *this*." I punctuated *this* with a snap of my hips.

He ground me into the bed, his belt buckle digging into my pelvis. "This is me loving ye the only way I can."

Oh, my fickle priest. What did I do with that answer? I crunched the muscles in my core and lifted to meet him. "Then this is me loving you back." Knowing it would only end in more pain.

Our hips rolled together, found the right spot, the right pace. I gave myself over to the sensations, the solace of his touch, the pull of our bodies rubbing and climbing together.

"There. Right there." I clung to his shoulders, consumed by his mouth.

His grinding hips slowed. One twist. Two. His body shook and he threw back his head, eyes squeezed shut. "Unghhh."

Seeing him like that, losing himself to something as simple as dry humping, it pushed me over. I screamed out my release.

He clamped a hand over my mouth and laughter bellowed from his chest. "I hate to quiet ye, love, but knowing wha' those cries do to me, it'd be a bugger to stir up the same reaction from the wankers on deck."

"Kiss me then," I murmured through his fingers. And damn, he did in a frantic feasting. Open-mouthed and urgent, his chin scratched against mine. Then he tilted his head, deepened the feeding. His hands moved over my neck, my breasts, down my thighs, always returning to knead my ass.

He raised his head, looked down at me. "Ye den' know how bad I've been gummin' to do this." His nose traced the length of mine. "I've been a right perv thinking about us a' it."

I licked his swollen lips. "I missed you, too. This shit with your vow, with Michio"—I hugged him, poured my heart in it—"it fucking hurts."

"I promise ye, I'll bind me soul to Satan for a thousand years in a bottomless pit if it means you'll never hurt again."

Those jade eyes bored into me with such stark focus that my mouth went dry and my bones softened. "Then stop fucking me around. You chose your vow. Yet here you are. Again."

He dropped his forehead to mine. "There's a balance between reason and faith. I'm going arseways about it, but I'll find it. Ye wait in that balance. I need ye, Evie."

"I don't know about the balance, but you can have me without the orgasm."

He groaned. "Right ye are. I survived thirty-three years without one. One buck with ye and I'm banjaxed beyond all help."

"Voodoo vagina."

He burst out laughing. I could get high off that sound. "Lay this out for me. Tell me how you see us going forward."

"I see ye leaving me with me head hanging like Beelzebub's ball sac."

I gasped. "Never that."

Our lips collided in more laughter.

"This." He held my face between his hands. "This is how I see us, Evie."

My smile filled my face and tingled through my body. "Okay."

"Hold that thought." He rolled off me and jogged to the bathroom. The water turned on, turned off. Then he returned with a scrap of paper and a pen in hand. "We're going to define our physical relationship. Our limits in regards to me relationship with God and your…other relationships."

My brow wrinkled. "My other relationships? Michio?"

"And the Lakota."

"Oh. We're not like that."

A laugh cascaded from his perfect lips. "Your arse and parsley. I spent a rake of time with that mentaller. He's lost the rag over ye."

Another Jesse puzzle to sort out. I wanted him with a heart already divided between two others. It felt wrong to love three men. But it felt more wrong not too. "Let's focus on us. You want to negotiate our relationship?"

"Our physical relationship." He joined me on the bed, facing me. "I wen' hurt ye again. I can make this work if we're on the same page." He nodded to the paper.

The desperation in his eyes and the plea in his expression would make me do just about anything. "Why are we writing this down? Just tell me what you want."

"So one answer wen' sway the other."

We sat cross-legged, knees to knees, heads down. I scrawled my only requirement and passed it to him, face down.

When he finished writing his on the other side, he pulled me into his lap and leaned against the headboard. The paper quivered in his hand.

I kissed his bottom lip. "You're nervous?"

He kissed me back. "Bloody terrified."

"We don't have to do this."

The paper floated to my lap. "Read them aloud."

I flipped to his elegant penmanship. "You want to maintain your relationship with God by refraining from intercourse." I looked up. "I already know this. This is what you were fretting over?"

A swallow bobbed his throat. "It's what's not on there. I want everything else, love. The holding, the touching, the kissing—"

"The ejaculating in your boxers."

A quirk touched his lips.

"I'm pretty sure just thinking about any of those things breaks your vow."

His thumb meandered over my knee. "I'm redefining me relationship with God. By refraining from the temptation of intercourse, by touching your fit body everyday knowing I'll never fully have ye, I'm still holding back a part of me self for Him. He understands me need to be physically comforted by ye amidst this devastating world. And He understands I'm still making a huge sacrifice. You're me biggest temptation, Evie. I promise, this will be a continual test of me faith."

"Fair enough."

"And your limit?"

I turned the paper over and held it up. "Accept my sexual relationship with Michio. My open affection with him. I won't be sneaking off to make out in dark corners."

His thumb jerked on my leg. "Nor will I. And all you're other relationships?"

"I told you—"

"You're the only woman in the world, love. There will be others." His arms went around me and he pressed a kiss into my hair. "We have our terms."

"That's it? After your possessive display yesterday?"

He pulled me closer. "I thought your relationship with Michio meant the end of ours. It scared me."

"He hasn't barged in yet. Admit you misjudged him and behaved like a belligerent child."

"Right." His smile was back. Maybe it would stay put. But as he rolled me over and buried his face in my neck, I wondered if Michio would sympathize with Roark's new definition of celibacy.

That night, a hum tingled low in my belly. I opened my eyes. Michio's steady breath brushed the top of my head. Roark's chest rose and fell against my back.

The buzz increased, spiraled up my spine. I raised my head and rubbed my eyes. A black figure blotted out the middle of the room. The shape expanded, stretched sideways.

My heart thundered in my ears. I blinked, adjusted my eyes to the dark. My throat closed up.

Transparent wings spread from wall to wall. Onyx eyes drank in the shadows. Lips curled back and fangs extended. "Now we finish where we left off, Eveline."

I am not afraid... I was born to do this.

Joan of Arc

CHAPTER THIRTY-NINE: THE ARC

All at once, I was alone in the bed. The clash of steel on wood rang out. Shadows writhed in the doorway and moved out of the room.

I jolted up and barreled into the cabinet that housed the carbine.

Empty clip. Next clip. Empty. Shit. I grabbed the USP, ejected the mag. A strip of brass peeked out. Adrenaline surged. I chambered a round, pivoted, elbows locked, and lined up the sights.

Roark leaned over his sword, chest heaving. And the Drone....

"Where is he?" He couldn't be far. I ran through the door and crashed into Michio.

His arms enfolded me, his staff nudging my back. "He's gone."

"His wings. Did you see—"

"Yes." He tucked my head under his arm. "He flew away."

"I didn't dream that? He can fly?" My voice pitched on the last word.

His other arm hooked around my waist, pulled me closer. "Yes," rattled from his chest, against my face.

I jerked from his hold, heart racing, and skin crawling. Slivers of wood jabbed my feet as I darted back to the cabinet. "We're surrounded by water. No messenger bugs. How did he find us?" If he could find me on a boat in the Ligurian Sea, he could find me anywhere.

The Drone's right hand man, member of the Shard, doctor with a hypothesis for everything, stared at me, eyes blank.

Not good. "Obviously, he learned our route. But how—" No, no, no. The hungry guards, the dungeon, meat hooks, torture. My hand went to my breast, to the turquoise stone there. "Oh God…Jesse."

"Don't jump to conclusions, Evie." Michio's knuckles blanched around his staff. Steel spikes protruded from the end. No blood.

The tip of Roark's sword dug into the teak floor, its sharp edge clean as well.

"How did the Drone get past you?" So quickly and uninjured?

"He flashed." Roark pointed the sword at the door. "He moves faster than ye doing that blurry thing when you're lamping bugs."

Knew that after two months on the painful side of his flashing fist. "Tallis and Cliff?"

"They saw him fly off starboard." Michio hauled on jeans and a shirt, the blades gone from the staff in his hand.

"And they didn't get a shot off? Harpoon his ass with their fishing gun? Nothing?"

Brows collided over black eyes. "It's dark."

"He flew all the way here, just to be chased away? He's fucking with us." I strapped on my arm sheaths and four knives. Jesse must have collected my spares from the Humvee. "How close is Genoa?" Goddammit, Jesse better be there. In one piece.

"On the horizon." Michio kissed my bare shoulder and draped a tee over it. "I'm going up." The door snicked behind him.

Roark leaned against the cabinet beside me. I scoured the racks for mags, filled the ones I found with ammo, unable to ignore the weight of his gaze. "What?"

"Ye were just gonna hurl along up there after the Drone in the nip, were ye?" His eyes made a perusal over my nude skin, stopping on the only thing I wore. Michio's boxers, rolled at the waistband, determined to give up their fight against gravity.

I tugged them up and slammed my pistol in the holster. "Survival before modesty."

His eyes darted to the shirt flung over my shoulder. "Think your doctor disagrees."

A shaky sigh escaped. "Add it to our list of disagreements."

His slouch against the cabinet grew taller. "That so?"

We didn't have time for melodrama, but my fragile relationships wouldn't work without communication and honesty. I turned toward him and traced fingers around his curling ones, intertwining our hands. "He knows about our negotiation. We talked after you went up on deck last night." Talking wasn't the only thing we did.

The tic in his cheek told me he caught the flush in mine. I straightened the strap on my holster, stalling. "We'll work it out. Nothing to worry about."

"Tell me wha' I'm not worrying about, then." His expression, so open and full of affection, made it easy to bare all, give him all.

"Okay." I raised our laced hands, pressed a kiss to his scarred knuckles. "It's the touching."

His eyes darkened, locked on my mouth. "What about it?"

"The intimacy you and I share…he's wants to draw lines at—"

He tossed his hands in the air. "Then throw us a bloody Sharpie, why den' he? We'll just draw 'Do Not Enter' zones on your body. Is that wha' he wants?"

"Stop making him out like a barbarian. It's not any different than the lines you and I drew. And don't forget, he just left us alone down here, with me wearing only underwear." I stretched out my arms, baring the reminder.

Cheeks splotched, he dropped his head and asked the floor, "Wha' do *ye* want?"

I stepped into him and raised his whiskered chin with a cupped hand. The worry bracketing his gorgeous eyes was my undoing. "I want you, you fickle, fucked up, beautiful man."

His lashes dropped through a ragged inhale and snapped back up. "Ye want the doctor."

My selfish heart jumped to my throat, choked my response. "Him, too." When he tried to look away, I hardened my grip, waited for those eyes to focus on mine. "And if he loves me like he says he does, he'll understand that nothing is worth holding on to like the love we share in touch. I won't let anyone take that from us, okay?"

"Bloody hell." His face softened, as did his body. We melted together, forehead to forehead, palms holding cheeks, and let our mingling breaths seal my vow.

I perched between Roark and Michio against the starboard bow. Cliff monitored port side. Tallis stretched behind the wheel. A cigarette sagged from his brazen lips as he steered us into Genoa's harbor.

Pale-breasted gulls screeched into the early morning twilight. Piers fingered from the shoreline, buried under concrete and metal. Disemboweled ships leeched the decrepit docks.

My grip on the railing clenched. In that moment, with the defensive walls of a dead city collapsing around us and the jaws of death echoing through the devoured streets, I felt so very far away from home. My breath caught in my throat, clinging to a lost hope.

One little girl.

My past followed me to every city, weighing me down. Surrounded by a foreign horizon, I lost the fight to keep all things familiar buried. Maybe it was the countdown to docking, the dread that came with the dangers waiting on land. Maybe it was the empty wharf, the sickening feeling that Jesse didn't make it. When I released a long-held breath, it escaped with an unobtainable wish.

One little boy.

I longed for wings. To let the wind carry my feet. To fly home, to the brick and boarded husk of the life I once had, to the woman I used to be. I ducked my head, didn't want them to see me, crumbling like the ships in the harbor.

A hand settled over mine on the railing. Sandalwood breaths stirred my hair. "Let it go."

"As if it were that easy." My voice wobbled. I swallowed the weakness, hardened it. "Did you let…someone go?"

"Parents. Brother." Michio's fingers curled, straightened, stroking between mine. "My girlfriend."

I cleared my throat. "What was her name?"

"Isabella."

Beside me, Roark closed his eyes and hooked his pinkie around my free one. Words didn't comfort, didn't undo what was done. So I said nothing.

Michio dropped his forehead to my temple. "Everything sad, everything dead, the past brought us here, alive."

The blades on my arms glinted against the sparkling ebb of the sea. "It's unforgiving."

His lips feathered my earlobe. "It's living."

"Living is relative. And not always ideal." I steeled my shoulders against the glaring empty wharf. But where would I be without Roark's faith in me, Jesse's loyalty, and Michio's strength. Things would be much, much worse.

Distant barking fluttered across the harbor. I jumped.

Cliff's voice ripped through the tension. "The dog's our green light to berth."

My heart panted as I leaned over the railing and squinted. A blur of black and tan streaked across the pier. I shoved my way to the port side. Darwin squatted on the edge of the dock, tongue lolling, tail whipping.

A man loomed on the shore, his back to us. He glanced over his shoulder and the first rays of sun caught the copper in his eyes. Then he returned to his watch, bow and arrow at his side. A position that would allow lift and release in one breath. My pulse sped up.

The yacht docked. I scrambled down the ramp and dropped to my knees in a furry reunion. Lathered in puppy kisses and dog hair, I caught the amusement cartwheeling across Roark's face. "What?"

He shook his head and gestured up the dock with his chin. "Ye gonna give your Lakota the same greeting?"

Tallis and Cliff walked the perimeter, rifles raised. Jesse leaned against a pier support, hands stuffed in the pockets of jeans hung low on his narrow hips. He didn't have Roark's height or Michio's bulk, but his trim physique was solid and intimidating all the same. He watched me with his usual bored expression.

Roark's hand found mine and gave it a squeeze. I loped up the pier with Darwin bouncing at my heels and stopped an arm's length away.

Last time I saw him, he was saving my ass on Dover pier. And there we were, another pier, another ass saving. There was so much to say, yet the only thing my mouth could produce was a weak smile. Definitely not a high-confidence moment.

"The doctor give you my message?"

I missed that smooth Texan accent. His gaze floated to my shirt where my scar curved above the low neckline. His copper eyes darkened under furrowed brows and his mouth dipped in a scowl.

"You weren't responsible for what happened in Dover. Or River Tweed."

His jaw clenched and his fists went to his hips. "Fuck if I wasn't. *I was there.*" Such pain in his voice.

We stared at one other, paralyzed in time, gazes fused in a war of emotions. I wasn't sure who moved first, but when we did, we collided, entangled, hugging as if it were our last. Standing there, wrapped in Jesse, invoked a sensation so long anticipated, I felt it from my crown to my toes. I felt safe.

"The Drone got away." His voice pulsed against my neck, arms banded around my waist.

"I know. But so did I." I pulled back, met his eyes. "Thank you."

Footsteps approached. He looked behind me, the moment gone. "We need to go."

Our cavalcade comprised of the Humvee and two Harley Davidson army bikes. Roark's eyes narrowed on Cliff, who straddled the enduro that had carried us from Lloyd's pub that cold night six months prior.

I nudged his arm. "If you wanna ride, kick him off."

He pinched my chin, gave it a jerk. "Naw, love. I stay with ye." He pushed me into the back of the Humvee with Darwin and all our gear then climbed in the front with Michio behind the wheel. Tallis mounted the other bike.

The minute the engines turned over, my insides jerked in the toils of vibrations. The pounding of boots neared my open door. Jesse fell in, bow arched, and landed in my lap. "Step on it, Doc. Go, go, go."

A claw followed him in, attached to his leg. Then the aphid was on us. Its jaw snapped open and the spear shot toward Jesse's chest. His arrow released, sunk a bulging eye, and exited the back of the head.

I kicked at the torso skipping over the cement with the Humvee's momentum. It let go and I slammed the swinging door, longing for the safety of the boat.

The whine of the enduros led the way. Aphids scurried from crowded high-rise buildings and spread over the lot. Darwin barked, claws curled against the rear window. Jesse climbed into his own seat and spit arrows out his window. Roark and I used our side-arms to pick off the aphids blurring too close to the bikes.

The bounce of the Humvee over debris and bodies jostled our aim. I needed Yang. Next to me, Jesse's arm flew in a stream of arrows. His back muscles waved through the movement. It probably wasn't the best time to explain why he and I needed to remove our shirts and press up against each other.

I switched to the carbine and held it steady at my shoulder. Exhale. Squeeze. Squeeze. Bugs squealed and rolled around us.

When the enduros zipped far enough ahead, the swarm fell back. Gravel shot up from our tires. Soon, the only thing trailing us was a haze of dust. A collective sigh washed through the Humvee.

A few minutes into the drive, I turned to Jesse. "Tell me what happened with the Drone."

Roark stirred in the front seat. Jesse didn't budge his head from the feather he was attaching to an arrow shaft.

"Jesse?"

He frowned without looking up. "What do you want to know?"

"You can start by telling me how he got away."

He tossed the arrow aside and raked a hand through his wavy russet hair. "I cornered him in the chamber at the top of the main tower. His army was barricaded outside. I was feet away, arrow nocked..." He palmed his nape.

I waited several heartbeats then cleared my throat.

"What do you want me to say? He just disappeared. It was dark as shit, but I know there was nowhere for him to go."

"But up?"

He stared at me.

"You were in *my* chamber. It has open rafters." I met Michio's eyes in the rearview mirror. "He flew away."

Jesse blinked, his lips in a thin line. "When he disappeared, the aphids scattered, wandering mindless without his control. Maybe one of my arrows hit him after all."

"He was on the yacht last night."

His face turned scarlet. "He what?"

"He slipped in while we slept." Michio's tone was cool as he walked through the event and brushed over what we knew about the Drone's metamorphosis.

"And where the fuck were Reynolds and Dilman?"

"The Drone sneaked into the stateroom," I said. "Came after me while I slept between two capable bodyguards."

Jesse dug a fist into his brow. "This is unacceptable. I hired them to do a job. Either they do it or I'll—"

"You'll do what? While we're on the subject of threats," I said, "you need to stop. Scalping, strangulation, castration?"

"They're not threats."

I groaned. "I don't understand you. You've been pissed at me since the day we met, yet you spent the last year and a half protecting me."

He steepled his fingers over the bridge of his nose and stared at the back of Michio's head.

"Then you told Tallis I was..." What would I accomplish by embarrassing him?

"Breathtaking," Roark supplied from the front seat.

I softened my tone. "Breathtaking. Is that what you think, Jesse?"

He closed his eyes.

Fine. I'd break down that wall another time. "What are you doing with Darwin?"

He dropped his hands and met my glare with his own. "When you left West Virginia, I followed you by car to Boston, but I knew I'd be tracking you on foot. I brought Darwin to help." He scratched him behind the ears and Darwin nudged his big head into Jesse's lap.

The shared affection tightened my chest. I wasn't sure if I was envious of the dog or of Jesse. "I never saw anyone following me in the states."

"You wouldn't."

I narrowed my eyes. "Why did you follow me?"

He gathered up the maps at his feet. "Doesn't matter."

"What's your job?"

"To keep you alive."

"You've invested a lot of energy in this. In me. I want to know why."

"No. You don't."

"Yes. I do."

Silence.

"Who do you work for?"

"No one." He put his nose in the maps and turned his back to me.

"What's your problem?"

Darwin's heavy chuffs ticked off the passing seconds.

"Wow, you know, I realize I owe you my life," I said to his back, "but would it be so hard to work on your approach?"

Nothing.

"Forget it. Just one more question then I'll leave you to your arrogance. Where are we going?"

"We're meeting my pilot at Aéroport Lyon Saint-Exupéry." The vowels rolled off his tongue as if French was his native language. He tilted his head, gave me his profile. "My pilot knows his way around the airport and the grounds will be easier to defend." He grabbed the arrow he was making, stabbed the point in a map and shoved it at me. "We'll spend the night in the valley of the Arc."

The arrow head pierced a green-shaded area surrounded by a white blotched mountain range. *Saint-Jean-de-Maurienne* labeled the nearest dot.

"Tomorrow, we'll fly from Lyon and go anywhere you want." His tone was void of emotion.

I gave Darwin a pat on his head, climbed over the wheel space and settled in Roark's lap. Michio watched the road, but must have felt my stare, because he reached across the space between us and settled a hand on my thigh. I held his hand there with my own and looped my other arm around Roark's neck. "Well?"

Roark's brow bunched. "Ye heard him. He's offering a vessel to save yourself, those ye love, and perhaps…humanity."

At least Roark and Michio agreed on something. And as much as I wanted to go home, I knew I never would. "Next you'll tell me we'll be boarding this vessel in pairs."

He held my glower in earnest. "Think on it, love."

I already had. "We're going to Iceland."

A clement breeze teased through the cracked window. Satiny pastures swallowed the shriveled husks of vineyards. The stone archways and blond skeletons of Tuscan homes littered the rolling horizon.

Several hours later, the hills steepened and the trees stood taller. A pebbled trail branched from the road and with it came a stinging sensation behind my breastbone.

Roark's arms wound across my midriff. "Evie?"

We passed the trail and the pinch in my chest inflamed. A pinch I hadn't felt in months. "I don't know. I feel something...here." I raised his hand, placed it over my heart.

Michio cut his eyes to me. "Aphids?"

I shook my head. "This is different."

Roark's big hand circled over the twinge, his brogue soft. "Ye babes?"

I nodded, hope swelling inside me.

Jesse angled out his window and released an arrow. It wobbled in the trunk of a cone-bearing tree marking the entrance to a side road. The enduros turned off and we followed. The pull in my chest vibrated.

Wider than the path, the Humvee shoved through the heavy brush of larches. Foliage and fuchsia sprayed the windshield. Several kilometers in, we broke through the trees and emerged on a high plateau.

Snowcapped mountains layered the landscape. We bumped along trickling ravines and descended to the mouth of a river. The blue water glimmered under the dipping sun, swaddled by jutting crags and frothy waves. A single ranch-style cabin waited at the bottom.

"The Arc River." Jesse reached for the door handle. When we skidded to a stop at the porch, he jumped out. "Looks abandoned. Stay put while we sweep."

Roark and Michio followed him. I reclined in the seat and concentrated on the nudge inside me. Like an unseen hand, it had a hold of me, pulling me back toward that trail.

Tallis poked his head in the door. "All clear."

I shuffled after him, into the house. Passed a couch, a chair, a bed, more chairs. The one-room space was large, with an equally large fireplace, which is where I found Jesse talking to Michio and Roark.

He watched me approach, expression unreadable. "Your guardians just filled me in on your connection with the aphids."

My guardians. "Then I'll save your boys some time. This area is free of bugs."

"Yeah, we made sure of that, but it'll be a damn nice security feature to have going forward."

My chest tugged, pulled my bones with it. "I saw a trail on the way here I need to check out. I'll take a bike and won't be gone long."

I could have sliced the dead air with my dagger.

Jesse's face transformed into an iron mask. "The answer is no."

My smile was brief and not a smile at all. "Good thing I didn't ask a question."

His lips pulled away from grinding teeth. "You stumble onto one, two, five aphids, yeah, I'm sure you got that, no problem. What happens when you run into a swarm? You carry enough ammo to escape that?"

"Watch and learn, Lakota." I spun toward the door, toward Roark's enduro, trusting my internal radar to alert me long before I encountered more than I could handle.

Since my hair had grown halfway to my waist, I looped it up in a ponytail. Carbine strapped on the bike's mount, I jumped on and fired up the single cylinder. The vibration seeped through my body and carbonated tingles to my fingers and toes.

Jesse stood over me. "Scooch."

"Get your own bike."

Muscles jerked under his scowl.

Behind him, Roark tucked his hands in his pockets. "Remind me to tell ye about the time she threw herself from that bike onto a street full of snarlies."

Jesse grumbled something inaudible and stalked to the other bike.

Roark's face filled my horizon. Droves of demands burned in his jade stare.

"Need a cage for that canary?" I asked.

"Do wha' ye have to do, love, but if you're gone long, I'll come after ye with a whole flock of them."

I ran a finger down the buttons of his cassock. "You think I'm a wanker."

His sun-kissed face ruptured in a smile. "If you're a wanker, I'm a wanker. Just keep your eyes *up*." He brushed his lips over mine and stepped back.

Michio squatted on the porch, scratching Darwin's muzzle. His eyes rose to the sky and flicked back to me. Unlike the others, he wouldn't argue or hover. He was too sneaky for that. No doubt he planned to trail us, stealthfully protecting me from myself.

I gave him a smile he didn't return. Hmm. My tongue made a slow swipe over my top teeth. Ah, there it was. The world's rarest smile.

Jesse rolled next to me. "Stick to my side."

I punched the gas, fueled with expectancy. By the time I hit fourth, my heart fluttered with the bike's purr and my top curled up my back. I followed Jesse along a ravine and though a grassland curtained by electric green hills and valleys. When we hit a straight stretch, I revved ahead. A flock of Greylag geese cackled above us. The wind whistled through my hair in a bouquet of grapes and loam.

Several acres ahead, a cement water tower rose above the meadow. Tattered fabrics flapped around a small form bound to the ladder. I sucked in a breath. A body? I'd come across bodies everywhere I'd traveled, but few were human and even fewer were children.

Jesse flanked me and we gunned it, slipping our tires over the gravel.

A tiny torso came into focus. My muscles locked and my skin bumped up. I skidded the bike sideways and rolled from it as it toppled over. My legs staggered through each step toward the tower.

Strips of denim hung from protruding bones and baked skin. Chunks of matted brown hair pasted a ghastly head. And tucked in the elbow of an ashen arm was a lovingly-worn teddy bear.

*Wakan Tanka, Great Mystery, teach me how to trust my heart, my mind, my intuition,
my inner knowing, the senses of my body, the blessings of my spirit.
Teach me to trust these things so that I may enter my sacred space and love beyond my fear,
and thus walk in balance with the passing of each glorious sun.*

American Indian Lakota Prayer

CHAPTER FORTY: MIND, BODY, AND SOULFUR

"Aaron?" Jesse said, frozen at my side. "Aaron, wake up."

I unholstered the USP and spun. "What the fuck did you say?" I shoved the barrel in his face.

He held his hands up, eyes on mine, blank and cold. "Put the gun down."

I stepped back, gun trained at his head. "You see him?" My voice cracked. "You can see my boy?"

My feet tangled in dried vines. Branches snapped. I stumbled but kept my footing. The gun shook in my hand as Aaron's hollow-eyed face ripped out my heart.

"We're here because he has something to show you." Jesse's voice scratched at my back.

I swung the pistol around. "Don't fucking talk about him like you know him. Stay back. I mean it."

Vines twined through the sunken torso and bound him to the ladder. Bark gnawed into gangrene skin. His head lolled to the side, eyelids stretched and dusty. I clawed one-handed at the woody stems, pulled at his body.

"If you only look with your eyes," Jesse said, "he'll be forced to use that."

Miasma burned my nose. I freed the unnaturally bent arm and Booey tumbled to the ground.

Scrape. Scrape-scrape.

Eyelashes broke off, dusted his gaping shriveled lips. A bulge moved under the lid of one eye. The dry skin splintered. A needle-like leg punched out. Then another and another. A spider wiggled free from the socket with a wet suction sound. Its body was all-white, Aaron's all-white eye. A tiny pupil dotted its back.

My throat closed up. My arms wouldn't work. Spiders crawled out of the torn collar of his shirt and covered him in a boil of shiny black bodies.

Not real. Not real. Not real. My heart pumped at a dangerous velocity. Still, I couldn't pull myself away.

"Aaron, we've seen enough." Jesse was closer, his voice stern.

Aaron's remaining eye snapped open. A dark bead welled in the corner and painted a crimson stripe down his cheek. The yellow-green iris darted between us and the orb-bodied spider on his shoulder.

The spider teetered, legs twitching. Then it popped in a hiss of smoke. A succession of smaller pops followed as the remaining spiders exploded with tiny sparks.

My pulse beat a wild tattoo through my veins. "Oh Jesus, how do I not look with my eyes?"

A firm hand clasped mine. "Look with your heart." Another hand gripped my jaw, turned my head. Copper eyes imprisoned mine. "It's time to leave this world. We'll go together." His voice was authoritative, echoed with power. My knees buckled.

He caught me around the waist and sat me in his lap on the ground. His fingers curled around the pistol and yanked it from my fist. The tug at my thigh told me he holstered it. I laid my head against the muffled thump of his heart and lifted my eyes.

The weathered corpse of a nymph sagged in the bindings where Aaron had hung.

"I'm fucking losing it," I whispered. "You must be too, since you saw…"

"Aaron's spirit."

"How—" I shook my head. "It wasn't real."

He shifted, settled me deeper into his lap. "I'm a spirit walker. Just like you."

"You sound like Akicita. I don't believe in that shit." A lump filled my throat. "No offense."

He cupped my head against him. "Your othersense, what you see in the spirit world, is a gift, the consciousness of the Great Mystery. It's up to you to discover the meaning."

I pushed his chest. His iron grip tightened.

"They're hallucinations." I rubbed my temple. "There's something wrong with me."

"The spirits show me things, too." He sighed. "They brought us together in West Virginia. I followed them to you."

My body stiffened. "You followed who, Jesse?"

"The energy from memories of those who have passed can give spirits a tangible form in the spirit world. Annie and Aaron's memories are potent. Their spirits are strong."

I jerked and his thighs and arms formed a cage around me. The way he looked at me made me want to break eye contact. I didn't. "How do you know their names?"

"I'll tell you, but don't pull away."

I nodded.

"Annie's ghost visited me the day after the outbreak. That was the first time. When did she die?"

Blood roared in my ears. I lowered my eyes, just an inch, to the sharp line of his cheekbone.

"She persuaded me to leave Europe," he said, "to reunite with my people in North Dakota. From there, I followed Aaron to the

Allegheny Mountains." The corner of his mouth crooked up. "He'd leave that bear in the damndest places for me to find."

A burn shot from my chest and spread behind my nose.

He stroked my hair. "The night you chased Annie into our camp, I was there. I was chasing her too." He stared at our laps. "I've grown attached to them over the past two years. Their lives were short, but very full. They've given me a reawakening. And more importantly"—he lifted his head, eyes raw—"they led me to you."

A kind of isolation I didn't realize I carried lifted away. I padded a fingertip over the blade-sharp angle of his jaw. "Why didn't you tell me? All this time?"

His hand shackled my wrist, pulled it from his face. But he didn't let go. "The veil between our realm and theirs shows me other things, darker things. Things I must keep from you."

I laughed and it rang of hysterics. "Darker than this?" I tilted my head toward the nymph's decayed body.

"Yes."

"Remember the nightmares I had in the mountains? They featured the Drone. This was *before* I'd met the bastard. Imagine my surprise when he showed up at River Tweed. How do you explain that?"

"If he's amidst transformation between human and other, maybe his spirit is caught between realms and your consciousness sensed him."

"There is nothing scientific about that answer. In fact, it reeks of bullshit."

"Spiritualism explains what science cannot."

He looked away from my glare and laid a hand over my stomach. "Maybe he was closer than you thought and was able to project through your shared communication."

"Maybe." A stiff breeze stirred up the nymph's decay. "Why would Aaron show himself in such a horrific way?"

"Sometimes it takes an extreme action to spur reaction. You'll get better at interpreting the visions." He studied me for a moment. "When you see them, can you leave them at will?"

"I don't think so. I don't want to."

"Most spirit walkers require a partner to hold their hand in the spirit world. There's danger of not returning. I'll guard your mind, Evie. I'll make sure you always find a way back."

"There have been times I didn't want to find my way back." When I wanted join my A's and Joel.

"It can be a trap in the mind." His fingertips brushed my brow. "Trust me with yours?"

Trust mind, body and soul. Your guardians.

"Oh my God. *You're* the guardians." I relied on Michio to care for my physical health and Yang. "Of course, a doctor guards my body."

Annie called Roark my heart fixer. He was my believer, my sense of direction and... "The guardian of my soul."

"The priest," Jesse said.

I met his eyes. Jesse saw my ghosts which meant I wasn't crazy. He would protect me from madness. "A Lakota guards my mind."

"Yes."

"You knew this. What else are you not telling me?"

He stood and tugged me up by my arm. "We should go. I guarantee your body and soul are hunting my head as we speak."

"What are you hiding?"

He righted my bike and seated me on it. His fingers slipped over the turquoise rock between my breasts. "Not even a close comparison to the stunning complexity of your eyes, but you give it depth. I knew you would."

The stone dropped on my sternum. He straddled his bike, his lips in a pale line. When our enduros coughed to life, his shot forward and blazed a trail through the meadow. I snapped my molars together and sped to catch up.

A shadow blotched the trail and swept over us. The dark shape stretched and rippled. I whipped my head skyward. The sun blinded me and the enduro wobbled. I slowed and regained my balance.

Jesse swung his bike around. "A plane? We're not far from the airport."

Golden ribbons streaked the sky. "Maybe."

"Let's pick up our pace."

We hit the high plateau and Jesse crawled to a stop. Michio stepped onto the path before us, knuckles jutting around his cane.

"Put your *shinobi-zue* away, Doc. We made a stop. She's fine."

Michio never took his eyes off me. "Evie?"

"I'm fine." I scooted back and patted the seat.

He slipped the cane in a loop on his belt and cradled my face in his palms. "I'll let you tell that to your priest. He's scouring the mountain, convinced that you've hurled yourself into battle again."

I touched my lips to the hard-edges of his mouth. The tension there said Roark had convinced him as well. He clutched my thigh and saddled in front of me. I slid my hands over his chiseled abs and buried my face in sandalwood. "What did Jesse call your stick? A shinobi what?"

A quiet chuckle danced over his shoulder and the bike plunged down the hill. Jesse didn't follow.

"Evie?" A groggy shake. "Evie, wake up."

I snapped to my feet, dagger out.

Roark fell back with a gasp in the dark. "Jaysus, love. One of these nights, you're gonna flay me nose."

I sheathed the knife and rubbed my eyes. "Shit, sorry. My turn, huh?" We'd agreed to split the night watch in pairs. Jesse and Roark. Tallis and me. Cliff and Michio.

"If you're not up for it," Michio said from the bed we shared, "I'll take yours."

"I'm good. Sorry I woke you."

Roark handed me the carbine and thigh holster. His lips moved against my forehead. "Den' forget to—"

"I know. Watch the sky."

I stepped over Cliff's blanket-wrapped body and trudged to the door. On the porch, I was greeted with a swipe of drool between my fingers.

"Hi boy."

Darwin's tail whipped back and forth, dragging his rear with it. Tallis leaned against the far-side of the house. When he saw me, he jogged over.

"Hey." He puffed on a hand-rolled cigarette and held it out to me.

I inhaled, let it soak in my lungs, and handed it back.

"Keep it." He lit another.

I finished the final drag. "Where's Jesse?"

"Tree line. Twenty yards in. Two o'clock."

The mountains shadowed the evergreens and reduced them to a prickly smudge against the gray sky. "I take it he's not going to share the bed with Roark and Michio."

Tallis dropped his head back, expelling smoke and laughter into the night sky.

"Shh." I started toward the trees. "I'll be right back."

He grabbed my wrist. "You can't."

"I can." I twisted my arm free.

"He's the master at evading detection."

"Well, shit. Bastard's evaded me all night."

"For what it's worth, I think he's trying."

"Trying is a great way to describe him."

He bowled another laugh, stopping abruptly when he caught my glare. "All right." He flicked his squashed cig. "You want his attention, tell me to kiss you."

"What?"

He cocked a lopsided grin. "You have to lure the beast out of hiding before you can tame him. Tell me to kiss you."

"I'm sure you have balls, but I don't want to see the evidence hanging in the Humvee."

"As much as I love you thinking about my balls, let me worry about them." The moon cast a spotlight on his blinking blue eyes.

"Oh, what the hell." I angled the carbine to the side and raised my chin. A deep breath. "Kiss me."

A smile spread over his face and his rifle creaked in his hands. He bent his head and his full lips swept over mine. His body moved closer and his mouth parted. Jesse had full lips. Would they feel like—

A fist shot out of the dark. Tallis' head snapped to the side.

Dammit. "Jesse, stop."

They rolled over the weeds in a whirlwind of flailing arms. I chased them, carbine banging against my back. Jesse landed atop, knuckles poised for a strike.

I trapped his forearm with mine, locked it between my thighs and brought his body to the ground. My other hand pressed his jugular. A little more pressure and—

His movements froze. "You're a dead man, Reynolds."

Nose to nose, I leveraged my weight and tacked on more discomfort to the arm bar. His jaw clenched.

"We talked about your threats. Besides, he had my consent. Acknowledge your mistake."

Tallis squatted next to us sporting a bloody nose and a smug expression.

Jesse's throat bobbed against my fingers as he looked daggers at the other man. "*Wanunhecun*, you dead fucking dickhead."

I inhaled his breath. Under the hickory was all man. "Tallis, can you take the watch by yourself for a bit? Jesse and I have some things to discuss."

"You bet." He wiped his face on his sleeve and planted a kiss on my temple. A growl erupted under me.

"Okay, Jesse. I'm going to release you, but you're going to promise two things. One, you won't touch Tallis and two, you'll talk."

His glowing eyes bored into me and stoked the heat where my thighs locked his arm.

"I'm waiting."

Emotions paraded across his face, none of them submissive. "You have my word on both things."

The tension in my fingers loosened from his throat. His arm pulled free and his body twisted. In the next breath, I was flipped and straddled. The carbine clunked at my side.

Chest against mine, elbows other either side of my head, his breath smothered my face. "What do you want to talk about?"

I shut my eyes and girded myself for temptation. Then I engaged his gaze. "I want to get back to your motives. How do I sever the link between you and my ghosts?"

A storm raged in his eyes. "You think I'm here because of *them*?"

"It's obvious."

His expression thawed with his voice. "Obviously, it's not." The back of one finger traced my face from brow to chin. His lashes fanned down as he watched the slow caress. "What I feel for you has nothing to do with Annie and Aaron."

The inches between us vanished. His lips touched mine. I had to strain to feel the contact, yet it caught my body on fire.

He trembled through jagged breaths and slipped his hand between our chests. "Everything I want is right here." His fingers spread over my breastbone. Then he pushed up.

I yanked him back by his shirt. "Then why do you keep pulling away?"

Pain flashed through his eyes. "Dammit, Evie." Steam huffed against my mouth. "I'm fucking drowning in my desire to be near you, to touch you"—he dropped his brow on mine and inhaled—"to be *inside* you."

My own desire exploded in my womb and sizzled through my veins. We lay there in silence, his heart knocking against mine, his mouth, close enough to taste his breaths, but too far to savor his lips. I arched to reach him. The hand on my chest held me down.

Too soon, he raised his head, the resolution in his gaze diluted by mystery. "I've seen things. Things I can prevent if I keep distance between us."

"Distance? What are you saying?"

His palm circled my left breast. "I'll never be farther than a heartbeat."

Emotional distance then. "This is about your visions. The dark ones."

He shoved off me. "I can't talk to you about that." His eyes clouded over as if he'd traveled to another time, another place.

"Okay. I trust you. But you know that partnership you mentioned?"

His face slacked.

"It goes both ways, Jesse. I won't let you get lost in their world."

"I know." He backed away, his muscular frame blending amongst the treed silhouettes.

When I turned toward the house, I wasn't surprised to see the dark shadow blackening the porch. Even darker was the face attached to it.

"You okay?" Michio leaned against the doorjamb.

"Yeah." My small smile agreed. "Thanks for not interfering."

He crossed his arms. "I was two seconds away from losing your gratitude."

Despite his schooled posture, I knew he was thrumming to run to me, sweep me back to bed. I blew him a kiss. "Go to sleep, gorgeous. I've got your back."

As I paced to the perimeter, my steps lightened, knowing that even on my watch, Michio would always have my back.

We stood under the dome hangar in Lyon, France, wide-eyed and gape-jawed. The mass of metal before us bristled with cannons and barrels protruding from side-firing hatches. Four turboprops turned in the breeze.

Roark's brogue cut the silence. "Who the hell's gonna fly this deadly bird?"

"*Je suis.*" A man stepped around the nose gear and made a beeline to me. His long white-blond hair slicked into a ponytail at his nape. The color of his beady eyes matched the plane's gunmetal armor. His skin clung to his hollow cheeks, crinkled with age and weather. "*C'est l'AC-130 Spectre* gunship."

"Meet the pilot," Jesse hollered as he rummaged in the Humvee.

"*Je m'appelle* Georges Prideux." He lifted my hand to his mouth and pressed cracked lips against my knuckles. "Madame Spotted Wing. *Merde. Tu es de toute beauté.*"

Jesse breezed past us. "Don't let him fool you. His English is better than ours."

Georges waved a hand after Jesse. "*Ta gueule,* Monseigneur Beckett." Then he tugged me to the gunship, pointing at the black dots painted under wings. "You like it, *oui*?"

Jesse hunkered over our packs on the rear loading ramp. "Apparently, I didn't keep you busy enough in Malta, Georges. Is the gunship fueled?"

"*Bien entendu.* We go to Iceland, *non*?"

Jesse looked at me, brows arched. Roark and Michio stood at my elbows in silent support. Did I harbor a sliver of hope that the Shard could validate Michio's hypothesis about my blood? About the cure?

I nodded to Georges.

We transferred the remaining gear and weapons from the Humvee to the ramp. A wave of aluminum soaps and jet fuel hit me in the face as I made my way to the cargo hold. Cliff buckled Roark and me in the jump seats. Michio followed Jesse and Georges to the flight deck.

Cliff handed Darwin's leash to Roark and shouted over the whine of the propellers, "You'll have to hold him. It might get bumpy. And whatever happens, do not unbuckle those belts." Then he settled next to Tallis behind an instrument panel and strapped earphones on his head.

The gunship soared down the runway and launched to the air. Five minutes into the flight, dials and gauges flashed on the panel in front of Cliff. He yelled into the headset, "Incoming. Incoming."

All the air seemed to rush from the cabin. We dipped and my stomach landed in my throat. Roark's hand found mine. The engines screamed and the plane shot upward, hard and fast. Through the tiny window, the steel body of another aircraft flickered by and dropped from view.

"Are we under attack?" The shrill of alarms drowned my voice.

My body bounced in the restraints and Darwin's nails scraped along the metal floor. Minutes toiled by as the plane readjusted speed and height.

Tallis shouted over the beeping electronics. "Nineteen thousand feet…twenty…twenty-five…"

We leveled off. Tallis swiveled in his seat and slid his headset off one ear. "Near collision." He shrugged. "Uncontrolled airspace and Beckett makes a lousy co-pilot. But we're cool now." He turned back to the weapons panel.

"Wow, that makes me feel so much better," I mumbled.

The next six hours were uneventful in comparison, but I didn't let go of Roark's arm, even as we came to a stop on the Reykjavik airstrip.

Footsteps clattered down the ladder and Michio was on me, hands framing my face. "You okay? That was…it was rough up there." He brushed hair from my brow. "I was so worried. Six hours, all I could think about was you. Wondering if you were banged up, hurt, scared. I wanted to get to you so badly."

The concern in his voice caressed places it had no business touching, especially as I clung to another man's arm banded across my lap.

Michio flattened a hand on the headrest beside my face and leaned into it as he lowered his mouth to mine. "Nothing can happen to you."

Of course he didn't want anything to happen to the potential cure. Something vulnerable flared inside me and I pressed into the seat, putting space between our lips. "Would suck if you had to return to the Shard empty handed."

A fog clouded his black eyes, dulling the corners, and I wanted to kick myself. But just as quick, the clouds cleared, replaced with an impenetrable glare. "I get it. You don't trust this." He thumped the spot above my left breast. "You can fight it, try to push me away." That determined stare narrowed, seeing too much. "It won't work, *Nannakola*."

Then his mouth covered mine and I had nowhere to go, nowhere I wanted to go. The attack on my lips skipped sensual and went straight to erotic. He kissed me as if trying to embed the truth of his intentions into my taste buds. Our tongues rolled together, drenching our lips, spiking my pulse, and the arm in my grip hardened. Oh damn, Roark. The heat from his gaze cooked my face.

A throat cleared and Michio took his time pulling away to glance over his shoulder.

Jesse dumped some insulated clothes on the floor, the skin above his turtleneck exploding in red.

All eyes shifted to me. The cavernous space suddenly felt too cramped for the four of us.

"Change your clothes. It's just above freezing here." Jesse eyed us, making a slow journey between our faces, his revealing nothing, and disappeared through the hatch.

I stifled the urge to sigh. My affection with Michio was a discomfort everyone needed to get used to. I turned back to him and caught the twitch kicking up his swollen, wet lips.

"I adore the transparency in your expression." He pressed a kiss against my open mouth and followed Jesse out.

A pair of cargo pants swung into my view. Roark shook them at me. "I'll wait with ye while they clear the area of aphids."

"Roark—"

"He's good for ye." He squatted in front of me, fingers working the laces on my boots.

I nudged his hands away. "Roark—"

"They're both good for ye, if I were honest." His forearms dangled over his bent knees. The position stretched the fabric of his trousers over his thighs, magnifying the bulk of muscle beneath. "I want ye to be happy. Whatever or whomever it takes."

"I'm difficult. And high-maintenance. Might take all three of you."

His delicious smile found its way to my womb. "Whatever ye want."

I trailed a finger over one golden eyebrow, hypnotized by how the glow in his gaze flooded all my worries. "I want to fall asleep every night wrapped in your warmth, beneath the blaze in your eyes. My own private sunset."

His breath sawed out, oaky and warm. "Ye got it."

"I think we're getting there. All of us."

Another heady bite of oak fanned my lips. "I think your Lakota's got a ways to go."

The hatch swung open and Tallis poked his head in. "Boss cleared us to leave."

Outfitted with enough artillery to make Joel proud, I jumped onto the tarmac and sucked in the cool Icelandic air. My hand flew to my nose against the onslaught of rotten eggs.

Michio stepped in stride with me. "Sulfur. The water underground is heated by lava and there's a leak." He jerked his head toward a bus standing on end and half-swallowed by a fissure in the ground. Water spouted from under it, spinning airborne tires.

Rusted debris scattered the broken clumps of concrete. Faded tail numbers rose from charred and twisted metal heaped on buildings and spread across the overgrown brush. Bones—human and other— poked out of scum covered rain puddles.

My nape prickled. "So, you know where the scientists are?"

"Yes. Beckett's arranged the transport—"

A roar pulsated the concrete under our boots. Hazy figures emerged on the horizon. I raised the carbine only to be walled off by three large frames. "Move. You're blocking my aim."

My guardians didn't move. Not when the rumble of dozens of motorcycles vibrated my chest. Not when foreign shouting carried through the sulfur-laden air. And not when the first boom of a rifle went off.

And give me silence, give me water, hope.
Give me struggle, iron, volcanoes.
Let bodies cling to me like magnets.
Come quick to my veins and to my mouth.
Speak through my speech and through my blood.

Pablo Neruda

CHAPTER FORTY-ONE: CONNECT THE DOTS

"*Komagnor.* I dare you," Jesse shouted. He stood in front me, feet shoulder width apart, arrow nocked. With Michio and Roark on either side, they formed a wall, blocking my view.

Twenty yards away, Cliff lay in prone position, rifle trained on the commotion I couldn't see. Where were Georges and Tallis?

"*Snub.* Go back where you come," a voice bellowed in a heavy German-like accent.

The volume of sputtering V-twins told me we were outnumbered, but that wasn't what locked up my muscles. It was the familiar buzz curling through my belly. Beside me, the hair on Darwin's ruff stood on end.

I wedged through Jesse and Michio. A line of motorcycles stretched across the horizon. Close enough to see the knotted beards and weathered goggles protecting human faces.

Pressed between battle-ready muscle, I whispered to Jesse, "I feel aphids."

He didn't move, didn't look at me. "We cleared the area of them."

My teeth clicked together. "Then you missed some, asshat."

The bikers jerked heads in my direction and the man in front held up his hand. "*Kona.*" He gestured to the riders on his right and thrust his finger my way. The men on his left raised rifles.

Violent shudders rocked my body, shaking my hold on the carbine. "What's *Kona?*"

The red-hue in Jesse eyes, aimed at the leather-clad men, sparked to flame. "Woman."

I fought the need to swallow. A shroud of stillness settled over us, each man waiting for the other to move.

A gurgling cry broke the silence. Followed by another and another, morphing into a symphony of terror. On the outskirts of the line, bikes tumbled. Bodies dropped, dodging jaws, and failing.

Aphids darted out of overturned trucks and shredded hangars. Screams and bullets tore across the airstrip.

I targeted white eyes and squeezed the trigger. Crimson misted the cloud-stuffed sky and stained the tarmac.

Roark's sword swung to my left, slashing through aphids breaking from the fray. Arrows flew on my right. I could feel the smooth glide of Michio's movements against my back.

"Are we surrounded?" I shouted over my shoulder.

"Eyes forward, Evie. I've got your back."

The carbine popped in my grasp. Bikers bucked on the ground beneath bone-crushing jowls. Soon, the motorcycles were abandoned and the owners lay gutted and drained, awaiting transformation.

Heaving bodies bent over their food, sucking and slurping, then raised hungry eyes to us. Mouthparts retracted and they stood as one.

My companions backed up, all but Cliff. "Where's—"

A few yards away, he clung to a mutated body, clenched in an embrace.

"Oh, no, no. Fuck no," Jesse screamed, releasing an arrow.

The aphid dropped. Cliff rolled with it, his chest cavity open, hooked by the mutant's mouth. Angling his head, his tortured eyes snared mine, his jaw convulsing in a silent scream.

I didn't think, just aimed the carbine and pulled the trigger, ending his life before the teeth of un-life took hold.

A floodgate of nausea released in my gut. The spurting hole in Cliff's head. Jesse's bloodshot eyes latched on his friend. The twenty or thirty aphids, snarling and sprinting toward us. I swapped mags, choking down bile, and raised the carbine.

The windup of propellers whistled across the tarmac. The gunship rolled into view and turned. The side-firing barrels rotated as the minigun plowed through the approaching swarm. I hit the ground and cupped my ears against the deafening jackhammer noise. After a few minutes, the minigun fell silent.

The nearby fissure hissed sulfur into the air. Sheet metal rippled above the hangars. Blood soaked the turned up snow. Darwin paced a circle around me and sat on my boots.

When the propellers slowed to a stop, I raised a brow at Michio.

"Tallis and Georges." He slid his cane inside his leather duster. "Quick thinking."

I gave into a much needed swallow and found my mouth dry. Jesse pulled me to my feet, eyes on Cliff's body. Then he spun on his boot heel and pitched over his shoulder, "Ivar waits."

Ivar. Jesse's no-last-name-non-English-speaking contact spoke one word we all knew. *Aphid.*

We met him on the outskirts of the airfield, where he corralled a dozen Icelandic horses. The man soared at around six and a half feet. His mammoth bone structure was prominent in his square face and I bet his untamed mane kept him warm on Iceland's cold nights.

He was mirrored by his four sons who stood next to him, taking up a shitload of space. I didn't catch their names, but they all ended in a gruff *arrr.*

Michio and Jesse knew a few Icelandic words and we collectively understood the Ivar family's terse grunts and distrusting glares.

Roark leaned down from where he towered on his mount. "Where'd your Lakota find these quare hawks and why are we hoofing it?"

"I don't know, but look at the size of their horses. What the hell's in the food supply around here?"

Michio sidled his horse alongside Roark. "We're *hoofing it* because there are no roads where we're going." He stretched out his hand to me.

"Um...I counted," I said. "There are enough horses for everyone."

"And what will you do when we run into aphids?" Michio's hand waited.

"Rip off my clothes and ride naked through the streets? Might get me a Yang volunteer."

He didn't encourage me with a response. I clasped his hand and he swung me in front of him.

A few minutes into the trek, his hand found the hems of my coat and shirt and slipped beneath. His fingers flattened over my ribs and traced the underside of my breast. "I'm making love to you as soon as we find shelter."

"If we live that long."

"Decide you want to live, and you will."

A tingly feeling spread under his fingertips. "If I let myself dream, I see a long life. With you. And this guy"—I reached for horse beside us and snatched Roark's hand from his thigh—"and maybe even with that guy up there."

Jesse turned in his saddle and met my gaze. His grin shocked me as much as it pleased me, shooing away some of the doubt I harbored about the future.

When Michio's hand retreated, I grabbed it, held it in my lap, and lowered my voice so only he could hear me. "I look forward to making love to you tonight. And every night after."

His fingers flexed, clutching my waist, pulling me close.

Hooves clopped along the barren streets of Reykjavik in the dim light of dusk. Ivar and sons led, strapped with axes welded to long hafts. Darwin sprinted ahead with ears back and tongue slapping to the side. Jesse's hired hands brought up the rear.

The cavalry grew edgy as the shadows slithered over the multicolored roofs. The darkening buildings seemed to animate with the same flux that pulsed in the air. Every time the wind creaked a door or a hoof kicked debris, an ax swooshed up.

Jesse pulled back to ride beside us, his boot tapping mine.

"You didn't tell the barbarians I can sense the aphids?" I asked him.

"No translator. Makes conversation limited."

"But you were able to contact them and tell them we were coming?"

He nodded, eyes on the sky. "I still have a network of contacts and a means to leave messages." His gaze rested on me. "Don't worry about it, Evie."

"It's not worry—"

Tremors pinched my insides. My muscles went taut and I knew Michio could feel the vibrations under his hand. He snapped open the buttons of my coat. I balanced the carbine on my lap and pulled my arms out of the sleeves. My sweatshirt went next. A shiver raced to my core.

Michio's bare chest covered my back. He wrapped his arms and my coat around the front of my sports bra. "How many?"

Murmurs hissed through my bloodstream. The linked tentacles spread in all directions, pitching and swaying. "Too many to count."

Jesse nocked an arrow and Roark's horse moved closer. His hand slipped under my hair, curled around my neck. "Which way, love?"

I scanned the dark structures looming over us, but I saw with my gut. "They're approaching from the side streets. Stay on this road. I'll hold them."

The horse jerked under our thighs, expelling heavy chuffs. The other horses side-stepped, tried to back up.

Ivar wrestled with his mount's bucking head. "Aphid."

The alleys lit up with the glow of green flames. I drew from the strength touching me and breathed, *Stay*.

The aphids quivered. Some tumbled onto the main road. *Stay* rolled off me in a steady drum.

There were grunts of surprise at seeing the mutated Icelanders glued to the road. Then the arrows flew, the rifles boomed and axes swung. I held the aphids in an execution style line-up as our horses thundered past.

Green bodies splattered and dropped. Eventually, the volley and swoosh of weapons quieted, as did the hum inside me.

The corridor of buildings began to space further apart. Soon, there were no buildings at all.

Michio pulled our mount to a stop in the center of a snow-covered plain. We slipped back into our shirts and coats, my limbs moving through a fog. Michio's hand pressed against my brow then rested on the pulse at my throat. I gripped the withers to balance against a bout of chills and dizziness.

"Her heart rate—" He dropped his hand and shouted, "Beckett."

Jesse was there with a pouch in his hand. "What does she need?"

"Sugar." Michio leaned my back on his chest.

Roark's eyes burned through the icy dark, creased with worry. I intertwined my fingers with his. "Stop that. I'm getting better at this."

His thumb made shaky whorls on my wrist.

Jesse shook a canteen and tipped it at my mouth. The sugary orange drink thickened in my throat, but within a few minutes, my senses came back on line.

He replaced the cap. "Is it always like this?"

I lifted a shoulder. "When there are too many bugs or not enough energy."

"She had a seizure when we escaped Malta." Michio's hands clenched on my thighs.

The tightness in Jesse's shoulders bled into his eyes. When his horse stomped a hoof, he snapped out of it. "We'll camp against that bluff." He gestured across the plain before us, his hand faltering as we digested the red and white vista.

As far as we could see, human, aphid, and unidentifiable beasts lay where they fell, bones exposed and gnawed by weather. A patchwork of pristine snow, shadowed mounds, and moonlit splashes of crimson.

I hugged the carbine as we wound our way through the frozen graveyard and set up camp on the other side.

Michio erected our tent, ushered me inside, and lit a candle. "You need to eat."

I curled into a ball on the bedroll, chilled from the temperature and side-effects of aphid control.

The tic in his jaw triggered a smoldering war in his expression. He straddled my hips, hands on either side of my head, and lowered his head. "I want nothing more than to feed you, strip you and feast on every inch of your body." Another tic. "But given the exertion you underwent, we're sticking to food."

I rolled to my back. "Don't be dramatic. We can—"

The tent flap zipped open. Roark pushed through and froze, eyes locked on Michio.

Michio sat back on his heels. "If you brought food, your timing's perfect."

The waft of roasted meat followed him in and my stomach growled in greeting.

"Ye should be resting," Roark said as he and Michio bandied glares.

"Knock it off. Both of you."

Roark didn't break the stare down, but his shoulders relaxed. "Doc, Beckett and I will take turns keeping watch."

"What about the five woolly mammoths wielding axes of unusual size?" I asked.

"They're quare." Roark said, as if that was answer enough.

I propped up on an elbow. "Then I'll take a shift."

"No," they said in chorus.

I slumped to my back and sawed my teeth.

Roark leaned around Michio and kissed my bottom lip. "Get cheesed off all ye want. This isn't negotiable."

"The sun will be up before three A.M." Michio's eyes didn't waver from Roark's. "You need to sleep while you can."

I swiped a hand over my face, hating their rivalry. "Can we just—" Could we what? Hold hands around the campfire and sing Kumbaya?

Two pairs of eyes watched me, waiting.

"This is going to sound girly—"

"Can I just point out that ye are a girl?"

I narrowed my eyes at Roark. "You both have managed to weasel your way into my heart"—which was somersaulting over the idea—"and that's a complication by itself without the I'm-gonna-stab-you-when-she's-not-looking glares defiling your pretty faces."

Michio burst out laughing. "No one's stabbing anyone."

Roark stared at his lap. "We wen' kill each other, love."

I blew a wayward hair from my eye. Fine. If they weren't concerned, neither was I.

Roark set a crumpled tin plate on my stomach heaping with shredded meat burnt on the ends. Funny how survival had wiped out my vegetarianism. I had no clue what we were eating, but between the three of us, the meat vanished within minutes. The last chunk lodged in my throat. I would not becounting the horses again.

Beneath a fur-lined blanket, I hunkered between Roark and Michio. Heat rolled off them and chased away my shivers. And I slept.

Sometime during the night, I woke bleary-eyed and chilled despite Michio's warmth on my front. His body rose and fell through deep breaths of sleep. I uncurled from him, slipped on my coat, boots, and artillery.

Outside the tent, Roark bowed over a bent knee, forehead resting on clasped hands. I crouched beside him, taking in the curve of lashes feathered over his cheeks, the full lips moving in soundless reverence, the pearlescent rosary beads winding over scarred knuckles. "Keeping watch with your eyes shut? Some guardian you are."

He leaned in and pressed his smile against mine. Then his eyes blinked open, roamed my face. "Why are ye up?"

Darkness closed around us. The sky was starless, but could very well be full of things lying in wait. "Where's Jesse?"

He sighed, but his finger rose and pointed where the shadows slanted over the lava-formed bluff. "Go on. I'm watching."

The frozen wool grass crunched under my boots, making a racket in the heavy silence. I passed one of Ivar's sons and nodded. The fume of cigarette smoke signaled Tallis' proximity.

Jesse's huddled form took shape at the foot of the cliff. His arms wrapped around his knees. His bow lay at his feet.

I stopped a foot before him. "Don't be a child. Sleep in the tent. If not mine then one of the others."

Cracking ice groaned across the barren terrain.

I swooped up his bow and walked back. Halfway there, he lifted the bow from my grip, but kept his stride in step with mine.

At the tent, I let my fingers rake through Roark's hair and crawled under the flap. Jesse lingered at the entrance.

"Come on, Jesse. Michio can sleep between us. I won't touch you." I paused, smiled. "Of course, I can't speak for him."

Michio's eyes cracked and his lips tugged up. Even tenuous, that smile curled my toes. I made a mental note to tease him more often.

I shed my coat and boots and Jesse did the same. Then I nestled into the warmth of Michio's chest. A moment later, Jesse floated over us. He stretched behind me and his pelvis cupped my backside. My breath caught.

"Don't you dare wiggle." He rested his hand on my hip.

"Wouldn't dream of it." But dream of it was exactly what I did.

In the light of daybreak, I opened my eyes to find Jesse watching me from inches away. Thoughts shifted in the depth of his gaze. Lost in his secrets.

I could tell by the height of the man at my back that Roark was curved around me.

"Did I wiggle?" I whispered.

The air between us thickened. He touched my cheek, his thumb padding my bottom lip. "You make things damn difficult, darlin'." His husky Texan accent shot my heart to my throat.

I crooked up my mouth and took his thumb with it. "I try."

He dropped his hand and raised his eyes to the ceiling where the sun pierced through the seams. "Wake your snoring priest. We need to keep moving."

The spirally patterns of rhyolite formations guided us through the mountains. Our mounts kicked up the volcanic soil and nibbled at the sparse vegetation. The ever-present risk of following the pebbles down the steep unpredictable ledges kept us alert. Falling to our deaths seemed to be the only threat. Still, my pulse roared with the occasional clap of wings or the flash of a shape sprang by the shading slopes.

That night, we camped beside a geothermal spa. Everyone took turns bathing and guarding. Then we slept along the edge on the soft bed of moss. Jesse, Roark and Michio split the guard over me. When it was Jesse's turn to sleep, he took Roark's position at my back.

On the third day, we guided our weary mounts over glaciers, sand, grass and volcanic rock. A terrain battling for identity, the plains and buttes pushed steam from its pores and blotted the horizon with billows of vapor.

We followed the sound of moving water and when we reached the river, we stood in awe of the powerful surge dropping in towering multi-level waterfalls.

Michio pointed to a charred rock wall near the lowest level. "We're here. Landmannalaugar."

Amidst the geologic chaos, a leafy-covered steel door hung from the face of the ridge. My eyes followed the hyaloclastite ledges up, up, up to the ice-capped peak.

"The labs are through there." Michio pointed at the door and alighted the horse. "Inside Hekla volcano."

Of course they were. His hands clutched my waist and he slid me down. Then he turned toward the door, fisting his cane. The tip glinted with blades.

A tumult twined my insides, something I hadn't felt since Reykjavik. We hadn't seen an aphid since then. Why was that?

I released the carbine from its mount on the horse and Michio tapered his eyes at me. The tingling dimmed. I shook my head.

"Evie." Roark appeared in front of me. "Wha' is it?"

"I don't—"

A giggle bounced along the rocky backdrop and raised the hair on my nape. I'd recognize my daughter's sweet laugh anywhere. My shoulders bunched to my ears. "Where's Jesse?"

Roark hovered so close his breath wisped my hair. "Den' ye get buggered looking for him all the time?" He raised my chin and read my eyes. "Talk to me."

I swallowed around a lump. The door to the labs blew open and snicked closed. "Something's wrong. Why didn't they come out to greet us?"

"The tunnels are deep and there's no surveillance," Michio replied. "But I agree. Something feels off."

Annie's singsong chant tiptoed across the lava field and carried above the roar of the waterfalls. Her high-pitched vibrato brushed by me. The door swung open again and slammed.

Jesse's fingers interlaced mine. "Annie wants us to follow her in."

I flinched. "Would she lead me into danger?"

Roark placed a hand on my elbow. "Good thought. She did lead ye to the Lakota."

Jesse grinned and waved his hand toward the door. "After you, priest."

Shoulder to shoulder, Michio, Jesse, Roark and I crept through the icy tunnel. Darwin slinked by, nose to the ground. Tallis and Georges trailed. Ivar and sons guarded the entrance.

We moved deeper into the volcano. Eventually, the frost melted from the walls and the air warmed. The dirt below our feet ended. Metal platforms stretched over the sloping ground to the flickering lights ahead.

Michio raised his voice over the clanking of our boots on the grates. "I haven't been here for six months, but there were forty scientists when I left. We should've run into someone by now." He nodded at the bend ahead. "We're approaching the hub."

Weapons at the ready, we stepped around the corner and onto an expansive balcony overlooking a pit. Scaffolding layered the multiple levels below. Tunnels and rooms branched in every direction.

We approached the railing. Our boots crunched glass. Broken equipment and workbenches were tossed across every level. Bullet holes chipped the rock walls, the metal platforms, and the furniture. I strained my eyes, scouring every nook and shadow. Not a single body, dead or alive.

"*Zut alors*," Georges whispered from behind us.

"Let's split up," Jesse said. "Tallis, Georges, back here in thirty."

We dispersed. Artificial light splashed over empty hallways and labs. We tossed bunks and tore out storage rooms. The facility was a shambles, the scientists gone. I leaned against the railing on the bottom level and rubbed my temples.

Jesse perched at my side. "It was the Drone's army, wasn't it?"

Michio nodded, lines fanning from the corners of his eyes.

A thrum bloomed in my chest and set my teeth on edge. Annie's voice drifted from the hallway behind us with eerie clarity.

Connect the dots. La. La. Lala.

Jesse shot his eyes to me. Heat rushed to my ears. Then our heads turned toward the hall. The tail of a skirt whipped around the corner. We darted after her.

"Evie?" Roark called after me.

"It's Annie," I shouted over my shoulder.

Hm. Hm. Hmmm.

Connect the dots...

Every bend brought us another empty corridor, but Annie's rhapsody didn't falter.

We skidded at a dead end. Tiny pale fingers curled around the frame of the last doorway. The fingers whisked away. We followed with Michio and Roark on our heels.

Inside was another a storage room. Her voice muffled from within a tall cabinet.

La. La. La. La.

I trained the carbine on the cabinet door and swallowed. Jesse opened it. An entrance to another room. We stepped through, Jesse first.

A beaker crashed next to his head. Then a keyboard hit him in the chest. He nocked an arrow.

A spindly man hovered in front of a cage. He held a shaky soup can over his head. "Be gone." His voice trembled.

"Michio," I whispered, "Do you know this man?"

He stepped around me and shook his head. "You understand English?" he asked him.

The man nodded.

"I'm Dr. Michio Nealy. I work for the Shard. I've been on an undercover mission. You might have heard—."

"Aiman Jabara?" He dropped the can, eyes bulging.

"Yes." Michio took a step closer. "And you are?"

He thumped his chest. "Njall." His eyes darted to the cage behind him and his chin dropped to his chest as he stepped to the side. "Her name Frida." His English broke through a heavy Icelandic accent. "My wife."

A hiss sprayed from the cage. Dull hair webbed her pallid face in thin strands. A hospital gown clung to her sunken frame. Tiny pupils flicked between us and a heavy rasp pushed from her lungs.

My heart banged against my ribs. Her gaze moved my feet closer. Until she opened her mouth. A tube slid in and out. Finger-like bits wiggled over the moving parts.

"I come after you left, Dr. Nealy," Njall said as we stared at the cage. "For my wife, you see."

"What happened here?" Michio eyes remained fixed on Frida.

"Lots of boom boom. I hide here. A week, maybe."

Damn. We missed them by a mere week?

"*Kona.*" He pointed to me. "She cures? The Shard hoped." He grabbed Michio's arm, pulled him toward the cage. "Please."

"Her name is Evie." Michio's tone was possessive as he stretched to his intimidating full height. "I've only tested her blood in the lab. Frida would be an experiment. You understand?"

"Please." Puffy red skin weighted his eyes.

Michio searched my face. "Evie?"

"What do I need to do?"

He made a list of supplies and sent Jesse and Roark down the hall to collect. They returned a few minutes later with syringes, vials and a dart gun. Then he pricked my arm, filling a hollow reservoir of a tranquilizer dart with my blood.

Capture gun loaded, he aimed it at the cage. Njall shoved his fist in his mouth.

The dart sailed and landed in the nymph's throat. She thrashed and dropped to her knees and a painful spasm erupted in my gut.

The next few moments bludgeoned by. Every sound, every stir was punctuated by a pounding in my head. Frida writhed on the floor of her cage. Annie's chilling hum crept through the hall. And hundreds of vibrating strings knitted over my ribs, around my spine and fisted my stomach.

My lungs wheezed. I clutched the pain in my belly and ran toward the door. An army was coming.

Annie's lilt chased me through the corridor. So did Jesse and Roark.

At the platform, Roark's arm blocked my advance. "Aw Jaysus, your eyes."

I didn't give a shit how freaky my eyes looked. I fisted his cassock. "There's an army outside. Help me stop them."

His muscles stiffened. "Damn the devil's hairy bollocks."

Jesse stood next to him, brows drawn and jaw jerking. I snapped my fingers in his face. "I'll need you, too."

Roark's sword swooshed as he slid it from his leather scabbard. "Get bloody on with it then."

We united with Tallis and Georges on the balcony and updated them as we flew down the tunnel. I shed my coat and top as I ran. Roark and Jesse did the same.

The ringing in my gut whirled in a circular motion and spun up my spine. How many spots would I walk away with? Oh hell, I just needed to walk away.

"*Alis volat propriis,*" Georges panted at my back. "They say you fight like them, Spotted Wing. I will *savourer le show.*"

I huffed and burst through the door. Sweet lord, it was so cold I had to force my limbs to cooperate.

Across the field, two aphids looked up from a hollowed out body turned on its side. Daylight shined through the hole in the chest. Long blond hair swam around it. Goddammit. Ivar? His son?

One aphid snarled. The other clicked back. Their orbs turned to me.

Human screams rode in on the wind and my bones shivered.

"Stay with her, Beckett," Roark said. "Tallis and Georges with me." They darted for the river, where the shrieks quieted.

Oh, Roark. His name jumped into my throat and died there. He could handle himself. He'd come back.

Hundreds of insectile bodies shimmered on the horizon. A mile away? I trained the carbine on the two feeding. Could I hit the eyes at that distance? Jesse's feathered arrows shifted in the quiver on his bare back.

"Give me an arrow, Jesse."

He scowled at me.

"Can you make the kill shot from here?"

"Can't you hold them while I run over there?" he asked.

"And give the army time to move closer?" I held out my hand.

He plucked out an arrow and pressed it into my waiting palm.

I punched the ice pick tip into the crease of my elbow. The burn reached my fingertips.

"You're mad," Jesse said.

Blood flowed onto the point. Then I handed it back to the still scowling Lakota. "You don't have to hit the eyes. Trust me."

He nocked the arrow and let it fly. It pierced the widest target, the chest of the closest one. The bulging body jerked. A flickering current danced through me.

The aphid flopped to the ground and exploded in a fountain of innards.

The remaining bug raised a claw. It snapped and snarled with quivering jaws. The approaching army stopped.

A howl barreled next me. Jesse was actually laughing. I wanted to laugh with him until I saw Roark sprinting back, his face twisted in rage.

"Beckett," he yelled. "It's Ivar, his sons."

Jesse stilled beside me. "They're all dead."

Roark skidded before us. "Something like that. I'm sorry."

My heart sank.

"Evie?" Michio's voice turned me around. He scanned the horizon then my face. "How are you holding them?"

I shook my head. "I'm not. They're nervous. It won't last. What about the nymph? Did it work?"

My answer shuffled out of the door behind him. Njall carried his wife, both squinting in the sun. Her face was sallow and her arms hung, but blue irises glowed in her human eyes.

"It worked, *Nannakola*. Just one injection of your blood and Frida's human genes reactivated. She's confused...doesn't remember anything since the infection took over. I'll run some tests—"

Whoosh. Whoosh.

My stomach turned over violently. A cold voice swept up my spine. *Eveline.*

I jerked up my head. From out the sky, a black form shot toward us. Waspy wings blurred in flight. Muscles jerked under a soaring sable cape. Claws and teeth shot out.

My guardians appeared in front of me, weapons raised. But the Drone's onyx eyes were locked on Frida. His body turned in mid-air and Njall screamed.

Deep in the fundamental heart of mind and Universe there is a reason.

Douglas Adams, *The Hitchhiker's Guide to the Galaxy*

CHAPTER FORTY-TWO: LIFE, THE UNIVERSE, AND EVERYTHING

Frida's cries joined Njall's as they rolled away from the outstretched talons of the swooping shadow.

The Drone landed in a crouch, wings tucking under his cape, his body blocking the door to the lab and Njall's intended escape.

Njall scrambled back, regained his footing, and half-walked, half-ran toward the waterfalls, his gait hindered by Frida's limp body bouncing in his clutch.

I drew myself up as tall as I could and sighted the carbine around the swell of muscle flexing against me. I steadied the aim on his chest. Squeeze.

The bullet skidded somewhere behind him as he rose from a crouched position he hadn't been in two seconds before. "Try harder."

Exhale. Squeeze.

That one pinged off the door. He stood beside it, the sun ringing his black eyes in red, their maddened depths locked on the lumbering escapees. "She's human." A hiss pushed past his fanged jaws. "So why is she emitting a pulse like one of my own?" He cocked his head. "It's residual. Fading." He bored his eyes into mine and floated forward. "There's only one explanation."

Jesse's bow stretched beside his cheek. "Back the fuck up." His arrow plinked off the rock wall, missing the Drone's side-stepping blur.

A blast of wind grabbed hold of the Drone's cloak and thrashed it against his boots. "You murdered my brother, Eveline."

Roark raised his sword in a two-handed grip. "Aw now, me girl might've taken the ballbeg's knob, but 'twas me who relieved him of his cranium."

A roar ripped from the Drone's throat. "Even you, *priest*"—he spat the word— "are not immune to Allah's judgement. It will be an honor to cast you into hell's fire." His eyes jerked across the lava field, targeting Njall's retreating back. "But first, I must deal with the creature who carries Eveline's blood"—he glanced at Michio— "for she, too, now sustains the missing element for my serum."

The terrifying truth of his words robbed my arms of strength and the carbine took a nose dive. He didn't want a cure, just an antidote for his own fucked up mutation. Then he would resume the design of his perfect race. I grappled to readjust the barrel. A wall of muscle supported my back as Michio stilled his most effective weapon, his body.

The Drone had been faster than me in every confrontation. But was he faster than a bullet? I aimed the carbine—God, Buddha, the Great Mystery, fucking make me a believer—and squeezed the trigger, again and again.

He shot to the sky in a snap of wings, bullets dusting where he'd stood. Mother fuck. His hellish shape whipped across the field and dove past the swarm of aphids chasing Njall. Then he rose from the chaos, Frida's body lolling from his grip in a misshapen arch, Njall arms stretching skyward and clawing at air. His gut-wrenching lament for his wife turned to gargles as heaving shadows fell upon his back.

I fired rounds from too far away. My heart sprinted as did my feet, a string of Irish curses chasing me.

The distance closed, aphid eyes bursting with black blood under the spray of my volley. The flex of Roark's shoulders followed the fluid swing of his sword. Bodies separated at the neck. Purpose tightened his freckled face and hardened his jade eyes. The fierce protection he put into action swelled my chest. It wasn't just the heart of the world's last woman that propelled him. His fight was born long before the virus, on the sectarian streets of Northern Ireland where young boys were beaten by the cruel fists of soldiers.

We slaughtered our away through the pile and reached the center. Gone was Njall's torso. In its place, a still-quivering knot of mutilated organs.

A tremor moved through me and the dagger's hilt wobbled in my hand. I soared it end-over-end, ceasing another mutation. Another loss to mourn later.

Between my rounds and Jesse's arrows, we annihilated the last of the immediate threats as the distant horizon swelled with more.

Above the carnage, the Drone bounced between the air and the ground in an oddly insectile movement of legs, and landed on a steep ledge over the highest waterfall.

I retrieved the blade from Njall's eye socket and reloaded the carbine. "The added weight is slowing down his flight. We can catch him."

My guardians exchanged looks.

"What will he do to her, Michio?" I glanced at the Drone atop his rock belfry. How far away he was up there, but close enough to see his black soul dancing in his eyes.

"He'll imbibe her blood, if he hasn't already. Since it's treated with yours, it could cure him. Strengthen him. Or maybe it'll kill him."

Jesse stiffened beside me. "And if we let him get away, we won't know. Evie will never be able to take her eyes off the sky." He scratched a whiskered cheek. "Let's cut off his wings, Spotted Wing."

I wanted to respond with a fist pump. Instead, my body buckled with the sickening buzz of hundreds of aphids beating a rhythm inside me. I knew it well. It had crawled under my skin enough to become a part of me. "They're coming in droves." I backed into a crevice in the cliff, shaking. "Is this why we haven't seen aphids since Reykjavik? The Drone gathered them here?"

"Could be the dearth of mammals left on this glacial island." Michio shrugged out of his coat and shirt. "Maybe the scent of food—our horses, or us—led them here. I have a plan to diminish their numbers."

Tallis sprinted along the river with Georges at his heels. "Better hurry," he shouted through heavy breaths. Then his eyes widened and he pointed over my shoulder.

A vibrational draft whipped my back. I spun, instincts jerking me out of a spell of hesitancy. The sharp point of a mandible stabbed the air. I swung my forearm, redirected it. The tiny pupils dilated, brimmed with a knowing. I sunk the blade.

Strong arms encompassed me. Hickory breath warmed my cheek.

I let my forehead fall against the naked ridges of Jesse's chest and waited for my heart rate to slow. His was a steady beat against me. I held tight to the moment, wishing it was another time, another place, that heartbeat pounding beneath me with the labors of desire. His chin lifted. I followed his gaze.

A sea of green bodies filled my vision.

He dodged the dance of pincers and striking jaws. Where his arrow struck, blood spouted.

Someone grabbed my arm, handed me my recovered dagger. "Take them, Evie." Michio's calm voice. "Take them over the falls." Then he screamed over his shoulder, "Jesse. Roark."

To free my hands, I dropped the carbine on its sling. My guardians encircled me, bathed me in warm muscle. I didn't know where one chest ended and the other began. Their hearts thundered with the torrent of water chuting off the icy bluffs.

Rifles boomed around us as Tallis and Georges protected our huddle. Michio pressed us onto a rock ledge. "If they get close, we jump."

Water rushed by, spraying froth at our boots. Spasms rioted beneath my skin and the army pushed closer in battle ready lines, the sun's golden reflection at their backs.

The tide crashed off the ledges above. Moss covered cliffs jutted on all sides and guided the crash of melt water over multiple tiers. The Drone watched, Frida hooked under his arm, his body vibrating.

"Anytime now, darlin'." Jesse's chin, buried under stubble, sawed side to side.

My waiting energy—my Yin and Yang—uncoiled from my backbone. I exhaled the image, the destination, like an emotional sigh.

The army continued their race toward us. I needed to turn them ninety degrees. Goose pimples cropped along my arms. My body temperature dropped. Roark pressed closer at my back, his whiskers scrubbing my hair.

I tried again, visualizing my breath as it escaped through my nostrils. I cleared my mind of all thoughts except the image I projected. Then I felt, rather than saw, the army turn.

The chill locked up my limbs. Michio rested his cheek against mine in welcome support. The threads battering me, itching my skin, spiked with fear and bristled the hair on my arms. The army reached the water's edge. The front line wavered.

I focused on the ranks behind. *Push, push, push* pulsed from my chest.

They fell like dominos over the ledge. A barrage of rifle fire picked off the stragglers escaping my command. The icy wind carried dozens of squeals as the aphids plunged into the rushing falls.

My muscles ached from strain and my hold on the threads slipped. The Drone leaned over his perch and bellowed, "Nooo."

I pushed harder, reaching through the electrical veins invading my mind. And there, at the center of the intangible web, the Drone fought me. For every link I grasped, he pulled three away. Nausea swished in my stomach. The threads untangled, snapping free from my hold, and the thrum in the air gathered strength.

"What's happening?" Jesse's hand in mine clenched to pain.

"The Drone." My lungs labored. Arms held me vertical. "He's out-Yanging me."

Roark cupped my face. "Deep breaths, love. Most of the snarlies are dissolving in the river."

The soft pads of Michio's fingertips glided along the strap of my sports bra, followed it over my shoulder, and traced new spots. "Let them go. The rest are scattering—"

A woman's scream followed the rush of water down the crag. A black flash blotted the sun. Then Frida's body plunged headlong over the highest fall. "Helllp meeee."

Her plea sent me barreling from the iron grip of my guardians. The terror in her eyes, as blood spurted from the puncture marks in her throat, arched my body into a dive.

I tensed for the frigid onslaught of water. It never came. The howling river rushed away as I was yanked into the sky in a whir of wings.

Beneath my dangling feet, Frida's body slammed into the cliff and battered back and forth against boulders, bloody and broken.

Numbness encased my heart. I bucked, pulling up my knees to bring the carbine closer.

It wasn't there. I scanned the rapids, a useless search, fighting back the scream in my throat as my hands twisted in the Drone's claws.

He dropped from the sky and my stomach bottomed out. Moments before hitting ground, he rose again, wings pumping, his grasp digging into my arms. He bobbed through the air and righted his flight. With each wrench of my arm, his grew tighter, more painful, until it hurt to breath.

Panicked shouts chased us toward the tip of the sun as it began its six hour repose. Without the carbine, vulnerability fisted my throat. If I could free a hand, I could reach a blade.

The Drone's talons dug deeper, rending my wrists. The arctic wind enveloped us, carried us up and away from the black sand terrain and the ripple of aphids following by segmented foot.

I strained to see my companions as they fought through the throngs, maintaining their pursuit. They were but tiny dots, growing smaller as my captor followed the slope of the earth. He soared higher over dikes and trails etched into the steep faces of rock, darting into the maw of the volcanic mountain.

Sulfuric gas steamed from fissures, filling my lungs and burning my eyes. The closest ledge waited hundreds of feet below. Why hadn't he bitten me yet? Was he haughty enough to think he'd made it? That he'd have plenty of time to consume his precious serum?

If I twisted free, if I injured him, I would fall to my death. But as our elevation dipped, I knew my chance was moments away.

We rounded a tabular rock cliff and I rolled in his hold to face him, my arms twisting in an awkward way. Arrogance arched his brows. He knew I had nowhere to go and adjusted his hands to my nape and backside.

I wrapped my legs around his waist and breathed through the queasiness brought on by our intimate position.

The violet bands of dusk sharpened the angles of his face. Unruly black curls whipped around his head. And his eyes, cruel in their complexity, sucked me in, attempting to devour the last of my bravado.

I held my arms still, wrapped around my waist, as to not remind him of their unbound state. "Watch where you're flying."

Too much intelligence worked in those eyes, colder than the wind itself and fixed on me. "We're almost to my plane. Just the other side of the mountain." A vile curve transformed his mouth, yanking back his lips and revealing a jaw full of inhuman teeth.

"Prayer time has come. Once on board, we will exult in Allah together."

He was panting from exertion when we reached a gorge, where the earth's crust fractured and wretched apart. Beyond it rose a massive basalt bluff. I sucked in a breath. "The only prayer I'm reciting is the Hail Mary."

A vein bulged in his forehead. "Mary?"

The bluff passed below. Plumes of gas billowed, engulfing us in a blinding smog. I gripped my opposing forearms, released the daggers, and drove them into his neck.

Silence. A sulfuric haze of agonizing silence. Then the cloud cleared.

His eyes blazed as my name gargled low in his throat. Dagger hilts protruded from each shoulder. I didn't have time to curse my aim before I was free from the cage of his arms and falling.

The bluff caught my hip, my shoulder. Pain exploded, threatening to steal my vision. I planted my feet on the slanting pitch, followed the rocks down on my back, feeling every bump like a punch in the spine.

My hand caught hold of a groove in a rock shelf. I shuffled my boots backwards, seeking purchase.

I clung there, fingers straining to hold on. The gray sky deepened the shadows waiting in the gorge below. Overhead, the Drone tumbled through the air, ripping the daggers free, and plummeting on the other side of the bluff.

Strength seeped from my fingers. One by one, they lost their hold. I slid down the bank, picking up speed, and landed in a heap in the pitch black gullet, my entire body throbbing from the impact.

I rummaged through my pockets and holsters, knowing what I'd find. Two daggers. No flashlight. No guns. Joel would have my ass if he were there. If only—

A gust of dank air smacked my face. "Eveeeline." The Arabic bawl bounced along the canyon walls.

My heart propelled to a furious roar in my ears. I wobbled to my feet, felt along the rocky crag. My palms explored the rough edges, my footfalls echoing along on the slick floor. The moist atmosphere laded my nostrils with the stench of rotten eggs.

I followed the wall around endless bends, a maze of stone tunnels. Where the darkness seemed blacker, thicker, I slowed, blood freezing in my veins. Skittering sounds rustled around me, above me. What sort of creatures dwelled in volcanic caves? I strained my eyes for the tell-tale glow of aphids and focused on the biological alarm inside me.

The deeper I hiked, the more disoriented I became. How many forks had I unknowingly taken? Were Michio and the others still following me or were they halted by the remnants of the army?

A tapping noise trickled from the depths of the cavern ahead. The shadows there writhed, clustered together. Sweat slicked my palms and my throat dried up.

Something tickled my fingers. I raised my hand to my face. Tiny orbs peered back, as many eyes as legs. Its fangs grazed my knuckles. I flicked the furry body, felt more tickling on my other hand and both of my arms. I shook my limbs free of spiders, dread knotting my gut.

A shape emerged from the dark, filling the narrow space, expanding until wings brushed the walls. A rustle of fabric. Then a green glow exploded around me, blinding me.

I pressed against an overhang, dropped my last two daggers to the tips of my fingers, and waited for my eyes to adjust.

Mother, have mercy. The brilliant flicker of the Drone's naked body pulsated beneath the caul of thousands of squirming spots. Eight-legged spots, falling over one another, rippling down his torso, his legs, over his feet.

The fire in his eyes sparkled across the wet walls. "Little fly, you cannot escape my web."

Translucent abscesses bubbled over his abdomen, shimmering with a gray oil, festering, gasping. Then they blew. Gossamer strings erupted, spitting through the tunnel, stretching for me.

I ran. Back from where I came and into the black ink. Sticky threads clutched my shoulders, jerked me backwards. I slashed the blades through the air, cutting them away, and flung myself forward.

Volcanic dust kicked up, thickened in my mouth. I bumped against the grimy walls, groping through the dark, and slammed my brow against a jutting protrusion. My head swam. I blinked through the wet warmth slathering one eye and choked on the scream clawing in my throat.

It wasn't footsteps that followed me. It was the drag of wings along the cavern walls and the pullulation of a thousand tiny legs moving over the rocky surface, below my feet, above my head.

My lungs wheezed and my feet moved faster. Fire enveloped my banged up muscles and dirt caked my nostrils. Would my blind run send me falling into a fissure? Or crashing into a sharp ledge, decapitating myself?

Something scratched my shoulder. Oh Jesus. Oh fuck. Don't look back. I picked up my pace. Sharp mantels and outcrops snagged my hair and tore at my arms.

Another turn. Another tunnel. More darkness. The icy breeze warmed, clotted with steam. A bronze glow illuminated ahead. My legs pumped harder even as unease harried my focus.

Why wasn't the Drone gaining? He should've caught up. Something was wrong. Then I felt it. A handful of insectile pulses branched through me. In the next breath, they doubled, strengthened with their proximity. I waved the daggers through the dark, fumbling for an outlet. Where were the aphids? Would they pour out of hidden burrows? Would my guardians be close behind?

The reddish light danced on the curved wall, growing brighter. Then, as if the glow inhaled with a great heave, the wind leapt past me and all the oxygen seemed to be sucked with it.

"You are trapped, little fly." The chilling voice crept from the caldron of shadows chasing me.

I gulped air to fill my lungs and increased my pace toward the light. The air turned dry, scorched my face. My tank top felt hot against my breast. I whipped around the corner.

The ground disappeared. I pitched forward, balancing on the ledge of a rift, staring headfirst into a fiery molten river. With the last of my strength, I twisted back and away. My heart labored to catch up.

An eerie sucking noise tiptoed from the cave, as if flesh was sighing apart and melding back together. I found my footing and spun to face it, blades raised before me.

The red glow from the lava river washed over the Drone's skeletal body as he floated forward. Pus sputtered from the leaking growths that covered his naked torso. His wings appeared harder, more shell-like, as they scraped along the ground behind him.

I inched back until my boots reached the edge. "What did Frida's blood do to you?"

Madness seeped from the black wells of his gaze. "You adapted." His eyes roamed over the spots on my shoulders. "Her blood, enhanced with your essence, enabled me to do the same."

"So, now you're what? An arachnid ladybug?" Would explain the alteration in his wings. "Can you fly with beetle wings?"

The wings divided into two, one fluttering more awkwardly than the other. "Consuming your unfiltered blood will strengthen me and secure Allah's chosen race."

A whisper drifted over my shoulder.

Ladybird, fly away!

My heart beat out of control as I turned my head. Annie rose above the fiery gorge, her hair wisping around her in a blaze of fire, her body swallowed in a wrap of flames. Her golden eyes sparked, seizing mine.

Your house is burning
Mother is crying

Father sits on the threshold

The lapping flames muffled her song.

"Step away from the ledge, Eveline." The Drone watched me, not once moving his gaze to the burning vapor over my shoulder.

Relief that he couldn't see her waged with my need to face her and risk revealing her presence.

Her voice wavered through the sweltering heat.

Fly into Heaven from Hell

"You have nowhere to go." The Drone offered a mutated claw. "Come."

A wrenching pain stitched behind my eyes. I felt the cancer of his soul crowding my head, like he was gouging his way in. He was trying to control me, and he was stronger.

Soprano warbled.

Ladybird thought, "Some wisdom I'll show."

Something moved in the shadows of the tunnel. Then a body lunged and crashed into the Drone. The unbearable pain in my head disintegrated.

The tunnel became alive with the hiss of a sword, the whistle of arrows, and squeal of dying bugs. I catapulted forward with aphid speed, skidding on my knees to Michio's side as he struggled atop the Drone's prone body.

A growl rumbled through the Drone. In a flash of movement, he stabbed his incisors into Michio's shoulder. Hands scratched at the Drone's face. Mine. Michio's. His fangs hung on.

"Your ouchie, Mama." Annie spun in a circle, rotating faster and faster with tornado speed, spraying sparks of embers. "Lure the beast. Send it to hell."

Her twirling slowed and she swiped her brow in a deliberate movement, eyes on me. I reached for my own, mimicking her gesture. The gash on my head wet my palm. I was bleeding worse than I realized.

Then she twirled again, arms pointed overhead like a macabre ballerina.

Never again need I hear as I turn,
Your house is on fire! Your children will burn!

Her chant dissolved as she melted into the lava river, fire popping and spurting from her smoldering frame.

The sound of slurping drew my attention away from the agony of my heart ripping at the seams. The Drone's mouth moved against Michio's throat, the muscles in his wings flexing and stabbing my ribs as they shuddered.

I held my blood-drenched hand up to the monster's flaring nostrils. "Bite me."

Either Michio was too weak to protest my plan or he trusted me. His body lolled motionless in the Drone's embrace.

A weakness lay beneath the viciousness of the onyx eyes studying me. His arrogance would be his ruination. He retracted his teeth and shoved Michio away. Before I could roll after him, the Drone twisted, his claw shackling my throat.

I landed on my back, hands under my legs. "Do it."

His jaw stretched, his body arched. Then he lunged. I caught his chest with my knees, my feet in his gut, caging the dagger I thrust into his chest.

He stared down at it, wide-eyed. I twisted the blade and pushed with my feet. He stepped back. A step he didn't have.

The blazing fissure swallowed his fall. I scrambled to the edge, squinted my eyes against the ribbon of fire, waiting for the tormented scream that never came. I hung there, muscles preparing to battle a roasted skeleton bursting from the flames.

Michio's silken voice brushed over my back. "He's gone, *Nannakola*."

I rolled over and hugged him. "Tell me you're okay."

He looked up at me, his smile brimming his gorgeous eyes, a hand clasped to his throat. "Just a bug bite."

"Did my stoic warrior just make a joke?" I rubbed my breastbone where it tingled. "How does one fight monsters and still look so damn beautiful?"

A scarlet flood drowned out his pallor. He shifted me up his chest, the movement sluggish. "You would know."

The stomp of boots burst from the tunnel. Strong arms dragged me to my feet, the essence of oak enveloping me. Beyond Roark's broad shoulders, Jesse lingered in the shadows.

Seeing them returned some strength to my wobbly legs. Dammit, my arms itched to wrap around them and hold on tight. But if I did that, even for brief moment, I'd fall apart. So, I dropped my hand to my cocked hip and said, "About time you showed up."

A clump of gore plopped from Roark's sword, at odds with his flirtatious eyes as they roamed my face with too much perception. He grinned. "Been a little busy, love."

I wanted to give into my own smile, but, "Georges and Tallis? Darwin?"

Michio gripped Roark's offered hand and stood. "Guarding the entrance." His scorching lips found mine, caressing, lingering. "Let's go home."

My eyebrows climbed up my forehead. "Home? Where's that?"

Jesse stepped away from the wall. "Nymph Mountain."

Nymph Mountain. Where we could deliver the cure and save a life. Where we could heal under Akicita's care.

Jesse held my gaze. "Say yes, Evie."

The lazy roll of lava pushed between the canyon banks, its surface burnished and undisturbed. I limped toward the tunnel, lips in full tilt. "Yes, Evie."

The nymph's cabin emitted an eerie calm. Its interior was ominous through the small window despite the glare of the late sun. Having been neglected by my ghosts since leaving Iceland, I shuddered at the memory of how I stumbled upon the isolated shack.

Aaron loitering on the porch. His blood-drenched Booey clutched to my chest like a talisman.

A month had passed since the Drone's fall. We carried a heavy burden on that walk back to the gunship. The weight of our gear. The deaths of our friends. But we also carried a cure, a hope that pushed us forward.

The gunship made one stop on its flight to the states. Georges knew of an underground supply of jet fuel in St. John's, Newfoundland. From there, we flew to Camp Dawson, West Virginia and purloined another Hum-vee. Jesse led us through the Allegheny Mountains without compass or map. When we reached the foothill, I too remembered the trails to the sandstone wall that towered the tiny shack.

"Looks empty." Roark leaned on his sword and rubbed the stubble roughening his cheek.

Small animal carcasses, fresh and old, scattered the porch and lawn. "She's here." Besides, she wouldn't have left her children. "She'll feel threatened if we go in. I'll try to call her out."

Michio stepped before me, armed with the capture gun loaded with my blood. "Please be careful." He kissed me.

Ow. I pulled back, touched my mouth. Blood dotted my fingers. I reached up and peeled back his lip. Normal human teeth.

His tongue swiped out, caught the bead of blood on my finger. Something flashed in his eyes. What the fuck? He backed up and walked to the cabin.

"Wha' in under feck was that?" Roark asked from my side.

"Glad you saw it. For a second, I thought I was having a flashback."

"Ready?" Michio shouted from his position behind a tree.

Roark curled his tall frame around my back. Jesse slipped in front of me, his back to my chest, his arrow ready. Tallis, Georges and Darwin walked the perimeter.

Swaddled by skin, I felt my energy gather. Then I called the nymph from her damnation. *Come.*

After a few patient pushes, she loomed in the doorway. I bathed the link in consoling thoughts. Her feet slid over the rotten boards, creaking them as she stepped off the porch.

Michio released the dart. It struck her throat and she clawed at it, wailing.

"Evie?" Roark's voice behind me.

She thrashed on the ground, her fear stabbing my gut. I released the connection. "I'm fine. Go help Michio restrain her."

Roark held her as Michio checked her vitals and sedated her with Kampo herbs. She would survive the reversal. She'd have a doctor and guards to ensure it.

Overcome with a heavy weight in my chest, I paced away, pulling out my music player and adjusting the buds in my ears.

A sharp draft bumped up my skin. Jesse's fingers slid over mine. At the tree line, Annie and Aaron flickered, took shape, holding hands in their pajamas. I schooled my breathing.

Aaron leapt forward. Annie grabbed the shirt of her runaway brother. He giggled as she tucked him under her arm. The human gesture made it difficult to remember they were just the remnant energy of my children's memories.

I covered the distance between us, Jesse at my side.

"Mama," Annie trumpeted through a stifled yawn. From the corner of my eye, I glimpsed Jesse smiling at her.

"The day is over," she said. "We have to go nighty-night."

A sharp stab burned in my chest. It was an innocent comment. Still, her tone held finality. "What do you mean, sweetheart?"

She shrugged. "We have to go, but Dada says we'll see you again someday."

Their forms faded and solidified again. Then they vanished.

Gone. I waved my arms around me and strained my eyes, searching the air, aching to feel, to see a remnant of their presence. There were no dissolving bones, no animated inferno, no blustering vortex. They were just...gone. I dropped to my knees and screwed my eyes shut.Air pushed from my lungs in heavy rasps. They were dead, I reminded myself. I watched them die.

I curled my nails in the loose dirt. Directed my thoughts to the earth. Away from the need to scream their names. I wanted to hold them and never let them go.

When I opened my eyes, a solid frame blocked my view. Jesse pulled me to his chest. He held me as the air crackled around us, as the synergy of their memories dissipated into the surrounding realm of living things.

I sucked in a deep breath. It was warm, lively, as if their energy had melded with the oxygen I inhaled. "They're gone," I whispered.

"We all have a responsibility to the earth." Jesse held me tighter. "What we take from it in life, we give back in death. When you feel a snowflake on your cheek, when you hear the whisper of the wind at your back, when you see the ribbons of mist hovering a pond, you'll know it's them. Their energy. One blood."

I released a choppy breath. When the wind blew back, I wondered.

Jesse turned me to face the western horizon where the afterglow of the sun's departure lit up the mountains. His lips moved at my ear. "Just like day and night, we heed the seasons of birth, life and rebirth."

Unearthing the mysteries of life and death was an unobtainable wish. I walked so many roads in two years. Left behind so many dead. Made so many mistakes, beginning with Joel's death. Then the young sailor, Ian. And Frida. Oh God, she was so close to happiness.

The music player powered on beneath my restless fingers and I queued up Bob Dylan's *Blowin' In The Wind*. Jesse's palm tapped my hip as if he could hear the croon from my ear buds.

A shadow fell over my lap. "It worked," Michio mouthed, eyes glittering. He sat at my side, Roark at the other. Their hands settling on my knees.

Jesse's heart beat against my back. Near the cabin, Tallis cradled the woman's head in his lap. A faint smile creased her face in sleep.

One cured woman gave me no illusions of salvation, but for one day, it was enough. The sun would return and when it did, we'd begin again. Humanity might be dependent on the most unlikely of heroes, but I had the Yang to my Yin, the Adam to my Eve. Three guardians. Three reasons to care, to fight, to live.

Together we watched the sun bow below the horizon in veneration for the eve that followed. The eve of the beginning.

5000 miles away...

A symphony of unearthly cries blanketed the island, *l'Isola del Vescovo*. At the center of the Mediterranean, there was nowhere for them go, nothing for them to eat. But their resilient bodies wouldn't starve. The aphids would roam the confines of the water's edge in an endless haze of hunger. And across the ocean, when the last mammal on Earth released its last breath, aphid cries would consume every island, every continent. But there was little concern for that.

Labored breaths sawed in and out of ruined lungs. The voice was an abrasion, scratching the raw tissue of an unhealed esophagus. "Forgive me, brother. I failed us."

The Drone fingered the silken webbing that covered the wall of his lab. "But I will fix this. My messengers will find her again, and when they do—"

Agony ripped through his midsection where the boils festered and wheezed. More velvet threads spun forth and wove around the hanging cocoon.

Nerve endings throbbed beneath charred skin as he willed his feet to slide toward the wall.

"When they find her," he rasped, stroking what was left of his brother's moldering scalp, "she will offer herself like Allah Almighty willed it, and finally we will live in perfect harmony."

Gossamer threads suspended his brother's disembodied head at eye level. The zigzag scar was the only recognizable feature in his decomposed face.

Red clouded his vision. He slowed his rising heart rate with measured breaths and side-stepped to the web-wrapped husk swaying beside the head. The effort ripped pangs through his dermis and into underlying muscle and bones.

"My wings will heal and they will be stronger, more durable than before." Their newly acquired armored exterior had sheltered his body from the worst of the burns and carried him to the passageway tucked beneath the overhang he fell from.

Her blood gave him that indestructibility, by way of the Icelandic woman. Imagine what he would become if he drank from her directly. But to catch the fly, he must heal. He must feed.

He summoned the strength to climb the cocoon, his claws and feet clinging to the sticky strands. When he reached the neck, his fangs pierced through layer after layer of diaphanous netting, sinking into the leathery flesh beneath. Then he drained the remains of his brother's carcass.

Trilogy of Eve

Dead of Eve
Blood of Eve
Dawn of Eve

Acknowledgements

Thank you to my friends at critiquecircle.com, for smacking me over the head with the writing rulebook, and for telling me to ignore the rules when they get in the way.

To John Pfannkuchen, for teaching me the importance of writing a novel not to be read, but writing one to be read again and again.

To Lindsey R. Loucks, for turning every page of my embarrassing first draft. Your succinct and timely critiques showed me how to strip to my briefs and get to the point.

To J. Andrew Jansen, for protecting Evie's butt-kicking manly men from becoming hunched shouldered, purse-holding, standing outside the women's restroom men.

To C.K. Raggio, for calling out my awkward phrasing, and for cheering Evie from beginning to end. I want to design an Evie Halloween costume just for you.

To David Bridge, for editing my American English, for advising me on the nuances of regional vocabulary within the U.K., and for not kicking my arse if inaccuracies remain. Any misrepresentations of Irish slang are entirely my fault.

To Lindy Winter, for showing me where my brevity worked against me, and for drafting my blurb when brevity was beyond me.

To Dana Griffin, for your "The Between Chapter" reflections. Your ingenuous thoughts and generous nudging kept the fire burning under my ass.

To my husband, for being my inspiration in Joel's creation. I hope his character is a worthy portrayal of you.

About the Author

Pam Godwin lives in Missouri with her husband, their two children, and a foulmouthed parrot. When she ran away at eighteen, she traveled fourteen countries across five continents, attended three universities, and married the vocalist of her favorite rock band. Now, she resides in her hometown, earning her living as a portfolio analyst, and living her yearning as a writer.

Java, tobacco, and dark romance novels are her favorite indulgences, and might be considered more unhealthy than her aversion to sleeping, eating meat, and dolls with blinking eyes.

You can follow her at pamgodwin.com

Made in the USA
San Bernardino, CA
16 April 2014